FROM THE DEAD

FROM THE DEAD

Mark Billingham

McArthur & Company
Toronto

First published in Canada in 2010 by
McArthur & Company
322 King Street West, Suite 402
Toronto, Ontario
M5V 1J2
www.mcarthur-co.com

First published in the UK by Little, Brown & Co. Ltd

Library and Archives Canada Cataloguing in Publication

Billingham, Mark
From the dead / Mark Billingham.

ISBN 978-1-55278-871-4

I. Title.

PR6102.I44F76 2010   823.92   C2010-903945-9

Typeset in Plantin by M Rules
Printed and bound in Canada by Webcom

10 9 8 7 6 5 4 3 2 1

For Peter Cocks.
We'll always have Mijas . . .

PROLOGUE

For a few seconds after the petrol tank goes up, the woods are shocked into silence.

At least that's how it seems, as though it takes those moments of quiet and stillness after the whump of the explosion for every bird and insect and small mammal to release the breath it has been holding. For the wind to begin moving through the trees again; although, even then, it dares do no more than whisper. Obviously, as far as the men watching the burning car are concerned, it might just be that it takes that long for the ringing in their ears to die down.

And, of course, the man inside the car has finally stopped screaming.

Ten minutes earlier, dragging him towards the Jag, the younger of the two men had needed to slap the poor bugger a few times to keep him quiet. As soon as he'd been bundled into the passenger seat, though, there was no shutting him up. Not when he'd seen the handcuffs come out and the petrol can that had been taken from the boot.

Not once he'd realised what they were going to do.

'I didn't think he'd make such a racket,' the older man said.

'They always make a racket.' The younger man sniffed and smiled. 'You're not normally around for this bit, are you?'

1

'Not if I can help it.' The older man shoved his hands deep into the pockets of his Barbour jacket, looked up at the trees crowding in on the small clearing. The light was already starting to go and the temperature was dropping fast.

The younger man grinned. 'Don't worry, it'll warm up in a minute.' He opened the back door of the Jag and started sloshing petrol around.

The man who was handcuffed to the steering wheel threw himself back and forth in the front seat, the cuffs rattling against the walnut steering wheel and the spittle flying on to the dash and windscreen. He started shouting, begging the man with the petrol can to stop. He told him he had a family, told him their names. He said, 'You don't need to do this.' Then, 'For Christ's sake!' and 'Please . . .'

The older man winced, like he had a bad headache, and told his colleague to close the door. Shut the bloody noise out a bit. The younger man did as he was told, tossed the empty petrol can back in the boot, then walked across and offered his employer a cigarette. It was refused, but he still took out a Zippo and lit one of his own.

'Happy?'

The man in the Barbour nodded. 'Just needed to get the details right. The clothes, you know? Jewellery, all that.'

The younger man nodded towards the car. 'Shame about your watch.'

The older man glanced down at the outline of a wristwatch, pale against a Barbados tan. 'It's all just . . . stuff, isn't it?' He shrugged. 'Watches, cars, what have you. Means nothing at the end of the day. Living is what counts, right?'

The younger man drew smoke deep into his lungs then hissed it away between his teeth. He took two more fast drags then flicked the nub-end into the trees. Said, 'Shall I get this done, then?'

He took out the lighter again and a rag from the other pocket, which he twisted between his fingers as he walked back to the car.

The man inside the Jag was crying now and banging his head against the side window. His voice was rasping and ragged and only audible for as long as it took to open the door, fire up the lighter and toss the burning rag on to the back seat. No more than a few seconds, but it was easy enough to make out what was being said.

Those names again. His wife and son.

Said for nobody's benefit but his own this time, and he repeated them, eyes closed, until the smoke stopped them in his throat.

The two men moved back towards the trees and watched the fire take hold from a safe distance. Within ninety seconds the windows had blown and the figure in the front seat was no more than a black shape.

'Where you going to go?'

The older man nudged the tip of his shoe through the mulch. 'Now, why would you think you need to know* that?'

'Just asking, is all.'

'Yeah, well. Just think about the worthless crap you'll be spending your money on.'

'*Your* money, you mean.'

'Right. Can't be too many like this, can there? How many times you been paid twice for one job?'

'Never had a job* anything *like this one—'

That was when the petrol tank caught and went up . . .

Half a minute later, they turn and walk back to where the second car is parked; away from the sounds that have begun to roll and echo around the clearing after those few dead seconds. The wind and the leaves and the creak of branches. The crackle and hiss as flames devour flesh and leather.

A hundred yards or so from the main road, the older man stops and looks up. 'Listen . . .'

'What?'

He waits, then points when he hears the sound again. 'Woodpecker. Can you hear him?'

The younger man shakes his head.

'Great spotted, I'm guessing. He's the commonest.'

They start walking again, the woods growing darker by the minute.

'How do you know stuff like that?'

'Reading,' *the older man says.* 'Books, magazines, whatever. You should try it some time.'

'Yeah, well, you'll have plenty of time on your hands now, won't you?'

3

The younger man nods back in the direction of the car, the blaze clearly visible a mile or more behind them, through the dark tangle of oaks and giant beeches. 'You can read about fucking woodpeckers till the cows come home. Now you're dead . . .'

PART ONE

A DECENT
TRICK

ONE

Anna Carpenter had eaten sushi only once before, when some bloke she'd gone out with for about five minutes had been trying to impress her, but this was her first time in one of these conveyor-belt places. She thought it was a good idea. It made sense, having the chance to look at the food before you took the plunge, and it didn't matter if you let it go by half a dozen times while you made your mind up, because it was cold anyway.

Fiendishly clever, these Japanese . . .

She reached for a plate of salmon *nigiri* from the belt and asked the man sitting next to her if he could pass the soy sauce. He slid the bottle towards her with a smile, then offered her the pot of *wasabi*.

'God, no, that's the really hot stuff, isn't it?'

The man told her it was just a question of not overdoing it and she said that she'd rather not risk it, that she was something of a novice when it came to eating raw fish.

'This your lunch hour?' the man asked.

'Yeah. You?'

'Well, I'm my own boss, so I usually manage to sneak a bit more than an hour, if I'm honest.' He expertly plucked what looked like a small pasty from his plate and dipped it into some sauce. 'You work nearby?'

Anna nodded, her mouth full of rice, grunted a 'yes'.

'What do you do?'

She swallowed. 'Just temping,' she said. 'Trying not to die of boredom.'

A waiter appeared at her shoulder with the bottle of water she'd ordered and by the time he'd left, she and the man sitting next to her were all but strangers once more. Anna felt as awkward as he obviously did about picking up their conversation, and neither needed any condiments passing.

They ate and exchanged smiles. Glanced and looked away. A nod from one or the other when something was especially tasty.

He was in his mid-to-late thirties – ten years or so older than she was – and looked good in a shiny blue suit that probably cost as much as her car. He had a crinkly smile and had missed a bit just below his Adam's apple the last time he'd shaved. He looked like he worked out, but not too much, and she guessed he was not the sort who moisturised more often than she did.

He was still sitting next to her by the time she had finished.

'Maybe I'll be brave and try the *wasabi* next time,' she said.

'Sorry?' He looked round at her in mock-surprise, as though he had forgotten she was there.

Anna wasn't fooled for a second. She had been aware for the last ten minutes that he had finished eating. She'd seen the pile of empty plates next to him, watched him eke out a cup of green tea, and known very well that he was waiting for her to finish.

She leaned in close to him. 'We could go to a hotel.'

Now the surprise was genuine. He had not been expecting her to make the first move. He opened his mouth and closed it again.

'Seeing as you can sneak more than an hour.'

He nodded, but could not make eye contact with her.

'Why don't we find out how much you *really* like eating sushi?' It was deliberately crude, and she felt herself redden as she said it, but she could see straight away that it had done the trick.

He muttered, 'Christ!' as the crinkly smile became a stupid grin. He waved the waiter across, pointing to Anna's empty plates as well as his own to indicate that he would be paying for both of them.

The hotel was a five-minute walk away. Tucked behind Kingsway and within conveniently easy reach of Holborn Tube Station and a well-stocked chemist. A notch or two up from a Travelodge without being silly money.

He took out his wallet as they approached the reception desk.

'I'm not a hooker,' Anna said.

'I know that.'

'I'm perfectly happy to pay my share of the room.'

'Look, it's not a problem,' he said. 'You said you were temping, so . . .'

'Fine, whatever.' She caught the eye of the young man behind the desk. He nodded politely, then looked away, sensing he should not show any sign that he had seen her before. 'If you *want* to be flash, you can order us a bottle of something,' Anna said, then turned and walked across the lobby.

In the lift, he finally asked her name.

She shook her head. 'Ingrid . . . Angelina . . . Michelle. Whatever turns you on the most. It's more exciting that way.' She closed her eyes and moaned softly as his hand moved to stroke her backside.

As the lift juddered to a halt at the first floor, he said, 'My name's Kevin.'

The room was larger than she had been expecting – a decent-sized double – and she guessed that he had splashed out, which made her feel oddly sorry for him.

'Nice,' he said, slipping off his jacket.

She headed straight for the bathroom. 'Give me a minute,' she said.

She sent the text while she was using the toilet, then stood in front of the mirror and wiped away the excess make-up. She could hear him moving around on the other side of the door, heard the bedsprings creak and imagined him pushing down on the mattress, testing it out like some sitcom gigolo, with that grin still plastered to his face.

9

When she came out, he was sitting on the edge of the bed in his boxer shorts, his hands in his lap.

'Where's that sushi, then?' he asked.

'Aren't we going to have a drink first?'

As if on cue, there was a knock at the door and he nodded towards it. 'They didn't have champagne,' he said. 'So I got some sparkling wine. It's more or less the same price, actually . . .'

Anna moved quickly to the door and opened it, then turned and saw Kevin's face whiten and fall when his wife stepped into the room.

'Oh, shit,' he said, one hand still covering the rapidly dwindling erection, while the other scrabbled for shirt and trousers.

The woman watched him from the doorway, clutched her handbag to her stomach. Said, 'You sad wanker.'

'She picked me up, for heaven's sake.' He jabbed a finger in Anna's direction. 'I was just having my bloody lunch, and this . . . *tart* . . .'

'I know,' his wife said. 'And she had to drag you here kicking and screaming, right?'

'I can't believe you did this. That you set this up.'

'What, you can't believe I didn't *trust* you?'

Anna tried to squeeze past the man's wife towards the door. 'I'd better get out of your way.'

The woman nodded quickly and stood aside. 'The money's already gone into your firm's account,' she said.

'Right, thanks . . .'

'You bitch,' Kevin shouted. He was still struggling to yank his trousers on and almost tumbled, bracing himself against a chest of drawers.

Anna opened the door.

'And don't flatter yourself either, love. It was only because it was on offer.'

The wife had tears in her eyes, but still managed a look that was somewhere between pity and rage. It seemed to Anna that both were aimed as much at her as at the woman's husband.

'I'll leave you to it,' Anna said.

She stepped quickly into the corridor as Kevin began shouting again, and winced as the door slammed shut behind her. She walked quickly past the lift and took the stairs down to the lobby two at a time.

Tried not to think of his face and his pale, hairless body and the things he must have thought they were going to do.

The words he'd shouted after her.

'You're kidding yourself, love,' he'd said. 'If you think you're not a hooker.'

On the tube back to Victoria, Anna picked up a tattered *Metro* and tried to read. Did her best not to think about her afternoon's work.

You're kidding yourself . . .

She knew that the man whose marriage she had probably screwed up was bang on the money in more ways than one; that almost everything about what she was doing was wrong. She'd seen some of the flashier websites and knew how the bigger and better agencies handled the more radical end of 'specialist matrimonial investigations'. There were always at least two investigators involved in any honey-trap operation. The well-being and safety of the investigator were always put first. There were hidden cameras and microphones and pre-arranged secret signals.

Yeah, right.

She could see the sneer on Frank's face; hear his gravelly voice thick with sarcasm.

'So, why don't you sod off and work for one of the *bigger and better* agencies, then?'

She imagined herself calmly dishing it right back. Blithely announcing that one of these days she just might do exactly that. The truth was, though, even if she had walked into that sushi restaurant with armed back-up, a concealed tape-recorder and a pen that squirted acid hidden in her knickers, she would not have felt any better about what she was doing.

The direction her life was taking.

Money might have helped a little, might have eased her discomfort, but there was not a great deal of that, either. In one of those rare moments when Frank Anderson had not been angry or pissed or unreasonably vituperative, he had sat Anna down and tried to explain the financial situation.

'I'd love to pay you a bit more,' he had said, sounding almost, just for a second or two, as though he meant it. 'I'd *love* to, but look around. Everything's gone tits up in specialist services like ours and this credit crunch is biting us all in the arse. You understand?'

Anna had considered reminding Frank that she had a good economics degree, but guessed where the conversation would end.

'So, why don't you sod off back to that flashy bank, then?'

That was a tricky question to answer.

Because you promised me things. Because I thought this would be a challenge. Because I was bored stupid playing with other people's money and you told me that if there was one job that was never predictable, that was always interesting, it was this one.

Because going back means giving up.

Anna thought back to the day she'd phoned F.A. Investigations, excited about the ad she'd seen in the local paper; keen as mustard and green as grass. Eighteen months and a lifetime ago. What the hell had she thought she was doing, walking out on a well-paid job, on friends and colleagues, for . . . *this*?

Ten pounds an hour to make tea and keep Frank's accounts in order. To answer the phone and come on to men who couldn't keep it in their pants.

And yet, despite the way things had panned out, Anna knew that her instincts had been right, that there had been nothing wrong with her ambition. How many people were stuck, too afraid to make a change, however much they yearned for it?

How many settled for jobs, partners, *lives*?

She had wanted something different, that was all. She had thought that in helping other people she would help herself. That, at the very least, it would stop her turning into one of those hard-faced City bitches who click-clacked past her all day long in their Jimmy Choos.

12

And, yes, she had thought it might be a little more exciting than futures and sodding hedge funds.

Kidding herself.

Same as she had been when she picked up the leaflet about joining the army, or when she'd thought about a career in the police force for all of five minutes. A year and a half ago, several of her friends had described her radical career shift from banker to private detective as 'brave'. 'Braver than me,' Angie, a triage nurse, had said. Rob, a teacher in a rough north London school, had nodded his agreement. Anna had suspected they really meant 'stupid', but she had relished the compliment all the same.

A soldier, though? A copper? Certainly not brave enough for *that* . . .

Anna stood as the train pulled into Victoria and caught the eye of the woman who had been sitting opposite. She tried to summon a smile but had to look away, convinced suddenly and for no good reason that the woman had got the measure of her. Could see what she was.

She felt over-wound and light-headed as the escalator carried her up towards the street; desperate now to get back to the office and change. She wanted to get out of the stupid heels *she* was click-clacking around in and back into her trainers. She wanted the day to end and the dark to wrap itself around her. She wanted to drink and sleep. It wasn't until she got to the ticket barrier and fumbled for her Oyster card that she realised she had a torn page of the *Metro* crushed into her fist.

The office was wedged between a dry-cleaner's and a betting shop; a cracked brown door with dirty glass. As Anna was reaching into her handbag for the keys, a woman who had been hovering at the kerb walked towards her. Forty-odd, and something fierce in her eyes.

Anna backed off half a step. Got ready to say 'no'. The typical London response.

'Are you a detective?' the woman asked.

Anna just stared. No, not fierce, she thought. *Desperate.*

'I saw your ad, and I need a bit of help with something, so . . .'

There was no light visible through the glass, and Anna guessed that Frank's lunchtime drink had turned into several. He would have diverted any calls for F.A. Investigations to his mobile and would almost certainly not be back for the rest of the afternoon.

'Yes,' Anna said. 'I am.' She took out her keys and stepped towards the door. 'Come on up.'

TWO

Had they been sitting side by side or staring at each other across the table in an interview room, the crucial difference between the two men might not have been obvious. Not to the casual observer, at any rate. Had one not been standing in a dock and the other in the witness box, it would have been tough to tell cop from killer.

Both were wearing suits and looking unhappy about the fact. Both stood reasonably still and, for the most part, stared straight ahead. Both seemed collected enough and, although only one was talking, both gave the impression, if you searched their expressions for more than a few moments, that there was plenty going on behind the façade of unflappable calm.

Both looked dangerous.

The man on the witness stand was well into his forties: stocky and round-shouldered, with dark hair that was greying a little more on one side than the other. He spoke slowly. He took care to say no more than he needed to as he gave his evidence, choosing his words carefully, but without letting that care look like doubt or hesitation.

'And there was no question in your mind that you were dealing with a murder?'

'No question whatsoever.'

'You have told us that the defendant was "relaxed" when he was first interviewed. Did his demeanour change when you questioned him subsequent to his arrest?'

As Detective Inspector Tom Thorne described the five separate interviews he had conducted with the man on trial, he did his best to keep his eyes fixed on the prosecuting counsel. But he could not quite manage it. Two or three times, he glanced across at the dock to see Adam Chambers staring right back at him; the eyes flat, unblinking. Once, he looked up for a few seconds to the public gallery, where the family of the young woman Chambers had murdered was gathered. He saw the hope and the rage in the faces of Andrea Keane's parents. The hands that clutched at those of others, or lay trembling in laps, wrapped tight around wads of damp tissue.

Thorne saw a group of people united in their grief and anger, and for whom justice – should it be meted out to their satisfaction – would be real and raw. Justice, of a sort, for an eighteen-year-old girl who Thorne knew beyond any doubt to be dead.

Despite the fact that no body had ever been found.

'Inspector Thorne?'

His voice stayed calm as he finished his testimony, reiterating dates and times, names and places: those details he hoped would linger in the minds of the jurors; combining to do their job as effectively as those precious, damning strands of blonde hair, the lies exposed by a mobile-phone record, and the smiling face of a girl in a photograph, taken days before she was killed.

'Thank you, Inspector. You may stand down.'

Thorne slipped his notebook back into the pocket of his jacket and stepped from the witness box. He walked slowly towards the rear doors of the courtroom, a fingertip moving back and forth across the small, straight scar on his chin. Eyes moving too, as he drew closer, towards the figure in the dock.

Thinking:

I don't want to see you again . . .

Not in the flesh, obviously not that, because you'll be banged up, thank God, and growing old. Watching your back and feeling that great big brain of yours turn to mush and staying on the right side of men who'd be happy to carve you up for looking at them funny. Because of what you are. I don't want to see you at night, I mean. Hanging around where you're not wanted and messing with me. Your smug face and your croaky 'no comment' dancing into my dreams . . .

As he passed beneath the dock, Thorne turned his face towards Adam Chambers. He paused for a second or two. He found the man's eyes, and he held them.

Then he winked.

Thorne shared a ride back to Hendon with DS Samir Karim. As Exhibits Officer on the case, Karim was responsible for the evidence chain and for maintaining the integrity of its key pieces.

A hairbrush. A mobile phone. A glass with Andrea Keane's fingerprints.

It was a typical February day that had begun for Thorne by scraping frost from his windscreen with a CD case, but still he opened his window and leaned towards it as the car moved slowly out of central London in heavy traffic. Over the rush of cold air, he could hear Karim telling him how well he had done. That there was no more he *could* have done. That it was as good as in the bag.

Thorne hoped the sergeant was right. Certainly, without the most conclusive piece of evidence, the Crown Prosecution Service had to be pretty confident of securing a conviction before they would go to trial. On top of which, Thorne and the rest of the team had done everything that was asked of them. They had worked as hard as Thorne could ever remember to prove the three things vital to securing a conviction in a 'no-body' murder case.

That Andrea Keane was dead.

That she had been murdered.

That she had been murdered by Adam Chambers.

Andrea Keane had disappeared eight months earlier, after a judo lesson at a sports centre in Cricklewood. Adam Chambers, a man with a history of violent sexual assault, had been her instructor. When he was initially questioned, he denied that he had seen Andrea after the lesson had finished, though later, when forensic evidence was found in his flat, he admitted that she had been there several times in the past. While Thorne and his team began to build a case against him, Chambers maintained that he had not seen Andrea the night she went missing, claiming that he had gone straight round to his girlfriend's after his lesson. It was an alibi that the girlfriend confirmed, up until the point when cell-site data proved that Chambers had phoned her that night from his own flat. Then the story changed. Andrea *had* come round after her judo lesson, Chambers had said, but had only stayed for one drink before he'd told her she needed to go. She had been a bit emotional, Chambers told them, ranting at him about his girlfriend.

He had leaned across the table in an interview room at Colindale station, with a leer that Thorne would need a long time to forget.

Said, 'She had a thing for me. What do you want me to say?'

From the moment he and his girlfriend had been charged and the lawyers had been appointed, Chambers changed his tactic. The ebullient swagger was replaced by a sullen refusal to cooperate; the wide-boy patter by two words.

No comment.

Thorne started a little as Karim leaned on the horn, cursing a cyclist who had jumped the lights ahead of him. Karim turned to look at Thorne. 'Yeah, in the bag, mate,' he said again. 'I'm telling you.'

'So, what are the odds?' Thorne asked.

Karim shook his head.

'Come on, you're not telling me you haven't worked them out.'

Karim was something of a gambler, and often ran a book on the result of a major case. It was officially frowned upon, but most of the senior officers turned a blind eye, had the occasional flutter themselves.

'No point,' Karim said. 'Odds against are *way* too long. Besides, who's going to bother?'

Thorne knew what his colleague meant. With a case like this one,

18

with a defendant like Adam Chambers, nobody would want to bet, or be seen to bet, on an acquittal.

Nobody would want to tempt fate.

Karim slapped out a drum-roll on the steering wheel. 'It's solid, mate, this one. *Solid.*'

As the investigation had gathered momentum and the circumstantial evidence had begun to mount up, Thorne had set about the task of proving that Andrea Keane was dead. Checks were run with every medical facility in the city. Unidentified bodies were re-examined and eliminated from the inquiry. Phone and financial records were analysed, CCTV footage was studied, and all travel companies supplied the documentation to prove that Andrea had not left the area voluntarily. While a massive search continued nationwide and all the major social networking sites were monitored round the clock, a criminal psychologist constructed a detailed and credible profile of a young woman with genuine ambition.

Someone who had made plans for her future.

Someone with no reason to run away or take her own life.

The media had, of course, been utilised extensively, but as was often the case, had proved to be more trouble than it was worth. A good deal of time and effort had been wasted chasing up dozens of 'sightings' phoned into the incident room every week after appeals on TV or in the newspapers. Each one, including those from overseas, had to be thoroughly checked out and discredited, but that had not stopped Chambers' defence team seizing upon them. Had not stopped his bullish, female solicitor suggesting in court that while Andrea Keane was still being spotted on a regular basis, it would be frankly ridiculous to convict anyone of her murder.

Thorne had stood his ground, drawing the jury's attention to the 'Presumption of Death' chart – a fourteen-page document outlining every inquiry undertaken to support the assertion that Andrea Keane was no longer alive. He had brandished his copy, looked hard at Chambers' solicitor, and told her it was frankly ridiculous to believe that Andrea Keane had *not* been murdered.

He had lain the document down again as calmly as was possible, aware of the movement, the noise of a muffled sob or grunt from the public gallery. He had kept his eyes on the chart, swallowed hard as they fixed on a highlighted bullet-point in the clinical psychologist's report:

Hopes and Aspirations

- The missing girl was variously described by friends as 'happy', 'full of beans', etc.
- She was looking for a flat to rent.
- She was training to be a nurse.

'Stick some music on, Sam.'

Karim leaned across and flicked on the radio. It was pre-tuned to Capital, and Karim immediately began nodding his head in time to some soulless remix. Thorne toyed with pulling rank, but decided he could not be arsed. Instead, he closed his eyes and kept them shut, tuning out the music, tuning out everything, for the rest of the journey north.

When they finally turned into the car park at the Peel Centre, it was almost lunchtime. Walking towards Becke House, Thorne was trying to decide between braving the canteen or a pub lunch at the Oak when an officer on his way out told him that he had a visitor waiting.

'A private detective.'

'What?'

'Good luck.'

The officer clearly thought this was hilarious, and that Thorne's reaction made it funnier still: a groan and a slump of the shoulders as Thorne continued, with no enthusiasm, up the steps and into the foyer at Becke House.

Thorne spotted his visitor immediately and made his way towards him. Fifty-ish and unkempt, a symphony in brown and beige with dirty hair and Hush Puppies, confirming just about every prejudice

Thorne had about sad little men who drove Cavaliers and stuck their noses into other people's business for a living.

'I'm DI Thorne,' he said.

The man looked up at him, confused. 'And?'

'You're not much of a detective, are you?'

Thorne turned at the voice from across the foyer. He saw a young woman take a step towards him, reddening as she did so.

'I think you're looking for me.'

Thorne reached instinctively for his tie and loosened it. 'Sorry.' He could sense the man he had spoken to smirking behind him. 'I've been in court all morning, so . . .'

'Did you get off?'

Thorne just stared as the woman reddened still further.

She mumbled, 'Sorry, stupid joke,' and proffered a business card. 'My name's Anna Carpenter, and—'

Thorne took the card without looking at it and gestured towards the security door. 'Let's go up to my office.' He swiped his ID and gave the finger to the desk sergeant, who was still chuckling as Thorne ushered Anna through the door.

THREE

Thorne stared down at the card and the photograph on the desk in front of him. He tapped a finger against the dog-eared business card. 'F.A. Investigations'. The name 'Frank Anderson' beneath and an address in Victoria. It looked like one of those you could get printed up in batches of fifty from DIY machines at railway stations. Thin card and a font that made the lettering look like broken-down typing. A cheesy picture of a bloodhound with a magnifying glass.

'Don't you get your own card?' Thorne asked.

The woman sitting opposite picked at her thumbnail. 'Mr Anderson keeps saying he'll get around to it,' she said. 'And he makes the administrative decisions. Right now, I think he's got more important things to spend his money on.'

Thorne nodded his understanding. Like keeping his Cavalier on the road, he thought.

'This is my case, though.' She waited until Thorne looked up and across at her. 'I mean, Donna's *my* client.'

Thorne could see the determination clearly in Anna Carpenter's face, could hear it in her voice. A desire to impress, to impose herself, even if she didn't quite look the part in jeans and a black corduroy jacket. Like a superannuated student, Thorne's father would have said. She was late twenties, Thorne guessed; round-faced and pretty. When she wasn't picking at her fingernails, she tugged at a strand of long, dirty-blonde hair and shifted around in her chair like someone who found it difficult to keep still for more than a few seconds at a time.

'I never said she wasn't,' Thorne said. He looked down again, turned his attention to the photograph. A man was squinting into the sunshine, grinning at the camera and holding up a glass of beer. He was probably mid-fifties, with the hair on his head a little darker than it would have been naturally, judging by the grey tangle on his flabby, nut-brown chest. The sky behind him was cloudless, with the jagged line of a mountain sloping down to a dark blue streak of sea in the background, a small sail-boat in the far distance. He might have been sitting on a boat himself, or at the end of a pier. In a restaurant near the water's edge, perhaps.

'Greece? Spain? South of France?' Thorne shook his head. 'Florida, maybe? Your guess is as good as mine.'

'It's not Birmingham,' Anna said. 'That's about as far as I've got.'

The man's eyes were all but closed against the glare, but the grin seemed unforced, effortless. 'He looks happy enough.'

'Got every reason to be,' Anna said. 'Actually, I thought you might recognise him.'

Thorne looked closer. A bell was ringing, but faintly. 'What's your client's name?'

There was a pause, the hint of a satisfied smile. 'She was sent that picture last December.' Anna moved her chair forward until she was tight against the desk. 'That was two months before she was released from prison.'

'What did she do?'

'Conspiracy to murder her husband.'

'How long?'

'Twelve years. She served ten.'

'*Langford?*' Thorne stared at her. The penny had dropped, hard, but it made no sense. 'Your client is Donna Langford?'

23

Anna nodded. 'She's using her maiden name now, but, yes, she was.'

'Somebody's winding you up, love.'

'I don't think so.'

'You know what she did?' Thorne stabbed a finger at the photograph. 'Why this can't possibly be who she thinks it is?'

'She told me some of it.'

'Let me tell you all of it,' Thorne said. 'Then we can both stop wasting our time.'

Thorne had worked on cases within the last six months that he could not remember as clearly as this one, even though it had been more than a decade since Alan Langford was murdered.

They'd called it the 'Epping Forest Barbecue' in the office.

Langford had always been a man who made news. He had kept a good few journalists busy over the years, crime and business correspondents both; his property empire growing as fast as his competitors retired suddenly, vanished or met with unfortunate accidents. He finally became front-page fodder when his charred remains were discovered in his burned-out Jag in Epping Forest. Then the column inches became feet and yards when it emerged that his wife had arranged his murder.

Donna Langford, an immaculately turned-out businessman's wife, patron of several local charities and lady who lunched, had paid someone to kill her husband.

'She used her old man's own contacts,' Thorne said. 'Maybe the bloke she hired was in Langford's address-book . . . under "H" for "Hit-men".'

'Look at the picture again,' Anna said. 'It's him. You must remember what he looked like back then. You can see that he's aged, surely?'

Thorne glanced down. 'Yes, well, he's certainly looking a lot better than the last time I saw him.'

'If you're talking about the body in the car, that wasn't him.'

'Donna *identified* him.' Thorne was doing his best not to sound patronising, but it was a struggle. 'It was *his* car and *his* jewellery. That was pretty much all that was left, mind you . . .'

'She never knew that was how he was going to do it,' Anna said. 'The man she hired.'

'She never asked.' Thorne leaned back in his chair. 'She calmly paid an Irishman called Paul Monahan twenty-five thousand pounds. He used a few quid of it to buy some petrol and a pair of handcuffs.'

'When did you know she had been involved?'

'About thirty seconds after I met her,' Thorne said. 'When she came in to identify the body. I've seen people react in all sorts of ways, but she just stood and . . . shook. I asked her if she was all right, and she more or less made a confession on the spot, with her old man still stinking like overcooked meat in the corner.'

'How did you catch Monahan?'

'Donna gave us his name and then we matched his DNA to a cigarette butt we found at the crime scene. It couldn't have been more straightforward in the end.' Thorne slid the picture across the desk towards Anna. 'Trust me, cases as piss-easy as that one don't come along every day.'

Anna nodded and cleared her throat. 'Donna's served ten years in prison, Inspector.'

Thorne took a few seconds, gathered together some papers on his desk. He summoned the same calm expression he had been relying on in court all morning, but he could still remember the smell of that Jag, the taste of the smoke and the ash that was not just ash, and the pale globules of fat that were stuck to the seats.

'She got off pretty lightly, if you ask me,' he said. 'She pleaded guilty, which always does you a favour, and it didn't hurt that her old man was a scumbag who was probably knocking her about when he wasn't busy having people's legs broken. Yeah, Alan Langford got what was coming to him, probably, but it was still a seriously nasty way to go.'

'Look at the date,' Anna said, She pushed the photo back towards Thorne. 'Bottom right . . .'

Thorne picked up the photo. The date had been stamped automatically by the camera: a little over three months earlier. 'They can do that sort of thing with Photoshop,' he said. 'Besides which, this could be a photo of *anybody*.'

'Donna says it's her husband,' Anna said. She shook her head, searched for something else, but in the end she just shrugged and said it again. 'She swears it's Alan.'

'Then she's lying.'

'Why?'

'Because . . . Look, maybe she went a bit funny inside. She wouldn't be the first. Maybe she wants money. Maybe she's trying to get some big "miscarriage of justice" thing off the ground.'

'She doesn't even know I'm here,' Anna said. 'She came to me because she *doesn't* want the police involved.'

Thorne was taken aback. 'OK, so how are you going to explain this conversation to your client?' He could not suppress a smile and felt more than a little guilty as he watched her start to fidget and redden again.

'I'll just be honest and tell her that I was getting nowhere,' Anna said. 'That I couldn't think what else to do. I'll tell her I've spent a fortnight staring at that sodding photo and that I'm none the wiser.'

'Why *did* you come to see me?' Thorne asked.

'I thought you might be able to get a bit more information from the photograph.' She looked at Thorne, but got no response. 'Don't you have ways of . . . enhancing pictures, or whatever? I mean, there must be some way to tell where this picture was taken. I don't know, geographical profiling, a computer programme or *something*?'

'This isn't *CSI*,' Thorne said. 'We haven't even got a photocopier that works properly.'

'I also thought you might be *interested*.' Anna was leaning towards him suddenly. 'Stupid of me, I can see that, but it seemed like a decent idea at the time. It was your case, so I hoped that if you saw the photo you might at least think that maybe it wasn't . . . finished.' She stared at Thorne for a few seconds longer, then sat back and reached for a strand of hair to pull at.

'It's a waste of time,' Thorne said. 'I'm sorry, but I've got more important things to worry about. Actually, I can't think of anything that *isn't* more important than this.' He pushed back his chair and, after a moment or two, Anna got the message and did the same.

'I'll get out of your way, then,' she said.

She took a step towards the door.

Thorne thought she looked about fourteen. 'Look . . . I'll run it past my boss, all right?' He saw her expression change and raised a hand. 'He'll only say the same as me, though, so don't hold your breath.' He picked up the photograph again, nodded down at it. 'Could do with a bit of that myself,' he said. 'Sun and sand.'

'Tom?'

Thorne looked up to see DI Yvonne Kitson standing in the door-way. They shared the office and most of the time Thorne was happy enough with the arrangement. He certainly liked her a lot more than he had back when she was a high-flier, and suspected that she felt the same way about herself. Like Thorne, she could still put noses out of joint without much effort, but it was hard not to admire the way she had rebuilt a career that had plunged so calamitously off the tracks after an extra-marital affair with a senior officer.

'Like a self-assembly wardrobe,' she had once said to Thorne. 'One loose screw and the whole thing fell to pieces.'

Now, she had one eye on Thorne's visitor. He gestured towards Anna, the photograph flapping between his fingers, and introduced her.

Kitson nodded a cursory greeting and turned back to Thorne. 'I just thought you'd like to know that the jury's gone out.'

'Right.' Thorne stood and moved around the desk.

Anna was doing up the buttons on her jacket. 'The case you were in court for?'

Thorne nodded, thinking about the wink he'd given Adam Chambers. 'One that isn't quite so . . . piss-easy,' he said.

DCI Russell Brigstocke's office was twenty feet along the corridor from the one Thorne shared with Yvonne Kitson. When Thorne walked in, Brigstocke was on the phone, so Thorne dropped into a chair and waited. He thought about an eighteen-year-old girl whose bones still lay waiting for an inquisitive dog and about a man who had died screaming, handcuffed to the wheel of a car in the middle of nowhere.

He tried to separate the two murders, committed so many years apart. To tease out the tangle of pictures, real and imagined.

He wanted to worry about the right thing . . .

Brigstocke put the phone down and reached for a mug of coffee. He took a sip, grimaced.

'You know the jury's out?' Thorne asked.

Brigstocke nodded. 'No point thinking about it, mate,' he said. 'I heard it went really well this morning.'

'Sam tell you it was in the bag, did he?'

'I'm just saying we've done everything we could.'

'Everything except find her,' Thorne said.

He felt chilly suddenly, aware of how thin and flimsy his suit was, missing the heavy familiarity of his leather jacket. As it went, most coppers dressed the way he was at that moment. It was as if each one graduated to a plain-clothes unit and instantly acquired the fashion sense of a low-end estate agent, but Thorne had always resisted the pull of the off-the-peg M&S two-piece, the easy-iron shirt and shiny tie.

'It's bloody cold in here,' he said.

Brigstocke nodded. 'There's air in the radiator and nobody's got a key.'

Thorne got up and walked across to the radiator, bent and put his hand to the metal, which was no better than lukewarm. He stood up, pressed his calves against it. Hearing a sound he had come to recognise and dread, he looked round and saw Brigstocke shuffling a pack of cards.

'I've got a new one for you.'

'Do you have to?' Thorne asked.

For reasons nobody could quite fathom, Brigstocke had developed a keen interest in magic over the previous few months. He attended classes at a club in Watford and had started performing close-up magic for beer money at assorted Met parties and conferences. He also insisted on trying out new tricks on anyone who could not escape quickly enough.

'Just think of a card,' Brigstocke said, slipping into the patter. 'Don't tell me, though. I mean, what kind of a trick would *that* be?'

The trick was pretty good, and Thorne did his best to sound encouraging, but he had never really seen the point of magic. He had no real interest unless the magician explained how a trick was done. Russell Brigstocke was a decent copper, but he was certainly not a wizard.

'Who was the girl in your office?' Brigstocke asked, putting away the cards.

Thorne told him about Anna Carpenter and the Curious Case of the Suntanned Corpse. Brigstocke had not worked on the Langford inquiry, but he remembered the investigation well enough.

'Coming back from the dead,' he said. 'Now *that's* a decent trick.'

'It would be impressive.'

'Anything in it?'

Thorne took the photograph from his pocket and passed it over. 'God knows what Donna Langford's up to,' he said. 'I just hope that detective agency's screwing a decent wedge out of her.'

'Does it even look like him?'

Thorne stood at Brigstocke's shoulder and looked again. The dyed hair, the squint, the grin. That faint bell was ringing a little louder now, but surely that was just because Anna Carpenter had told him who it was *supposed* to be. 'Looks like a lot of people,' he said. 'Looks like a bad actor playing a gangster on his holidays.'

'What did you tell her?'

'That she was wasting her time and we couldn't afford to waste any of ours.'

'Absolutely right,' Brigstocke said. 'Not when we've got the latest Police Performance Assessment Framework to read and twelve-page reports on Standard Operating Procedure to complete by the end of the day.'

Thorne laughed and felt it take the chill off.

They talked about football for a few minutes, then families. Thorne asked after Brigstocke's three kids. The DCI asked Thorne how on earth his girlfriend was handling her job on the Kidnap Unit and managing to share a flat with someone who supported Spurs and listened to country music.

'How does she cope with all that pain and stress, day after day?' Brigstocke asked.

Thorne shook his head and let the punchline come.

'And the kidnaps must be even worse . . .'

They joked and chatted. Piss-takes and bullshit. Killing time and pretending not to think about the twelve strangers arguing in a room on the other side of the city.

FOUR

Anna bolted her dinner.

It was always fairly awkward when it was just her, Megan and Megan's latest boyfriend – on this occasion the admittedly gorgeous, but palpably brain-dead, Daniel – and it didn't help that Megan had done the cooking. Anna's housemate could only really manage pasta, and usually just threw in whatever happened to be lying around in the fridge. Her latest creation involved carrots, tinned peas and hard-boiled eggs, and watching Daniel slather brown sauce all over it didn't do much for Anna's appetite. Half a plate was filling enough, in the end.

It still tasted better than sushi, though . . .

After ten minutes' idle chat, during which nobody asked how her day had been, and ten more growing increasingly annoyed as Daniel sprawled on the sofa, smoking and dodging the washing-up, Anna went upstairs to her room. She lay on the bed and watched TV. Channel-hopped through the local news, a quiz show that left her utterly baffled, and a pointless remake of a sitcom that had been point-less first time around.

That had to be a sign of getting old, Anna thought: when they remake something you've grown up watching. It had to be a *bad* sign, surely. Looked at objectively by almost anybody – her parents, for example – it made her present circumstances seem that much sadder.

Working for peanuts and living like a student.

The house was only a couple of minutes' walk from the office which, along with the lower-than-average rent, justified for Anna the fact that she hated the area. It helped her forget, some of the time at least, that she had nothing in common with her nineteen-year-old housemate and had actually lived in a far nicer place when she *was* a student.

Back then, of course, her parents had been happy to chip in a little and help her do the place up. They had arrived unannounced, beaming on the doorstep with the radio she was always borrowing when she was at home and a brand-new microwave. They sent funny letters and food-parcels. Later, though, all of that had changed.

'What the hell did you think you were doing?'

Her father did not often lose his temper, and seeing him looking so lost, so genuinely confused, when Anna had announced that she had thrown in her job at the bank had been hugely upsetting. She felt ashamed just thinking about it; prickling with sweat and as close to tears as he had been when she'd told him.

'What are we supposed to think, your mum and me?'

Her mother had risen slowly from her seat as soon as Anna had begun saying her piece, but had made no response. She had just stared, red-faced and breathing noisily, as though she were trying her very best not to march across the carpet and slap her daughter.

'I'm really sorry you're upset,' Anna had said. Standing in her parents' overheated front room, she had heard her mother's voice in her own. The tone that had been reserved for those occasions when Anna or her sister had done something more than usually idiotic. 'But I think I'm old enough and ugly enough to make my own decisions, don't you?'

Her father had opened and closed his mouth. Her mother had just sat down again.

My own seriously stupid decisions . . .

Detective Inspector Tom Thorne knew nothing about Anna's history or her questionable lifestyle decisions, but clearly he thought she had been stupid to take on Donna Langford as a client. Thinking through their conversation on her journey back south of the river, she had decided he'd been pleasant enough, if a little condescending. No, more than pleasant, but he had made his scepticism and his *distaste* perfectly obvious, so she had not been holding out much hope.

A text message had been waiting for her when she came out of Victoria Tube Station: '*Like I thought. Not much we can do with this. Good luck with Donna.*'

She was halfway through a reply, trying to word a jokey comment about Thorne's broken photocopier, when she changed her mind and erased what she had typed.

Luck was hardly likely to help her, Anna decided. She could not imagine where it might come from and how it would turn things around. It would not prevent her having to make the phone call she was dreading; giving back the money she'd been paid in advance and admitting to her client – her *only* client – that she had run out of ideas.

Downstairs, housemate and housemate's stupid boyfriend had put on some music. Anna turned up the volume on the TV. She flopped back down on the bed, muttered a barrage of swear-words and slapped her palms repeatedly into the softness of the duvet.

I've got more important things to worry about, Thorne had said. Well, *she* hadn't. She needed the money and she needed something to get her blood pumping a little faster. Whatever Tom Thorne thought about her, Donna Langford had nowhere to turn and she was even more desperate than Anna had guessed when she'd first laid eyes on her.

There was something about Thorne, too; something that told her she could not quite write him off. She had seen it in his face when she'd challenged him, when she'd told him she thought he might be interested. When she had shamelessly done her very best to sound disappointed.

She sat up and reached for the remote. Smiling now, thinking about her poor put-upon father. He was a man who could always be relied upon for a decent homily, whether one was needed or not.

If you want something doing, gift horses and the price of politeness. Always wear clean underwear in case you're in an accident, that sort of thing.

You make your own luck . . .

'He's got a point,' Louise Porter said.

'Yeah, right.' Thorne had told her about Russell Brigstocke's joke: the kidnaps and the country music.

Louise held out her wine glass and Thorne topped it up. 'It's a wonder I don't throw you out.'

'It's *my* flat.'

'I'm fully expecting the Pope to make me a saint.'

'I think that only happens once you're dead.'

'See? Everything Russell said is true *and* you're a smartarse.'

They had spent more evenings together recently, at Thorne's place or occasionally at Louise's in Pimlico, than was usually the case. Louise's team on the Kidnap Unit was less busy than it had been in a long time and Thorne had not caught a murder that necessitated too much over-time. Certainly nothing as all-consuming as the Andrea Keane inquiry.

He had picked up a takeaway en route from Hendon, ignoring the Bengal Lancer – his usual port of call – and opting instead to try a new Greek place a little further south on the Kentish Town Road. The food had been fine, but looking down at what was left of his chicken sou-vlaki, Thorne wished he had not been so adventurous.

It wasn't like him, after all.

They drank their wine and a silence grew between them, while Louise flicked through the *Evening Standard* and Thorne watched the ten o'clock news. It was comfortable enough, as it should have been, more than two years into their relationship. But since Louise had lost a baby the year before, Thorne had found it hard to take anything for granted.

An equilibrium had returned, but it felt precarious.

Often, it seemed to Thorne, they moved too cautiously around one another, circling their loss like wild animals. Curious, but wary. She got angry if she felt that he was treating her differently, and he would overcompensate, storming around the flat and taking out his bad day, his foul mood, his grief on her.

It was difficult.

The mildest of disagreements, a furious row, a fuck . . .

Sometimes it felt wrong to Thorne how easily one could lead to the next, and that any of them was really about a hundred different things. He had tried to explain it to Phil Hendricks – his closest friend and a good one to Louise, too – one night in front of Sky Sports.

'I bet the row lasts longer,' Hendricks had said.

'I just can't bear the thought of her in pain,' Thorne had said, at which point Hendricks had stopped joking.

'Tom?'

Thorne looked over and saw that Louise was watching him over the top of her paper.

'There's no point worrying about it,' she said. She laid down the paper and reached for the cat, curled up next to her on the sofa. 'There's nothing you can do, unless you fancy trying to nobble a couple of jurors.'

Thorne sighed, nodded. He knew she was right, but it wasn't helping. 'A couple of them are no older than Andrea was,' he said.

'So?'

'So, you worry they can't make a . . . mature decision.'

'"Mature" meaning "guilty".'

'That they won't see what Chambers is really like.'

'You want to raise the legal age for jury service? To what – twenty-one? Forty?'

'I'm just saying.'

'You don't think an eighteen-year-old knows exactly what the likes of Adam Chambers is capable of?' She jabbed a finger at her *Standard*. 'Kids half that age are doing worse things every day of the week. Knifing each other for an iPhone.'

Thorne shook his head.

'Come on, you've dealt with enough of them.'

'Not the same,' Thorne said. 'You're right . . . but most of the time there's a reason at least. I'm not justifying it, course I'm not, but it's not the same as what Chambers did to Andrea Keane.'

'You don't know what he did.'

'They don't *enjoy* it.'

Louise picked up her paper again, read for a minute, then asked Thorne if he'd remembered to put the leftover souvlaki in tin-foil. He was on his way to the kitchen when the doorbell rang.

Louise asked the question with a look. Thorne shrugged a 'no idea' and moved towards the door.

'Look, I know I should have called, so I'm sorry if it's a bit late . . .'

Thorne's flat was on the ground floor, but the entrance to the building was half a dozen steps up from the street. He peered down at his visitor from the edge of the half-open door, his expression making it abundantly clear that he was cold and less than delighted to see her.

'How did you get my address?'

She smiled. 'I'm a detective.'

Thorne waited.

'I've got a friend who works for the DVLA.'

'*Used to*,' Thorne said. 'She just lost her job.'

'Oh come on—'

'What do you want, Anna?'

She climbed a couple of steps, then leaned towards Thorne and held out a hand. He took the piece of paper she was brandishing.

'It's Donna's address.'

'Haven't we been through this?'

'Just go and see her,' Anna said. 'Please.'

'There's no point.' Thorne rubbed at his bare forearms, shook his head. 'Look, I don't want to see her and I very much doubt she'd be too keen on seeing me.'

'I phoned her. She knows I've spoken to you.'

'So, phone her again. Tell her I'm not coming.'

'Just go round there for half an hour.' Anna took another step up towards the door. 'That's all I'm asking. If you still feel like it's a waste of time, fair enough.'

'I will.'

'Meaning you'll go, right?'

'I thought you were just misguided this morning,' Thorne said. 'Now I think you're misguided and pushy.' He looked down at the slip of paper. An address in Seven Sisters.

'You got changed.'

Thorne looked up. 'What?'

'This morning,' Anna said, pointing, 'you looked like you couldn't wait to get out of that suit.'

Thorne suddenly felt rather self-conscious in his rattiest jeans, socks and T-shirt; even more so when he sensed Louise at his shoulder. He opened the door a little wider, so that she and Anna could see each other, made the introductions.

'I'm really sorry to disturb you,' Anna said. 'I'm just being pushy.'

'It's OK,' Louise said, not really getting it. 'And you're welcome to come in, you know. I might go to bed, but if the pair of you have got stuff to talk about . . .'

Anna mumbled a thank-you and looked at her feet.

'It's fine,' Thorne said. 'We're about done.'

FIVE

For a few uncomfortable seconds, before reaching into his pocket for his warrant card, Thorne could only stare at the woman who had opened the door. She had short, bottle-blonde hair and a blank expression, her face thin and hard in spite of the bronze foundation and dark brown eyes.

Thorne was trying to keep the reaction from his face, the amazement that Donna Langford could have changed quite so much, when a second woman appeared from a doorway a few feet down the hall. Realising his mistake, Thorne nodded his recognition and she did the same. She said, 'It's OK,' and the woman at the door stepped back, her face finally softened by a sly smile, to let Thorne inside.

'You haven't changed much.' Donna said.

The flat was in the middle of a two-storey block on a busy road between the stations at Seven Sisters and South Tottenham. There were ornamental plastic animals – rabbits, turtles, herons – lined up along the path to the door and scattered around a front garden almost completely cast into shadow by a giant satellite dish. The orthodox Jewish community of Stamford Hill lay half a mile away, with the up-and-coming middle-class enclave of Stoke Newington a few minutes further south, but Donna Langford was living in one of the few areas in London where you could still buy a place for less than six figures and the pound shops outnumbered the Starbucks.

As comedowns went, it was steeper than most.

Donna introduced the blonde woman as Kate and asked Thorne if he wanted tea. While Kate went to the kitchen to fetch the drinks, Donna led Thorne into a smoky living room. As Thorne took it in – a small leather sofa and matching armchair, a plasma TV that all but filled the wall above the gas fire – Donna sat down and reached for the pack of cigarettes lying on a low, glass-topped table.

'Housing association,' she said. 'Kate found it.'

Thorne nodded. He could still hear the working-class Essex upbringing in her voice. If anything, it was stronger now than it had been before, the result of ten years inside trying to pretend she was tougher than she was. He thought about the last time he had visited this woman at her home – a surprisingly tasteful mock-Tudor pile in the Hertfordshire countryside. 'You couldn't even fit your old kitchen inside this place,' he said. He remembered the echo and the gleaming, dust-free surfaces. 'Never seen so much marble in my life.'

Donna blew out a plume of smoke and tossed the disposable lighter on to the table. 'I probably cooked in that kitchen three times,' she said. 'Never knew where anything was.'

'What happened to the house?'

'Gone. Same as everything else.'

'Right, yeah.' Thorne sat down on the sofa. He remembered that Donna had been the main beneficiary of her husband's will, that for a while this had been considered her motive for wanting him killed. As it had transpired, there was far less to inherit than anyone had thought – the majority of Alan Langford's assets turning out to have been paper – with the little that was tangible seized by the Serious Organised Crime Agency before Donna had even been sentenced. 'So, not a lot to come out to?'

'I had plenty,' Donna said. She shrugged, reached for a large glass ashtray and pulled it towards her. 'My priorities had changed.'

Kate shouted from the kitchen, asking if Thorne wanted sugar. He shouted back, letting her know that he did not.

'Actually,' Donna said, 'you've put on a bit of weight.'

'Yeah, well.' Thorne smiled, unamused. 'We've all changed.'

She too was heavier than she had been ten years before, puffy-faced and jowly, while her hair, which Thorne also recalled that she had been inordinately proud of, was grey and far from perfectly coiffured. She was still prison-pale and, on top of the smoking habit, she had acquired a wariness that Thorne had seen in many with a few years inside under their belt. She shifted focus every few seconds, the circles beneath her eyes as blue-black as bruises.

She might have been the mother of the woman Thorne had last seen a decade earlier.

'Her Majesty does pretty good makeovers,' Donna said, seeing what Thorne was thinking. She nodded towards Kate, who was coming through the door with three mugs and a packet of biscuits. 'Not *that* bloody drastic, though.'

Thorne looked from Donna to Kate. 'Sorry.'

Donna leaned over, smirking, to stub out her cigarette. 'You thought she was me, didn't you?'

Thorne looked again and saw that Donna's companion was at least ten years younger than he had originally taken her for, ten years younger than Donna herself. He also noticed the delicate swirls of blue that snaked up from below the neck of her T-shirt. He could just make out a 'D' and an 'O' and guessed what the rest of the tattoo spelled out. Now he could see that there was no physical similarity whatsoever between the two women. What had seemed familiar to him was merely something they shared in their expressions: a suspicion, a challenge, an invitation to judge.

He had simply recognised an ex-con.

Kate smiled as she handed Thorne his tea, that invitation even clearer this time. 'Me and Donna met in Holloway, a couple of years back.'

'I'm thrilled for you,' Thorne said.

'I was released nine months ago. Got all this set up for us.'

'It's quite lovely.'

Kate bent down and took a cigarette from the packet on the table. 'Donna *said* you were a wanker.'

'Sorry, I just don't give a toss,' Thorne said.

Kate shrugged, like that made sense, and lit the cigarette. She took two good, deep drags. 'So, you going to find her ex, then?'

Thorne held up his free hand. 'Look, I'm just here because someone asked me, OK? And because I'm an idiot.'

Kate took two more cigarettes from the pack and slipped them into her shirt pocket. 'I'll leave you to get on with it.'

'You don't need to go,' Donna said.

But Kate was already at the door, her back to them, waggling her fingers in a goodbye.

When the door closed, Donna said, 'I couldn't do this without her.'

'Do what?'

'You saw the photograph of Alan.'

'I saw a photograph,' Thorne said.

'Come on, you know it's him.' She leaned forward in her chair. 'You know Alan's still alive.'

Thorne took a slurp of tea. Deciding he might just as well stay until he had finished it, he went over some of the same ground he had covered with Anna Carpenter. Donna had received the photograph two months earlier in a plain brown envelope addressed to her at HMP Holloway. There had been no accompanying note. Two more pictures had followed, both delivered in the same way. Then, a fortnight ago, after her release, a fourth had arrived at the flat.

Donna showed Thorne the three other photos. They were all from the same batch, dated three months earlier, each shot showing the man in more or less the same pose, holding up his glass of beer or drinking from it. The same triumphant grin. The same sea and sky, the same black mountain and distant boat.

'No helpful postmark, I suppose?' Thorne asked.

'All posted in London,' Donna said.

41

'You keep the envelopes?'

'I didn't think. Sorry.'

Thorne stared down at the photographs laid out on the table, listened to the rustle and click of the lighter, the faint hiss as Donna lit another cigarette.

'Why didn't you come to us straight away?' Thorne asked.

'Because I knew you'd be like this. Suspicious. I knew you'd think I was full of shit.'

'But you didn't mind when Anna came to see me?'

'She's a nice girl,' Donna said. 'But to be honest, I don't think she does much more than fetch and carry. I'd rather you lot weren't involved, no point me pretending otherwise, but if it's the only way I'm going to find out . . .'

'Find out why the photos are being sent?'

Donna nodded. Her eyes were closed and smoke drifted from the corner of her mouth.

'And who's sending them?'

'Where he is,' she said. 'I want to know where that bastard is.'

Thorne fought the temptation to make some crack about knowing *exactly* where Donna's ex-husband was, about there not being an awful lot left of him, seeing as how he had essentially been cremated twice. He watched as Donna reached for another stack of photographs from a small sideboard, flicked through them, then passed a couple across.

These were much older. Donna and Alan Langford dressed up to the nines on an evening out. Black tie for him, cocktail dress for her, and best smiles for the camera.

'Looks fancy,' Thorne said.

'Some charity bash or other.' Donna spat the words out as if she now saw what a sham her life had been back then. The contented wife. The gangster masquerading as philanthropist. She pointed from one image of her ex-husband to the other; from a photograph taken a dozen years earlier to one dated a few months ago. 'You can see it's him, can't you?'

Thorne looked. He could not deny the resemblance.

'Alan had a scar,' Donna said. 'He got knifed in the belly when he was a teenager, some ruck in the local pub.' She pointed again at the photo of the older man and Thorne saw the mark: a pale line just above the crinkled waistband of the swimming shorts, clear against the sagging, brown gut. 'I reckon he's had a bit of work done – something around the eyes is different and he's dyed his hair – but it's definitely him.'

'All right, for the sake of argument, let's say it's him . . .'

'Christ Almighty!' She sighed, dropped back in her chair. 'Your eyesight going as well, is it?'

'Look, *if* it's him, it's a fair bet he's not spending his time playing bowls and doing the gardening, right?'

She nodded. 'He'll be into something dodgy.'

'So, I'll put in a word with SOCA and see what they want to do with it, OK? I can't really do any more than that.'

'If it's him, don't you want to know *how*?' She knocked the worm of ash from her cigarette. 'How he can still be alive, swanning around in the sunshine, when he burned to death ten years ago in Epping Forest? If it's him, don't you want to know whose body was in that car?'

Hypothetical as he still believed – *just* believed – the question was, it had been rattling around in Thorne's head ever since Anna Carpenter's visit to Becke House. *Somebody* had been handcuffed to the wheel of that car, even if it had not been Alan Langford. Somebody's flesh had spat and melted on to the leather seats.

'Granted,' Thorne said, 'there are reasons why we might want to find Alan Langford if we thought he was the man in these pictures. But why do *you* want to find him? I'm guessing you're not looking to kiss and make up, see if he's got room on his yacht for you and your girlfriend.'

'Me and Kate are fine as we are.'

'I'm pleased for you. But even so, you've got good reason to be ever so slightly pissed off with him.'

'Life's too short.'

'For some more than others,' Thorne said.

'I was angrier with him when I thought he was dead than I am now,' Donna said. 'I could have happily killed him a dozen times over. It's not about that any more.'

'So why, then?'

'I want to find him,' Donna said, 'because I think he's got my daughter.'

Thorne had completely forgotten that there had been a child. A memory stirred and came quickly into focus: a young girl standing at the fridge in that cavernous kitchen, pouring herself something to drink, asking her mother who Thorne was and what he wanted.

He struggled to remember the name. Emma? Ellen?

'I'm listening,' Thorne said.

'Ellie was only seven when I went inside, and there was no one to take her. Nobody who wanted her at any rate. Nobody who Social Services considered fit for it.' She leaned forward, mashed her cigarette butt into the ashtray, and told Thorne that with no grandparents to step in, her daughter had eventually been taken into long-term foster care. 'My younger sister would have taken her if she'd had to, but we never got on that well. Besides which, her old man wasn't keen. The only other option was Alan's brother, but he had even more form than Alan, which didn't make him an ideal candidate either. So . . .'

Thorne felt a niggle of guilt that he had not known any of this, nor taken the trouble to find out. But it was the way things worked. Though not always successful, he tried not to think too much about those he put away or the people they left behind. His concerns were generally reserved for the dead and their relatives. But in this case, of course, he had not cared a great deal about the victim, either.

'When did you last see her?' Thorne asked.

'The day I was arrested.'

'What? I don't understand.'

'Obviously she was way too young to visit,' Donna said. 'I was told she'd gone into care, that she was doing OK and that Social Services would consider allowing visits when she turned sixteen. Meanwhile, I got photos.' She reached for yet more pictures and passed them across to Thorne. 'Three or four times a year. Occasionally they let her put a note or a drawing in with them.'

Thorne saw the girl he remembered from Donna's kitchen growing up over the course of a dozen or so finger-smeared photographs. A gawky-looking child cradling a puppy. A girl with long, blonde hair posing with her friends in netball kit. A sullen teenager, the hair now cut short and dyed black, the practised and perfected expression somewhere between boredom and resentment.

'When she was sixteen,' Donna said, 'Social Services wrote and told me that, considering the severity of my offence, they had decided it would not be in my daughter's best interests to visit until she was eighteen. Then, last August . . .' She stopped and took a deep breath, swallowed hard. When she spoke again, it was barely above a whisper. 'I got a letter telling me that she'd gone missing.'

'What happened?'

'She vanished, simple as that. According to her foster parents, she went out one night and never came home. They were upset, obviously, but since she was eighteen the police weren't interested and that was that.' She picked up the cigarette packet, then dropped it back on to the table. The whisper had darkened. 'Social Services said they thought I'd like to know. *Thought I'd like to know.* Can you believe that?'

'If she went missing last August,' Thorne said, 'that was only a few months before you received the first photograph.'

'She didn't go missing. She was *taken*.'

'Don't you think the two things might be connected?'

If Donna heard the question, she showed no sign of it. She just stared at Thorne, her breathing heavy and her eyes filling as she reached for her cigarettes yet again, turned the packet over and over in her hands. 'I need her back,' she said. 'I was taken from her. Now she's been taken from me.' She looked at Thorne. 'Can you find her?'

Thorne could not hold the look. He dropped his eyes to the table-top, to the changing face of Ellie Langford.

'Can you?'

An eighteen-year-old girl, gone. Missing.

Another one.

The phone buzzed in Thorne's jacket pocket and he stood up quickly. He saw that it was DS Dave Holland calling, told Donna he needed to take it, and stepped into the corridor.

'It's Chambers,' Holland said. 'It's not good news.'

'Oh, Jesus.'

'Bastard's on TV right now.'

Thorne walked back into the living room and asked Donna if she would mind turning on her television.

It was actually the bastard's solicitor doing all the talking, posing on the steps outside the Old Bailey and issuing a statement on his client's behalf because 'Mr Chambers' was 'too overcome to speak'. Family and friends were thanked, as were those who continued to believe in his client and to have faith in a just outcome. Chambers himself stood a few feet behind and to the right. He kept his head down, nodding in agreement, looking up only once to wave at the rank of photographers who were shouting his name.

He smiled shyly. He'd already taken off his tie.

Kate had appeared in the doorway behind Thorne. 'He definitely did it,' she said, nodding towards the TV. 'I said that right from the start, didn't I, Don? He killed that poor girl and hid her somewhere. Look at him, you can *see* it.'

'You can't see anything,' Donna said. 'You can never tell.' She shook her head. 'Not everything's what it seems, is it? I mean, I thought Alan was dead.'

'Thanks for the tea,' Thorne said.

SIX

Unexpectedly running into his chief superintendent could provoke a wide range of emotions in Tom Thorne. Revulsion, horror and fury were among the most common. But seeing him with his feet under Russell Brigstocke's desk, today of all days, caused Thorne to feel nothing but a wash of bog-standard bemusement.

Thorne was spotted hovering in the doorway, beckoned into the office and instructed to close the door.

As a man who normally kept well away on days such as this one, blithely wafting the stink of failure in the direction of others, Trevor Jesmond was the last person Thorne expected to see. Had the Chambers result gone the other way, of course, it would have been a different story. Jesmond would have been the first one cracking open the supermarket Cava and saying his finely honed piece to all and sundry.

Failure, though, did not touch the likes of Trevor Jesmond. Not in any sense.

Thorne walked towards the desk, nodding to Brigstocke, who was seated near the window, as he went. Even before he had sat down, Jesmond was shaking his head, then raising his arms in theatrical disbelief and giving it his best, matey 'What can you do?' expression.

'No sense to it, Tom,' he said. 'No sense at all. Just chalk it up.'

Chalk it up? You pathetic, pussy-arsed tosser.

'Right,' Thorne said.

'You did everything you could. You did a fantastic job.'

So, it's *my* fault? thought Thorne. 'Thanks,' he said.

'Just put it behind you. Get back on the horse.'

Why are you *here*?

'Now, obviously, I came in to gee the team up a bit in the wake of this Chambers fiasco, but seeing as I'm here . . .'

Here we go . . .

Jesmond leaned forward, leafing through the papers in front of him on the desk. He nodded towards Brigstocke, and Thorne noticed that the bald patch was that little bit bigger than last time; that even though there was less hair, the production of dandruff only seemed to have increased.

'I've been talking to Russell about this Alan Langford thing.'

Thorne glanced at Brigstocke, whose barely perceptible shrug told Thorne everything he needed to know. DCI was a tricky rank; caught in an uncomfortable limbo between the lads and the brass. 'Like a cock in a zip,' Brigstocke had told Thorne once. 'Up or down, it's a world of pain.'

'What *thing* are we talking about?' Thorne asked.

'No need to be arsey, Tom,' Brigstocke said. 'You're not the only one around here in a bad mood.'

Jesmond waved away the DCI's concerns. He had not stopped smiling. 'The same thing that took you to Donna Langford's this morning.'

Thorne watched Jesmond's smile widen as he enjoyed his moment or two of triumph; watched him shake his head as though it meant nothing.

'I checked the log,' Jesmond said. 'No big mystery. I saw the address you'd signed out to for the morning was the same as the one I've got in front of me.' He picked up a sheaf of papers. 'I started doing my homework yesterday, putting a small dossier together as soon as Russell had filled me in on this photo business.' He straightened the

48

papers, laid them down again. 'So, what do we think, Tom? Is Alan Langford still alive and kicking?'

'I reckon so,' Thorne said. 'Either that or he's got a double.' It was strange how saying it made Thorne realise that he'd known who the man was from the first moment he'd clapped eyes on the photo. That without quite understanding why, it had been easier to pretend otherwise. But having acknowledged the simple and seemingly harmless fact of it, he still felt as though denial might have been the safer option. As though he were no more than a step or two away from a terrible drop.

'Well, I don't think there's any reason to panic,' Jesmond said. 'Russell?'

Brigstocke was cleaning his glasses. 'No reason at all. There's no way a miscarriage-of-justice suit would stick. I mean, regardless of whether the man she wanted dead was the man who actually died, Donna Langford *did* conspire to kill her husband. She's certainly not denying that, so there's no worries on that score.'

'What about Monahan?'

'Same thing,' Brigstocke said. 'We know he killed *somebody*, so I can't see an appeal with any legs coming from that direction either.'

'Looks like we can all sleep easy in our beds, then,' Thorne said.

Jesmond missed the sarcasm or chose to ignore it. 'I'm not sure that's quite true, Inspector. In the light of these developments, we have to look at the Langford inquiry again and it seems obvious to me that, in retrospect, we might have done one or two things differently.'

So, this one's down to me as well, is it? Thorne thought. He cleared his throat. 'Such as?'

'Well, DNA and dental checks are the obvious ones.'

'She identified him, for Christ's sake!' Thorne saw Brigstocke raise a hand in warning. He raised his own to make it clear that he was perfectly in control, that he was unlikely to throw himself across the desk and start throttling the chief superintendent just yet. 'The body was the same height as Alan Langford and wore Alan Langford's jewellery. And Alan Langford's wife formally identified it.'

'Even so—'

'And if all that wasn't enough, she knew it was him handcuffed to the wheel of that Jag because she had paid somebody to do it. Bearing that little lot in mind, sir, aside from the formality of the post-mortem, there seemed no reason to trouble the boys in the white coats.'

'However it might have *seemed*, a belt-and-braces approach is always advisable. And it would certainly have paid off in this instance.'

Thorne could not suppress a grin, remembering something. 'On top of which, I seem to recall a memo from yourself which was widely circulated at the time, implementing a Command-wide cost-cutting scheme.'

'Hang on . . .'

Thorne leaned forward, enjoying it. '"Any non-essential procedures involving payment to external bodies or individual specialists must be carefully considered and if at all possible . . ." Blah blah blah, bullshit like that. With respect. Sir.'

Jesmond's smile was long gone, although Thorne noticed one creeping across Brigstocke's chops. 'We need to cover ourselves.'

'How?' Thorne asked.

'Take the case,' Jesmond said. 'Treat it as though you've just caught the Epping Forest Barbecue all over again. We desperately need to ID the body, and as there's now every reason to believe that Alan Langford had something to do with the murder, we need to find him. What do you think the ex-Mrs Langford wants out of all this?'

Thorne told them about his conversation with Donna Langford, about the daughter that had gone missing and Donna's belief that her ex-husband was responsible.

'Well, that clearly needs to be another element of the inquiry,' Jesmond said. 'We need to keep her happy.'

'Do we?'

'She may not have a leg to stand on legally, but she might decide to make a few quid by selling her story. If she went to the press or wrote a book, we could be made to look like idiots.'

Thorne bit his tongue.

'Let's give her what she wants,' Brigstocke said. 'After all, it's what we want too, near enough.'

Thorne had no real objection, at least not when it came to searching for Ellie Langford. Her mother's concern was genuine. And it was not the first time Thorne had looked at photographs of a missing girl and found it hard to catch his breath for a few seconds. 'OK, whatever,' he said.

Jesmond nodded and grunted enthusiastically. 'But let's try to keep it all as low key as we can, all right? Make this a priority, but we don't want any bulls in china shops.'

Thorne did not need telling which particular bull his superior officer was talking about. 'What about Anna Carpenter?' he asked. Jesmond glanced down at his papers. Clearly the homework had not been that thorough. 'The private detective.'

'Right.' Jesmond thought for a few seconds. 'She could embarrass us too, if she felt like talking to the papers.' He looked over to Brigstocke, received a nod of agreement. 'What does she want?'

'This case,' Thorne said. 'Well, *any* case, I'm guessing, but she's keen to do something.'

'OK, let her get involved,' Jesmond said. He saw Thorne open his mouth to object. 'Or let her *think* she's involved. Tell her she can shadow you?'

'You're joking, right?'

'As long as she knows when to keep her mouth shut, it shouldn't be a problem. Fair enough? Russell?'

'I can't see it doing any harm,' Brigstocke said.

Thorne shook his head. 'Yeah, well, you're not the poor sod who'll be stuck with her.'

Jesmond stood up, said that he needed to crack on. To get into the incident room and do whatever he could to build morale, bearing in mind what had happened. On his way out of the door, he told Brigstocke and Thorne that he was pleased they were all singing from the same hymn sheet.

'What a racket *that's* going to be,' Thorne said.

The Royal Oak was unlikely to attract anyone for whom great service or a friendly atmosphere was important, but it was five minutes' walk from both the Peel Centre and Colindale Station. As such, and with an ex-DI's name above the front door, it was always going to be a pub where the Met's finest, and its decidedly less fine, were in the majority. Tonight, though, any punter without a warrant card would have been well advised to open a few cans at home instead.

It was wall-to-wall Job.

The clientele could equally well have been bikers, football fans or braying, pissed-up City boys. Friends, colleagues or strangers, it hardly mattered. Something in their shared experience, in the unspoken bonds between these men and women, caused feelings to run high and wild as bewilderment turned to anger and sorrows were drowned many times over in white wine, Stella and Jameson's. Had it not been for the stronger smell coming from the toilets, the whiff of testosterone might have been overpowering, drifting above the pockets of aggression and self-pity as Thorne pushed his way to the bar. Walking back to the table with another Guinness for himself and lager-tops for Dave Holland and Yvonne Kitson, he was accosted several times by those keen to give vent to one emotion or another; to pass comment on the only topic of conversation in the room.

'Bad luck, mate . . .'

'Don't worry, he'll get what's coming to him.'

'Wankers!'

Thorne handed Holland and Kitson their drinks and sat down, wondering exactly who that last half-cut philosopher had been talking about. The members of the jury? Adam Chambers and his legal team? Thorne and his? Himself and every other copper in the pub for not making a better job of the case?

Whichever it was, Thorne wasn't arguing.

'Cheers,' Holland said.

Thorne nodded and drank.

'They're like arseholes,' Kitson said.

'What are?'

'Opinions.'

Holland swallowed. 'Every bugger's got one.'

Thorne looked from one to the other. 'So, what's yours?'

Thorne had spent a good deal of the morning with Russell Brigstocke, speculating as to what might have happened in that jury room, but he had yet to sit and talk things through with anyone else whose opinion he valued. He had tried to get hold of Louise, but she had been in and out of meetings all day and able to do no more than leave a message saying how sorry she was.

Kitson was a damn sight less cautious than she had once been when it came to speaking her mind; and Holland, though not quite the wide-eyed innocent he used to be, could still usually be counted upon to say what he thought.

'It's hard enough getting a conviction at the best of times,' Holland said. 'You've got the judge instructing the jury, banging on about reasonable doubt and the weight of evidence, all that.'

Kitson nodded. 'So, when you haven't got a body and there's a brief who knows what he's doing, you're really up against it.' She looked at Thorne. '*We're* up against it.'

'Nothing else you could have done,' Holland said.

Thorne blinked slowly and imagined Adam Chambers celebrating, pissing it up the wall in some West End bar where there were far fewer police officers knocking around. He pictured the jubilant friends and family and supposed that, in a way, it was a let-off for them, too. There would be no need to lie to work colleagues or rewrite their personal histories. They would not have to duck difficult questions when journalists came knocking every year on Andrea Keane's birthday, insisting that they must know something about what happened to her. Now they could happily let their own doubts about Adam Chambers' innocence – and Thorne knew they had them – shrivel, until they seemed like something only dreamed or imagined.

'We've just got to crack on,' Kitson said.

'Life's too short, right?' Thorne necked a third of his pint, swallowed back a belch. 'But a lot shorter for some than it is for others.' He thought about two eighteen-year-old girls. The memory of one sullied by injustice. A chance, perhaps, to find the other. And to make himself feel a damn sight better, to salve a conscience scarred by his failure to find the first.

The horse that Jesmond thought he should get back on.

They were joined by Sam Karim, who brought another round to the table just as Russell Brigstocke stood up and made a short speech. The DCI thanked everyone for their hard work, told the team they were the best he had ever worked with, and said that one day, if something new turned up, they might get another crack at it. There were cheers and some half-hearted applause, then the pub drank a toast to Andrea Keane.

'God bless,' Thorne said. It was the kind of thing a copper with a drink inside him came out with at such a moment. Even one without a religious bone in his body.

The Oak was hardly the sort of establishment to get done for after-hours drinking, but there was no more than fifteen minutes' official drinking time left when Thorne spotted someone he knew walking out of the Gents'. Gary Brand had been a DS on the original Alan Langford inquiry; had sat in on a couple of the Paul Monahan inter-views, if Thorne's memory served him correctly. He had stayed in the Homicide Command for another eighteen months or so afterwards, until a vacancy for an inspector had come up elsewhere, and was now working south of the river, as far as Thorne could remember.

Thorne thought it might be an idea to run a few things past some-one who had been part of the team ten years earlier. Moving through the crowd, he felt the drink starting to take hold. He took a few deep breaths. There was no way he was driving home, but that didn't matter a great deal. He had spent the afternoon on the phone, making the necessary arrangements, and he would not be needing the car much, if at all, the following day.

Brand looked pleased to see him and immediately reached for his wallet. They made for the bar. Thorne took a half, though he knew it was already a little late for caution.

'Hardly your local any more this, is it, Gary?'

Brand was a slim six-footer and a few years younger than Thorne.

His light hair was cut close to the scalp and he wore the kind of thin, soft-leather jacket that Thorne thought looked better on a woman. 'Well, obviously I know quite a few of the lads on the Chambers inquiry, and I've been following the case.' He was originally from the West Midlands and it was still clear enough in the flattened vowels and the downward intonation at the end of each sentence. As a result, he often sounded despondent, even if he were in the best of moods. He shrugged. 'Couldn't think of anywhere else I'd rather be tonight.' He raised his glass, touched it to Thorne's. 'What an absolute shocker.'

'We've had a few of those.'

'Right enough.'

'Talking of which . . .'

Thorne told Brand about the visit from Anna Carpenter and the photographs. About a case that had come back to life as miraculously as Alan Langford himself appeared to have done.

'He was always a slippery sod,' Brand said. 'The type that enjoyed making the likes of you and me look stupid.'

'The type to snatch his own daughter?'

'I don't see why not.'

'And what about the photos?'

Brand told Thorne that he had no idea why they might have been sent to Donna. 'So, what are you going to do?'

'See if I can get anything out of Paul Monahan.'

'Good luck,' Brand said. 'I don't remember that animal being particularly talkative.'

'Maybe he's mellowed in prison,' Thorne said. It was banter, no more than that. Thorne had checked Monahan's record that afternoon and discovered that he had hardly been a model prisoner. His sentence had been increased twice since his original conviction.

'Yeah, course he has.'

'He might be one of those types that takes degrees and spends his spare time making quilts for Oxfam.'

'My money's on the gym and homemade tattoos,' Brand said. 'But let me know how you get on . . .'

They exchanged mobile numbers and Thorne went back to his table. Holland asked if he wanted another, but faced with a straight choice between heading home now or fighting for a taxi later with half of Homicide Command, Thorne decided to make a move. He said as few goodbyes as he could get away with and headed out to the car park, grateful for the cold against his face and the fresh air.

He called home on his way to Colindale Tube Station and heard his own voice on the machine. He guessed that Louise had gone to bed or back to her own flat, but he left a message anyway.

Then he called Anna Carpenter.

He was suddenly aware, as he heard the call connect, that it was probably way too late to be ringing, that he should have called on his way *to* the Oak, or just sent a text. Then again, a part of him was hoping that she would not answer, or if she didn't, that she might not get the message he was about to leave.

When Anna's voicemail cut in, Thorne spoke a little more slowly than he might otherwise have, careful not to slur. 'This is Tom Thorne. Just calling to say, if you're still up for this, meet me at eight o'clock tomorrow morning outside the WHSmith at King's Cross Station. Bring your passport. And you might want to wear something that's a bit more . . . *severe* or whatever.'

SEVEN

Though there had been a prison on the same site since 1595, the majority of the current building dated from two hundred and fifty years later, with a brooding neo-Gothic gatehouse and wings arranged in the typical mid-nineteenth-century radial system. Like most Victorian prisons, HMP Wakefield had certainly not been designed to be beautiful, but approaching it, as he had done several times before, it seemed to Thorne as though every blackened brick and each barred window had been infused by those that had built it with something poisonous. Something subtle and dark that might leach from the building's brutal fabric into those inside and slowly kill off hope; *harden* them. Or perhaps it was the other way round. Was it the people within its walls that made the place so ugly?

Whether it was a Victorian monstrosity like Pentonville or Strangeways, or a pale, concrete, US-style penitentiary like Belmarsh, Thorne was never wholly comfortable stepping inside a prison.

He could see that Anna Carpenter felt the same way.

He watched her cheerfully handing over her passport at the first of three checkpoints they would have to pass through before being admitted into the main body of the prison.

'Trust me to get the wrong end of the bloody stick,' she said, nodding towards Thorne. 'There I was thinking that when he asked me to bring my passport, he was going to whisk me off on some glamorous, last-minute holiday.'

The man-monkey checking her details did not so much as glance up from the paperwork. Anna turned to Thorne, rolled her eyes. She was rattled, he could see that, and overdoing the nonchalance.

'Nice to chat,' she said, when her passport was handed back.

She was right to be apprehensive, though. Thorne knew that better than most. The outfit she was wearing – a suitably understated dark skirt and jacket – would lead any prisoner to assume she was a copper. She would feel studied and hated, just as much as Thorne always did. But, as a woman, she would also feel things that were a damn sight more unpleasant.

'He was a cheery so-and-so,' she said, as they moved on.

Rattled as she might have been, Anna seemed in a better mood now than she had been two and a half hours earlier at King's Cross, marching up to where Thorne stood slurping from a takeaway coffee at one minute before eight o'clock.

'A bit of notice would have been nice.'

'You're very punctual,' Thorne said. 'I like that.'

'And I don't like being told what to wear.'

'You should consider yourself lucky. I was dead set against you coming at all.'

'So why am I here?'

'Because I do what I'm told.'

'Why don't I believe that?'

Thorne blew on his coffee, began walking towards the platform.

'Coming where, anyway?' she asked, following. 'Do I get to find out where I'm going, or is that classified information? I'm guessing it's not Hogwarts.'

Thorne told her.

'Bloody hell.'

'"Bloody hell" is right,' Thorne said. 'Now, here are the rules . . .'

Once they were through security, they moved towards the Visits Area. Even though the route kept them well clear of prison landings and association areas, the atmosphere worsened. Wakefield was a high-security lifers' prison, and the air tasted a little different when so many of those breathing it had nothing to lose and no reason to give a shit. Anna was clearly still thrown simply by being there, maintaining an all but constant stream of frivolous comments as they walked.

'You need to turn it down a bit,' he said.

'Turn it down?'

'The volume. All of it. I know you're nervous, but—'

'I'm fine.'

'And I certainly don't want any chit-chat when we see Monahan. Fair enough?'

'Sorry,' she said. 'I talk too much, I know that. Always have. Overcompensating, I suppose.'

'For what?'

'All sorts.'

They rounded a corner and entered the waiting area. Two dozen people sat clutching torn-off, numbered tickets as though they were queuing at a supermarket deli counter. Thorne showed his authorisation to the officer at the desk, and he and Anna walked straight through to the Visits Area. The room was large, bright and airy, with several rows of clean tables and simple metal chairs. A prison officer sat near the doors at either end, while a third moved slowly up and down between the tables, leading a bored-looking sniffer-dog. The carpet smelled new and Thorne wondered if that made the dog's job any harder. It can't have helped, surely. How many visitors were able to waltz in with wraps of crack shoved up their arses for weeks after Allied Carpets had been in?

There was a supervised play area in one corner, and a few smaller rooms for private visits at the far end. As they moved past a refreshments counter towards one of these, Anna asked, 'What about building a rapport?'

'What?'

59

'No chit-chat, like you said, but don't we need to make him relaxed or whatever?'

'*We* don't need to do anything,' Thorne said. 'And trust me, you don't want any kind of "rapport" with a man like Paul Monahan.'

He was waiting for them, looking agitated, if not exactly nervous. His face and hair were both greyer than Thorne remembered, and he had filled out a little beneath the blue and white striped shirt he wore with standard HMP-issue jeans and training shoes. He stabbed at his watch. 'You're late.' The irritation was clear enough under the nasal Derry twang.

'Somewhere else you'd like to be?' Thorne asked. He took off his jacket, laid it across the back of a chair. Anna did the same.

'Got a class.'

Thorne nodded. It looked like he, rather than Gary Brand, had been closer to the mark when it came to guessing at Monahan's prison hobbies. That said, it might have been a class in cage fighting. Like most prisons, aside from a bewildering assortment of treatment pro-grammes, Wakefield had an enormous range of activities and educational opportunities on offer. Thorne happened to know for example that those working in the engineering workshop spent their time making security gates, grilles and fencing. Even *he* had to admit that sounded like taking the piss. 'I thought you might have a hot date.'

'You were funny as cancer ten years ago,' Monahan said. 'You've not got any funnier.'

'Nice to see you again, too.'

Monahan looked at Anna for the first time. 'Who's this?'

'Detective Carpenter,' Thorne said. Not a lie. Not exactly. He saw Monahan's eyes wander across Anna's body, lingering where they shouldn't. 'Let's crack on, shall we? Seeing as you're so busy.'

Monahan shrugged, leaned back.

'You know your former employer's out and about, don't you?' Thorne let it hang for a few seconds. 'I'm talking about Donna Langford, obviously.'

Another shrug. Monahan might have known, or known and not cared.

'Sorry, when I said "employer", did you think I meant Alan Langford?'

The hesitation was brief, but it was enough. 'Why would I think that?'

'Well, you did some work for him too, once upon a time. Before Donna hired you, I mean.'

'So?'

'So, I'm just trying to avoid any confusion.'

'You're the one who's confused, pal. How can *he* be out and about anywhere?'

'Of course. He's dead meat, isn't he?' Thorne shook his head in mock-annoyance at his own mock-idiocy. 'Seriously *overdone* meat, now I think about it, but certainly dead. Stupid mistake on my part. Don't know what I was thinking.' He looked hard at Monahan, watched the eyes move back to Anna.

Less about lust this time. More an attempt to change the way the conversation was heading.

'Isn't it kind of annoying?' Thorne asked. 'Donna on the out while you're still stuck in here, doing your GCSEs or whatever.'

'Not thought about it,' Monahan said.

'I don't think I believe you.'

'Believe what you like.'

'Not that you've done yourself a lot of favours, mind you. All that extra time getting whacked on to your sentence. Assaulting prison guards, trashing your cell . . .'

'Why should you care?'

'I couldn't give a toss, but it's not clever, is it?'

'I get wound up.'

'You must love that Seg Unit.'

Monahan's head dropped a little, one hand pulling at the fingers of the other. 'Can't do anything about it.'

'What have you got, another seven or eight years, minimum?'

A nod. His chin inching closer to his chest.

Thorne was about to speak again when Anna cut in. 'Sounds like it could get a whole lot longer if you're not careful,' she said. If she was aware of the hard look Thorne gave her, she chose to ignore it. 'You need to sort yourself out.'

Monahan raised his head, sniffed. After a few seconds he looked away from Anna, sat back in his chair and crossed his arms. Cocksure again and waiting for them to get to whatever it was they had come such a long way to talk to him about.

'There are ways to *reduce* your sentence,' Thorne said. 'Radical idea, I know.'

Monahan smiled thinly, with just a hint of prison teeth. 'Getting to it now, are we? What you actually want.'

'What? We can't just pop in to see how you are?'

'Like I said, funny as cancer.'

'It's really no big thing,' Thorne said. 'Just a little help with a murder we're trying to solve. Not even that, actually, because we know very well who the murderer is. It's more a question of trying to identify the victim.'

'Why should I know anything?'

'Well, because it was you that handcuffed the poor bastard to the wheel of that Jag and set fire to it.'

Monahan stared for a few seconds, then began to shake his head and show a few more teeth. 'You're mental, you know that?'

'Barking,' Thorne said. 'Completely off my trolley. But let's see just how mad I am, shall we? I mean, let's think for a minute about how this might have panned out. I'm guessing that Alan found out what his dearly beloved was up to. Overheard her on the phone or talking in her sleep, it doesn't really matter. Then he comes to you before you get a chance to do what she's paid you for and makes you a better offer.'

Monahan looked at Anna, nodded towards Thorne. 'Who did you piss off to get stuck with *him*?'

'So, you had to find someone to take his place,' Thorne said. 'Did you do that or did Alan find someone? Had to be someone roughly the

62

same height and general appearance, I suppose. Not that it really mattered by the time you'd finished with him.'

Monahan was still looking at Anna. 'Seriously, love, you want to put in for a transfer.'

'Thanks, I'll bear it in mind,' she said. 'Now tell us who you got to replace Alan Langford in that car.'

Thorne turned, ready with another hard stare of admonishment. Then he saw the look on Anna's face, and Monahan's reaction to her simple, straightforward question, and decided to save it for later.

Monahan composed himself. Took a deep breath. 'Alan Langford is dead, OK? Jesus, why do you think I'm in here? His missus paid me to get rid of him and I did what I was good at back then. Fair enough?'

'Well, it would be,' Thorne said. 'If I hadn't just seen a photo of Mr Langford looking ever so well.' Monahan swallowed and looked away. 'He's alive and kicking, Paul, and we all know it.'

'So, no need for any more bullshit,' Anna said.

Thorne nodded, sat back. 'Yep, that's another one on the out, getting himself a very nice suntan while you're rotting in here, the colour of a manky spud. I mean, we've got to presume he's been making it worth your while all these years, you saying nothing. Something nice to look forward to when you come out, I shouldn't wonder. And he's probably taking care of your nearest and dearest, right? Keeping up the mortgage payments, all that.'

'This is stupid,' Monahan said quietly. '*You're* the ones who are bullshitting.'

'Has it really been worth it, though?' Thorne almost sounded as if he meant it. 'I mean, you've already been in here a good long while, no matter how much you might cop for when you get out.'

Monahan stared above their heads, chewed at something.

'You've got a son, haven't you?' Anna asked.

Thorne took the cue without a beat. 'What is he now, mid-twenties?'

'Be nice to get out that bit sooner and see him,' Anna said. 'Don't you reckon?'

Monahan reddened, and as his hands tightened around the arm of his chair, in the few seconds before he dragged himself closer to the table, it was easy to see why he had spent so much time in segregation. He leaned towards Anna and whispered, 'I *reckon* that I'll be thinking about you a bit later.' His hand dropped to his groin and squeezed. 'When I'm lying on my bunk with my cock in my hand.'

Anna moved closer to him. 'That's nice to know, because I'll be thinking about you too, Paul.'

Thorne raised a hand. 'Anna . . .'

If there were any nerves left, she showed no sign of them. 'And I'll be having a good laugh, because I'll just have been shagged stupid by a bloke who can do whatever he wants, whenever he fancies it, and doesn't have to shit in a bucket.' Her smile developed as quickly as Monahan's disappeared. 'But you go ahead and enjoy yourself too.'

Monahan stood up quickly and Thorne moved with him, ready to step in if need be. For a moment, it looked as though Monahan might snap, but then he sucked his teeth and grinned, as though it had been no more than a cosy chinwag, before turning and walking to the door.

A guard appeared and Monahan told him that he was done.

'Have fun in class,' Thorne said.

EIGHT

They caught the two-thirty train back to London. As soon as they were settled in a relatively quiet carriage, Thorne gave Anna a ten-pound note and sent her to the buffet car for hot drinks and sandwiches. Once she had gone, he phoned Brigstocke.

'Well, I don't think we were telling Monahan anything he didn't know,' Thorne said.

'Other than the fact that *we* know.'

'Right.'

'That shake him?'

'I think so. We'll need to come back at some point, have another crack at him, but in the meantime we can gather a bit of ammunition. We need to look at his family. Get their bank statements, check out new cars they shouldn't be able to afford, where they've been going on their holidays, usual stuff.'

'I don't think it'll be as simple as that,' Brigstocke said. 'Probably all done in cash, nothing that can be traced.'

'You never know,' Thorne said. 'Give some people more than they're used to and there's always some idiot who can't resist flashing it around. The main thing is that word gets back to Monahan. As

65

long as he knows we're looking, putting on the pressure, he won't be quite so cocky next time we come to visit.'

'Course, he might not know much,' Brigstocke said. 'If Langford organised that side of it, he might have decided that the less people who knew the better.'

'Monahan knows something that's worth paying for. He could have made some sort of deal ten years ago, told us the truth and got himself a shorter sentence, but he swallowed it. Langford obviously promised him a decent whack in exchange for keeping his mouth shut, and I don't think he would have done that unless Monahan knew something . . . dangerous.'

'Like who was really in that Jag.'

'I reckon.'

Brigstocke told Thorne that he'd set up a meeting with somebody from the Serious and Organised Crime Agency, because trying to build a case against Alan Langford was likely to involve them at some point. They had departments that could uncover any financial irregularities or examine in forensic detail the business dealings that Langford – or whatever he was calling himself these days – had been engaged in since his 'death'. SOCA had money and manpower, but was not always easy to deal with and moved notoriously slowly.

'Be a damn sight simpler for everyone if we could just nail him for murder,' Brigstocke said.

'I'm doing my best,' Thorne said.

'And there's the small matter of finding him . . .' Again, Brigstocke explained that SOCA would have far greater resources available than any homicide team when it came to tracing overseas felons, but that they *did* need to know which country they should start looking in.

In the absence of the high-tech photographic facility Anna Carpenter had been talking about, Thorne had sent copies of the Langford photographs to a man he hoped would be able to help. Dennis Bethell was an informant of many years' standing. He was also something of a genius when it came to cameras and film development, albeit one who chose to use his talent in the production of hardcore pornography.

66

'I've told Dennis we're in a hurry,' Thorne said.

'How were things with your new partner?' Brigstocke asked.

'We need to have words.'

'That good, eh?'

When Thorne spotted Anna on her way back from the buffet car, he told Brigstocke that they were about to go into a tunnel, that he'd give him the details next time he saw him. Brigstocke told him not to bother coming back to the office, so Thorne agreed to call him from home.

'Have fun with young Miss Marple,' Brigstocke said.

Thorne took his tea and sandwiches and swore loudly enough to provoke disgusted looks from the elderly couple across the aisle when Anna told him there was no change from his tenner. He sugared his tea and lowered his voice and said, 'So, what the hell was all that about back there?'

'All what?'

'I told you not to say anything.'

'Come on, I couldn't just sit there like a plank,' Anna said. 'It would have looked really strange.'

'I don't care how it would have *looked*. I was there to question a potentially crucial witness and you were there to observe, that's all. I did not want you chipping in.'

'I thought we made a good team.'

'We're not any sort of team,' Thorne said.

'Whatever.'

'And what was all that stuff about his son?'

'That worked. You know it did. It got a reaction.'

'It's about getting the *right* reaction.' Thorne's voice was loud enough to have attracted the attention of the elderly couple again, but he was past caring. 'You were there as a courtesy, and you abused that.'

'Sorry—'

'It won't be happening again.'

'I said I'm sorry.'

Thorne sat back and bit into his sandwich. He lifted the bread and

67

peered down at the sliver of sweating ham. Rain was starting to streak the window, and the countryside moved past in blocks of brown and grey.

'Maybe you've got a problem working with women,' Anna said.

Thorne swallowed quickly. '*What?*'

'Some blokes do. The bloke I work for certainly does.'

'We were not *working* together.'

'You said that already.'

Thorne glanced across at the elderly couple and smiled. They both looked away. He lowered his voice. 'Anyway, that's bollocks. I've worked with plenty of women. I *still* work with plenty of women.'

'Are you married?'

'What?'

'I'm just making conversation. I mean, I presume that woman I met the other night . . .'

'We just live together,' Thorne said. 'Off and on. I don't mean that the relationship is off and on. I mean . . . we have our own places.'

'Sensible.'

'I'm glad you approve.'

'What does she do?'

'She's a police officer.' Thorne shoved the remains of his sandwich back into its bag. 'Not that it's any of your business.'

Anna held up her hands. 'Sorry.' She turned towards the window. '*Again.*'

Thorne wasn't sorry. It had needed saying, all of it. In spite of that, he started to feel a little guilty, watching her stare out at the damp and desolate Yorkshire landscape as the silence grew between them. She looked like a teenager who wanted to be older, trying hard not to show that she cared about being slapped down. She looked thwarted, and Thorne found himself thinking she was probably used to feeling like that. He also found himself wanting to know more about the 'bloke she worked for'. Wishing she would start jabbering again.

'Look, it *was* out of order,' he said, 'But you were probably right. That stuff about Monahan's son.'

She turned from the window.

'I'm not saying that I'd want you to do it again, OK? But, yes, it seemed to do the trick. It got the right reaction.'

She mumbled a 'thanks', doing her best not to look as delighted as she clearly was.

'That little speech at the end was pretty good, too. Were you just winding him up, or . . . ?'

'Meant every word,' Anna said.

'Prisoners don't *actually* shit in buckets any more, but aside from that it was very moving.'

Thorne had not seen her laugh before, not really. They were the best moments of an average day.

He wandered into the huge prison kitchen and made straight for the storage room at the far end. A couple of inmates he did not know well clocked him and went back to what they were doing, the less seen or said the better. Eventually, he caught the eye of the trustee he was looking for. He pointed towards the storeroom and patted his pocket. The trustee nodded, silently agreeing to watch the door in return for some future favour.

The deal was done with just a look, the smallest of gestures.

He shut the heavy door of the storeroom behind him, sat down alongside a rack of metal shelves stacked with catering-sized cans of soup, tomatoes and kidney beans. He took out the phone. It was small, out of necessity, and a basic model, but he did not need bells and whistles.

The call was answered quickly.

'You took your time,' the man said.

'It's the first chance I've had to call.'

'Busy schedule?'

Voices were raised right outside the door. He told the man to hang on, closed his hand around the phone, waited a minute. 'Sorry about that.'

'Where are you?'

'Don't worry, it's safe.'

'No point taking stupid risks . . .'

'Listen, there were coppers here today.'

'I know.'

'Visits Area still stinks of bacon.'

'Why do you think I sent the text?'

'So, what do you want me to do?'

The man paused, like he was taking a sip of something. 'I want you to start earning your money.'

Without feeling the need to check with Thorne, Louise had invited Phil Hendricks over. He arrived just as she was dishing up the pasta, a whiff of carbolic still lingering around him and cans of beer clanking in a plastic bag.

Thorne could see straight away that his friend was keen to kick back a little. 'Tough day at the office, dear?'

'I could do with a drink,' Hendricks said. 'Been cutting up a teenager all afternoon.' He took a can from the bag and opened it. 'I mean, obviously he'd already been cut up by several *other* teenagers.' He dropped his long black coat on to the sofa and sat down at the small dining table.

As Home Office-registered forensic pathologists went, Phil Hendricks was unusual, to say the least. Thorne had certainly not met any others with shaved heads, multiple body piercings and more tattoos than the average heavy metal guitarist. He had never met one as skilled either, or as empathetic to the victims he dissected. The jokes – delivered with immaculate timing in a flat, Mancunian accent – were often tasteless, but Thorne knew what was going on behind them.

He had seen his friend's pain up close and often.

'That smells fantastic, Lou.'

It had been a while since Hendricks had treated himself to a new piercing, something he usually did to mark the acquisition of a new boyfriend, but he was keen to show off his latest tattoo: a scattering of small red stars on his right shoulder.

'Looks like designer acne,' Thorne said.

Hendricks was chewing, so just stuck up a finger.

'Didn't fancy the "Sodomy" tat then?' Louise asked.

A few months earlier, a City-based chaplain had made headlines by saying that gay men should be 'marked' with government health warnings, like cigarette packets. His suggestion that they have 'Sodomy Can Seriously Damage Your Health' tattooed across their buttocks had caused predictable outrage and eventually forced the priest into hiding. 'I'm going to hunt the God-bothering little gobshite down,' Hendricks had said at the time. 'Damage *his* health.'

Now, he shook his head and grinned. 'Decided against it in the end,' he said. 'Mainly because I couldn't fit all those words across my perfectly tight little arse.'

Louise laughed and said that she would have had no trouble. In a decent-sized font. In capital letters.

Thorne talked about his trip to Wakefield, about Monahan's refusal to admit that the body in the Jag had not been Alan Langford's. About the need to prove that Monahan was being paid to keep quiet.

'If he's not going to cough, I don't see what else you can do.' Louise poured herself and Thorne more wine. 'You're only likely to get anywhere by following the money.'

'That won't get us very far though, will it?'

'Sorry, but you're not going to get it on a plate, darling.'

Ten years earlier, Hendricks had carried out the post-mortem on the body that had been found in Epping Forest. What had been left of it. 'You could always exhume the remains,' he said. 'There might be the odd blackened molar knocking around in the ashes. But even dental won't help unless you've got some idea who the victim was.'

'Which we haven't.'

'So, you're pretty much stuffed, mate. As long shots go, it's right up there with Tottenham getting a top-four finish.'

'Shouldn't you be heading home?' Thorne said.

They finished eating, opened another bottle and a couple more cans. Thorne put on a new CD of stripped-down Willie Nelson

71

recordings and Hendricks told him that it sounded as though someone was slowly feeding a cat through a mangle. Thorne pointed out that, as usual, Hendricks had now slagged off both his football team *and* his taste in music, and asked to be reminded exactly why Hendricks considered himself to be a friend. Hendricks said it was less about being a 'friend' and more to do with being the only person Thorne did not actually sleep with who was willing to put up with him.

Louise started gathering the plates, scraping at the leftovers. 'Who did you go up to Wakefield with today?'

'Sorry?'

'Boys' day out with Dave Holland, was it?'

Thorne looked for something other than simple curiosity in her face and felt blood move inexplicably to his own. He hesitated, began rubbing at a mark his glass had left on the table. 'Actually, I took that private detective with me,' he said. 'The one who popped round here the other night. *Had* to take her, in the end.'

'The girl?'

Thorne shrugged, pulled a face that he hoped would say, 'Ridiculous, I know,' and explained: 'Jesmond thinks we need to keep her on side, make sure she doesn't go blabbing to the papers about the fact that we screwed up with the Langford case.' He knew he was talking too fast, sounded as though he were lying. 'Pain in the arse, as it turned out, just like I told Jesmond it would be, but there we are. I got well and truly lumbered. What can I tell you?'

'You don't have to tell me anything,' Louise said, laughing. 'I just asked a simple question.'

She carried the plates out to the kitchen and began to load the dishwasher. Thorne looked over and saw Hendricks mouthing a 'What?' He waved the question away and stood up to change the CD.

Louise shouted from the kitchen: 'Do you want coffee, Phil?'

'No, I'm fine,' Hendricks said. 'I'll be up all night, and not in a good way.'

Thorne looked along the rack of albums, trying to decide whether Louise's laugh had been forced or genuine. He could not be sure

72

either way, but was fairly confident that the subject would resurface once Hendricks had left.

Louise appeared in the doorway. 'You sure?'

'I think I should probably be heading off.'

'I've got decaf.'

'Why don't you just stay the night?' Thorne asked.

Monahan's stomach had been plaguing him since late morning. He had been in and out of the toilets half a dozen times since the session with Thorne and his bitch of a sidekick, and whatever the hell was in the meat pie he'd had for dinner had made things a damn sight worse. He lay on his bunk, listening to his guts grumble and the voices echoing on the landing outside the cell door.

Animal noises.

When he was not in the Segregation Unit, this was his favourite part of the day. The hour he liked best. On his own, reading or smoking, while the other inmates got through association their own way, playing table tennis, working out or whatever. A bubble of peace, with the rest of the prison moving around him. He enjoyed the stillness – such as it was, with six hundred other blokes sharing the oxygen – but knew there was company just a few feet away, if ever he wanted it. He far preferred being alone in a crowd to those stinking, scratchy hours of genuine isolation, even though he'd always brought them on himself.

It was like he'd said to Thorne, though. Sometimes he just couldn't help himself.

Be nice to get out that bit sooner and see him.

He thought about what Thorne had said, the request for help that was really an offer. However tempting it might be, he knew it was short-term thinking. *Dangerous* thinking. The money being set aside every month for his release was a threat as well as a promise; he had always understood that. It put a price on his silence, but never let him forget what shooting his mouth off would cost him.

His life and his son's life, no question about that.

Living is what counts, right?

73

He thought about the man who promised and threatened so much, and above the sound of the acid bubbling in his gut, he heard the hiss and crackle of a fire. The *whump* of an explosion and the distant drumming of a woodpecker.

'Paul?'

There was a knock on the open cell door and Monahan sat up. Jeremy Grover was a con he got on with better than most. He did his time quietly enough and was fairly bright, as armed robbers went.

'Jez.'

'Thought you were coming to play cards.'

'Sorry, mate, my belly's a nightmare.'

'I'll have some tea then, if you're getting a brew on.'

Monahan swung his feet to the floor and walked over to where the kettle stood on a small table in the corner. He asked who was winning all the money, reached for a mug and promised to take all the lads to the cleaners as soon as he stopped shitting through the eye of a needle. Then he turned to say something else and stepped into a punch that pushed the breath from his lungs in an instant. Grover's breath hot and sour on his face.

'Jez . . . ?'

Only it wasn't a punch, course it wasn't, and there was already blood pooling on the floor as he slipped down to his knees and then dropped on to his side. It was hard to raise his head and he was scared to look at what was leaking into his hands. He saw Grover lean back against the door and then step forward as an officer pushed his way into the cell. He watched them speak while his guts slipped, warm between his fingers, but he could hear nothing, not really, until the officer had gone again and an alarm began to sound from a long way away.

PART TWO

HONEY-SWEET AND HELL-DARK

NINE

The man on the prison security desk had as little to say to Dave Holland as he had done to Thorne's more garrulous female colleague twenty-four hours earlier. There was no question of Anna Carpenter accompanying Thorne this time, not considering the reason he was returning to Wakefield.

Brigstocke had called just after 6 a.m., in no mood for going round the houses. 'Whoever was paying Paul Monahan to keep quiet can cancel the direct debit,' he said.

The Crime Scene Investigators from the West Yorkshire force had already been and gone, but the murder scene was still sealed off with blue tape that stretched from the cell door to the edge of the landing. Thorne and Holland were escorted on to the wing by a prison officer and met outside the cell by a grim-looking welcoming committee. Sonia Murray, an attractive black woman in her early thirties, was the prison's police liaison officer. She made herself known, then introduced Andy Boyle, the local DI, whose team had been on call when the incident had occurred.

Boyle seemed less than thrilled to meet his colleagues from down south. 'If we have to work together on this,' he said, 'I suppose we have to.' The Yorkshireman was clearly no shrinking violet, but he still had to raise his voice to make himself heard above the shouts and jeers that echoed along the landing. The entire wing had been confined to their cells for more than fifteen hours, since the body had been found, and the prisoners were not shy about making their feelings known. 'It's not ideal though, is it?'

'We'll try not to step on anyone's toes,' Holland said.

Thorne forced a smile, but was beyond caring if it was convincing. 'And if we do, we'll make sure we're wearing slippers.'

Paul Monahan's body was in the city mortuary, awaiting post-mortem. He had died on the way to hospital the previous evening, having been discovered on the floor of his cell with serious stab wounds. The prisoner who had been found inside the cell with Monahan had been taken to the local station, but he remained uncharged and had been returned to the prison that morning in anticipation of Thorne and Holland's arrival.

'So, here's the story,' Murray said. She emphasised the last word, making it clear to Thorne that they were now leaving the known facts behind and venturing into an area where all they had were possibilities, interpretation and bullshit. It was dangerous territory, and interesting. It was the part Thorne had always liked the most. 'A prison officer named Howard Cook entered Monahan's cell just after nine-thirty last night.' Murray was reading from a small notebook. 'He discovered a prisoner named Jeremy Grover covered in blood and bent over Monahan's body. Grover told Officer Cook that he had discovered the body a minute or so earlier, had been unable to find a pulse and was trying to perform CPR.'

'Good of him,' Holland said.

'Oh yeah, he's a regular good Samaritan is our Jez.'

'Except when he's waving sawn-off shotguns around in building societies,' said Boyle.

Murray returned to her notebook. 'Cook left the cell to sound the alarm, an ambulance was called and a Code Black was declared. Within twenty minutes, the wing was shut down and the police were informed.'

'We were here just after ten,' Boyle said. 'Monahan had already pegged it in the ambulance.'

Thorne nudged the cell door open and stepped inside. Everything except the bunk and the metal chair had been removed. The blood had run towards one wall, down the slope of an uneven floor. Dried, it looked almost black against the dark orange linoleum. 'Where's Officer Cook?' he asked.

Murray moved to the door. 'He was sent home and given a day's trauma leave,' she said. 'Standard practice after a Code Black incident.'

Thorne turned and walked back on to the landing.

Holland caught his eye and nodded towards the CCTV camera mounted high on the opposite wall. 'Should give us a bird's-eye view,' he said.

Thorne looked at Boyle. 'I presume you've checked the footage to see if anyone else went in there before Jez Grover?'

Boyle shrugged, satisfied that he knew something Thorne did not.

'The camera was not in operation,' Murray said. 'That wasn't established until the early hours of this morning.'

'Meaning it was broken or had been switched off?'

'No idea.'

'That's handy,' Holland said.

Thorne nodded, thinking. 'Murder weapon?'

Boyle shook his head. 'Turned the place upside down,' he said. 'Gave Grover a full body search an' all, just to be on the safe side, but no sign of it. Sharpened toothbrush, something like that, be easy enough to hide it where the sun don't shine.'

Holland winced. 'I don't suppose there were any other prisoners walking about covered in blood?'

'Not that we could find.'

'We'd best have a word with Mr Grover then,' Thorne said.

Murray said she would arrange to have Jeremy Grover taken down to the Visits Area. 'All visits have been cancelled,' she said. 'So you can pick a room out over there.'

Thorne said that would be fine and he and Holland followed

79

Murray down the landing. Those inside many of the cells they passed made it very clear what they thought of her. If she was upset by the vileness of the language or the suggestions, she did not show it.

As they walked down the stairs, Boyle caught up with Thorne. 'We've already had a pop at Grover,' he said. 'But if you think you can do any better . . .'

'Looks like I'd best get my slippers on,' Thorne said.

'Cheeky bastard.'

Thorne kept walking and did not stop smiling, but he made sure Boyle got a good look at his eyes and said, 'Why don't you piss off home and walk your whippet?'

It was the same room in which Thorne and Anna Carpenter had interviewed the man who had since become a murder victim. When Jeremy Grover was escorted in by a prison officer, he looked no more happy to be there than Paul Monahan had been.

'For Christ's sake, I've been through this already.'

Was no more happy . . .

Grover was taller and skinnier than the average armed robber, but his eyes were dead enough. There were flecks of ginger in the neatly trimmed goatee and a little grey in the curly brown hair. He was the same age as Thorne or thereabouts, but he looked lithe and wiry in regulation jeans and striped shirt. Thorne marked him down straight away as the sort who worked out not because he wanted to display himself, but because he enjoyed being fit. The sort who felt the need to stay keen and ready.

He looked past Thorne and Holland, who were seated at the table, towards Andy Boyle, who was leaning against the wall behind them. 'Any chance of getting my trainers back?'

Boyle said nothing, looking as though he could not bear to expend any more energy than was necessary to chew his gum.

'That's a "no" then, is it?'

Grover's bloodstained clothes had been taken and sent to the Forensic Science Service laboratory for testing. Nobody was expecting anything other than confirmation that the blood and scraps of stomach tissue belonged to Paul Monahan. Grover could not deny that he had been covered in it.

'Those look all right,' Holland said. He nodded towards the shiny white training shoes with which Grover had been issued. Grover glanced down at them then looked back at Holland as though he were something stuck to the bottom of one.

'So, you got your Boy Scout first-aid badge, did you?' Thorne asked.

'Come again?'

'Or maybe you just saw it on *Casualty*. Either way, very heroic – trying to save your friend's life.'

'You don't think about it, you know? You just do whatever you can.'

'You didn't think about alerting a prison officer? I mean, they're probably trained for it, right?'

'Like I said—'

'Oh, I forgot,' Thorne said. 'One came along pretty quickly anyway, didn't he?'

'Bit of luck,' Holland said.

'So, here's our problem,' Thorne said. 'And I'm sure it's the same problem Detective Inspector Boyle has.' He turned. 'Right, Detective Inspector Boyle?'

Boyle nodded.

'Thing is, the man who attacked your mate Paul, who killed him, as it turns out, seems to have vanished into thin air. Disappeared inside a high-security prison without so much as a spot of blood on his clothes *and* taken the murder weapon with him.' Thorne held up his hands. 'Any thoughts? I mean, you can see why we're a bit confused here, can't you?'

Grover sat back, stretched his long legs underneath the table. 'If you think I'm going to do your job for you, you're more than confused, mate. You're completely mental.'

'You sure?' Holland said. 'You don't know anything that might help us?'

Grover shook his head. 'Wouldn't matter if I did, would it? You know how it works in here. Paul was my mate, and if I find out who carved him up, they'll have me to answer to. But you still don't grass.'

'That's a real shame,' Thorne said. 'Because as soon as we clear this up, we can crack on with getting your good citizen medal organised.'

Grover seemed to find that genuinely funny, but told Thorne to go and fuck himself anyway.

'It also means we can't really do anything but jump to conclusions,' Holland said. 'I mean, we'd rather not, but when you've not got anything else . . .'

'What "conclusions"?' Wide-eyed and mock-innocent.

Boyle pushed himself away from the wall suddenly, clearly irritated by the back and forth. 'Like it was *you*, you poxy little wankstain. You strolled into Monahan's cell and shanked him.'

'Why would I want to do that?'

'Because someone paid you to,' Thorne said. 'You were contacted and told to get Paul Monahan out of the way. Now, if you could tell us who contacted you and how, it might make a difference when this comes to trial.'

'You think this is going that far?'

'I wouldn't bet against it.'

Grover let his head fall back and stared up at the ceiling, as though he were considering what Thorne had said. As though the accusations were perfectly fair and justified. When he looked at Thorne again, though, it was clear how little he cared if they were justified or not.

'I'll tell you what *your* problem is,' he said. 'This non-existent murder weapon.' He was full of himself now, leaning forward and pointing at Thorne. 'I mean, what am I supposed to have done with it? Did I stab Paul and then walk out of the cell covered in claret, nip off somewhere to get rid of the blade and then calmly stroll back in there again? Is that really what you think happened?'

'No,' Thorne said. 'I don't think that's what happened.'

'Well, until you can prove it happened any other way, you can kiss my arse.'

Thorne said nothing as Grover calmly stood and walked to the door. He knocked, then turned and smiled at Thorne and the others, waited until a guard arrived to take him back to his cell.

'That go like you wanted?' Boyle asked. He walked around the table until he stood in Thorne's eye-line. 'Happy with it?'

Thorne ignored him and turned to lift his leather jacket from the back of the chair.

'Cocky bastard knows we've got nothing,' Holland said.

Thorne stood up. 'Not yet.'

It was dry and cold, and Thorne stared out of the taxi window as the streets narrowed and the greys of office blocks and multi-storeys gave way to those of rutted fields and spindly trees, with the black ribbon of the River Calder twisting alongside. 'Whatever we turn up on Monahan money-wise is probably academic,' he said. 'Considering he won't be around to spend it. So, we need to look at Grover as well. Find what he's getting paid for doing Monahan and where it's going.'

'And where it's coming from, with a bit of luck,' Holland said.

'I don't think there's too much doubt about that.'

'Definitely Langford, you reckon?'

'Got to be.'

'But how's he organising all this?' Holland asked. 'We're presuming he's still out of the country, right?'

Thorne turned away from the window, stared over the driver's shoulder at the road unwinding in front of the car. 'Monahan was killed within hours of me talking to him,' he said. 'So, wherever the hell Langford is, he's tuned in to a seriously good set of jungle drums.'

Before they had left the prison, Boyle had told Thorne that he and his team would start getting stuck into Jeremy Grover and his family, see if there were any funds knocking about that could not be accounted for. Thorne told him that there might be a fair bit more to do, depending on how his and Holland's next appointment went. Boyle said the overtime would come in handy.

Follow the money, that's what Louise had said.

She hadn't said anything else the night before, at least not about Thorne's day out with Anna Carpenter. She had gone to bed early, leaving Thorne and Hendricks talking nonsense in front of the television. It was the way Thorne had been hoping the evening would turn out.

You're not going to get it on a plate.

She'd said that too, just before things had turned a little awkward, and, much as it pained him, Thorne knew she was right. There were too many hard-arses like Monahan and Grover and not enough luck. On a plate would have been nice, but he was happy to do things the hard way if it meant getting the right result in the end.

The taxi slowed as it drove into Kirkthorpe, a village four miles west of the city.

'Reckon you could live out here?' Holland asked.

Thorne looked out of the window again and shook his head. 'A bit too *Last of the Summer Wine* for my liking,' he said.

Holland laughed.

'Not nearly dirty and noisy enough.'

'Oh, I don't know,' Holland said. 'I can just see you coming down one of those hills in an old bathtub on wheels.'

Thorne looked at him. 'Sophie still trying to get you out of London, is she?'

'We're still . . . talking about it.'

As ever, Thorne could see that Holland was uncomfortable discussing his girlfriend. They both knew that she was not Thorne's greatest fan, and that she wanted to get Holland and their daughter Chloe away from more than just the city.

'As long as it's just talk,' Thorne said.

The driver found the address Thorne had given him quickly enough and pulled over. Holland paid the fare and hurried after Thorne to the door of a modern terraced house. Thorne rang the bell and stepped back, thinking: One of these buggers has got to give us *something*.

Howard Cook was older than they had been expecting. Thorne

84

guessed that the man who eventually answered the door, bald and blinking, was only a few years away from retirement.

A nice, cosy one.

Thorne and Holland showed the prison officer their warrant cards.

'I hope we're not disturbing you,' Holland said.

'This'll be about what happened last night, I suppose.'

Thorne said that it was.

'You'd best come in then,' Cook said. 'I've not long boiled the kettle.'

Thorne stayed where he was. 'I'll keep this quick if it's all the same to you, Howard. I just want to know where the knife is.'

'Sorry?'

The sounds of a TV show were coming from inside the house. A lot of shouting, gunshots.

'Knife, sharpened toothbrush . . . whatever Grover used. I just want to know where you put it once he'd passed it to you.'

Cook was shocked, or else did an amazing job of looking it. Thorne guessed it was more at the manner in which he had been confronted than the accusation itself.

'How dare you?' Cook said. 'How bloody *dare* you?'

'I know you've been through a trauma,' Holland said. 'So you might want to think about calming down.'

'I'm perfectly calm.' Cook folded his arms across his chest and swallowed. His lips were dry and white. 'And I'm *thinking* about how many shades of shit my solicitor is going to knock out of you two smartarses.'

'That'll be pricey,' Holland said. 'Hope you've got a bit of cash tucked away.'

A woman appeared behind Cook, asked if everything was all right. He didn't turn round; just said that he was dealing with something and told her to go back into the living room.

'If we dig hard enough, we'll find something,' Thorne said. 'You need to know that.'

'Have you any idea how long I've served as a prison officer?'

Thorne ignored him. 'We'll find the weapon. We'll find someone

85

who saw you dump it or saw you turn off the security camera. We'll find someone willing to turn you over—'

'Thirty years.' He pointed back towards the city, the tip of the cathedral spire just visible in the distance. 'Longer than most of the bastards in there. So, do you think I'm going to let you pair of clowns get away with this?'

'You're finished,' Holland said. 'Next time you set foot in a prison, you won't be coming home for your tea.'

'I'm saying nothing else, so you might as well save your breath.'

'We all know what happens to the likes of you inside.'

Cook shook his head like they were simply being silly. He reached down to a pot near the front door and began pulling the dead leaves from a plant.

'Anything you made on the take gets confiscated,' Thorne said, 'and you can forget about your pension.' He nodded towards the inside of the house. 'How's *she* going to get on when you've gone? What's she going to do with herself while you're getting spat at and watching your back on a VP wing?'

'Just tell us what you did with the knife,' Holland said. 'That would be a good start.'

Cook slowly straightened up and considered them. He crushed the dead leaves in his fist and tossed the pieces into the flower bed. Then he pushed his shoulders back and stuck out his chin. 'You go ahead and dig,' he said. 'Fill your boots. Get right down there in the muck and see what happens. Because I promise you *this*: when you're finished, you'll be covered in it.' He thrust his hands into his trouser pockets, rocked on the balls of his feet. 'You'll find bugger all, because there's bugger all to find. You'll look stupid, but from what I've been reading lately, I reckon you're probably used to that.'

'Are you done?' Thorne asked.

Cook stepped back and reached across to pull a tabloid newspaper from a table against the wall. He stabbed at the front page. 'This was your lot, wasn't it?' He gleefully turned the paper round to show them.

There was a picture of Adam Chambers on the front page.

'How much did that little fiasco cost?'

The day was brighter and still mercifully free from rain, so the view from the southbound train was less depressing, but Thorne felt every bit as frustrated as he had done the day before. Three men, each with a connection of some kind to Alan Langford. One dead and the other two – so far at least – saying nothing. Scared or just bloody-minded, it didn't much matter, as far as making progress in the case went.

Brick walls, as solid as any of those around Wakefield Prison.

Thorne looked across at the table opposite. A young couple sat where the elderly one had been a day earlier, and he wondered if he was in exactly the same carriage, on the same train. He sent Holland to the buffet car for coffees and told him to make sure he got a receipt.

Then he called Anna Carpenter.

She sounded pleased to hear from him. Thorne imagined her sitting alone in her office, bored and flicking through a magazine. He told her where he was calling from, where he had spent the best part of the day.

She laughed. 'Didn't trust me to have another crack at Monahan, then.'

'Monahan's dead.'

She said nothing for a few seconds, then spluttered a 'Jesus'.

'So, you know . . . things have changed.'

'What happened?'

'I can't really go into it,' Thorne said.

'OK.'

'I just thought you should be aware that it's all a bit more serious now.'

'I'm not with you.'

'Just, you might want to think about . . . Anna?' He realised that she could no longer hear him and put the phone down on the table. He stared at the handset, waiting for the signal to return, but unsure as to exactly what he would say when it did, or even why he'd called her in

87

the first place. After a minute or so, the icon reappeared on the screen and he called her back. 'Sorry, lost you. I was just saying—'

'Donna called me,' Anna said. 'She was really upset.'

'She got another photo.'

'How did you know?'

'It makes sense, that's all. Whoever's sending them hasn't got what they want yet.'

'Which is?'

'Pass.'

'She sounds like she's losing it. Keeps going on about how he's got her daughter.'

'What did you say to her?'

There was no reply and, after a few seconds, Thorne realised that the connection had been broken again. While he was looking at the phone, Holland returned with the drinks. He sat down and handed over the change and the receipt. Then, while Thorne was putting the money into his wallet, the phone rang.

'This is ridiculous,' Anna said. 'Why don't we just meet up for a drink tonight?'

'Right . . .'

'Any time is good for me.'

'We can sort it out later.'

'Or I could buy you dinner or something.' She laughed. 'As long as it's cheap.'

'A drink is fine.' He looked across, saw Holland pretending not to listen, staring into his tea.

'Have you got a decent local?'

'I'll come to you,' Thorne said.

TEN

When it came to bar snacks, Thorne preferred pickled eggs and peanuts to bowls of oversized olives at four quid a pop. And he was never likely to feel too comfortable in a place where conversations had to be conducted above the sound of tuneless jazz and the barmen looked like they belonged on the front cover of *GQ*. That said, it was preferable to the ersatz *bejeezus-ness* of an Irish theme pub, or even a 'proper' old boozer, where miserable old men propped up the bar and your feet stuck to the floor, where lager-top was considered to be a cocktail, and where, male or female, the person pulling the pints looked as if they'd once been a fair-to-middling heavyweight. In fact, Thorne only ever felt totally relaxed in the upstairs room of the Grafton Arms. Five minutes' staggering distance from his flat. Playing pool with Phil Hendricks until chucking-out time and putting the world to rights.

Football and music. Love lives and their attendant headaches. Spatter patterns, rigor mortis and knife wounds.

Anna Carpenter seemed to be in her element, though, with her hair tied back and dressed in the same corduroy jacket she had worn to her first meeting with Thorne. And she was certainly enjoying the olives.

'This place isn't as poncey as it looks,' she said. 'And the food's not bad, as it happens. You sure you don't want something?'

'I can't stay that long,' Thorne said.

'I mean, you get a few idiots in here sometimes, but you get them everywhere, and, if you ask me, when you're out somewhere it's down to the company as much as the place itself. Yeah, it's handy, 'cause it's midway between the office and my flat, but me and Rob and Angie, they're probably my best mates, we've actually had a few good nights in here. Had a laugh, you know?'

Thorne nodded. It struck him that she talked just as much when she was relaxed as when she was nervous.

'A couple of shit nights as well, admittedly, but they were with my flatmate and her latest boyfriend.'

Thorne reached for his glass. 'What about you?'

'What about me, *what*?'

'No "latest boyfriend"?'

'None worth talking about.' She used the edge of her hand to sweep the discarded olive stones into the empty bowl, then looked up at Thorne.

A full stop.

Thorne swallowed a mouthful of Guinness. 'Listen, like I said on the phone, I think you should probably step back from all this now.'

'You never said that.'

'It's what I was trying to say.'

'But it's my case,' she said.

'Not any more.'

'Donna came to me and I told her I would help. I took it on, and I can't just walk away from it now because things have got a bit heavy.'

'*A bit?*'

She shrugged. 'I took it on.'

'That was when it was just about a photograph,' Thorne said. 'Now it's a murder. A *new* murder.' He had already given her the headlines on the Monahan killing: the prime suspect from a few cell doors along, the missing murder weapon and the prison officer who was probably an accessory.

'I still don't understand why Monahan was killed,' she said. 'I mean, we'd already talked to him and he didn't tell us anything.'

'Langford didn't know that, though.' Thorne sat back, thinking out loud. 'Or even if he did, he didn't know what Monahan might decide to say further down the line, once he'd had a bit of time to weigh up his options. Monahan was the only person who could finger Langford for the murder ten years ago, or for conspiracy to murder at the very least. So, as soon as Langford found out he was on our radar again, he couldn't take that chance.'

'He was getting rid of a potential witness.'

'Right.'

Anna nodded, taking it in. She leaned towards her wine glass, then stopped. 'But how did Langford know?' she asked. 'That we'd talked to Monahan, I mean.'

'It's a very good question.' What had he said to Holland? *A seriously good set of jungle drums* . . .

'Maybe Grover told him?'

'Maybe.'

'That would make sense, don't you think? Let's say Grover was his mole inside the prison, keeping an eye on Monahan for him. Grover tells Langford that we've been in to see Monahan . . .'

'It's possible, but—'

'. . . then Langford tells Grover to kill Monahan.'

'It happened too fast, though.'

'Like you said, he couldn't afford to take any chances.'

Thorne was not convinced. 'The likes of Alan Langford try not to get too closely involved,' he said. 'There was probably a go-between. More than one, even.'

'What about the bent prison guard, then? Cook?'

'I reckon we'll find out soon enough,' Thorne said. He was in no hurry to head back up north and had been happy to delegate, to leave Howard Cook and Jeremy Grover to the less-than-tender mercies of his West Yorkshire counterpart. Much as he had taken a dislike to DI Andy Boyle, Thorne felt sure that when it came to putting the squeeze on, the Yorkshireman would make a decent job of it. He emptied his glass and caught the half-smile on Anna's face. 'What?'

'This is good, isn't it?' She moved her hand backwards and forwards. 'The pair of us batting ideas around, trying to work stuff out.' She finished her own drink. 'It's what I thought it would be like all the time, being a detective.'

Thorne went to fetch more drinks. He waited at the bar, wishing that the background music would fade a little further into the background and failing to catch the eye of a barmaid who was every bit as attractive as her male colleagues. He was finally served by one of the *GQ* boys and carried the drinks back to the table.

'What you said before' – Thorne handed Anna her glass of Merlot – 'about what you thought it was going to be like. Sounds like you've been disappointed.'

'I think I was just naïve,' she said.

'So, not the cleverest career move, then?'

She told him about how unhappy she had been working at the bank. How fearful. Drifting towards a future that had seemed mapped out, the pressure of it becoming increasingly unbearable and nudging her towards a potentially dangerous depression every day. How a move as rash and off the wall as the one she had eventually made had come to feel in the end like the only option she had left. 'I never fitted in,' she said. 'Not really. Never said the right thing, wore the right thing, *did* the right thing.' She thought for a few seconds. 'Never have, if I'm being honest.' She looked down and rubbed at the edge of the table with a finger. 'Fitted in, I mean.'

'It's overrated,' Thorne said.

'The stupid thing is that, for a while, I really thought I'd landed on my feet. Frank Anderson said he needed someone like me, and I felt . . . vindicated, you know? I thought he meant someone enthusiastic, eager to learn the ropes, all that. Actually, he just wanted someone who could keep the agency records straight and nip to the off licence when he ran out of Scotch.' She took a sip of wine, then another. 'Plus, he knew there was decent money to be made if he could get into the honey-trap market, and he couldn't really provide the honey himself.'

'Right . . .'

'So, back on with the slap and the high heels again.' Anna's face was not quite as red as her wine, but there was not a great deal in it. 'Who would have thought anything could be less sexy than banking, eh?'

Thorne laughed.

'Not to mention making me feel even less good about what I was doing for a living.'

'I gave up worrying about that a long time ago,' Thorne said.

'So, yeah, I've been *disappointed*.' She tapped a finger against the rim of her glass, staring down at a fingernail that Thorne could see was chipped and bitten. 'But not as disappointed as some.' She looked up. 'My parents weren't exactly thrilled.'

'You can see their point.'

'They couldn't see mine, though.' Her tone was casual enough, but there was tension around her mouth. 'My mum especially. We had words.'

Thorne struggled for something to say. He thought about some of the words he had exchanged with his father, both before and after the old man's death a few years earlier. He had learned since that the fire in which his father had died had not been accidental, that Jim Thorne had been targeted because of him.

Thorne still woke up sometimes stinking of sweat, tasting the smoke.

He looked across at Anna and thought about saying 'Sorry' or 'Be glad you've still got them.' In the end, though, he settled for an understanding nod and the safety of his beer glass.

'I think I'll go and see Donna tomorrow,' he said.

'OK, but I already told you what she told me.'

'Right, but I need to pick up this latest photo. And I want to talk to her about Langford. I know she hasn't clapped eyes on him for ten years, but she still knows him better than anybody else.' He caught Anna's look. 'What?'

'You sure about that?'

It was a fair point. Donna Langford had not known too much about what her husband was thinking ten years earlier. She had not known that he had rumbled her, that he planned to fake his own death and skip off with everything, leaving her to rot in prison. She had not known he would come back years later and snatch their daughter. 'OK, but she's the closest thing I've got to him,' Thorne said.

'Sounds like a plan, then.'

'This is what being a detective's like, most of the time. Making it up as you go along.'

'Can I come with you?'

'I don't think so.'

'Donna trusts me.'

'I told you, you need to back away.'

'Yes, I know, but—'

'Langford found out we'd been to see Monahan, so he'll also know we're talking to Donna.'

'I'm not scared,' Anna said.

Thorne could see that she meant it. 'Then you're stupid,' he said. 'And I need to get home . . .'

When Thorne came out of the Gents' she was waiting for him, standing by the bar's main door, with her hands in her pockets. He offered to run her home, but she reminded him that her flat was only a five-minute walk away.

'Good luck tomorrow,' she said. 'I mean obviously you'd get more out of Donna if I was there.'

'Obviously.'

'You wouldn't have to make up quite so much as you went along.'

'You don't give up, do you?'

She pushed open the door to the street and they both grimaced at the blast of cold air.

'That's something we've got in common,' she said. 'Isn't it?'

ELEVEN

He carried a bottle of decent wine out on to the balcony, sat and poured himself a glass, hoping it might help him relax.

When he was younger, marauding around the pubs of Hackney and Dalston, playing the big man, booze always fired him up; made a bad temper worse and turned a minor niggle into something worth pulling a knife for. Once he'd got into his thirties, with a few quid and a reputation behind him, alcohol started to have the opposite effect. Now, much to his and everybody else's relief, a good drink was more likely to put the brakes on and calm him down. He guessed that was because he was smarter than he used to be. Or just older. Then again, it could be down to the quality of what he was drinking these days.

Either way, it usually did the trick. And right now, he *needed* calming down.

He drank a glass, then another, and felt his mood gradually begin to lift a little. He stared down towards the lights of the town a few miles below, and the bright slice of moon reflected in the sea beyond.

Silly bastard, he was. Still playing the big man.

He had overreacted, he knew that. He should never have raised his hands, how stupid was *that*? He would apologise to the bloke, sort things out, send over a good bottle of single malt in the morning.

It wasn't as if nobody ever called him by his real name any more, or that he didn't occasionally hear it whispered in a bar. What did he expect? OK, it hadn't been what he'd called himself for ten years, and the face and hair weren't exactly the same, but 'Alan Langford' was still basically the bloke he saw when he looked in the mirror.

Only the name was dead.

Still, everyone close to him knew how it worked, same as those who had been here a while. They knew there were coppers and friends of coppers all over this stretch of coast like flies on a turd, and stupid things like the name you used could draw attention. Could end up getting you pinched. But a few faces occasionally got careless. Older types from the London days who turned gobby after a drink or two; or recent arrivals who were mooching about, looking to make the right contacts.

Tonight, it had been one of the older boys. A bloke he'd done some business with in the seventies. No harm in him, just a slip of the tongue, and the look on his face when he realised what he'd said was priceless. But still, he'd needed telling.

A week ago, he wouldn't have reacted the way he did. A quiet word would have done it. Now though, with the business back home, with these photographs and everything else, he had every right to feel a bit jumpier than he would be otherwise.

To feel cornered.

Below him, lights drifted across the water as a couple of boats emerged from around the headland and moved into the bay. Night fishermen, probably, nets bulging with squid and sardines.

All this grief because of a *photograph*. Jesus . . .

He could just make out the music drifting up from his favourite club on the seafront, the bass-line anyway, like a racing heartbeat. He knew there'd be a few of those in the place tonight – sweaty punters revved up on coke and ecstasy. Soft-top Mercs and Bentleys parked

96

outside and high-quality Russian hookers lined up around the dance floor.

He poured out what was left of the wine and lobbed the empty bottle into the swimming pool.

He was a long way from Hackney.

There had not been too much traffic on the way back from Victoria, and Thorne was home before ten o'clock. Louise had already gone to bed. He thought he had come in quietly enough, but standing in the kitchen, necking water from the bottle, he heard her call out from the bedroom.

He got undressed in the dark.

'I just conked out in front of the TV,' she said. 'Couldn't keep my eyes open.'

'It doesn't matter.'

'I can smell Guinness.'

He got into bed and turned on to his side. Said, 'I had a couple in the Oak with Russell.'

Had Thorne been asked there and then why he was lying, he could not have explained it. The night before, when Louise had asked about his first trip to Wakefield, he had felt as though he were lying when he was being truthful. Now, lying felt a lot less problematic than being honest.

He told himself that he was protecting her. That she was over-sensitive at the moment, had been since the miscarriage.

He knew it was nonsense.

He did not want an argument, it was probably as simple as that. Yes, Louise was more easily hurt these days, was prone to see offence where there was none intended, but so was he. He was still raw, and he was not up to a fight.

Louise rolled over and her arm moved across his leg. 'How many did you have?'

'Only a couple,' Thorne said.

'That's very responsible.'

'I was driving.'

'How early are you in tomorrow?'

Her fingers dropped to his groin and her breath was hot as she moaned softly into his shoulder. He had more or less stopped thinking about Anna Carpenter when he turned to her.

TWELVE

Thorne picked up Anna near Victoria Coach Station and they drove north, along Whitehall and around Trafalgar Square, across the Euston Road, up into Camden and beyond.

He did not bother warning her this time or issuing ground rules that he guessed she would break anyway. He was rather less cautious about this interview than he had been about the one in Wakefield Prison, on top of which he now thought she'd probably had a point the night before. He might well get more out of Donna Langford with Anna along for the ride.

Presuming there was anything to get.

They didn't talk much in the car. Thorne content to listen to the radio and Anna appearing to get the message. Waiting to cross the Holloway Road, Thorne slipped a CD into the player; a vintage blue-grass compilation. Lester Flatt and Earl Scruggs, the Louvin Brothers, Bill Monroe . . .

'Oh, I love this sort of stuff,' Anna said.

Thorne nudged the volume up as he accelerated away from the lights.

'My dad used to have loads of these records.'

He glanced across and was pleased to see that she did not appear to be taking the piss; nodding her head in time to the music and smacking out the rhythm on her knees. She had made all the right noises when she had first seen the BMW, too; something Thorne was not accustomed to. Certainly not from work colleagues, most of whom delighted in describing the 1975, pulsar-yellow CSi as the 'rusty banana' or a 'puke-coloured death-trap'. Anna told Thorne she thought it was 'cool'. He told her she had very good taste, but couldn't help wondering if she had held secret meetings with Holland or Hendricks, and had been comprehensively briefed on the best ways to wind him up.

'My mum hates it, though,' Anna said, smiling. She was still tapping along to the beat of the upright bass, the scratchy melody of the fiddle, and the syncopation, so delicately picked out on the resonator guitar.

'This Weary Heart' by the Stanley Brothers, honey-sweet and hell-dark, as the car turned off the Seven Sisters Road and slowed.

'Most people do,' Thorne said. 'I think it's one of the reasons I like it so much.'

Donna Langford did not seem overly keen on letting Thorne and Anna inside when they arrived. She was already pulling her coat on when she opened the door and stepped out quickly. 'Kate's got the right hump this morning,' she said.

Thorne and Anna exchanged a look as Donna marched past them down the path.

'It's a nice day. Let's go to the park.'

The day, though bright and sunny, was hardly warm, while the park, a five-minute walk from Donna's block, turned out to be a scrubby patch of green and brown no bigger than a couple of tennis courts. There was a pair of rusted swings and a set of goalposts without a net. A fire had scorched what might once have been a penalty area, and there was a collection of discarded cans and bottles scattered among the long grass behind.

The three of them squeezed on to a metal bench.

'What was your first thought?' Thorne asked. 'Back when you saw that first picture of Alan.'

A few leaves skittered half-heartedly at their feet, and for the few seconds before Donna answered they all watched as a battered Nissan Micra raced down the small road that ran behind the goalposts.

'I thought it was typical,' Donna said, laughing. 'Once I'd got over the shock, I mean. I started wondering why I hadn't thought he was alive before. Why I ever thought I'd actually managed to get rid of him.'

'Why "typical"?'

'Alan never did anything by halves,' she said. 'He planned things out, thought them through, you know?'

'So, this is all part of a plan?' Anna asked. 'The photos . . .'

'Christ, I don't know.' Donna suddenly looked very weary as she lit a cigarette. 'He used to tell this story,' she said, 'when he'd had a drink.' She turned to Thorne, rubbed her belly through her thick coat. 'Remember I told you about that scar he's got, where he was knifed?'

Thorne nodded.

'He'd bang on about how that only happened because he hadn't thought things through properly. Because he hadn't thought about the details. Basically, he was a cocky sod and he hadn't reckoned on the other bloke carrying a knife. But he always said it taught him an important lesson. After that he became obsessed with planning stuff out, working through every eventuality.' She sat back and screwed up her face, against the cold or an unpleasant memory. 'However vicious business got, however mental some of it seemed, it was all . . . thought through, you know?' She looked at Anna. 'My husband never did a spontaneous thing in his life, love. So, yeah, I reckon he knows exactly what he's doing.'

'Why did you want him dead?' Anna asked.

Donna let out a long, slow breath, threw a half-smile at Thorne.

'It's a reasonable question,' he said.

It was also one Thorne had never asked, not to Donna's face at least. As with so many cases, once he had got his result, in the form of Donna Langford's confession, he had moved on to something else.

There had been speculation about her motive, of course, not least in the *Sunday People* and the *News of the World*. But with a conviction more or less in the bag, Thorne had had neither the time nor the inclination to care a great deal about the 'Why?' Donna had not spoken in her own defence at the trial, her counsel fearing that she might come across as somewhat hard-faced and spoiled. Instead, her brief had spoken passionately about 'years of mental torment and domestic abuse'. In the end, though, the jury had been unconvinced.

Such provocation, the prosecution had countered at the time, might understandably lead victims to lash out with knives and hammers, or, at a push, to slip rat poison into the old man's shepherd's pie. But calmly planning and paying for a gangland-style execution was a very different matter.

'Alan was spontaneous enough when it came to using his fists,' Donna said. 'But even then he was usually smart enough to avoid hitting me where it would show.' She had been staring at her feet, but now glanced up towards Anna. 'I didn't like what it was doing to Ellie. What *he* might do to her.' She shook her head, as though correcting herself. 'I never saw him hit her, but I was starting to think it was on the cards, and there was no way I was going to let that happen.'

Anna placed a hand on Donna's arm.

'So, it wasn't about the money, then?' Thorne said. He saw the look from Anna but stared right back, hoping she would get the message.

I know this woman a lot better than you do.

'Look, I'm not going to deny that I thought I'd be all right when Alan was dead. That I thought I'd be comfortable.' Donna stared across the park. By now, the Micra was stationary and two young men, two *kids*, were leaning against it, smoking and laughing. 'That wasn't the reason I wanted him gone, though, I swear to you. I had money when I was with him and I was miserable as sin.' She shrugged. 'I wasn't remotely surprised that there was nothing left, either. I always thought he might be squirrelling it away overseas, somewhere the taxman couldn't find it. Now I know he's still alive, I'm damn well sure that's what he did. One more thing he was planning for.'

'Why the contract killer, though?' Thorne remembered the smell of cooked meat in the forest clearing, and the questions the prosecution had put to the jury during the trial. The same questions that were posed in a dozen magazine articles and a particularly salacious edition of *London Tonight*. 'Why bother with Paul Monahan? Why not just take a knife to him or batter him while he was asleep?'

Donna nodded, like they were fair questions. 'Of course, I thought about all those things,' she said. 'All my options. In the end, though, I was just terrified that I wouldn't hit him hard enough. That I wouldn't stab him in the right place, wouldn't get the dosage quite right, whatever. You wouldn't want to be the person who tried to murder him and saw him survive.'

'I imagine he wouldn't have been too thrilled,' Thorne said.

'The way I chose to do it, by paying someone to do it for me, felt like the safest bet.' She smiled, genuine enjoyment in it. 'Alan wasn't the only one who was concerned about details. Eventualities.'

Thorne glanced across and caught another look from Anna. There was enjoyment in her smile, too.

Maybe you don't know this woman as well as you thought you did.

'Monahan's dead,' Thorne said. 'You should probably know that.'

Donna blinked three or four times, her face suddenly pale. She stared at Thorne for a few seconds, then looked to Anna. 'When?'

'Day before yesterday,' Anna said. 'He was stabbed in his cell.'

Donna took another moment, then shrugged. 'Well, I'm not going to pretend I give a monkey's.'

'I wouldn't expect you to,' Thorne said.

They watched as a man came towards them walking a Jack Russell. He stopped a few feet away and waited, staring blithely into the distance while the dog curled out a good-sized turd in the middle of the path. Then he carried on walking.

As he passed the bench, Anna said, 'You should pick that up.'

The man turned, yanked his dog closer and told her to go fuck herself.

Thorne stood up and stepped across. 'That's not very polite.'

The man sighed and tried to walk past, but Thorne moved sideways and pushed the flat of his hand into his chest. The dog was jumping and scrabbling at Thorne's knees as he reached into his pocket and pulled out his warrant card.

'Shit,' the man said.

'Now.' Thorne held his ID inches from the man's face. 'Pick it up.'

'I haven't got a bag.'

'Use your hands.'

'*What?*'

'It's all right.' Anna stood up and took a crumpled wad of tissues from her pocket. She leaned across and handed them over. The man dragged his dog back along the path, picked up its waste, then walked quickly away in the opposite direction.

Anna watched until he was out of sight. Muttered, 'Arsehole.'

Thorne was still breathing heavily a few minutes later when the three of them began walking back towards Donna's flat. Donna nodded over her shoulder towards Anna, who was a step or two behind them. 'Looks like I picked the right girl for the job, doesn't it?' she said.

At the end of her path, Donna reached into her pocket and produced a brown envelope. 'The latest photo. London postmark, same as before.'

Thorne took out the photo, not caring about how it was handled. The other photographs had gone to the FSS lab the day before, and he reckoned if there were any fingerprints to be had, they were as likely to be found on those as they were on this one. He would send over the envelope, though. It would not be the first time DNA had been extracted from the back of a stamp.

The photo was from the same set as the others. Sun, sea, the usual.

'Why do you think he's doing this?' Thorne asked.

'Revenge,' Donna said. 'It's not complicated. What I said before, about not wanting Alan to survive and know that I'd tried to kill him? Well, that's what's happened, except that it's taken him ten years to do something about it.' She wrapped her anorak tight around her chest. 'To take Ellie.'

'So, why now?' Anna asked.

'It's the perfect time,' Thorne said. He remembered a case from a year or two earlier. A man whose girlfriend and child had been murdered just before his release from prison. It was as cold and brutal an act of revenge as Thorne had ever encountered, and it had gone on to cost many more lives.

Donna nodded. 'Couldn't be better, could it? He takes her just before I'm due to come out, when all I'm thinking about is being with her again.'

'You think he planned that, too?' Anna asked.

'Oh yeah.'

'Ten years ago?'

'You don't know him,' Donna said. Her voice dropped away as the anger took hold. 'First he . . . *takes* her. Then he sends these photographs to rub it in. To make sure I suffer as much as possible.' She had taken out another cigarette and was struggling with a disposable lighter. 'He's showing me how great his life is, now that I've got nothing.'

Anna stepped in and steadied Donna's hand so she could light her cigarette.

'Now that he's taken away the only good thing I ever had.'

'We'll find her,' Anna said.

'I'm dead if you don't, simple as that.' Donna sucked hard at the cigarette, her cheeks sinking with each draw. 'Dead in all the ways that matter, anyway. You lose a child, the best bit of you dies, that's all there is to it.'

Anna stepped back. She pushed her hands deep into the pockets of her coat and looked at the pavement.

'Any idea at all where he might be?' Thorne asked. 'I know you must have thought about it . . .'

'Spain's a bit obvious, but he did know a few people down there. Ex-business colleagues of one sort or another.'

'Remember any names?'

'You'd be better off asking some of your lot,' she said. 'The organised crime mob, or whatever they're called now. We had so many of

105

that bunch knocking on the door over the years that Alan was on first-name terms with most of them.'

If Langford *was* in Spain, it would certainly make sense to speak to the people Donna was talking about. These days that meant SOCA, so Thorne made a mental note to ask Brigstocke how he'd got on with them. Then he would chase up Dennis Bethell, see if his friendly neighbourhood pornographer had made any progress with the photographs.

'We'll be in touch,' Thorne said.

Donna took care to give Anna a hug before turning and walking up the path. Thorne did not even warrant a goodbye. Standing at the car door, he could see Kate looking down from an upstairs window, though whether she was watching him or Donna, he could not be sure.

Thorne started the engine, cranked up the bluegrass CD. Then he turned and saw the look on Anna's face.

'What?' He turned off the engine. 'Anna?'

There were no tears, but it looked as though they might be on the cards. 'It's just all that stuff about her daughter,' Anna said. 'It upsets me.' She shook her head, said, 'Stupid,' and glanced at him. 'I'm sure you have to get . . . hardened or whatever to that kind of thing, what with some of the stuff you see. I mean, it's just stories in the newspapers for the rest of us, you know? Dead kids . . .'

'You don't get hardened,' Thorne said.

'Sorry, I'll be OK in a minute.'

'Take your time.'

'Have you got kids?'

'No,' Thorne said. He started the engine again, told her he would run her back to Victoria.

'That's miles out of your way.' She rooted in her bag, pulled out a small pack of tissues. 'Haven't you got to get back to Hendon?'

'It's really not a problem.'

'I'll be fine,' she said. 'Just drop me at a tube.'

The argument picked up where it had left off; Kate on her way down the stairs as Donna came through the front door.

'How did that go?'

Donna ignored the question, threw her coat across the banister and walked past her girlfriend into the kitchen. Kate followed, asked the same question.

'Why would you care?'

'Come on, Don . . .'

'You've already made your opinion perfectly clear.'

Kate sat at the small table. 'Look, I was just warning you about getting your hopes up.'

'My *hopes*?'

'I don't want you to be miserable.'

'You're making me miserable, because you're not supporting me.'

'You're wrong,' Kate said.

'I don't need people being negative.' Donna slapped her hand against a cupboard door. 'I've had *years* of that. I need you to back me up.'

'I've always backed you up. I'm just saying go steady, that's all. You're pinning everything on that copper and that soppy girl and if you're not careful—'

'What?'

'You just might be in for a shock, that's all.'

'You think she's dead, don't you?'

'I never said that.'

'You think my Ellie's dead? I will *not* listen to that crap.'

'You're not listening to *anything* . . .'

Donna flicked the kettle on, paced up and down the five feet of worn linoleum. 'I know what this is about,' she said.

'It's not about anything, OK? I just think you need to be realistic.'

'You're threatened by her,' Donna said. 'You're threatened by Ellie.'

'Don't be stupid.'

Donna nodded, suddenly sure of herself. Spitting out the words. 'You think that if I had my daughter around, I wouldn't have time for you. You're scared shitless about being number two.'

'You're pathetic.'

107

'I should have worked it out before,' Donna said. 'Same as when we were inside. You were always a stupid, jealous bitch.'

'How can I be jealous of someone who isn't even here? Someone you don't even know?'

'I know you, though,' Donna said. 'I fucking know you!'

'You don't know anything.' Kate stood up and walked to the door. 'You don't know anything, and I can't help you.'

They stared at each other for a few seconds, until Kate turned and walked out. Donna leaned against the kitchen worktop, feeling the anger and the panic wheeze in her chest as the grumbling of the kettle grew louder behind her.

THIRTEEN

No more than a couple of days into it, Dave Holland had to face the fact that they might never discover the identity of the man who had died in Alan Langford's place.

It wasn't that the numbers were daunting. Although more than two hundred thousand people were reported missing each year, only a third of them were adults. Of those, the majority were found safe and well within seventy-two hours, and almost ninety-nine per cent turned up within a year. So the number still missing *ten* years on was in the dozens rather than the hundreds. The parameters within which Holland was working narrowed down the search even further. He was looking for a man of roughly the same height and build as Alan Langford, who had probably been reported missing a week or two either side of the body being discovered in Epping Forest.

Thus far, however, there was only one name on the list of likely candidates.

Jack Shit.

Holland had started from the assumption that, when faking his own death, Alan Langford had barbecued two birds in one Jag and got rid of someone he wanted dead. It was the ideal opportunity to knock off a business rival, or at the very least to get shot of someone who had simply pissed him off. But having cross-referenced the Police National Computer, the National Policing Improvement Agency's Missing Persons' Bureau and the relevant section of every police force website in the country, no obvious name had emerged. No gangsters, major or minor, no legitimate businessman who might have found themselves in Alan Langford's way, in fact nobody with any visible connection what-soever to him who had been reported missing around the time that the man himself had apparently been killed.

It was a shame, but hardly unprecedented in this sort of case. The optimism had been knocked out of Dave Holland long ago, and these days he was surprised when *any* aspect of an inquiry turned out to be a walk in the park.

With no obvious enemy fitting the bill, everybody else had to be checked out – those few dozen men of the requisite build who were still unaccounted for ten years after their loved ones had first reported them missing. After two days, Holland was already ranking this as one of the most unpleasant spells of donkey-work he had ever done. Calling the relatives of the missing men, he was always careful not to raise their hopes by suggesting that their loved ones might have been found, especially when that hope would quickly turn to horror as soon as the circumstances were explained. So he was as vague, occasionally as evasive, as he needed to be until he felt sufficiently confident to ask the person on the other end of the line if they would be willing to provide a DNA sample. 'This is purely to help us elim-inate your son/brother/father from our inquiries . . .' That usually did the trick. The sample could then be compared with tissue taken at the original post-mortem and now stored at the FSS lab in Lambeth.

But plenty of people could be ruled out before that stage. The PM report had detailed two metal pins holding together the bones of the victim's right leg and though there was little of *anything* left, Phil Hendricks had been unable to find any trace of an appendix in the victim's body. At the time, in light of Donna Langford's confession, no one had felt it necessary to check whether her husband had suffered a serious leg injury and undergone an appendectomy.

'You look like you could do with this.'

Holland looked up and smiled, relieved to see an attractive trainee detective constable brandishing a cup of coffee. She had been paying him a good deal of attention over the previous few weeks, but he couldn't decide if she fancied him or was just arse-licking. He was happy enough either way and certainly grateful for the drink.

'Bit of a slog, is it?'

Holland had just got off the phone with a woman whose younger brother, a soldier in the British Army, had disappeared after going AWOL from his unit.

'Can't you just tell me if he's dead?' The woman had sounded wrung out. 'It'd be so much bloody easier if we knew he was dead . . .'

'Yeah, a slog,' Holland said.

He had found himself constructing scenarios in a bid to explain the often baffling disappearances laid out in the files before him. The twenty-eight-year-old who had vanished on the way home from the pub during a stag weekend in Newquay could have been bundled into a car by Alan Langford or one of his cronies. Equally, he could simply have wandered off the road, three sheets to the wind, and tumbled into the sea from a cliff-top. The thirty-seven-year-old man with a history of mental illness last seen at a bus stop in Willesden could have been picked up by Langford. But he was more likely to have drifted into the shadows and lost himself, to die later in rather more banal circumstances than the man Dave Holland was looking for.

It was a long and laborious process: tracing the relatives; dispatching officers to collect samples; testing the DNA. With no guarantee of a result at the end of it. There was a real possibility that Langford had deliberately selected someone whose disappearance might not even be noted; someone who had already slipped through society's cracks and would not merit a missing person's report. It made a sick kind of sense, Holland understood that, and was far less risky than targeting

111

someone whose nearest and dearest would go running to the police as soon as he didn't show up for his dinner.

If that were the case, they might never identify the victim.

They might never pin the murder on Alan Langford.

Holland took the tea, asked where the biscuits were, then told the blushing TDC that he was only kidding. 'Pull up a chair,' he said. 'I'll take you through it.'

As soon as Thorne returned to the office, he called Gary Brand, the DI he had spoken to in the Oak a few nights earlier. Before being drafted into the Langford inquiry ten years earlier, Brand had worked on the old Serious and Organised Crime Squad. In fact, his expertise in that area had been the very reason why he had been drafted in.

Thorne hoped that same expertise might come in handy again.

'I heard about Monahan,' Brand said. 'Sounds like you've opened a right can of worms.'

'It was opened for me,' Thorne said.

'Doesn't really matter, does it?'

Thorne told Brand about his conversations with Jeremy Grover and with Cook, the bent prison officer. Brand did not seem remotely shocked at any of it, but he was more surprised when Thorne told him what Donna had said about the possibility of Langford being in Spain.

'Really? I mean, it was my first thought when you told me about the photograph, but you would have thought he'd be slightly more imaginative. The Costa del Crime's a bit bloody predictable, don't you reckon?'

'We'd never catch any of these buggers if they weren't *occasionally* predictable,' Thorne said.

Brand laughed. 'True enough, mate.'

'Look, it's a possibility, that's all, but she said he used to know a few people who were holed up over there. I wondered if you might be able to come up with some names.'

'Bloody hell, we're going back a bit . . .'

'I know, and it's probably a waste of time . . .'

'Let me make a couple of calls, see if I can dig out some old files.'

'Anything you can find.'

'I can't promise anything.'

'My shout next time you're in the Oak,' Thorne said.

Brand said he would get back to him by the close of play.

Once he'd hung up, Thorne wandered along the corridor and into Russell Brigstocke's office. The DCI had a selection of coins laid out in front of him on the desk. He was moving them from hand to hand and growing increasingly annoyed at his own less-than-impressive legerdemain. Thorne sat down and watched, thinking that Alan Langford's sleight of hand had been all but faultless. He had slipped away, leaving a mysterious body in his place. And, if Donna's suspicions were correct, he had returned ten years later to make his daughter disappear.

'Revenge,' Thorne said. 'That's what Donna reckons it's all about.'

'You buying it?' Brigstocke asked.

'If that's what it is, it's certainly worked,' Thorne said. 'She's in pieces.'

'Did you take Anna Carpenter with you this morning?' There was a slight smile on Brigstocke's face as he casually asked the question, but Thorne convinced himself it was because he'd just palmed one of the coins particularly well.

'I thought it was a good idea,' Thorne said. 'She's pretty close with Donna. Puts her at her ease, you know?'

'Makes sense.'

'Good.'

'I'm glad all that's working out.' Brigstocke opened his hand to show Thorne it was empty. 'Jesmond will be happy at any rate.'

'I wouldn't sleep well otherwise,' Thorne said.

While Brigstocke continued to practise, Thorne told him about the call to Brand, and the possibility of Langford having followed an old friend or two to Spain.

Brigstocke agreed that it sounded somewhat obvious, but suggested it was certainly worth chasing up. 'I'll put the SOCA boys on stand-by,' he said. 'It would be nice if we had something a bit more definite before you meet them, mind you.'

Thorne said he'd do his best.

'Any word from Bethell?'

'I've left two more messages today,' Thorne said.

Brigstocke admitted he was having no more luck with the FSS lab than Thorne was having with his own image-analysis 'expert'. 'I'll chase them up too,' he said. 'Tell them we need something by tomorrow.' He thought for a second, then spun round in his chair to study the chart of shifts on the wall behind him. 'Are you on tomorrow?'

Saturday.

The first since a long-forgotten and seemingly resolved case had come back with a brutal vengeance. Since a corpse had been revealed as a killer. Since one murder had become two, separated by ten years, but each orchestrated by the same man.

'Presuming you've managed to conjure up the overtime,' Thorne said.

'Makes you want to ring in,' Yvonne Kitson said. 'Put some of these idiots straight.'

'Would it make any difference?'

'Who cares?' She slammed shut a drawer in her desk. 'I tell you this, though, they'd need a state-of-the-art bleeping machine if I ever got on there.'

'There's a delay,' Thorne said. 'Thirty seconds or something, so the swearing doesn't get broadcast.'

Kitson thought about it. Said, 'Wankers.'

In their office, Thorne and Kitson had the radio tuned to 5 Live and were listening intently to a phone-in discussion about the legal system and the presumption of innocence.

The guest in the studio was Adam Chambers.

It seemed to Thorne that the show's host was fawning all over Chambers as though he were some hot-shot actor or pop star. Chuckling at every quip and grunting in sympathy each time her guest complained about how he had been treated by the police or pleaded for the tolerance and understanding that, as an innocent man, he believed was his by right.

'It's another example of trial by media,' one caller said. 'And the police just go along with it.'

'Adam?' the host simpered.

'That's spot on,' Chambers said. 'The police know very well that people are reading these stories, taking in all these rumours and allegations, and the truth goes out the window. Even if the truth *does* come out, which, thank God, it did in my case, you still have to deal with being . . . marked out and stigmatised. Tarnished by it, you know?'

'No smoke without fire, right?'

Thorne winced; the phrase, as it always did, setting his teeth on edge.

'Absolutely, Gabby,' said Chambers.

'I think I might be sick,' Kitson said.

Thorne felt pulled in two very different directions. He despised the 'no smoke without fire' brigade, the knee-jerk smugness of their tabloid-friendly mantra. He knew better than most that some people *were* convicted of crimes they had not committed. And he did his best to accept that, in principle at least, those who were innocent in the eyes of the law should be able to walk free, unburdened by any association of guilt.

But then there was Adam Chambers.

In his case it was not so much fire as a raging inferno.

When Sam Karim came in and said that Andy Boyle was on the line from Wakefield, Thorne told him to put the call through and turned off the radio.

'Bloody good job,' Kitson said. 'I was about to lose my lunch.'

Thorne would listen to the rest of the programme on his computer when he got home. Get worked up all over again. He felt sure that Andrea Keane would not even warrant a mention.

Boyle was in a marginally better mood than the last time Thorne had spoken to him, but it could not have been described as cheerful. Thorne doubted the Yorkshireman *ever* did cheerful.

'Thought you might like a progress report.'

'That's good of you,' Thorne said. 'So?'

'There isn't any,' Boyle said, his mood lightening further as he delivered the bad news. 'We've had another crack at Grover and we've had that bent screw in a couple of times an' all, but neither one's about to roll over.'

'What about trying to find the money?' Thorne asked.

'Well, you know what the sodding banks are like. Hardly falling over themselves to give us any records on the hurry-up. But I'm betting the payments were made in cash and never deposited, so we're probably wasting our time.'

Thorne had already come to the same conclusion about any money paid to Paul Monahan, but a detailed investigation into his finances had been put on the back burner since his death. There was not much point in pressurising a witness who was no longer around to give evidence.

'Even if we do find the cash,' Boyle said, 'there's no way of tracing where it's come from. Cook might have bought a new car more often than most, taken the odd flash holiday or whatever, but without a paper trail, there's bugger all linking either him or Grover to Langford.'

'They still have some explaining to do, though.'

'Best we can hope for,' Boyle said. 'I mean, they might not even have been paid yet for the Monahan job, and any money they pocketed before will probably be long gone. You just keep the cash under your bed and spend it as you see fit, right?'

'I wouldn't know,' Thorne said.

'These days you can pay for most things with readies, right? People are too grateful to bother asking questions.'

Thorne said he supposed so.

'I'm betting that whoever's handing the dosh over is going to wait until it's safe. They'd know damn well we'll be looking at Grover and Cook, so they'll bide their time and meanwhile that pair of arseholes can just bluff it out.'

116

'Grover's not exactly got a lot to lose by keeping his mouth shut, has he?'

'Right. He's never going to be convicted of doing Monahan without Cook's confession. And Cook's already done the smart thing and handed in his resignation, by the way. Claims his wife's poorly.'

'Well, there's an admission of guilt.'

'Yeah, you know that, and I know that . . .'

Thorne also knew that Boyle was right to be pessimistic. Wherever he was, as things stood, Alan Langford did not have a great deal to be worried about.

'I'll keep squeezing,' Boyle said. 'All I can do.'

'We'll find something.'

'The thing is, even if I could pin something on Cook, and even if he put Grover firmly in the frame for the Monahan murder, I don't think you'd get your man. Not directly, anyway.'

Thorne found it hard to argue with what Andy Boyle was suggesting. What had Donna said about her ex-husband considering all eventualities? Alan Langford was not stupid, and by getting Monahan out of the way so efficiently he had already proved just how careful he was. He would certainly not be dealing personally with the likes of Jeremy Grover and Howard Cook.

There had to be a middle man.

Thorne's mobile buzzed on his desk. He picked it up, saw the caller ID and told Boyle he'd check back with him tomorrow. 'Sorry about that whippet comment, by the way,' he said.

'Don't worry. If it weren't for the fact that I've actually got one, I might have clocked you.'

'That's all right then.'

'I'm joking, you twat.'

Thorne hung up and answered his mobile. 'About bloody time, Kodak.' His nickname for Dennis Bethell. 'I was on the verge of sending a few friendly vice-squad types round to kick your door in.'

'Yeah, sorry, only I didn't want to get back to you until I had something on these photos, you know?'

Irritated as he was, Thorne smiled at the familiar high-pitched squeak, the voice so at odds with the man's appearance.

'Let's have it, then.'

'Best if we meet up, don't you reckon? So we can sort out the cash and what have you.'

'I've not got time to piss about.'

'Tonight's good for me.'

'I'll have to owe it you.'

'I'm a bit strapped, if I'm honest, Mr Thorne.'

Thorne sighed and rolled his eyes at Kitson. 'Right, when and where?'

FOURTEEN

Anna could not say that she had ever seen Frank Anderson roaring
drunk. She guessed that he had a tolerance borne of many years' practice and could put away a fair amount without it becoming obvious,
but she was often aware that there was drink *on* him. She could smell
it, the sweetness not quite hidden by the gum or extra-strong mints,
could see the flush in his face after one too many glasses of red at
lunchtime. The songs sung under his breath and the slight tremor in
his hands.

The singing aside, her mum had been much the same.

It had been apparent an hour before, when Frank had returned
from a three-hour lunch meeting with a prospective client, that a good
deal had been drunk. Anna was not surprised, but did not know
whether his ebullience was down to the booze or to landing the job.
Frank preferred to conduct such interviews in the swanky bar across
the road, and though Anna could understand his reluctance to let
clients see the unimpressive office, she often wondered if the prodi-
gious consumption of alcohol might be even more off-putting, might
cost him more in the long run than he would ever earn.

She had never bothered voicing her concerns.

Since four o'clock, while Anna had been stuffing tacky A5 adverts into envelopes – 'F.A. Investigations: Peace of Mind Needn't Cost the Earth!' – Frank had been hunched over his computer or making calls. He had chased a couple of late payments, trying and failing to sound fierce, then phoned half a dozen competitors, posing as a prospective client and arranging time-consuming meetings at distant locations.

'Anything that gives us a bit of a leg up,' he'd told Anna when she'd first caught him doing it.

She looked at her watch and saw that it was almost quarter-past five. 'Can I get off now, Frank?'

He looked up, glanced at his own watch and shrugged. 'You've had a fair amount of time off lately . . .'

'I've been ill—'

'What about this morning?'

'That was a family thing. I told you.'

'I don't think I'm being unfair asking you to make it up.'

Anna had not told Frank about Donna; about her meetings with and alongside Tom Thorne. He would not have been pleased to discover she had taken on a client behind his back. Actually, if she were being honest with herself, she could not be sure how he would react, but she was certain he would at least insist that she hand over the majority of the fee.

She stared back at him across the small office, thinking, Sod *that*!

'A *lot* of time off.'

'It's not like you've been run off your feet,' Anna said.

Frank nodded slowly, went back to his computer. Anna slotted two more flyers into envelopes. The Association of British Investigators logo was reproduced on the bottom. F.A. Investigations was not a member of the ABI, and any client would only need to visit the association's website to discover that, but Frank was unconcerned. Few ever bothered, he had assured Anna, and besides, maintaining a punter's confidence was more important than complete honesty.

Frank was happy to play fast and loose with the concept of transparency where business was concerned. Anna had known him to take money for jobs he had no intention or was incapable of carrying out properly. She remembered a distraught widow who had probably read one too many crime novels and was convinced that her husband's death in a car crash had not been accidental. Frank took the consultation fee and two weeks' expenses, sat on his backside for a fortnight, then reported back that, after extensive investigation, there had been nothing suspicious about the man's tragic death. Of course, he was unable to supply a shred of documentary evidence to support this assertion, but he assured the woman that, as no law appeared to have been broken, it would have been 'unethical' and 'against ABI policy' to provide details of his research.

Such obfuscation, or what Frank called 'blinding them with science', usually did the trick.

'Nothing you're not telling me, is there, love?'

'Like what?'

'I don't know. Just that we spend our time sniffing around for other people's dirty secrets, so we shouldn't have any of our own, should we?'

'You're bonkers, Frank.'

Three more flyers, three more envelopes.

'Who's Donna?'

'Sorry?'

'Someone called Donna phoned for you yesterday.'

Anna tried to make sense of it. Donna normally used the mobile number, had been *told* to, and had called Anna on it the day before to tell her about the latest photograph. She must have rung the office beforehand by mistake. 'I don't know who that could be.'

'Didn't sound like one of your mates,' Frank said. 'Sounded . . . older.'

Anna shook her head, as if struggling to recall the name. Perhaps Frank was a better detective than she took him for. She shrugged. 'Well, she'll call back if it's important.'

'So, this new client sounds promising,' Frank said.

'Really?' Anna had become used to tangential jumps in conversation. She put it down to the drink. Something else she recognised.

'It's a matrimonial job, so you might need to dig out the slinky frock again.' He was grinning now, enthusiastic. 'Thinking about it, you should maybe get another outfit or two, go to town a bit. This is a growth area, I'm telling you.'

Another honey trap.

Anna felt sweat begin to prickle on her neck and chest. 'Come on, Frank.'

He held up a black-and-white photo. A head shot. The man's face was ordinary, unmemorable. 'At least this one's not some lardy old bugger, so you know, not too bad.'

'I don't care what they *look* like.'

'Fair enough, but I thought you were a bit fussier than that.'

'Piss off, Frank.'

He laid the photo down and raised his hands in mock-surrender. 'All right, love, steady on.' He turned back to the computer screen, muttered, 'Time of the month, is it?'

Anna reached for more envelopes and watched the second hand crawling around the dial of her watch. Wondered how easily she could unplug the keyboard from her computer and throw it at him, whether he would have time to get his fat, red head out of the way. Wondered how much longer Donna would continue to pay her now that the police were involved and making a far better job of the case than she was.

Wondered if 'Time of the month, is it?' was the kind of thing that Tom Thorne would say.

In jeans and a thin sweatshirt, Donna Langford stood shivering outside the back door of the flat, staring out at the cheaply paved postage-stamp that passed for a garden, the outline of trees beyond and a scattering of stars against the blackness above.

The house in which she had lived ten years before had come with a garden that she could not see the end of. There had been ponds and statues that were lit up at night and a paddock for Ellie's pony. There had been parties in marquees. Donna closed her eyes for a few seconds, willing away those memories that had come to feel like images from a film she had seen once upon a time.

The story of somebody else's life.

She had always hated those stupid statues anyway and the sky was bigger now than it had ever been at Holloway or Peterborough and Donna wondered if this was where she had always been destined to end up. In this life, somewhere between luxury and lock-up. It seemed a fair enough result, given all the stupid decisions she had made in her life.

She was certain now that, with the exception of Ellie and Kate, most of her decisions *had* been terrible ones. None more so than when she had decided that she and her daughter would be better off with her husband dead. When she had emptied her savings account and sought out Paul Monahan.

'This is a turn-up for the books, I'll say that.' The man she was asking to commit murder for her had stood up and asked her if she wanted a drink. He had hesitated, smiled. Said, 'I don't know what to call you.'

'I don't much care,' she had said. 'And I'll have a large gin and tonic.'

Donna could still remember the exact date when she had walked into that bar; an anonymous hotel a mile or so from Gatwick Airport. It was just a week after the bash at which she had first been casually introduced to Paul Monahan, along with another dozen or so of her husband's more dubious friends and acquaintances. A party from which she had later been dragged after Alan had put away a few too many drinks. After a joke she had not laughed at hard enough and a look or two in what he had decided was the wrong direction.

He had screamed at her across the roof of the Jag. Called her an ungrateful whore. He had smashed a vase when they got home and when that was not satisfying enough he had pushed his way into the bathroom and broken three of her fingers.

She had known exactly what Monahan *was*, even as she had watched him chit-chatting and putting away the canapés, and his was

123

the number she had searched for frantically on her husband's mobile phone the following morning as he showered; that she had dialled a few days later with one of her undamaged fingers.

'This is a seriously big deal, love. You sure you've thought this through?'

They had moved to a small table in the corner of the bar. Away from prying eyes and a noisy group of businessmen on the lash. Monahan had nursed his Guinness like he was on any ordinary night out and had turned on the blarney; leaning close and flirting with her, safe in the knowledge that she would not go running to her husband. As though it might enable him to bump up his price when they got to talking about the money.

Cheeky bastard . . .

'I've thought about it.'

'OK, only you don't want to be going down this road on the spur of the moment, you know what I mean?'

'I don't need advice.'

'You can't undo it. That's all I'm saying.'

'I've told you.'

'It's not like taking back one of your fancy pairs of shoes—'

'I just need to know if you'll do it.'

'I'll do anything if there's enough money involved,' Monahan had said. 'Only, considering what you're asking, I wouldn't go trying to pay me with your old man's credit card . . .'

She had walked out of the bar thirty minutes later thrilled and terrified in equal measure, and though she never met with Paul Monahan again, it would be five months before the Irishman finally got the job done.

Or pretended to . . .

Four times Donna gave the go-ahead and four times she lost her nerve and called to cancel the contract, telling Monahan that he could keep the down payment. She had almost decided to forget the whole thing, convinced herself that she must have been out of her mind even to consider doing it. Then, one day, Alan lost out on some business deal or other, came home scowling and pressed her hand between a pair of heated hair straighteners.

She had called Monahan that evening and told him to get on with it.

'Don . . . ?'

She turned to see Kate standing in the doorway, brandishing a mug of tea that Donna guessed would be stone cold by now. Donna said sorry, that she would only be another minute or two, but she was still thinking about Monahan, twinkly-eyed and full of himself.

This is a seriously big deal, love.

Later, she had become convinced that it was Monahan himself who had called Alan. Had probably called him as soon as she had walked out of the bar. Got himself paid twice.

She turned and walked back inside, imagining the cocky so-and-so now, sewn up and stiff in a freezer drawer. She smiled and thought: I'm not the only one who didn't think it through properly. But the smile evaporated as she thought about her daughter. Her only consolation was that, whatever else her ex-husband might be capable of, at least he would never hurt Ellie. Would he? Surely just taking her would be enough . . .

She felt Kate move up close behind her, her lover's hands rubbing the tops of her arms. But it was no longer the chill in the air that was making Donna shiver. It was everything she knew about the man she had believed to be dead. The man Paul Monahan was supposed to have killed.

She glanced down at a ten-year-old scar on her hand.

Thought that a few photographs might only be the start of it.

FIFTEEN

Thorne drove into the West End just before six, waiting for ten minutes on the north side of the Marylebone Road to avoid the congestion charge. He parked on Golden Square and walked towards Soho. It was considerably milder than it had been earlier in the day – hardly balmy, but bearable – and the working women in the strip-lit doorways of the Brewer Street bars were showing a little more flesh than of late.

Considering the other risks they ran every day, a few goose pimples were neither here nor there.

Gary Brand called back as Thorne was walking, said he'd managed to dig up a few names from Alan Langford's past who had probably been in Spain at one time or another. It was all a bit vague, he admitted, apologising, but the best he could come up with at such short notice. Thorne thanked him anyway and scribbled down the names, his mobile wedged between chin and shoulder.

'So, Spain still favourite, is it?'

'With a bit of luck I'll know a lot more in a few minutes,' Thorne said.

He had already arrived at one of several shops in the area popular with both bargain hunters and dirty old men. It sold cut-price books and

CDs on the ground floor, with adult entertainment – magazines, DVDs and a small selection of sex toys – a few steps away in the basement.

Thorne stopped at a set of shelves just inside the door. He looked at the back cover of a thriller that he thought might be good for his next holiday – whenever the hell that might be – and leafed through a coffee-table history of the Grand Ole Opry that was a steal at £6.99. Then, ignoring the knowing look from the woman on the till, he jogged down the stairs to where the volumes on display boasted a few more pictures, and Dennis Bethell would almost certainly be browsing.

He was not hard to spot.

Pumped up and powerful, six feet four, bleached blond hair and diamonds in both ears, Bethell would have stood out among an average crowd at White Hart Lane. There were only half a dozen punters in the basement. Five men and a woman.

'One of yours, Kodak?' Thorne nodded down at the magazine in the photographer's hands.

Bethell continued to turn the pages. He was wearing tight jeans and an even tighter T-shirt beneath a silver Puffa jacket. 'I do hope you're kidding, Mr Thorne. My stuff's *way* classier than this. I mean, look at how this cowboy's lit this rubbish . . .'

Thorne studied the explicit double-page spread that Bethell was helpfully holding only inches from his face, aware of the eyes on both of them; the heads that had turned, same as they always did whenever Dennis Bethell's voice was heard for the first time.

'I'm not sure that anyone really gives a toss,' Thorne said. He nodded towards the customer closest to them, a man in a brown suit who looked like Central Casting's most in-demand 'seedy accountant'. 'You think *he* cares about the lighting or the composition?'

'I know what you're saying, but you've got to have some pride in what you're doing, surely?'

Thorne said he supposed so, struck as ever by the contradictions in the man before him: the bouncer's torso and the helium voice; the genuine passion for his craft and the seeming lack of care or concern for those who took their clothes off for his camera. On a more basic level,

Thorne had never figured out Bethell's own sexual leanings, coming to the conclusion that he probably didn't much care either way.

Man, woman, fish, whatever. None of the images conjured up was particularly pleasant.

To Bethell's right, the only woman in the place was looking at the back of a magazine sealed in plastic. Bethell caught Thorne's look, leaned in close and lowered his voice. 'You'd be surprised, Mr Thorne. A lot of women go for this stuff these days.'

Thorne pointed to the magazine that Bethell was still holding. 'Not *that* stuff, surely?'

'No, you're right, it's more of a specialised market. Material that's a bit more aimed at them, a touch more sensitive or what have you. Believe it or not, they like a *story*, you know what I mean? If it's a film where the hunky plumber comes round, him and the horny housewife usually talk for a while before he starts giving her one. They might even have a cuddle afterwards.'

'That's disgusting!' Thorne said. 'Does he offer to sleep in the wet patch as well?'

Bethell laughed, high-pitched and scary. The woman looked round, a little alarmed. Thorne smiled and she quickly turned away again.

'So, let's have it,' Thorne said.

Bethell reached into a shoulder-bag and produced a large brown envelope. 'Right, well, it's almost certainly Spain.'

'You serious?' Thorne fought to keep his voice down. 'We'd pretty much got to that point ourselves.'

'Hold on, Mr Thorne. I might be able to tell you which part as well.' Bethell pulled four large colour prints from the envelope and handed them over. 'I managed to isolate and enhance the bits of the photos with the boat. Remember the boat in the background?'

Thorne looked at the pictures. 'I remember. Go on . . .'

Bethell pointed. 'That's the Spanish flag. By law, every boat registered in Spain has to fly it. Now, we might be unlucky. I mean, it's possible that some Spaniard was sailing about off the Greek islands or something, but I doubt it. So, like I said, I reckon Spain's a fair bet.'

'You said you could be more specific.'

'Well, I think you can find out from the registration.' He pointed to an indistinct black smudge on the boat's hull, then took out another print in which this section had been blown up to fill the entire frame. Now a series of letters and numbers was blurred but legible. 'There's no name, but I reckon this should be all you need. A mate of mine had a boat in Lanzarote and the Spanish are shit-hot when it comes to keeping records about all that stuff.'

From the corner of his eye, Thorne could see the seedy accountant staring, clearly keen as mustard to know what was in the photographs.

'It's because they charge extortionate taxes,' Bethell said. 'Mooring fees on the boats, harbour taxes, all that. Now, you should be able to trace the owner of this boat and, with a bit of luck, he'll be able to tell you where he was on this date.' Just to be extra helpful, Bethell produced a final print in which the date that had been stamped on the original photograph had been blown up. 'See?'

'You're wasted in porn, Kodak.'

'Nice of you to say, but I don't think I'm cut out to be a copper.'

'No, probably not.'

'They *are* some of my best customers, though.'

Thorne slid the prints back into the envelope. 'Nice one, Kodak. I think this may be one of those rare occasions when you've earned your money.'

'Talking of which . . .'

'Sorry, I didn't bring any cash with me. I thought I'd just make a donation to an appropriate charity.'

'What?'

'Something for the blind, maybe?'

'Funny, Mr Thorne.'

Thorne reached into his jacket pocket and took out the four fifty-pound notes he'd signed out from the CHIS fund. These days, only stubborn old sods like himself still used the word 'snout'. In a prime example of corporate wank-speak, the likes of Dennis Bethell were now officially known as 'covert human information sources', even though there was nothing remotely covert about Kodak. Besides which, on this occasion, he was acting more as an expert witness. Not that Thorne or anyone else would ever consider putting him on the stand, of course. Even if Bethell changed his appearance and his occupation went unmentioned, any iota of credibility would disappear as soon as he opened his mouth.

'Who's the bloke in the photos anyway?' Bethell squeaked.

'A ghost,' Thorne said.

He thanked Bethell again and Bethell thanked him right back, reminding Thorne that he was always available for this kind of work and handing him a fistful of business cards. 'Give them out to some of your colleagues, if you get the chance,' he said. 'Either for this sort of thing or, you know, I can fix them up with any other *material* they might need.'

Thorne put the cards in his pocket, wondering if Yvonne Kitson might be in the market for a hunky plumber/horny housewife DVD. With added cuddling.

'I'm very discreet.'

'You couldn't be discreet if your life depended on it,' Thorne said.

He moved away, stopping at the foot of the stairs and beckoning the seedy accountant across. The man looked nervous but could not resist the invitation. Thorne drew him close then glanced around to check that the coast was clear, before teasingly pulling out one of the photographs of the boat.

'Look at the mast on *that*!' he said.

Friday evening, and the main routes out of the West End were predictably snarled up. Sitting in traffic on Regent Street, Thorne called Brigstocke and told him about the meeting with Bethell. He gave him the registration number of the boat and Brigstocke said he'd get on to it straight away.

'I wouldn't bank on getting hold of anybody before Monday, though, even if it was a British boat,' the DCI said. 'And we're dealing with the Spanish here, mate. *Mañana, mañana*, all that . . .'

Thorne told him he was a racist and to let him know as soon as he heard anything.

The BMW moved a few feet forwards, then stopped again. Thorne had tuned into talkSPORT, but was only half listening to a discussion about the following day's football fixtures. Mostly he was thinking about Ellie Langford.

Had her father really spirited her away to Spain?

Thorne realised he knew next to nothing about the missing girl. What had her life been like before she disappeared? What had her plans been? She was eighteen. Had she been planning to go to college or did she already have a job? Was there a boyfriend?

Thorne needed to find out.

He had managed to get across Oxford Street and was waiting at the traffic lights by Broadcasting House. Drizzle had just begun to fall and some pundit or other was talking about Arsenal's leaky defence when Thorne glanced to his left and saw the woman crying in the car. She had parked twenty yards past the Langham Hotel in a blue Peugeot 405, and at first, Thorne thought she was rocking with laughter at something on the radio or a hands-free call. Then he saw that she was racked with sobs.

He stared . . .

After fifteen seconds or so, he began to feel slightly uncomfortable just sitting there and watching her cry, but he could not look away. He felt the urge to pull over to the kerb, to knock on the window and ask if she was all right. But he sensed that she would not welcome the intrusion; that, although she was parked on a busy street, she would have been horrified at the idea that she had been observed.

He saw her shake her head as though she were arguing with herself, or thought she were being silly.

He watched her cry and cry and cry.

As the lights up ahead changed to amber, Thorne saw a girl – fifteen, maybe less – come out of a house a few yards further up the street and run to the car. He guessed that she was the woman's daughter, and that the woman had been waiting for her.

Was she collecting her from a friend's house? From a party?

The woman leaned across the front seats to open the door, then turned away quickly as the girl jumped into the car. Rubbed at her face. Not wanting the girl to see her tears, or at least the extent of them.

It was at that moment, just *for* a moment, that Thorne caught the woman's eye. Through the rain streaked on his window and on hers, before she turned back to her daughter and Thorne began to pull slowly away.

For the rest of his journey home, past the Nash terraces on the perimeter of Regent's Park and down Parkway into Camden, he thought about her. Wondering how sudden her collapse had been and if it had happened before. What might make someone sit in a parked car and howl?

Bad news of some sort. A loss, recent or imminent. A diagnosis . . .

Or had it been something more general? Something she was stuck with or settling for? Something about which she could do nothing but sit alone and weep in rage and frustration.

He was still thinking about the woman when he turned off the Kentish Town Road and pulled up outside his flat. He saw Louise's silver Megane parked a few spaces up on the other side of the street. He was about to get out of the car when the text alert sounded on his phone.

It was a message from Anna Carpenter: *Sorry about being upset outside Donna's place earlier. Feeling v. stupid! Please don't think I'm flaky or whatever. I want u to know that I'm up for all this. I'm stronger than I look :0)*

Thorne switched the engine back on. He turned the radio off and the heating up. Then he called her.

SIXTEEN

Friday was the biggest night of the week and, as usual, the club was packed. The dance floor was solid. Even though there was barely room to move, sweat glistened on tanned shoulder-blades and showed in dark patches against expensive white and cream linen. He chatted for a few minutes with the owner, a man he had known for almost as long as he had been in the country, necked a bottle of San Miguel at the bar, then took a complimentary bottle of champagne through to the VIP area.

The gorillas flanking the velvet rope smiled as they let him through and tucked the cash he'd palmed them into their pockets.

He knew most of those who were already there; exchanged smiles and a handshake or two on his way to one of the booths. There might occasionally be some lower-tier footballer knocking about with a glamour model in tow, or a mainstream comedian scrabbling for the tourist euro, but most of those deemed to be 'very important' in this neck of the woods had earned the label the same way he had.

There were all sorts of ways to be well known.

He had arranged to meet Candela here. She liked to dance and he liked to show her off. Theirs was an on/off arrangement, nothing too serious, but he enjoyed her company, loved what she got up to in bed and thought the feeling was mutual. Tonight, they would have dinner and a few drinks before heading back up to the house. They would sleep late, then, after breakfast, he would take her shopping for something nice.

It was important that some things remained uncomplicated, that a sense of normality was maintained, in spite of what was happening back at home.

One of the many gorgeous waitresses stopped at the booth to open the champagne and pour him a glass. They chatted for a minute or two. She had got down on her knees for him the previous week, earned a *very* good tip that night, but he could not remember her name.

Back at home . . .

It was funny that he still thought of the UK, of London, as home. Strange, because he wasn't one of those soppy buggers who were forever dreaming about HP Sauce and warm beer. He had happily settled down and got on with his new life, because he'd had no choice. Still, there was an attachment, of course there was, and he wouldn't be human if he didn't miss a few things.

Strangest of all, though, in spite of everything that had happened – was still happening – he continued to think fondly of Donna.

He could clearly remember the moment when everything had fallen apart. That helpful voice at the end of a phone: 'I think you should know what your old lady's up to, Alan. Who she's met up with.' At the time, fired up and raging, he had thought about dishing out the same kind of treatment to Donna that Monahan eventually received a couple of days ago, but that would only have aroused suspicion. It might have scuppered all his plans and caused some copper to start looking at things a bit harder.

He remembered the coverage in the papers after they'd found the car in the woods. The copper in charge: Thorne. He'd looked the type that might have enjoyed a bit of digging.

So, he'd let the anger go and, in the end, as far as Donna was concerned, he'd almost come to admire what the silly cow had done. To understand it, anyway. All that time dressing up and tagging along after him, playing the dutiful wife like a good girl, she had been *learning* . . .

Candela finally appeared looking suitably stunning, and they sat pressed up against each other while she told him about her day. She worked for one of the smartest independent estate agents in the region and was very excited about a Russian businessman who seemed keen on one of her luxury villas in the next town.

'Him and his friends have *three* viewings,' she said, holding up her fingers.

Three guesses what kind of business he was in.

When the champagne was finished, Candela went to dance and he moved to the edge of the floor to watch her. He enjoyed seeing the young men trying to get close and the older ones – all those saddos who thought they could still cut it – with their tongues hanging out. He would never dream of dancing himself, that had never been his game, but he wasn't worried about the competition. Even if some bloke didn't know who she was with and tried to make a move, she wouldn't give him the time of day.

She knew where her bread was buttered. Besides which, he reckoned he still looked pretty good for his age. He'd had a little work done – some orthodontics and a dye job, just enough to help with the new ID – but it was mostly about keeping fit. Not eating like an animal, the way some of them did. Full English breakfast like it was going out of fashion and lager with everything.

Candela closed her eyes, shook her hips and ran her hands through her long hair for him. She was gorgeous, no question, but at that age Donna had been every bit as spectacular, in her own way.

And Ellie looked a lot like her mother. Same temper on her, too, which didn't make things as easy as they might be.

Looking around, he saw a few faces he'd been wanting to get close to for a while and decided that he might do a little business before the evening was over. It was the ideal place. A few drinks, a handshake and the deal was done, which was how he preferred it. The money and the merchandise would be moved by others later, and there would be no need for him to get his hands dirty.

That had been the secret these last ten years.

It was becoming increasingly difficult, though, what with everything that needed doing back in the UK.

Candela waved and he waved back, but his thoughts were far away. Suddenly darker and more troubling than he was comfortable with.

If he wanted to stay free, it would get harder to stay clean.

SEVENTEEN

Traffic was moving on the M25, which was about the best you could expect even on a Saturday. Thorne's passenger was keen to chat – about her flatmate, her flatmate's thick boyfriend, people she'd known when she worked at the bank who had been high-fliers and lost everything when the economy had gone belly up – but he was happy to let her do most of the talking.

To watch the road and think about other things.

He had been unable to shake the image of the woman crying in the blue Peugeot; wondering who she was and what had happened to make her world so unbearable, for those few minutes at least. It had been on his mind since waking, and he and Louise had barely spoken during a snatched breakfast.

'Will you be late?'

'See how it pans out.'

'Fine. I've got a lot on myself, so . . .'

The truth was that aside from the lovemaking two nights before – slight and unexpected – there had not been a great deal of closeness between them in recent days. Weeks, even. There were fewer calls made or texts sent and seemingly no real desire to connect. There was less interest.

As Louise had said, though, they were both busy . . .

He had called Russell Brigstocke on his way to pick up Anna, to tell him he would not be coming into the office. To let him know about the visit he would be making instead.

'Not much worth coming in for anyway,' Brigstocke had said. 'Like I thought, as far as this boat business goes, getting any joy out of Madrid on a Saturday morning is like pulling teeth. I mean, it *might* have helped if I'd been able to find a bloody translator.'

Thorne had told him he would check in again later, and had listened to Brigstocke rant for another minute or two.

'Do you know how many Albanian speakers there are on the Home Office books? Or Turkish? Or Urdu? Dozens, mate. But could I find one who spoke Spanish? I would've done it myself, but beyond knowing the names of a few Barcelona players and being able to ask for a beer, I'm a bit stuffed . . .'

Seeing the exit they needed coming up, Thorne swiped at the indicator stalk and swung the BMW into the middle lane.

'So, it looks like walking away from the bank might not have been such a stupid move after all,' Anna said. 'I mean, at least *I*'ve got a job.'

'Right,' Thorne said.

'Some of those flash bastards I used to work with are living on benefits now.' She grinned, looking out at the fields that stretched away from the motorway. 'Cheers me right up sometimes.'

Thorne indicated again and drifted into the inside lane. Anna said something else, but he was still thinking about the woman in the blue Peugeot as he pulled on to the slip road and began to slow for the roundabout.

Twenty miles south-west of central London, in the well-heeled heart of the Surrey countryside, Cobham is the archetypal commuter town. Its exclusive private estates are home to a number of Chelsea footballers whose training ground is nearby, but Maggie and Julian Munro were rather more typical inhabitants. He worked at an architectural practice in Clerkenwell and she taught at the local independent secondary school. They lived in a detached house opposite Cobham Mill and drove his and hers Volvos. They had a nine-year-old son who played rugby for the county, they kept a flat-coated retriever, and for ten years, until she had suddenly gone missing six months before, they had been foster parents to Ellie Langford.

Maggie Munro showed Thorne and Anna into a large sitting room. She offered them tea, but Thorne said they did not want to take up too much of their time.

The dog was barking in another part of the house.

'I was probably somewhat . . . *manic* when you called,' Maggie said. The fixed smile and the way her hands moved in her lap told Thorne that she was still far from calm. 'Only, as soon as you said who you were, I thought maybe you'd found her.'

'I'm sorry for the misunderstanding,' Thorne said.

Julian Munro came in and Thorne and Anna stood to shake his hand before everyone sat down again. It was all rather formal, despite the invitation that Thorne and Anna should make themselves at home and the Munros' Saturday casuals: jeans and rugby shirt for him; powder-blue tracksuit for her.

'I must admit, I thought you'd be older,' Thorne said. He had been genuinely shocked to find that the Munros were in their late thirties, having got it into his head that fostering was only ever done by fifty-something women whose own kids had flown the nest.

'We'd been trying for a baby for a while,' Julian said, 'but for one reason or another it hadn't worked out. So then we thought of adoption, but the process was incredibly long and drawn out.'

His wife had been nodding along and now she took up the story. 'We thought we'd try fostering just to see if bringing up someone else's child was something we were cut out to do. And we got Ellie.' She smiled. 'As it happened, a few months later, I fell pregnant.'

It was Thorne's turn to smile. 'Falling' pregnant only ever seemed to be something the middle classes said. 'Fell' rather than 'got'. Despite this, he thought he had heard the trace of a northern accent from both of them and for no very good reason had quickly formed an impression of a couple who had not been given anything on a plate. Who had worked hard for everything they had.

'Ellie was thrilled to be getting a little brother,' Maggie said. 'And when Samuel came along, we were a family.'

'He's training,' Julian said, explaining their son's absence. 'Every Saturday morning.'

Anna hunched her shoulders and shivered theatrically. They had been talking about snow on the radio as she and Thorne had driven up. 'Poor little lad'll be freezing,' she said.

Julian shook his head. 'He's pretty tough.'

The husband and wife were sitting a few feet apart on a large sofa, while Anna and Thorne sat in matching armchairs, facing them across a low table strewn with glossy magazines.

Maggie leaned forward and cleared her throat, as if she were about to deliver a prepared speech. 'The fact is, we're very glad to see you,' she said. 'Nobody ever took Ellie's disappearance seriously, not really. She was eighteen, so legally she was responsible for herself, and they just kept telling us she must have run off with some boyfriend or other. Kept saying that she'd show up when she got bored or ran out of money. It was so frustrating.'

'Was there one?' Anna asked. 'A boyfriend?'

Maggie shook her head. 'Nobody we knew about. Nobody special, at any rate.'

'The police *did* keep in touch fairly regularly,' Julian said. 'At the beginning anyway. But only to tell us there was nothing to tell us, if you see what I mean.' His jaw tightened and he breathed out noisily through his nose. 'Some family liaison officer or other would sit where you are now, scoffing our bloody biscuits and bleating on about coun-selling, but singularly failing to tell us what anybody was actually doing to find our daughter.' He looked at his feet, one of which was tapping angrily against the carpet. Maggie leaned across and took his hand.

'Tell us about the day Ellie went missing,' Thorne said.

Maggie glanced at her husband. He nodded. *You tell it.*

140

'She'd been out celebrating her A-level results. She'd done really well. She and some of her friends went to one of the pubs in the centre of town.' Maggie shrugged. 'That's it. Just a bunch of teenagers having a drink and letting their hair down. All her friends told us she was fine when she left to get the bus. She never came home . . .'

Thorne thanked her and said he understood how difficult it must be, going over it all again. She told him it had become second nature; one or other of them had told the story a thousand times by now.

'What were the results?' Anna asked. 'You said she did well.'

Maggie looked slightly taken aback before her face broke into a beam. It was clear that nobody had ever bothered to ask. 'Two Bs and a C,' she said. 'Bs in English and History, C in French.'

Thorne knew that the Munros were exaggerating somewhat in claiming that the police had done nothing, but he understood why. If he were the parent of a missing child, he would want every police officer in the country on the lookout twenty-four hours a day. The truth was that those in charge of the inquiry had done as much as possible before running hard into a brick wall. Ellie Langford had quickly become just one of several thousand missing teenagers.

Thorne had spoken to one officer from the case who suspected drug use of some sort. Said most of his team expected Ellie to be on the streets somewhere, London most likely. Sitting here and talking to the girl's foster parents, Thorne doubted that, but he knew he was no expert. He did know that no images of her had shown up on CCTV footage and that her mobile phone had not been used since the night of her disappearance. He also knew that if she had left the country, she had done so illegally.

'She didn't take her passport,' Thorne said.

Maggie shook her head. 'No. We told the police that. Her passport was still here, and all her clothes. She hadn't been planning on going anywhere.'

The implication was obvious. She had been taken. Of course, the Munros had no way of knowing that Alan Langford was still alive, so they could not have suspected that Ellie had been taken by her own

141

father. Their fear was far worse, far harder to wake up with every morning.

That their daughter had been abducted by a stranger.

'She's dead.' Maggie addressed the words to Anna. Simply and without emphasis. 'Isn't she?'

'Why do you say that?'

'Because if she was alive, she would have got in touch to let us know she was OK. She would have wanted to talk to us, to talk to Sam.'

'We've got no reason to believe she's come to any harm,' Thorne said. He knew that the Surrey Police had checked at the time and that they were still routinely checking all unidentified bodies as well as calling A&E departments as part of a regular monthly review.

'Nobody ever said as much, but I think those people who believed she'd run away weren't particularly surprised.' Julian sat back, calmer now. 'As though it was only to be expected that she'd have some kind of breakdown sooner or later. After what happened with her parents, I mean.'

The surprise must have registered on Thorne's face.

'We knew who they were.' The man fought to keep the distaste from his expression, but it was clear in his voice. 'We knew all along who Ellie's father was, and why her mother went to prison.'

Thorne shrugged. 'I just didn't think they would have told you everything. All the details, I mean.'

'Well, they told us a little of it at the time and we pieced together the rest once it all broke in the media. I think they wanted us to know the basic facts in case Ellie had been . . . *affected*, you know? They were worried she might show signs of it in her behaviour, of being traumatised.'

'Did she?' Anna asked.

Maggie shook her head. 'You would never have known,' she said. 'She was the calmest little girl. Never lost her temper, never had a tantrum. Even when she hit thirteen, fourteen, and all her friends were going through that awful hormonal stage.'

'Boyfriends and bitching,' Julian said.

'She just seemed to be removed from it somehow. Like she was above it all.'

'She never talked about her mother coming out of prison?' Thorne asked. 'What might happen then?'

The Munros shook their heads.

'You do know she's been released, don't you?'

The look on both their faces made it clear that they did not. Social Services might have decided that they had no need to know. Or they might just have screwed up and neglected to call them. Either way, it was an awkward moment. Looking at them, Thorne suddenly felt under pressure; as if he were being invited to declare where his loyalties lay.

'How long?' Maggie asked.

'Just over a month,' Thorne said.

He looked through a glass door that led to a small conservatory and the garden beyond. There was an almost full-sized football goal in one corner and a huge trampoline in the other. Thorne thought this must have been a good place to grow up, and not too much of a comedown from the place Ellie Langford had lived in before. Not as much as the one her mother had faced at any rate. Then, just before he turned back to Julian and Maggie Munro, he found himself thinking about another missing girl. About the very different house in which Andrea Keane had been raised.

Four siblings scrabbling for attention and a garden barely big enough to bounce a ball in.

'Have you still got Ellie's computer?' Thorne asked.

Maggie nodded. 'We've got everything.'

'Is it OK if we send an officer round to pick it up?'

'They already looked at it,' Julian said. 'The week after Ellie disappeared.'

'I know, but we're making progress with that stuff all the time, so it might be worth a try. I can barely manage an email, but you can get all sorts of information off a hard disk now, so . . .'

'It's no problem,' Maggie said. 'Just let us know.'

Thorne gave Anna a small nod, and reached down for his briefcase. 'Well, if you think of anything else . . .' He stood up, shaking his head. 'Why do coppers always say that?'

'You've read the statement we made at the time?' Julian asked.

'Yes,' Thorne lied. He had asked for it to be faxed across. With luck, it would be waiting for him back at the office, along with statements from the friends who had been with Ellie in the pub the night she vanished.

'Well, you know as much as anyone, then.' Julian walked slowly to the door, with Anna, Thorne and Maggie a few steps behind. 'The pub, her friends, the woman. All of it.'

'Which woman?' Thorne asked. 'I don't recall . . .'

'I saw her talking to a woman,' Julian said. 'An older woman. This was a couple of weeks before she went missing. I thought it must have been one of her teachers, but then I could see . . . Well, she didn't *look* like a teacher.' He leaned against the door jamb. 'I saw them twice, actually: once at the end of the road when I was coming back from the office, then a few days later in one of the cafés in town. They were sitting at a table in the window and I thought they were arguing.'

'About what?' Anna asked.

'I've no idea.'

Anna leaned forward, excited. 'But there was definitely some sort of argument?'

'Look, I was driving past, so it wasn't like I watched them for a long time, but that's what it looked like.'

'Did you talk to Ellie about it?' Anna asked.

'She didn't really want to discuss it. At least, that's how it seemed when I thought about it later. Afterwards, I mean. She said something about it being of one of her friends' mums and that was the end of it. I didn't really think about it again until after Ellie had disappeared. You rack your brains for anything, you know?'

'I know it's in the statement,' Thorne said, 'but can you give us a description?'

★

'*That's* why I left the bank,' Anna said in the car outside. She smacked her palm against the dash for emphasis. 'Why I wanted to get into this kind of thing. To get that feeling, that buzz.'

Thorne looked across at her. She was virtually bouncing up and down in her seat.

'I mean . . . does that happen often?'

Thorne started the car.

'Oh, come on, don't say you didn't feel it as well.'

'I felt it,' Thorne said. 'And no, it doesn't. Not often enough, anyway.'

'When he described the woman Ellie was with, I almost wet myself.'

'Well, you'll need to do something about that.'

'I haven't the faintest idea what it means, mind you. *Her*, talking to Ellie.' She looked to Thorne for an answer.

'Not a clue,' he said.

'So, what now?'

'We go back to Seven Sisters and find out.' He swung the car around and waited for a gap in the oncoming traffic. The first car flashed its lights to let him in. It was nice to be out of London. 'Lunch first, though,' he said. 'I think I saw a decent-looking pub a mile or so back.'

'Oh, OK.' Anna sounded a little disappointed. As though she wanted to maintain the momentum they had generated; to hold on to the unfamiliar rush for fear it would dissipate.

'I think you need to calm down,' Thorne said. 'Besides which, this is going to be an awkward conversation. Best not to have it on an empty stomach.'

EIGHTEEN

Thorne's dislike of the typical English country pub was as fierce as the one he harboured for trendy bars. Thankfully, though, there were no horse-brasses in evidence, nor any wizened old buggers with their own tankards, and the place did not fall *completely* silent when they walked into the saloon bar.

They sat at a round, copper-topped table with a bottle of sparkling water, two bags of crisps and a couple of yesterday's baguettes. At the bar, the landlord and two middle-aged women were watching *A Place in the Sun* on a small television mounted high in the corner.

'People must lie to you all the time,' Anna said.

They had been talking about the woman they would shortly be visiting ever since leaving the Munros' house.

'To be fair,' Thorne said, 'she couldn't really give a dishonest answer to a question we never asked her.'

'You know what I mean.'

'She just didn't mention it.'

'A lie by omission, then. She must have known it was relevant.'

'Let's just see what she's got to say.'

'I'll know if she's lying again,' Anna said. 'I'm good at spotting it.'

'I'm listening,' Thorne said.

She leaned towards him. 'It's all about body language and the small-est changes in expression. Like that TV show, the one with the actor from *Reservoir Dogs* . . . God, I'm *so* rubbish at names. Anyway, he helps the police by letting them know when someone's lying, but it's a curse as well as a gift, because he can also tell when the people he loves are lying.' She swallowed. 'And that's not always . . . a good thing.' She reached for a beer mat and began methodically tearing it into tiny pieces. 'Are you good at telling?'

'I thought I was once.' Thorne puffed out his cheeks. 'But I've made enough mistakes to be a bit more careful now.'

'As long as you learn from them, right?'

'People lie for pretty basic reasons,' he said. 'They're scared or nerv-ous or they've got something to hide. Sometimes they lie to spare somebody's pain, or at least that's what they tell themselves they're doing.' He looked past her, up at the television. 'We all do it dozens of times a day, most of us. Some people lie even when they've got no reason to, because they just can't help themselves. Each time they do it and don't get caught, it's a little victory. It's what gets them through the day, I suppose. Then, there are the ones whose lies are a little more serious.'

On the screen, an elderly couple was being shown around a farm-house in Tuscany or Carcassonne or somewhere. Louise watched the show whenever she got the chance, but Thorne had never seen anyone actually buy one of the places they were shown. 'They're just in it for a free holiday,' he told Louise. She said she didn't care and told him to shut up.

'Are you thinking about that man who got off?' Anna asked. 'The one who killed the girl. Chambers?'

'He didn't kill her,' Thorne said. 'Not in the eyes of the law.'

'But you think he did.'

'I don't want to get into it.' With no beer mat of his own to tear up, Thorne leaned forward and swept crumbs from the table on to his plate.

'I lied to you,' Anna said.

'When?'

'In the car, outside Donna's place. I told you I was upset about her and Ellie, but it was really all about me and my mother.'

'You had words,' Thorne said. 'You told me. After you left your job.'

'It was more serious than that.' She smiled, reddened a little. 'You see, there you go, another lie. The truth is that we haven't spoken since. Not for a year and a half.'

'Blimey.'

'It's always been tricky with me and my mum.'

'What about your father?'

'He's fine about it now, or at least *says* he is. We talk once a week, something like that, but whenever I call, she refuses to come to the phone.'

'It sounds like she's the one who's behaving like a child, so why are you feeling guilty?'

Anna didn't argue. 'Listen, I know she's being melodramatic and that she should be supporting me, but it's complicated. She drinks, OK, and I don't think what I'm doing is helping matters.'

'How bad is it?'

'It *was* getting better. That's the point. But I think my . . . change of career kind of set her back a bit. And now my dad's not coping very well.'

Thorne poured out the last of the water. 'What you said before, about knowing when people are lying . . .'

She nodded, knowing that he'd worked it out. 'Mum was really good at it, but I learned to read the signs. I knew that she'd had four glasses when she said she'd had just the one, I knew where she was hiding the empty bottles, all the usual stuff. So, you know, I'm not exactly like the bloke in that TV show, but I can spot a porky more often than not.'

'I'll bear that in mind.'

'Where did you get the scar?'

She pointed. Thorne reached up and traced a finger along the straight, white line that ran across the bottom of his chin.

'I'll know if you're bullshitting, remember,' she said.

'It was a woman with a knife a few years back,' Thorne said. 'Or a man wearing a signet ring who punched me when I tried to arrest his brother. Or I ran into a coffee table when I was five.'

She narrowed her eyes. 'Knife,' she said. 'I'm right, aren't I?'

'You had a one-in-three chance.'

'I should also tell you that it makes me a very good liar.' She sat back, folded her arms. 'And a shit-hot poker player.'

'You kidding?'

'It saved me having to work behind a bar when I was at college.'

Thorne nodded, genuinely impressed. She was certainly naïve, this girl, and gobby and over-exuberant.

But she kept on surprising him.

The look on Kate's face when she opened the door gave Thorne the impression that she knew, or at least had a good idea, why he and Anna had come. She certainly did not appear overly shocked when he told her.

The three of them were in the living room and each tensed at the sound of footsteps on the stairs. Donna came in drying her hair. Nobody had bothered to sit down.

'What?' she said.

Thorne ran through it all again for Donna's benefit. Then he turned back to her girlfriend. 'Julian Munro saw the tattoo, Kate,' he said. 'Not in any great detail, though I'm not convinced the name would have rung any bells with him anyway.'

'It rang quite a bell with us, though,' Anna said.

Kate's hand moved to her neck, to the elaborate lettering that curled below the collar of her shirt. She nodded. 'It was boiling that day,' she said. 'I remember the two of us sitting there sweating in that café and I had this stupid little vest on . . .'

Donna was just standing there, the towel dangling from her fist, the anger building to the point where it looked as though she might use it to strangle the woman she loved. 'You saw *Ellie*? Why the hell didn't you say anything? Why did you think it was any of your business?' She shouted, furiously spitting out the questions one on top of the other, while Kate turned her face away and tried desperately to interject. '*Why* did you see her? Christ, why am I only hearing about this *now*?'

'I'm sorry.'

'All that rubbish the other day, you swearing blind you were on my side. I was right, wasn't I? About you being jealous. Were you trying to warn her off?'

'No—'

'Did you tell her I didn't want to see her?'

'God, *no*. Why would I want to do that?'

'How the hell should I know? Because you're sick in the head?'

'You should try and calm down,' Thorne said.

Donna wheeled around. 'You can piss off as well. I can see how much you're enjoying this.'

'Don't be stupid.'

Donna turned to Anna, jabbing a finger in Thorne's direction. 'He fucking loves it, look at him.'

'Why did you go to see Ellie, Kate?' Thorne asked.

Kate stepped back until her calves were pressing against the sofa, then she dropped on to it. 'Look, it was stupid,' she said. 'I knew that. But I also knew how much you were looking forward to seeing her. So when I got out, I just wanted to . . . I don't know, pave the way or something. See if I could help.'

'What did she say?' Anna asked.

'What the hell did *you* say?' Donna marched across and stood above Kate; glaring down, demanding answers. 'What did you say to my daughter? "You don't know me, but I've been shagging your mother in prison for the last few years"?'

'I told her I was a friend.'

'Some *fucking* friend,' Donna said.

Kate looked up at Thorne. 'It didn't go very well, OK? Like I said, it was stupid and I don't really know what I was expecting.'

'You didn't hit it off, then?' he asked.

'I just freaked her out, I think.'

'Julian Munro said you were arguing.'

'It was a bad time for her, that's all. She was waiting for her exam results and was all stressed out about it. She got upset, and . . . Look, it was just bad timing, OK?'

'That was the last time you saw her?'

Kate nodded.

'You never saw Ellie Langford again after that meeting in the café in Cobham?'

'No, that was it,' Kate said. 'It was only a few weeks later that she went missing.'

Donna suddenly swung the towel violently, slapping it hard against the cushion next to Kate, who flinched when it came down. 'I cried on your shoulder. When you came to visit, the day after I'd heard about Ellie disappearing. I cried like a baby and you just sat there. You'd *seen* her, and you just sat there and said nothing.'

'You know why I'm asking, Kate,' Thorne said. 'Why I *have* to ask?'

Anna looked at him, her lack of understanding obvious. Thorne continued to stare at Kate.

'The girl you killed was about the same age as Ellie, wasn't she?'

Kate's eyes met Thorne's, something desperate in them now. 'You can't be serious.'

'That was a case of bad timing too, wasn't it?'

'You're out of order.'

'Someone else who didn't react the way you were expecting.'

'It was nearly twenty years ago.'

'What were you and Ellie arguing about?'

Kate looked up at Donna, leaned towards her and clutched at the wet towel as though her life depended on it. 'Don, you're not taking any of this shit seriously, are you? You're not listening to this, right? Ellie just disappeared, I swear.' She pulled on the towel, but Donna stood firm, her knuckles as white as the cotton, her eyes fixed on the floor. 'Tell them, will you? Tell them this is out of order, Don, for Christ's sake . . .'

★

'She *killed* someone?'

Thorne nodded, walking quickly away from the front door that Donna had slammed behind them. 'Like she said, we're talking almost twenty years ago. She was only a teenager.'

'Who was it?' Anna asked.

'A girl she was in love with who was already involved with someone else.' Thorne had looked up Katharine Mary Campbell's record after his first visit to Donna's flat. 'Kate hit her more than twenty times with a lump hammer.'

'Jesus . . .'

They could still hear the shouting from inside the house as they reached the car.

'So, what do you reckon?' Thorne asked. 'Is she lying?'

'God knows,' Anna said. 'Ever since this whole thing kicked off, I've started to think that almost everybody's lying about something.'

Thorne opened the car door. '*Now* you're starting to think like a detective,' he said.

NINETEEN

Thorne and Louise walked down into Camden and mooched around the market, as busy as any other Sunday morning, despite the near-freezing temperature and the threat of rain. Although Louise still spent an evening or two a week at her own flat in Pimlico, they had been talking vaguely about doing up Thorne's place a bit and she was on the look-out for decorating and design ideas.

'Something a bit more colourful,' she'd said. 'Something funky.'

As it was, nothing caught her eye and anything approaching a purpose was quickly forgotten. They trudged around aimlessly for the best part of two hours while Thorne moaned about being cold, ate freshly made doughnuts from a stall near Dingwalls, then walked up towards Chalk Farm to meet Phil Hendricks for lunch.

As close as he and Hendricks were, a few months ago Thorne might have resented his friend's presence – the intrusion on a few precious hours alone with his girlfriend. He could not recall which of them had made this particular arrangement, but it hardly mattered. He did not feel the same way any more and seriously doubted that Louise did, either.

They ate mussels and chips at Belgo and drank bizarrely named

Belgian lagers: Satan Gold, Slag and a sickly concoction called Mongozo Banana, which Louise could not finish. Hendricks was happy to help her out. He thought it was hilarious that some of the most lethal-sounding ales were brewed by Trappist monks.

'I bet they've got plenty to say after a few pints of that,' he said, dipping a chip into a pot of mayonnaise. 'They must at least manage "I love you, you're my best mate."'

'Or be able to ask where the nearest kebab shop is,' Thorne said.

'Trust me, they get up to all sorts inside those monasteries with gallons of free beer knocking around. Maybe they can't speak because their mouths are full . . .'

Hendricks was on fine form and the three of them laughed a lot. He talked about some of his fellow pathologists – 'humourless morons' – and the boyfriend situation – 'deader than the buggers on my slab'. He seemed to sense that Thorne and Louise were desperate for the company and the entertainment, that both were going through stressful periods at work and that things weren't a whole lot better at home.

When Louise was in the toilet, Hendricks asked Thorne how things were going. Work had been off limits all day and it was clear that he was not talking about Adam Chambers or Alan Langford.

'I think I'm getting on her nerves,' Thorne said. He looked at Hendricks and saw that his friend was not quite buying it. 'We're getting on *each other's* nerves.'

'You should try and get away,' Hendricks said. 'First chance you have.'

'Right, so we can get on each other's nerves somewhere a bit warmer.'

'It's about spending some decent time together, that's all.'

'Maybe . . .'

'You should do something about the living arrangements. Make it more official or whatever.'

'Have you written that best-man speech already?'

'I'm just saying, maybe Lou should get rid of her flat. Or you could sell both places and get somewhere bigger.'

They had been considering both of these options before Louise had lost the baby. But like a great many other things, changing their living arrangements had become something associated with the pregnancy, and, as such, was no longer talked about.

'It's just a blip, mate,' Hendricks said.

Thorne looked up and saw Louise walking back from the toilets. She looked tired and distracted, in no great hurry to return to the table, and Thorne suddenly understood the unconscious association he had been making in his head over the last two days. He pictured Louise sitting in her silver Megane, parked up somewhere and crying her heart out.

He thought: It's me.

Something she was stuck with or settling for.

A blip.

Hendricks leaned across the table. Said, 'My best-man speech would be *hilarious . . .*'

After lunch, they returned to the market and while Hendricks and Louise wandered in and out of vintage clothing shops and looked at retro furniture, Thorne walked back up the main road to the Electric Ballroom in search of second-hand CDs.

He browsed for a few minutes, then sent a text to Anna Carpenter: *the series is called 'lie to me' and the actor is tim roth!*

He was looking at the track listing on an Alison Krauss compilation when she called him back.

'You're a genius,' she said. 'That's really been annoying me.'

'I meant to tell you yesterday.'

'Listen, there's this pub quiz which a few of us go to on a Sunday night. I wondered if you fancied it.'

'A quiz?'

'It's a good laugh and we could do with you on the team, to be honest.'

Thorne stood to one side so that a fellow browser could flick through the box of Johnny Cash bootlegs. 'Sounds a damn sight more fun than paperwork, but I've got a ton of stuff I need to catch up on before tomorrow.'

'Come on! Two free pints for each member of the winning team.'

'I'd be rubbish anyway,' Thorne said. 'If it isn't music, football or obscure TV shows.'

'There's always stuff like that, and anyway it doesn't really matter if you don't know the answers. It's just a good night out.'

'I'd better not.'

'OK, well, call if you change your mind.'

Thorne said he would and with fifteen minutes to kill until he was due to meet Louise and Phil, he went back to the CD racks. He wondered why the conversation had made him so nervous, and if Anna was quite as good at spotting lies as she thought she was.

He had no paperwork to do. And he'd looked up the actor's name on Google.

On Fridays, if he fancied a night on the town, he would see Candela or one of his other girls. But Saturday night was usually reserved for the boys. The previous night, he and a few of the lads had taken one of the boats, motored out a mile or so on a calm sea, then dropped the anchor. Somebody had brought along a decent-sized bag of charlie, which got the party started, and they did a bit of business and necked red wine until nobody could talk sensibly about anything.

So, as was often the case, Sunday morning meant a long lie-in. Once he was vertical, a stumble on to the patio to drink tea and listen to one of the English-speaking radio stations. Then, when he was starting to feel vaguely human again, he stretched out by the pool to sweat out the over-indulgences of the night before.

He flicked through *El Sur in English*, a free newspaper that was delivered every week. There were details of a foiled ETA jailbreak on the front page, a few familiar faces in the local news section, but nothing that really grabbed his interest. Later, he would drive down to pick up the overseas editions of the *Mail on Sunday* and the *News of the World*. He missed the supplements, but enjoyed catching up with the sport and doing the crosswords.

He had books of crosswords and sudoku in every bog in the place; they kept his mind sharp.

The breeze made reading the newspaper tricky, so he reached for a paperback that had been sitting beside his bed for several months, that he had picked up at the airport on his last trip across to North Africa. It claimed to be a 'gritty gangland thriller' and promised to 'pull no punches'. It sounded like just the thing to take his mind off what was happening in the real world.

He needed a laugh.

It was the same with most of the films. All that million-miles-an-hour geezer-garbage the bloke who used to be shacked up with Madonna churned out. Gangster chic, or whatever they called it.

Gangster shit, more like.

He supposed it was entertaining enough, if that's what you were looking for, and it certainly gave him and the lads a few good giggles. But it was about as true to life as *Lord of the* effing *Rings* . . .

The book was much as he expected – sharp suits and sawn-offs – at least those few pages he read before the words began to blur and he felt himself drifting away. He flattened the sunlounger and pulled the towel over his head. There was an old Rolling Stones song on the radio and the sucker-thing slurped and ticked as it hoovered the bottom of the pool, and when he woke up an hour later, his head was thumping.

He kept the towel on his face and lay still. He was desperate for something to drink but unwilling to get up and walk to the kitchen, or even shout through to the maid who was pottering around inside. It was hot and white behind his eyes, the sweat was slick on him, and the worry turned to anger as the sun crept higher in the sky. His mood became sour and murderous when he thought about what was happening, the moves he was being forced to make.

So much trouble over a few poxy snaps . . .

Somebody had it in for him, that was clear enough, but finding out *who* might not be so straightforward. So, as well as trying to sort things out back in the UK, he'd put the word out locally. There were a few in the frame: a town councillor he'd maybe squeezed a little too hard; a

Moroccan supplier who thought he was being underpaid; a jumped-up used-car dealer from the Midlands who'd arrived six months before and had been put in his place when he'd tried to throw his weight about. There were those, and more than a few others who might have resented his closeness to their wives and girlfriends. Any one of them could have sent the pictures, stirred up trouble.

Of course, it would help if he could see the bloody photographs. Then he might have a better idea about who was playing silly buggers. One way or another, he'd find out eventually and get it sorted, but until then it was all about damage limitation.

Fortunately, he'd always been good at that.

He tried his book again, but it got no better, then deciding the paperback was good and heavy if nothing else, he hurled it at the sliding doors as hard as he could. It thumped against the glass and dropped to the deck. He lay there watching as a few of the scattered pages were picked up by the breeze and blown towards the water.

They bought cakes from a patisserie on Camden Parkway and took them back to Thorne's flat. Louise dug out a teapot from somewhere and poured milk into a jug, despite Thorne's curmudgeonly protestations that hot soup and toasted crumpets would have been more suitable, considering the testicle-free brass monkeys that were knocking about.

Hendricks told Thorne he was a soft southern bastard. Thorne ignored him. Louise only took issue with 'soft'.

Once tea was done with, the wine came out and they sat and drank as the Sunday evening doldrums kicked in early. The light faded outside, and when the conversation turned equally dark, Louise announced that she was going to have a bath.

Thorne opened another bottle. 'I should have worked harder at school.'

'You what?'

'Got enough qualifications to go to university. Got myself a job that didn't make me feel like this quite as much.'

'I shouldn't worry about it,' Hendricks said. 'I doubt you were bright

158

enough anyway.' He smiled, raised his glass. 'This is almost certainly all you're fit for.'

It was a trick Hendricks had used a good few times before. The banter and the piss-take as ways of easing Thorne out of a black mood. It worked more often than not, but tonight Hendricks had an uphill struggle, and Thorne told him so.

'Who said I was joking?' Hendricks asked.

'You're probably right,' Thorne said. 'I wouldn't have stuck it for so long otherwise.'

'Maybe you need to move up.'

'As in . . . ?'

'You've been an inspector since I was a sodding medical student.'

'Suits me.'

'What's so wrong about an extra pip and a better parking space?'

'Nothing . . . if I want to sit on my arse all day. Spend most of my time having to crawl up Jesmond's.'

'Get you out of the firing line for a bit.'

'I'd rather wash a corpse.'

'I can arrange that,' Hendricks said. He refilled both their glasses, nodded towards the bathroom. 'Listen, you should be in there scrubbing her back instead of sitting out here talking crap with me.'

Thorne manufactured a smile, but he was thinking about the enthusiasm that fizzed up and out of Anna Carpenter. He had felt the same thing, had *probably* felt it, back before he had stood over the body of a dead child. Before he'd watched a man tortured and done nothing. A lifetime or two before he'd seen a murderer waltz out of a courtroom to be fêted by the media.

'Why not sit the exam at least?' Hendricks asked. 'Might take your mind off stuff.'

Five minutes later, the pathologist was getting to his feet, complaining that the Northern Line would be even slower than usual thanks to weekend track repairs. At the front door, he pulled Thorne into their usual awkward embrace and winked. 'With a bit of luck, that bathwater will still be warm.'

Thorne walked back into the living room and drained his glass. He looked up a phone number in his diary and dialled.

'Steve? It's Tom Thorne.'

Stephen Keane was not a man who said a great deal, at least not in Thorne's experience. Then again, Thorne had not known him long or in anything like normal circumstances. He might ordinarily have been as mouthy as all hell, there was really no way to know, but since his daughter had been murdered, he had been a man of few words.

Now, it took Andrea Keane's father a few seconds to find a couple.

'Oh. Hi.'

'I just called to . . . see how you were doing. *Both* of you.'

'We're OK.'

'I meant to call earlier, so I'm sorry—'

'Is this because Chambers was on the radio?'

'Did you hear it?'

'A friend called us, told us about it.'

'It was a disgrace. What can I say?' Thorne was sitting on the edge of the sofa now, shaking his head. 'If there was anything we could have done to stop it, we would have, I promise you that. You shouldn't have to sit and listen to that.'

'Look, I'm right in the middle of something, so—'

'No problem. Sorry to . . . Not a problem at all.'

There was a pause. Voices in the background at Keane's end. Thorne's breathing loud against the plastic handset.

'What do you *want*?'

'Like I said, I just wanted to see how things were going.' Thorne eased himself on to the floor. 'I don't know . . . I thought it might help.'

'Help you or me, Mr Thorne?'

Howard Cook held the car door open, waited as his wife walked slowly down the path from the restaurant, then gently took her arm and guided her as she leaned down and folded herself painfully into the passenger seat.

'In you go, love.'

The arthritis had been getting steadily worse, so there had been at least an ounce or two of truth in what he'd told that copper. He had known for a while that Pat would need a lot more care as time went on. What had happened at the prison might have speeded up his decision, but he had been thinking about retirement anyway.

It was basically a pub, but they did good food and it was only a ten-minute drive, so they treated themselves to dinner there a few times each month. Now and again, they came with friends – a couple Pat knew from the library or one of the other prison officers and his wife – and once they'd brought their eldest and his girlfriend, on one of the rare occasions when he'd deigned to visit. But they were happy enough on their own.

'How was your lamb, love?' she asked.

'Very tender. What about your steak?'

'A bit rare for me, if I'm honest, but they're so nice in there you don't like to say anything, do you? And the pudding was lovely.'

'Let's get home, shall we?' he said.

Heading back through the narrow, unlit lanes towards the village, they left the radio off, same as always. Happy enough to chat. In thirty-two years of married life they had never run out of things to say to each other. Plenty of people envied them, told them it was the secret to a long and happy marriage.

That and knowing when *not* to talk about certain things.

Driving home, they continued the conversation that had begun back in the pub, over steak and lamb and a bottle of rosé. They talked about the kids, and where they might go for a holiday this year and what they were going to do with Pat's mother, who was eighty-five and barely able to leave the house. They talked about almost everything except where the money was going to come from and the retirement which had been taken out of the blue, several years too early. Cook was relieved that his wife knew him well enough to leave it alone. When he had told her about his decision a few days before, he had made it clear that he was not at all keen to discuss it further. She had nodded, concerned but understanding, and he had drawn her into a reassuring hug.

'It's done and dusted, love, so what's the point?'

Just *how* done and dusted any of it really was remained to be seen, but he didn't think that Boyle and his team would be going away any time soon. Cook had brazened it out when they had first confronted him, not knowing what else to do. He had told that London copper to dig away to his heart's content, cocky as you like, but now he lived in fear of the knock at the door and a smiling Andy Boyle on the other side of it.

'Good news, Howard. Not for you, mind . . .'

The money he'd been given for those first few 'favours' – the mobile phone business and what have you – was already long gone, and there would certainly be no more cash until things had quietened down. But he had no way of knowing how careful everyone else involved had been. One slip and they'd all be buggered.

Pulling up outside the house, Pat was talking about making them both tea as soon as they got indoors, and Cook told himself to try to relax. These were people who knew what they were doing, course they were, who did their homework. He had often wondered if they knew him even better than his wife did. Asked himself if, back when they had made their first approach, they had known exactly how worried he was about making ends meet on a prison officer's pension.

That he would be unlikely to refuse their offer.

'Here we are, love . . .'

Christ, though, now he wished he'd refused. Back then, it had seemed like a lot of money for very little work or risk. A few bits and pieces of business in and out of the prison, and a bag full of tenners in the boot of his car.

'Wait there and I'll help you out.'

No talk of anybody being killed. No cell floors running with blood and homemade blades to get shot of. And no way for him to stay clear of it.

He was theirs by then, wasn't he?

162

He got out of the car and walked around to open Pat's door. She held out a hand and he was about to take it when the headlights broke across the brow of the hill.

The car was travelling at such a speed that he knew what was coming for no more than a few seconds. Just enough time to squeeze his wife's hand once before letting go. Before the car took him and the open door, then accelerated away, the roar of its engine dying as Patricia Cook's screams grew louder.

A few minutes later, kneeling over the body in the road, a neighbour phoned 999 while his wife tried to calm the distraught woman in the car. Once an ambulance was on the way, the emergency call was relayed to the on-call Homicide Assessment Team and one of their cars was immediately dispatched. Within an hour, as soon as the pathologist had made his initial examination and the identity of the dead man had been established, contact was made with the relevant unit of the West Yorkshire Homicide and Major Inquiry Team. Once the name had been run through the computer, details of the incident were passed to the senior investigating officer of the investigation with which Howard Cook appeared to be closely connected. Within two hours of the incident in Kirkthorpe, the case had been given a number and the necessary files had been opened.

A second murder inquiry had been launched.

Just before 11.30 p.m., driving towards the crime scene from his home on the other side of Wakefield, Andy Boyle called Tom Thorne.

TWENTY

'There's so much to do,' she said. 'To be organised and what have you. I haven't even had the chance to go to the shops yet or cook anything and the house is a pigsty. I wish you'd let me make some tea or something. I could easily nip down to the end of the road and pick up some cake . . .'

Pat Cook stopped, the thought trailing away as though she had just remembered something, and turned to look at the woman sitting next to her on the sofa. She seemed surprised to see the local WPC – sent to stay overnight and by her side ever since – and shook her head. For a moment or two, she appeared to be trying to work out what the woman, and two other police officers, were doing in her front room.

At least one of those officers was not entirely sure himself.

'Honestly,' Thorne said. 'We're fine.'

It was Monday lunchtime, but the curtains were drawn at the large windows and the only light struggled from behind the fringed, brown shade of a standard lamp. Pat Cook wore a padded blue housecoat and was clutching what looked like a man's pyjama jacket. She spoke slowly, each thought an effort, like someone who was not quite awake yet.

'Did you get any kind of a look at the car?' Andy Boyle asked. He was standing near the door, a similar position to the one he had taken when he and Thorne had interviewed Jeremy Grover. Thorne wondered if he did it deliberately, if it was some kind of status thing. 'The make or the colour?'

'It was dark,' Pat Cook said. 'And it was all so quick.'

'Not even when it was driving away? A glimpse of the number plate, maybe?'

'I wasn't watching the car, I was watching Howard. He seemed to roll over and over, for ages. Then, when he stopped, I could just see the door lying beyond him in the grass.' She turned to look at the WPC. 'It took the door clean off the car, did you know that?' The WPC nodded, confirmed gently that she did. 'I was looking at it, lying there all twisted, and I was thinking that they'd have one hell of a job to fix it back on the car. It's ridiculous, now I come to think about it. Don't you think that's ridiculous?'

'It's not ridiculous,' Thorne said.

He knew from experience that the strangest thoughts could fly into people's heads at the most extreme moments. He remembered a woman who had taken a carving knife to her husband and would not stop talking about how bad she felt for ruining his favourite shirt. A father whose young son had been the innocent victim of a drive-by shooting who became obsessed with finding the football his son had had with him at the time. 'It was his best ball,' the man kept saying. 'He would have been so upset if that had gone missing.'

'Could you even see if the car had one occupant or two?' Boyle asked.

As inconspicuously as possible, Thorne rolled up the sleeves of his shirt and loosened his collar. The room was far too hot, but none of the visitors had been brave enough to make any comment.

'I didn't see anything.'

Thorne found himself wondering if Howard Cook had been the one responsible for turning the radiators down; the one who complained about it being too stuffy and marched around the house adjusting the thermostat and throwing open windows. Thorne had yet to encounter a couple who agreed about such things.

Boyle asked a few more questions about the incident, but Thorne knew that it was all academic. The car would almost certainly have been stolen and, when it finally turned up, they would be very lucky if it yielded anything remotely useful. Based on the pattern of the inquiry thus far, even if they were to get *super*-lucky and pull in whoever was responsible, they would probably not be able to identify the third party who paid them to murder Howard Cook. Thorne knew who was ultimately responsible, of course, and he had it on very good authority that this was a man who considered all eventualities. These would surely include the arrest and questioning of the people he hired.

'It's to do with his job, isn't it?' Pat Cook asked suddenly. 'The money.'

Boyle took half a step away from the door. 'What about it?'

'When I asked him, and this is going back to last year now, he said he was doing a lot more overtime.' She shook her head at what she clearly believed was the littlest and whitest of lies. 'But I knew all his comings and goings, because I always cooked for him, always had a hot meal ready, you know? I knew his hours better than he did and it wasn't overtime.'

'What did you think it was, then?' Thorne asked.

'I knew it . . . wasn't overtime.'

Thorne nodded. 'So, how did you become aware of it?'

'A few little things, really. He bought me one of them TENS machines for the arthritis, and an orthopaedic bed, one of those as goes up and down. And they're not cheap. I checked. When the service was due on the car, there was none of the usual moaning, you know? Because they'll rob you blind, those garages, won't they? Crooked, the lot of them.'

Thorne and Boyle exchanged a look. The death of her husband had clearly not quite sunk in yet, so irony would almost certainly be lost on her.

'So you just accepted it? You didn't say anything?'

'I as good as forgot about it, tell you the truth. Howard always looked after things financially. He didn't like me to worry.'

I bet he didn't, Thorne thought.

'The bills were paid, we had our holidays. Everything went on as normal, you know?'

'Did you ever see him with anyone suspicious?' Boyle asked.

Pat Cook seemed to find that pretty funny. 'He was a prison officer, love,' she said. 'He spent eight hours a day with some of the most suspicious characters you'd ever come across.'

'Right . . .'

Once again, Thorne wondered what Andy Boyle was expecting: *Oh, yes, come to think of it, there was this one man . . . very shifty-looking he was, making sure nobody was watching, then slipping Howard this big brown envelope bulging with cash. Funny, because I didn't really think anything of it at the time . . .*

'So, what now?' she said.

'Well, we'll do everything we can to bring those responsible for your husband's death to justice . . .' It was the start of a small speech that Thorne had made many times before, one that he knew sounded convincing, but he stopped when he saw Pat Cook shaking her head.

'No, love, I mean about Howard.' She folded her hands together in her lap. '*Now*, will you leave him be?'

Afterwards, Andy Boyle drove them into Wakefield, then on to where his team was based in a sprawl of interconnected units on an industrial estate to the south of the city. Police facilities were rarely beautiful, but this one was grimmer than most, making Becke House seem positively charming by comparison. Thorne wondered if each force had some kind of exclusive deal with the same people who designed slaughterhouses and multi-storey car parks. Did these places really need to be quite so dismal? He wasn't holding out for thatched roofs or artfully incorporated water features, but Jesus . . . wasn't the job bad enough already?

167

It could hardly help the cause if those *doing* it felt depressed just walking into the place.

Thorne said as much on their way in, but the Yorkshireman said he'd never really thought about it and didn't give a toss either way. Thorne asked if he'd heard of sick-building syndrome, but Boyle just shook his head and led him into the incident room, gesturing towards the dozen or so men and women who were busy at cluttered work-stations.

'Sick-*bastard* syndrome, more like,' he said, pleased with himself. 'You want to hear some of the stuff this lot come out with.'

As he was being introduced, Thorne could see that, for all the cur- mudgeonly posturing, Boyle was not only proud of his team but rather fond of most of them. Certainly more fond than Thorne was of some he had the misfortune to be working with.

He was also struck, as he had been in similar situations before, by how coppers brought together in teams always seemed to fall into distinct and recognisable categories. There were the can-do types and the moaners. There were arse-lickers, loners and thugs. Thorne recognised an Yvonne Kitson and a couple of Dave Hollands and after a few bad jokes and off-colour comments, was able to identify the team's Samir Karim. Having spoken to almost everyone, he was unsure which of those he had met was the closest approximation to himself. He wondered if it might be Andy Boyle, but even as he con- sidered it his eyes drifted towards a surly DS who was sitting slightly away from the others. He had just grunted when Thorne was intro- duced and then turned back to his computer screen. He seemed vaguely disturbed.

Thorne spoke to the officers responsible for looking into the finan- cial affairs of Howard Cook and Jeremy Grover and was told much the same story he had heard already from Andy Boyle. Almost certainly cash. No paper trail so far.

'Buggers aren't daft,' one of them said.

Thorne remembered what Pat Cook had said to him before they left – the plea on behalf of her husband. He had dodged the question, unwilling to tell the painful truth. The fact was, though, until they had something – *anything* – better to go on, they would not leave him be.

'Keep digging,' he told the officers.

He made a small speech, outlining how the inquiry was developing from the London end. As far as tracing Alan Langford went, they were following up promising leads, but they still needed all the help they could get. 'When it comes down to it,' he said, 'the work you are doing up here is likely to prove crucial in gaining a conviction.'

'Stirring stuff,' Boyle said, when Thorne had finished. 'You'll make brass one of these days.'

'Over my dead body,' Thorne said.

'Talking of which . . .' Boyle nodded towards a tall man in an expensive suit who was striding towards them. He muttered, 'Here we bloody go . . .' then smiled and introduced Detective Chief Inspector Roger Smiley.

The DCI failed miserably to live up to his name as he shook Thorne's hand and told him how pleased he was with the way their two forces were working together. Thorne did his best to look as though he were paying attention and formulated an instant opinion. Same rank as Brigstocke, but probably not a Brigstocke. Way too much formality and, thankfully, no card tricks.

'We like to think that we can stay as ahead of the curve as you boys down south,' Smiley said. 'That's right, isn't it, Andy?'

'Spot on,' Boyle said, looking as if he hadn't the faintest notion of what or where this curve might be.

'So, we're particularly proud that this inquiry is such a good example of the CRISP initiative in action.'

'*Which* initiative?' Thorne asked.

Smiley finally smiled. 'The Cross-Regional Information Sharing Project.'

'Yes, well, it's a shining example.' No, not a Brigstocke, Thorne decided. Definitely a complete and utter Jesmond.

'I'm sure you've got plenty to be getting on with,' Smiley said. 'Andy can sort you out with an office, if you need one.'

Thorne thanked him, said he wasn't planning to hang around too long, but an office for an hour or two would be nice. When Smiley had left, Thorne turned to Andy Boyle. '*CRISP?* Is he having a laugh?'

'Does he look like the type?'

'Sometimes I think they come up with these half-arsed schemes just to fit the stupid bloody initials.'

'I suggested one of my own the other day,' Boyle said. 'The National Unified Tactical Service. Told him that way he could have CRISPS and NUTS.'

Thorne laughed.

'Didn't even crack his face,' Boyle said.

By the end of the day, Thorne had spent a couple of hours in a poky office, reading through everything that the West Yorkshire team had put together in the wake of the Paul Monahan murder and in the few hours since Howard Cook's. All information pertaining to the investigation would be accessible from London via a shared-database system, but it made sense for Thorne to review the material while those who had compiled it were on hand to answer any questions.

As it was, nothing worried or excited him.

Building a case, some called it, though the likes of Jesmond and Smiley probably had a far more convoluted description. To Thorne's mind, nobody was building much of anything, although that was understandable, given that they lacked most of the necessary materials and had no clear idea of what was being built.

Get Alan Langford. For Thorne, it had already become that simple.

And find his daughter.

He called and left a message for Louise, to let her know that he would be leaving soon and that, barring delays on the train, he should be back in time for a late dinner. He offered to pick up a curry on the way back from King's Cross.

He was ready to go and reaching for his jacket when he changed his mind and went back to the desk. He picked up the phone and called Donna Langford.

'What the hell do you want?'

'How's everything with you and Kate?' he asked.

'What do you care?'

'I care enough to ask, obviously.'

'We're beating seven bells out of each other. We're not talking. I'm moving out. Which of those would you like best? Which one would give you the biggest stiffy?'

'You're being stupid, Donna.'

'Look, it's not exactly love's young dream at the minute. Let's leave it there, shall we?'

'Kate had nothing to do with Ellie going missing,' Thorne said. 'You need to know that.'

There was a pause. 'So, why bring up all that ancient history the other day? Talking about what Kate did twenty years ago.'

'I was just trying to shake things up, all right?'

'*Shake things up?*'

'Pushing buttons, trying to find out what happened. It's what I laughably call "my job".' Thorne pulled across a piece of paper, grabbed a pen and began to doodle. 'I didn't mean to stir it up between the pair of you.'

'Now you're really taking the piss,' she said.

'OK, I knew it *might*, but that wasn't why I did it. That's what I'm trying to say.'

'This is all well and good, but I don't hear you saying sorry.'

Thorne had already got as close to an apology as he was planning. 'Look, you must have known when you started this that there might be some . . . pain down the line.'

'I didn't *start* anything.'

'Whatever, you know what I mean.' Thorne was actually dating things back to the receipt of the first photograph, and though it was a possibility he had briefly considered, he did not think Donna Langford had sent the photographs to herself. 'Since this thing started then . . .'

'I never thought it would be plain sailing,' she said. 'I'm not an idiot.'

171

'Two people dead is certainly not "plain sailing", Donna.'

Thorne got the silence he had expected. The incident in Kirkthorpe had yet to make the news. Donna knew about the murder of the hit man she had hired a decade ago, but she could not possibly know what had happened to the prison officer who had been an accessory to it. He heard a cigarette being lit.

'Who else?' she asked quietly.

'I can't go into the details, but I think it's safe to say that your ex-husband knows people are looking for him.'

'Jesus . . .'

'Which is why I want you to call Anna Carpenter and tell her you're not employing her any more.'

'It's a free country, isn't it? If I want to pay her and she wants the money—'

'Listen, we've both been around the block a few times, OK?' Thorne pressed the pen hard against the page, going over the same shape time and time again. 'We both know exactly what Alan Langford might do if he's threatened, what he's *already* done, and for various reasons neither of us has much say about whether we get involved or not. I want to put him away and you want your daughter back. But whatever Anna *thinks* she wants, she's not up to any of this. She's not much older than your daughter, for God's sake.'

The sigh was filled with smoke. 'Fine, I'll talk to her,' Donna said.

'Thank you.'

Ten seconds went by before Donna said, 'What are they like? The people who had Ellie.'

It took Thorne a moment to realise that she was asking about the Munros. 'They're nice,' he said.

'That's good.'

'And every bit as worried as you are.'

There was not too much else to say, and once Thorne had said he'd call again to see how the conversation with Anna went, Donna hung up. He sat back in his chair, thinking that a drink would be nice. That Kate and Donna seemed a solid enough couple to deal with the trouble he'd caused between them. That, despite Kate's past, she was by far the more straightforward of the pair.

He picked up the piece of paper and stared down at his scribbles: a house; a boat with an enormous sun overhead; a woman sitting in a car. Then he screwed up the page and dropped it in the bin on his way back to the incident room.

He found Andy Boyle at the photocopier, asked if there was anyone available to run him to the station. Boyle said he would do it himself. Then, 'Actually, I was wondering what you had on later.'

Thorne hesitated. He was about to trot out the paperwork excuse he'd used on Anna the day before, but Boyle did not give him the chance.

'I thought you might fancy a bite to eat.'

'Well . . . maybe we could grab something quick near the station,' Thorne said.

'I don't mean anything fancy. I've got a huge pot of stew in the fridge, that's all.'

'Oh.' Thorne realised he was being invited back to Boyle's house. 'Well, thanks, Andy, but I should probably be getting back. And anyway, I don't want to intrude.'

'No intrusion, pal.' Boyle leaned back against the photocopier. 'I could do with the company, to be honest, and the stew needs eating.'

Thorne glanced at Boyle's wedding ring. 'Right. I just presumed . . .'

Boyle looked at the ring himself, admiring it as though he had never seen it before. 'She passed away a couple of years ago.'

'I'm sorry.'

'It's a pretty decent stew, if I do say so myself.'

'I'm sure,' Thorne said.

'She taught me how to cook all sorts of things, those last few months.'

TWENTY-ONE

Boyle and Thorne drove down a busy main road crowded with shops, most still open even though it had gone six-thirty, and restaurants just beginning to serve dinner. The customers and the signs made it clear that the community was predominantly Asian.

Sitting at a set of lights, Thorne lowered the window and thought about the curry he could have been having.

Soon they entered a quieter neighbourhood and pulled up outside Boyle's modest terrace. 'City's had a lot to deal with the last few years,' Boyle said. 'Some of the lads that did the London bombings were from round here, so the anti-terror thing kicked off big time. Been a load of press about honour killings an' all, special initiatives, all that.' He opened the door. 'Personally, I don't give a monkey's *why* you're killing someone. You're an arsehole and I'm going to nick you, simple as that.'

Thorne followed Boyle up the narrow path, thinking that as a working philosophy went, it was as decent as any.

'Last train's about ten, I think,' Boyle said. 'I've got a timetable inside somewhere.' He leaned against the front door until it opened. 'I may not be in a fit state to drive you to the station by then, but there's plenty of taxis.'

'That's fine.'

'Sorry about the mess . . .'

The stew was as good as Boyle had promised, and Thorne made sure he said as much. The lamb was lean and nicely spiced, and there were dried fruits – apricots and sliced mango – which Thorne had not seen in a stew before but which went very nicely with the puy lentils. They ate in the kitchen and then carried cans of lager through to the living room. It was a decent size, but cluttered: a mass of papers on a low table, a pile of clothes that might have been clean or dirty on a chair. An enormous plasma TV dominated one corner, with DVDs stacked underneath and scattered on the floor in front. Thorne saw boxed sets of *Only Fools and Horses* and *The Fast Show*, and there was plenty of cricket in evidence: *England's Six of the Best*, *The Greatest Ashes Ever*, *Boycott on Batting*.

Andy Boyle could not be more of a Yorkshireman if he tried, Thorne thought.

'I tell you what cheers me right up,' Boyle said. 'The thought of Jeremy Grover sitting there shitting himself when he hears what's happened to Howard Cook.'

'Presuming he doesn't know already?'

'Yeah, somebody always knows somebody, don't they? Jungle drums.'

Plenty of those about, Thorne thought.

'Might make the little shitehawk a bit more talkative.'

'Or do the exact opposite,' Thorne said.

Boyle shrugged and agreed that was the more likely outcome, that warning Grover might well have been one of the main reasons Cook was killed in the first place. 'Don't get me wrong,' he said. 'I feel sorry for the wife, course I do. But it's hard not to think that Cook got what was coming to him.'

'I think that's a *bit* harsh.'

'Maybe, but he knew the risks. You take dirty money from that sort of pondlife, all bets are off.' Boyle shook his head. 'Cook was bent and that's the one thing I can never get past with people. Whatever else, you keep a straight bat, right?'

This was clearly something of a hobby-horse, so Thorne just nodded and said, 'Right.'

'Same as on the Job. I don't care whether it's a few quid here and there or if you're swiping kilos of coke left, right and centre, a bent copper's a bent copper and I don't want to know.' He gave a sly smile. 'I can tell which ones are bent, an' all.'

'You reckon?' He thought of Anna Carpenter and her in-built lie-detector. Now, here was someone else who thought he had a nose for dishonesty.

'Oh yes, mate.' Boyle pointed. 'I had *you* figured out within the first five minutes.'

'Go on . . .'

Boyle paused for comic effect. 'You're a wanker, but you're a straight wanker.'

Thorne laughed, held up his can when Boyle raised his.

They sat in silence for half a minute. It had just reached the point where Thorne was about to ask if they should turn on the TV.

'She was weird, though, wasn't she?' Boyle said. 'Cook's missus.'

'I've seen people react in stranger ways than that,' Thorne said.

'Oh yeah, me too.' Boyle took a long swig of beer and relaxed into his chair, clearly relishing the opportunity to swap war stories. Or perhaps just to talk. 'A mate of mine got slapped in the face once, when he had to break the news. This woman went mental and just smacked him good and proper, like it was his fault.'

'Everyone reacts differently,' Thorne said.

'Yeah, right, for sure.'

Thorne had seen sudden death affect people in more ways than he could count. He had known people laugh their way through the bad news, as though Thorne and whichever officer he had been with at the time were playing some elaborate practical joke. It took time to sink in with most people, but none he could remember were quite as *calm* as Pat Cook. Her denial was almost childlike, a game of pretend.

'It knocks you for six, even when you know it's coming,' Boyle said.

Thorne nodded, sensing where Boyle was going.

'Like with my Anne. I mean, for those last couple of months we were talking about it *all* the time . . . planning for it, because Annie didn't like loose ends, you know? But then, at the very end, it was still . . . bad.' He took another drink. 'You think you're prepared for it but you're not, that's all I'm saying. It's still like the world stops.'

'It must have been rough,' Thorne said.

'I can't tell you, mate.'

'How old was . . . ?'

'She was forty-two.' His fingers busied themselves on the arm of the chair, picking at a loose thread, a speck of dirt, or nothing at all. 'No bloody age, is it?'

'You seem to be doing OK, though, Andy,' Thorne said. 'I'm sure she'd be proud of you.'

'She'd be bloody *amazed*, mate.'

'I mean it.'

Boyle drained the can and crushed it. 'You get on with it, don't you? Nothing else you *can* do.'

Thorne wondered how it would be for Pat Cook in the coming weeks and months. For some, it was helpful to focus all their energy into a simple hatred for whomever they deemed responsible. For others, it was easier to blame themselves.

I should never have let him go out

I should have picked her up.

If only, if only, if only . . .

He wondered, too, which way Andrea Keane's family would go, now the justice system had decreed that Adam Chambers should be free to walk around, to breathe fresh air and talk to anyone he liked about the young woman they had lost. At least the law had given them a target; perhaps, for some of them, that would help.

'Do you want another?' Boyle asked, brandishing the distorted can.

'I've not finished this one.'

'You don't mind if I do?'

'It's your house,' Thorne said. He watched Boyle head towards the kitchen, still thinking about Andrea Keane's parents. Hoping that what had happened in that courtroom did not slowly destroy what little was left of them.

It was probably a vain hope, he knew that.

A single murder cost many lives.

Having flown in the face of all her instincts and been extra nice to Frank, she had still not been allowed to leave the office a minute before five-thirty, so Anna had hit the rush hour full on. It had taken almost an hour and a half to drive the eight miles from Victoria to her parents' place in Wimbledon. Plenty of time to ask herself why she was bothering.

And to build up her courage.

Even so, having pulled up outside the house, she needed another five minutes before she felt ready to go inside. She sat in the car and stared at what had once been her home: a four-bedroom house with a decent garden and views over the common, no more than a ten-minute walk from the All England Club.

'That'll all be yours one day,' her friend Rob had said.

'I think I've been written out of the will,' Anna had said.

Neither of them had really been joking.

Now, her father turned from the fridge and carried the milk across to where Anna was sitting at the kitchen table.

'Must be some weird, primal thing,' Anna said. 'Every time I come back here I get this urge to eat cereal.'

Her father smiled. 'I always make sure I've got some in.'

'Thanks.'

'I only ever have a slice of toast, and your mum . . .'

'Right, I know. If she *was* having Rice Krispies, it wouldn't be milk she'd be pouring over them.' Anna glanced up and saw the look on her father's face. 'Stupid joke. Sorry . . .'

She started eating.

'She'll be glad you've come, you know.'

'What?'

'I told her you were coming over and she *will* ask me all about it later, when you've gone.'

178

'When she's sober.'

'She'll ask me what we talked about.'

'If I said anything about *her*, you mean.'

Her father searched for the words but gave up and turned away. He picked up a cloth that was draped over the sink and began wiping the work surfaces. Anna watched him, thinking: This nonsense is making him older. It's ridiculous . . .

Robert Carpenter was still a year or two the right side of sixty, and until recently had worked full time at one of the city's largest accounting firms. But he had been going into the office less and less since his wife had begun drinking heavily again, and Anna knew that his firm's tolerance would last only so long. She felt guilty about it every day, although she knew very well that it was not her fault.

'She does talk about you, you know.'

Anna dropped her spoon and sat back hard in her chair. She saw that her father was startled, but she was too irritated with him to care a great deal. 'You've really got to stop doing that.'

'Doing what?'

'Talking about her in those ridiculous hushed tones, like she's the mad woman in the attic or something.'

'I didn't realise I was.'

'She hasn't lost her marbles . . . yet. She's just a stupid, stubborn old cow.'

'Don't get all worked up—'

'A stubborn, *pissed* old cow.'

'Please stop shouting.'

'I don't care if she hears me. She's probably listening anyway, if she's still conscious, that is.'

Her father turned back to his cleaning, but gave up after half a minute or so. He tossed the cloth into the sink and sat down opposite Anna.

'Sorry,' she said.

'It's fine.' He was wearing a smart shirt tucked into jeans, as though, Anna thought, he could not quite allow himself to relax. Or afford to.

'How's she doing?'

'A little better, I think. We had a couple of days up in the Lakes last week. A nice hotel. She really seemed to enjoy it.'

'Did she stay sober?'

A half-smile. 'More or less.'

'Is she taking all her tablets?'

'I think so, but I can't watch her all the time, you know?'

'I know.' Anna leaned across and patted her father's arm. 'And you can't blame yourself if she pours half a bottle of vodka down her neck while you're busy trying to make a living. To have a *life*.'

He watched her eat for a while. She had almost finished. 'You mustn't blame yourself, either . . . for any of this. It's not your fault.'

Anna tried to answer too quickly, dribbled milk down her chin. They both laughed and she had another go. 'It feels like it sometimes.'

'You were an excuse, that's all,' he said. 'The excuse she was waiting for. It's what addicts do.'

Anna looked at him.

'I got a couple of books on it. It's always better if they can make out that somebody's driven them to the drink or whatever it is. It's easier to hate somebody else rather than yourself.'

'You think she *hates* me?'

'No, course not, that came out wrong . . .'

Anna nodded and took the last couple of mouthfuls. 'She's not going to come down, is she?'

'I can go and ask again,' her father said. 'Try and persuade her.'

'She shouldn't need persuading, for God's sake, I'm her daughter.' She leaned back, the chair tipping on to two legs. 'And I'm *happy*, do you know that?'

'I know,' he said. 'And whatever's going on inside your mum's head, however bad all this gets, I'm pleased it's working out for you.'

'Well, I wouldn't go that far. I can barely pay my rent.'

'Do you need some—?'

'God, no, I just meant . . . I'm still learning the ropes, that's all. But this case I'm working on now is brilliant. The people are interesting, and fun. Back at the bank . . . Well, you know.'

She stopped, and they both pretended that they weren't listening to the heavy footsteps from the floor above, the door closing louder than it should have.

'Tell me about the case,' he said.

Anna nodded. 'You sure? I mean, it might only be interesting to me.'

'That's good enough,' he said. Then he leaned across the table to pour another helping of cereal into his daughter's bowl.

Andy Boyle was one of those drinkers who said less the more he had to drink. He still talked happily enough, but he tended to repeat himself, and the silences grew longer between his increasingly slurred and rambling pronouncements.

'You need to appreciate what you've got, is all I'm saying, because one minute everything in the garden's rosy, and the next you're buggered. You're bowling along, happy as Larry, you go to a doctor because you find a lump or whatever, and everything goes to hell. So, be bloody careful.'

'I will be.'

'All I'm saying . . .'

Thorne listened, made the appropriate noises, and glanced at his watch whenever Boyle looked away or closed his eyes for a few seconds. Finally, at around quarter-past nine, he asked where the train timetable was, and for the number of a local taxi company. Boyle directed him to a drawer in the hall table, then to a bowl in the kitchen. As Thorne squinted at the stupidly small font on the timetable, Boyle reached down to the side of his chair for another can, one of several he had brought back from his last trip to the fridge.

'You're kidding me.'

'What?'

'Do you know how long this last bloody train takes to get to London?' Thorne had looked twice, just to confirm that the 22.10 from Wakefield took nearly nine hours to reach St Pancras, with one change at Sheffield, then a four-and-a-half-hour wait for a connection at Derby.

181

'I know, it's ridiculous,' Boyle said.

'I could *walk* home in that time.'

'But have a look, mate . . . you can get one back at quarter to six in the morning, or even earlier if you can be arsed getting up. You'll be back at your desk by half eight. Problem solved.'

Thorne swore at the East Coast Mainline, Richard Branson and anyone else who seemed deserving of it for a minute or two. Then he picked up one of Boyle's cans and went into the hall to phone Louise.

'Sounds like he wanted you to stay the night all along,' Louise said, when Thorne had told her about the trains. 'Maybe he's going to murder you in your bed.'

'He might have even stranger plans . . .'

'Could have been Rohypnol in that stew.'

'How was your day?'

'Well, since you ask, it started with me stepping in cat sick and went downhill from there.'

'Oh, God.' Thorne had fed Elvis just before he'd left that morning, a good half-hour before Louise was due to get up. 'Sorry.'

'It's not your fault.'

'So, what happened at work?'

'Just dealing with this bitch of a DS who's been drafted in.' Now, the frustrations of her day were there in her voice. 'Spreading poison around, usual stuff.'

'What kind of poison?'

'It doesn't matter. Don't worry, I'll sort her out.'

Thorne grunted. He knew that she would. 'So . . .'

'Sounds like you've had a useful day, though.'

'I suppose so.' Thorne took another step away from the living-room door. 'Even if the last few hours have been closer to care in the community.'

'Your good deed for the year,' Louise said.

'I suppose I'll see you tomorrow night, then.'

'Actually, I was thinking I might go back to my place tomorrow. I've got a few things to do.'

'Oh, OK. I just thought it would be nice to . . .'

'You *can* come over to mine, you know.'

Suddenly the conversation felt stilted and odd; especially as they had made such simple arrangements a hundred times before.

'I'll do that, then,' Thorne said.

'Provided you make it through the night, of course . . .'

By the time Thorne went back into the living room, Boyle was asleep in his chair. Thorne shook him gently awake and suggested that he might want to get to bed, but Boyle insisted he was more than happy where he was. He scrabbled around blindly for the remote control and turned on the television. He opened his eyes wide and reached down towards his severely depleted lager stash.

'Right you are,' he said. 'So, where are we?'

Thorne called the taxi company and booked a cab for five-fifteen the following morning. He told the controller he *knew* it was stupidly early, and to make sure the car was on time. He picked up a few empties and carried them through to the kitchen, got a glass of water then said goodnight.

He could hear Andy Boyle quietly talking to himself as he walked upstairs in search of the spare bedroom.

TWENTY-TWO

Jeremy Grover lay on his bunk and listened.

There was always plenty of chat echoing around the wing in the hour after lock-down: earlier conversations continued and news shared; filthy jokes and songs bawled from behind cell doors that spread along the landing; rumours, curses and threats.

He listened out for Howard Cook's name.

A couple of the black lads had been talking about Cook while dinner was being dished up, pissing themselves in a corner and grinning happily across at the screws who were on duty. Grover heard them, caught the name and wandered across. They told him this was *big* news and funny as fuck. One of them said something about Cook's retirement being permanent, but a fat, ugly screw named Harris came over and broke up the conversation before Grover could find out any details.

Harris was a mate of Cook's and, from the look on the bastard's face, he had heard something, too.

Grover had gone right off his dinner, wandered back to the landing and crawled into his bunk. Happy to be on his own until lock-up and needing time to think. Hoping the flutter in his guts would settle. He had dug out the mobile from its hiding place and sent a text message to the usual number, making it clear that he needed to talk. Needed to be told.

Now the phone lay tucked inside the pillow case beneath his head; the same phone, ironically enough, that Howard Cook had given to him.

That was when Grover had found out Cook was iffy. That, when it came down to it, they were on the same team. It had come as a major surprise. If he'd been asked to guess, Grover would have marked down plenty of others, that fat sod Harris included, as a bent screw long before he would have picked out Howard Cook. He supposed it was the same as with the cons themselves. Often those who looked like full-on nutters wouldn't say boo to a goose, while the ones who sat good as gold in the library all day, would tear your head off if you took the piss out of the book they were reading.

Still, it had been a shocker definitely, finding out a jobsworth like Cook was on the take.

He remembered how it had been in that cell, the evening he'd done Monahan. Cook standing there in the doorway, clearing his throat like he was struggling to breathe and holding out his hand. 'Give it to me,' he'd said and Grover had handed over the sharpened toothbrush; wiped the blood off against his trousers first so Cook wouldn't get it on his uniform. For a second they'd just stared at each other and Grover could still remember how utterly terrified the screw had looked. His face was the colour of porridge, and at first he couldn't even get the toothbrush put away properly. Couldn't find his pocket because his hand was shaking so much.

From what Grover was hearing now, it seemed that Cook had been right to be afraid.

'The twat is dead, with tyre-tracks on his head,
Howard Coo-ook, Howard Coo-ook . . .'

The song rolled along the landing like a football chant. Aggression and exuberance in equal measure.

When he felt the vibration beneath his cheek, Grover started, then reached quickly to retrieve the phone. He slid off his bunk and stood flat against the wall to the side of the door.

Took a deep breath.

'What's the panic?'

'Tell me about Cook,' Grover hissed.

'Bloody hell, that was quick. They haven't finished scraping him up yet.'

'I don't understand.'

'Would you like me to explain, Jeremy? Words of one syllable, that kind of thing.'

'There's no way he would have said anything.'

'He was being given a hard time by that West Yorkshire DI, and, you know, better safe . . .'

Grover said, 'Hold on,' and pressed his ear to the cell door. Still plenty of noise and no way that he'd be heard talking over it. 'So, I'm supposed to be scared, am I?'

'Are you?'

'Tell me about the money I'm supposed to get. For doing Monahan.'

'We'll need to leave it a while longer, until the pressure's off, but there's no need to worry. It'll be sent where you wanted it to go.'

Grover thought about his son, and the woman who had given birth to him. He couldn't be sure that the silly cow wouldn't blow most of the cash on powder and booze when she finally got it, but it should certainly make life easier for them.

'By the way, it seems like a nice school. The one your son goes to. He's a pretty decent footballer too. You should be proud.'

Grover refused to rise to it, understanding well enough what was really being said, but he suddenly found it that bit harder to breathe. A belt pulled tighter across his chest. 'So, what . . . ?'

'Just keep your head down.'

'I always do.'

'We'll try to make things as pleasant as we can for you in there. Long as you know it *can* go the other way easy enough.'

'You've got nothing to worry about.'

'I hope so. I remember having much this conversation with Paul Monahan a long time ago . . .'

Grover said, 'Listen, you can relax, OK?' then realised he was talking to himself. He put the phone back in its hiding place and lay down again.

Outside, they were still singing about Howard Cook, inventive variations now on a popular theme, until a voice rose above the cacophony, shouting about the withdrawal of privileges and suggesting they shut up.

Fucking Harris.

TWENTY-THREE

Thorne felt like death warmed up. He tried to focus, but his brain was fuzzy and sluggish, and Russell Brigstocke had definitely delivered livelier briefings. Something was needed to ginger proceedings up a little, Thorne decided.

'So, let's move on to the incident in Kirkthorpe,' Brigstocke said.

Maybe he could saw one of the DCs in half, Thorne thought . . .

Having set the alarm on his phone, he had woken at a little after 5 a.m. feeling as though he had barely slept at all. Downstairs, Boyle had been asleep where Thorne had left him, but managed to surface just long enough for Thorne to ask if he could borrow some clean socks and underpants.

'I'll stick them in a jiffy bag tomorrow,' Thorne had said.

Boyle had grunted and mumbled, 'Thanks for stopping.' Still not properly awake.

With both taxi and train miraculously on time, Thorne had – as Boyle had promised – made it back to Becke House by half-past eight. There had just been time to grab tea and a bacon sandwich from the canteen. To think about the best way to deal with the text message he had received from Anna Carpenter as the train had pulled into King's Cross.

what the hell did you say to donna??

Now, he sat towards the back of the incident room, behind two dozen or so others gathered on chairs around a pair of desks that had been pushed together. Another ten officers had been drafted on to the team the day before, following the hit and run in West Yorkshire. Overnight, the operation had become 'more significant'. It was a convenient and sensitive euphemism.

It simply meant that more people were dying.

'The car that was used to run down and kill Howard Cook on Sunday evening was found late last night, having been set alight in a field between Wakefield and Castleford.' Brigstocke looked to the back of the room, caught Thorne's eye.

A burning car. Wasn't that where all this had started?

'As you can imagine, there wasn't a great deal left of it,' Brigstocke went on. 'Just enough to confirm that it was the vehicle involved. It had been stolen from a car park in Wakefield on Sunday morning. A forensic team up there is looking at it, but I don't think we should be holding our breath on that score.'

From one of the chairs near the front, Yvonne Kitson said, 'If whoever was in that car thought there was anything we might be able to use, they wouldn't have made it so easy to find.'

'Right,' Brigstocke said.

Behind him, the case was mapped out on a whiteboard: a series of names and images linked by thick black lines drawn in marker pen. On the left-hand side was a photograph of Howard Cook that had been provided by his wife. Above that was a shot of Paul Monahan and at the very top, a picture from the original post-mortem report of the very first victim. The blackened remains that had been removed from Alan Langford's Jaguar in Epping Forest more than ten years earlier.

A face, barely recognisable as such. The rest no better than body-shaped.

In the middle of the board was one of the many shots on file – all of which were at least a decade out of date – of Alan Langford himself. There were arrows from this photo to the pictures of the victims, and towards copies of the more recent photographs that had been sent to his ex-wife. Donna Langford's own photo and one of her daughter were on the right-hand side of the whiteboard.

Now and again as he spoke, Brigstocke stepped across and pointed to the appropriate picture on the case-map. It was a simple aide-mémoire for some of the less creative thinkers on the team. *This* murder victim. *That* missing girl. *This* dodgy-looking bastard who we'd like to speak to in connection with the death of *this* man.

'We're still no nearer to finding out who this poor sod was.' Brigstocke pointed to the topmost photograph. 'So, we're concentrating on tying Langford to the murders of Howard Cook and Paul Monahan.'

Thorne was struck, as he had been many times before, by how positive Brigstocke managed to sound, how good he was at maintaining a team's morale. Even when, as in this instance, 'concentrating on' could easily have been replaced by 'getting nowhere with'.

'As to his whereabouts,' Brigstocke continued, 'we've had some luck in tracking him down to the southern coast of Spain.'

Samir Karim raised his hand. Brigstocke asked what he wanted.

'Just volunteering, Guv.' Karim turned towards those sitting behind him. 'You know, if you're looking for people to go over there and bring him back.'

'I'll bear it in mind, Sam.'

'I could do with topping up this tan.'

There was a smattering of laughter, other voices chipping in and more hands raised.

Brigstocke smiled, said, 'Yeah, all right,' and waited for the group to settle. 'I've got information sheets for everyone and I'll be briefing DI Thorne in more detail later. There's every possibility, of course, that this is also where the missing daughter is located . . .'

Thorne looked at the picture of Ellie Langford, one of those that Donna had shown him. She looked more than a little surly, as though smiling were physically painful.

'. . . though we will obviously keep checking with all the usual agencies in case a body turns up.'

Thorne could not help but compare the image with the dozens he had seen of Andrea Keane over the previous eight months. He could not recall a single one in which Andrea had *not* been smiling. Age was all the two girls had in common, he decided, and some eighteen-year-olds had less to smile about than others.

After all, Andrea's mother had not gone to prison for conspiring to kill her father.

'We've also had a good result on the photos that were sent to Donna Langford,' Brigstocke said, tapping the appropriate place on the whiteboard again. 'The FSS have come up with some decent prints, and they're definitely not Alan Langford's. I don't need to tell you that finding out who *did* send these photographs is hugely important.'

Another hand was raised. One of the new boys. Brigstocke nodded.

'If we're presuming that Langford, or whatever he calls himself now, is up to his eyeballs in drugs or what have you over there, shouldn't we be looking at some of the other characters who are doing the same thing? Maybe one of *them* sent the pictures.'

A woman sitting next to him – another new face – nodded in agreement. 'Right. It's a clever way for one of his business rivals to try and get rid of him, isn't it? Send the pictures, the police start looking—'

'It doesn't make sense,' Thorne said. The woman turned to look at him. She was young, black, serious-looking. 'First off, this "business rival" would need to know that it *was* Langford. And even if he did, look at the pictures.' He waved a hand in the general direction of the whiteboard. 'He's smiling, holding up his glass, posing for the camera. He's like a pig in shit. Whoever's taking those photographs, Langford at least *thinks* they're a friend.'

The woman smiled thinly at Thorne and turned back to the front. Brigstocke thanked her and the other officer for their input and began to wrap things up. But right at the death, the woman – whom Thorne had already decided was destined for great things – had one more suggestion.

'I was thinking about tax evasion,' she said.

Brigstocke looked at her. Waited.

'I wouldn't bother,' Karim said. 'It's against the law, you know.'

'Seriously. If nicking Langford for these murders is going to be as tricky as it sounds, then we might get him for something like that.' She spoke loudly and quickly; nervous, Thorne decided, but hiding it well. 'Whatever business he's in now, I'm damn sure he's not declaring his earnings.'

The friend next to her said, 'It's how they got Al Capone.'

'Look, I want to get Alan Langford back here and put him away for *murder*,' Brigstocke said. 'For three murders, if at all possible. Having said that, if you want to liaise with Her Majesty's Revenue and Customs, that's entirely up to you. If I have to, I'll settle for him going down on whatever charge we can get.'

'I'll make a few calls,' Thorne said. 'See if he's got any library books overdue.'

Fifteen minutes later, Thorne was in Brigstocke's office. He read through the information sheet detailing how the location of the Langford photographs had been determined, while Brigstocke gave a blow-by-blow account for good measure.

'Every boat in Spain has to be officially registered, and each owner – the *patrón de yate* – has to obtain the necessary qualification to command his vessel. All this information is logged with the local *Commandancia de Marina Mercante*, and he feeds it back to the authorities who collect assorted taxes on pleasure craft. So—'

'I *can* read,' Thorne said.

'All right.'

'I'm impressed with the accent, though . . .'

Each stage of the process was laid out for him in black and white. Providing the appropriate government department in Madrid with the boat's registration number had quickly yielded the name of its owner. Interpol, liaising with the Guardia Civil, had then tracked down the man in question in a matter of hours. Señor Miguel Matellanes had been able to confirm exactly where he was on the day in question; that he always moored his eighteen-foot sailing cruiser in the small harbour at Benalmádena Costa on a Sunday afternoon. Something about the best *pulpo a feira* on the south coast.

'I'm just showing off,' Brigstocke said, pleased with himself. 'Been a long time since I did a decent bit of donkey-work.'

'*Pulpo* what?'

Brigstocke pulled a face. 'Some sort of octopus . . .'

Thorne shook his head. 'But this only tells us where Langford was that day,' he said. 'He might live a hundred miles from there.'

'It's somewhere to start, though.' Brigstocke was standing behind Thorne, looking over his shoulder, staring down at the information sheet. 'It's all been passed on to the relevant lot at SOCA. You've got a meeting with them at three o'clock.'

'Here or there?'

'There.'

'Good,' Thorne said. 'They provide a better class of biscuit.'

Brigstocke pointed at the sheet. 'Actually, they seemed to think this was a bloody good start. Better than the information you got off your mate Brand, at any rate. None of those names led anywhere.'

'This truly is some of the finest police work it's ever been my privilege to witness, Russell,' Thorne said, waving the piece of paper. 'Seriously, I really don't know how you're ever going to top it.'

'Yeah, all right.'

'Maybe you can pull a few coins out of your backside or something . . .'

Brigstocke wandered over to his desk. 'How come you're so bloody chirpy all of a sudden? You looked like shit when you came in.'

'Early start.'

'Taking out your bad mood on that new girl.'

'She's *good*,' Thorne said.

'Glad you think so. Because, providing you haven't scared her off already, we might get to keep her when this is all over.'

'I'll have a word,' Thorne said. 'Show her my charming, funny side. I think she's a bit in love with me already, to be honest.'

'You might want to calm down a bit first . . .'

In the quarter of an hour since the briefing had ended, Thorne had necked three cups of strong coffee and he was feeling good and buzzy. Just before going in to see Brigstocke he had found two minutes to text Andy Boyle. To thank him for his hospitality, to rave once again about the stew, and, most importantly, to suggest a new acronym to try out on his boss. A specialist unit for the investigation of contract murders.

Tactical Operations, Tasking And Logistics of Covert Organised Criminal Killings.

Or TOTAL COCK.

'Try and hold on to that good mood for a while longer, will you?' Brigstocke said. 'I had half an hour on the phone with our beloved chief superintendent this morning.'

The buzz began to wear off fast. 'I'm all ears,' Thorne said.

'Jesmond is making this a high priority now, which is why getting more resources is not a problem. He's fired up.'

'Oh, God help us.'

'With *certain* high-profile cases having gone against us recently, he wants to make sure this one turns out the right way.' Brigstocke ploughed on, talking over Thorne's attempts to interrupt, using his fingers to form quotation marks. 'He told me he wants us to "bounce back". That "not getting a result isn't an option" any more. Something like that.'

'What happened to keeping this "low key"?' Thorne mimicked the use of air quotes.

'All gone out of the window now a prison officer's been killed. He reckons the media's going to be all over it . . . and he's probably right.'

'Can't we quietly let the media know that Cook was on the take?'

'Do we have proof of that yet?'

'Come on, Russell . . .'

'Jesmond also seems to think putting that information in the press might tip Langford off that we're on to him.'

Thorne didn't know whether to laugh, cry or bang his head against the wall. So he settled for raising his voice. 'I think the fact that Langford has had two men killed in the last week might indicate that he already knows, don't you?'

Brigstocke raised a hand to make it clear that he agreed, but he did not appreciate being shouted at. Thorne mumbled an apology.

'What's happening with Anna Carpenter?' Brigstocke asked.

'What do you mean, "happening"?'

The hand was raised in warning again. 'Since things have got a bit more . . . serious, Jesmond is even more keen that we try to keep a lid on the mistakes we made ten years ago.'

'Which "mistakes"?'

'We've been through this, Tom,' Brigstocke said. 'I'm just telling you that he wants us to cooperate fully with *anyone* who has access to that information. Donna Langford, Miss Carpenter . . .'

'Still afraid they'll go running to the papers?'

'Nobody likes bad press, do they?'

However the case turned out, Thorne had no idea what Donna Langford might do down the line, and he found it hard to believe that Anna would ever sell the story. 'I've already spoken to Donna,' he said. 'Told her to tell Anna she doesn't want her involved any more.'

'Because . . . ?'

'Because *I* don't want her involved any more. This has gone way beyond spying on unfaithful husbands.'

Brigstocke nodded. 'No room for amateurs.'

'Plenty of those around already.'

'OK, well, I'm just passing on what Jesmond said. I'll leave you to think about the best way to handle it.'

Thorne said he would, though in truth he had been thinking of little else all day

Back in his office, Thorne tried hard to clear his desk and caught up with Yvonne Kitson. She asked what he thought of the new girl and he told her about the evening he'd spent at Andy Boyle's place. Just as he was thinking of heading out for his meeting at SOCA, a call from Julian Munro was put through.

For a moment or two, Thorne thought that Munro might have remembered something; that he was calling with some vital, new piece of information.

'I just wanted to see how things were going,' Munro said. 'See if you'd made any progress, you know?'

Thorne raised his eyebrows at Kitson. 'Obviously, we'll let you know if there's any news, sir, but you need to know we're doing everything we can.'

'OK,' Munro said. 'Thanks.' Then he cleared his throat. 'So, what would you say are the chances? I mean, do you think . . . ?'

'I'm hopeful,' Thorne said.

He would not normally have come out with something so optimistic. You always tried to keep things upbeat with the relatives, of course, but it made sense to keep your powder dry as much as possible. Generally, it was no more advisable to say, 'Don't worry, she is definitely alive,' than it would be to draw a finger across your throat and mutter darkly, 'Brown bread, mate, no question about it.'

I'm hopeful . . .

And he was. It had already struck Thorne that he was not thinking as much about Ellie Langford as he might otherwise have expected. Not with an eighteen-year-old girl missing, her foster parents bereft, the birth mother distraught. In fact, he was still thinking far more about Andrea Keane, a girl he had long since given up for dead.

But he thought he knew why.

He had come to believe that Donna Langford was right and that her ex-husband had taken their daughter. It was the only logical explanation for her sudden disappearance, coming as it did within weeks of the first photograph arriving. And if it *were* the case, Langford had surely been trying to hurt Donna and not Ellie. He was a man who would do whatever was necessary to survive and prosper, who could order the execution of others and who could stand by, so Thorne was starting to think, and watch while someone burned alive. But Thorne was not convinced that he would deliberately harm his own daughter.

He could only hope that this atypical bout of optimism was not just Anna Carpenter's naïveté starting to rub off on him.

TWENTY-FOUR

The London headquarters of the Serious Organised Crime Agency was on the south side of the river, near Vauxhall Bridge, a stone's throw from MI6, in a cream brick and glass building that looked out across the water towards Millbank. The IRA had fired missiles at the complex in 2000, and rumours persisted of a secret network of tunnels that ran beneath the Thames to Whitehall.

Becke House was far less interesting, Thorne reckoned, but probably a whole lot safer.

Walking from the tube station at Vauxhall, he called Gary Brand.

'You remember Trevor Jesmond?'

'Bloody hell, don't tell me you're still stuck with that wanker.'

'Afraid so.'

'I'm amazed he hasn't been beaten to death, or had a truncheon stuck where the sun don't shine.'

'I've thought about it,' Thorne said, before running Brand through the latest piece of Jesmond double-think, giving vent to a good deal of bottled-up aggression as he did so. Though Brigstocke was usually on Thorne's side where such things were concerned, it felt good to cut loose with someone who had no need to be diplomatic.

'I heard about the prison officer,' Brand said.

'Cook. Right . . .'

'Sounds like it's all getting seriously nasty.'

'Like you said, "can of worms".'

'Snakes, more like.'

'It's starting to look that way.'

The sky was a wash of grey, but the sun was struggling through in places and, walking north along the Albert Embankment, Thorne could see the top half of the London Eye beyond Lambeth Bridge, with the spires of Westminster just visible a mile or so away on the other side of the river. The spooks certainly had a decent view, he decided, when they weren't busy keeping the free world safe. Or whatever.

'Where are you?' Brand asked. 'Sounds like you're out and about.'

Thorne told Brand about his appointment with SOCA. Brand said that he hoped Thorne was ready to be talked down to, and asked if he had struck lucky with any of the names he had given him. Thorne told Brand that none of them had connected with Alan Langford thus far.

'Sorry, mate,' Brand said. 'It was the best I could come up with in a hurry. You want me to keep digging?'

'Don't worry about it,' Thorne said. 'I'm hoping these high-fliers at SOCA will have found something.'

'They'll make you kiss their arses before they give it to you, though.'

'I think my DCI's already done that for me.'

'So, you around for a pint later?' Brand asked. 'Sounds like you might need one.'

'Sorry, I'm at my girlfriend's place tonight.'

'Girlfriend?'

'Don't sound so surprised.'

'Russian mail-order kind of thing, was it?'

'Actually, she's Job.'

Brand laughed. Said, 'Good luck with *that*.'

Five minutes later, Thorne had passed through a rigorous security check and was presenting his warrant card to the bored-looking woman at a large reception desk. Behind her on the wall was a huge picture of a big cat – a jaguar, maybe, or a puma – its claws and fangs bared as it leapt across a stylised silver globe. The SOCA logo was presumably meant to show that the agency was fierce and powerful, that it had teeth, but Thorne thought it looked like something from the kids' TV show *Thundercats* which he remembered from the eighties.

'Take a seat,' the receptionist said.

The cushion of the black leather sofa settled beneath him with a soft hiss as Thorne sat back to wait in a lobby that would not have disgraced a five-star hotel. The effects of his morning coffee-fest had worn off hours ago and he was starting to feel sleepy again, and desperate for a hot shower. He made sure that the receptionist saw him looking at his watch, that she knew someone was late and that it wasn't him. He turned to look at the pictures on the wall behind him – splashes of brown and cream in random patterns – and flicked aimlessly through one of the magazines spread out on the glass-topped coffee table.

But he was unable to stop thinking about something Gary Brand had said. The phrase bounced around inside Thorne's head as he sat and waited and tried to stay awake.

Snakes, more like.

She caught the train from Waterloo, walked from the station and stopped when she reached the water mill. She sat on one of several benches, each with a small plaque inscribed in memory of someone who had loved the river or the view of it, ate the sandwich she'd brought with her from home and watched the house.

It was as good a place as any to spend an afternoon.

Initially, Anna had been reluctant to let her have the address, but once Donna had pointed out that she was still the agency's client and paying for the privilege, the girl had given her what she wanted. Then Donna had done what Thorne had asked her to do and dispensed with Anna's services.

That had not been the easiest of conversations.

199

The house was not as old as she'd been expecting, having got it into her head that the Munros lived in some kind of listed country mansion or other. It was big, though, with a good-sized front garden and pillars on the porch. There was plenty of space around it and she imagined a large garden at the back, sweeping away in perfect stripes from a sunlit patio, with access to fields beyond or at least a view of them.

That was what she'd wished for, what she'd wished for Ellie, during all those years inside.

A car was parked on the drive, a Volvo, but Donna had no idea if there was anybody inside the house. She finished her sandwich and continued to watch, and just once or twice she thought she saw movement. A shadow, a shape moving past an upstairs window. She had some notion that husband and wife both worked. If that were the case, then one or other of them would be home soon enough, but she was not sure if she would wait that long, if she wanted to see them.

After all, how would seeing them help?

Everything about Maggie and Julian Munro provoked strong, conflicting emotions that defined her for long and painful days on end. They made her a nightmare to live with, she was certain of that, and she was constantly amazed that Kate had not given her up as a bad lot a long time ago.

She was grateful for the home these people had given Ellie and she hated them for it. She was happy that her little girl had made them the family they wanted to be and she bitterly resented every moment they had spent with her. She understood their misery and she revelled in it, for it was not and could never be as real, as *valid*, as her own.

Donna stared at the Munros' house, as fine and cold in its way as the one in which she had once lived, and imagined a couple inside, awake in the early hours and driven apart by despair. One hunched over a polished kitchen table and the other alone upstairs, weeping into her pillow, while the space between them that was Ellie's absence grew bigger and darker by the day.

Ellie *Langford*, not *Munro*. Her name.

As Donna watched, the pillars on either side of the porch began to blur and swim as her eyes filled with water.

Silly cow. Stop it!

The photographs had helped, just a little. At least she knew what Ellie looked like, could see the ways in which her little girl's face had changed and how it had stayed the same. But so many other things left her distraught.

She could no longer remember what her daughter smelled like.

Thorne asked himself, as he had done many times before, if there ever came a time when men stopped sizing one another up like dogs fighting over a bitch. It was usually for no more than a moment, but it almost always happened when men first met. As well as taking in the superficial stuff – the clothes, the haircut, the approximate values of the watch and shoes – it often came down to the handshake, firm or otherwise, and those few awkward seconds of eye contact, and the simple, stupid, *childish* question of whether you could take them if it ever came down to a good, old-fashioned punch-up.

He had decided that the urge to compete in that way probably stopped at the same time a man stopped sizing up the *women* he met and wondering altogether different but equally stupid things.

It was ridiculous, Thorne accepted that, but it was also as natural as breathing and harmless enough for the most part. For those who knew where to draw the line, anyway. At that morning's briefing, he had looked at the new woman on the team for a little longer than was strictly necessary. Now he sized up the two SOCA agents who greeted him when he stepped out of the lift on the fourth floor, and as they led him along a corridor to a meeting room that smelled of new carpets and wax polish.

'There's coffee on the way,' one of them said.

'Biscuits?'

'I'll see what we can do . . .'

The three of them sat around a large blond-wood conference table. There was a jug of water and half a dozen glasses, notebooks in front of every chair. The taller of the two SOCA men, who had introduced himself as Nick Mullenger, began to spread an assortment of photographs, charts and blown-up map fragments across the table. He was in his early thirties, with thick, dark hair and acne scars, and a voice that sounded perfect for cheaply made radio adverts. His colleague had not bothered with the pleasantry of a Christian name, so Thorne could only guess that he was either short of time or simply trying to appear more enigmatic than he seemed. Silcox was shorter than Thorne but in the same ballpark, age-wise. He wore a suit and tie, as did Mullenger, but filled his out a little better than his colleague. He had less hair than Mullenger and rather less to say for himself and when he did speak, it was barely above a whisper, as though there were something badly wrong with his throat. It might have been a heavy cold or it might have been cancer, so Thorne did not bother asking.

'Right, Spain,' Mullenger said. He spoke cheerfully, as though they were a family who had finally settled on a holiday destination after a long discussion.

'It was always our best guess,' Thorne said. 'Even if it seemed a bit obvious.'

'There's a good reason for that.'

'Drugs?'

'Definitely,' Silcox said.

Mullenger pointed to a spot on one of the maps. 'The south coast of Spain.' He moved his finger slightly. 'The north coast of Africa . . .'

Thorne nodded and remembered what Gary Brand had said about being talked down to. But Mullenger seemed pleasant enough, so Thorne bit his tongue and wondered what else the SOCA man might deem it necessary to point out.

Notebook. Pencil. Water jug.

'Morocco's only forty miles away,' Mullenger said. He turned his palms up as though no further explanation were necessary, then proceeded to give one anyway. 'Started out with a few hippies bringing hash across on fishing boats and now it's a multi-million-dollar industry.'

'Billion,' Silcox said.

'Once upon a time, old-fashioned villains like your Mr Langford fought shy of the drugs trade, but that was before they saw how much money could be made. Now, almost every ounce of cannabis and cocaine that arrives in the UK has to come through Spain, so it's the perfect place to base a drugs empire. They use the marinas as cover and the authorities haven't got the manpower or the inclination to search all the yachts.' He sat back in his chair. 'It's a drug-smuggler's paradise.'

'It's not just about the beaches and the sangria,' Silcox said.

Thorne pulled one of the pictures of Langford towards him. 'Don't suppose that hurts, though.'

Mullenger laughed, said, 'No, indeed.'

'So, Langford's got a decent business going out there, you reckon?'

'Almost certainly,' Mullenger said. 'And it's not really a surprise that he's been reacting the way he has, now he knows these enquiries are being made. So *violently*, I mean.'

'It's how he does things,' Thorne said.

'How they *all* do things.'

Silcox tapped a pencil on the table. 'Wild West over there,' he said.

Mullenger nodded, reaching for a list of facts and figures. 'You've got the Brits, the Irish, the Russians, the Albanians, whatever, all fighting for a bigger slice of the action, so it's pretty much become a war zone. They set up a special unit in the late nineties to try to get to grips with it, and for a while things calmed down a bit.'

'"Marbella Vice",' Thorne said. 'I remember. I knew a few people who tried to swing a transfer over there.'

'Right, and for a year or two there was an unwritten agreement among the residents to tone things down, so as not to attract any more attention. They spent their time settling scores elsewhere. But once the Colombians started laundering drug money there, it all kicked off again, big time, and now there are shoot-outs on the streets every other week.'

'*Costa del Plomo*,' Silcox said.

Thorne looked to Mullenger for an explanation.

'That's the new nickname for the place,' Mullenger said. 'Spanish for "lead".' He made a gun with his fingers. 'Because of—'

'I get it,' Thorne said.

Mullenger had the good grace to look embarrassed, but Thorne caught the trace of a smirk from Silcox. Thorne stared across the table and Silcox stared back, his doughy features a picture of innocence.

'We've been working with the local police in southern Spain for the last few years,' Mullenger said. 'Trying to disrupt a few of the criminal networks and round up as many fugitives as we can. It's tricky, though, because some of the people who are supposed to be on our side aren't really on our side, if you know what I mean.'

'Corruption in high places?'

Silcox was still staring. 'High places, low places.'

'Last year, three local mayors and a couple of high-ranking officers in the Guardia Civil were prosecuted for laundering drug money.' Mullenger shrugged and picked up another piece of paper. 'We're making some progress, but just to give you an idea of the scale of what's going on over there . . .' He glanced down and read from the sheet. 'Last year, *Operación Captura* led to the arrest of forty-one people and the seizure of four hundred million euros' worth of funds, as well as over twenty yachts and private planes, forty-two cars and two hundred and fifty houses.'

'Pretty impressive,' Thorne said.

Silcox smiled. 'Us or them?'

'And that's in Marbella alone.' Mullenger laid down his list. 'So . . .'

There was a knock on the door and a man brought in the coffee: a Thermos jug and three cups on a tray. Mullenger did the honours while Thorne stood and walked to the window. He was still feeling fractious and fidgety, and decided that both he and the double-act assigned to brief him would be a lot happier were he to be nodding off aboard one of the pleasure boats he could see moving up and down the river two storeys below.

'We managed to get you your biscuits,' Mullenger said.

Thorne went back to the table and took his coffee. 'I was expecting chocolate ones at least,' he said. He bit into a digestive and pointed to one of the headed notepads. 'Obviously spent too much on your fancy logo.'

Mullenger forced a nasal laugh and said something about cost-cutting that was less funny than he thought it was. Thorne ate his biscuit and pretended to listen.

Thinking: *Thunder-Thunder-Thunder-Thundercats Ho!*

Mullenger pointed to a spot on a larger-scale map. 'I don't think the location where these photographs were taken is likely to be where Langford actually operates. It's a smallish town, not too many visitors.' He nodded to himself. 'But I shouldn't think he's too far away.'

'His business is likely to be based around a marina somewhere,' Silcox said. 'But a lot of the big players tend to live up in the hills or on one of the golf resorts. There's still plenty of building work going on all along that coast.'

'He's probably into some of that as well,' Thorne said. 'It's how he made his money over here.'

'Always pays to diversify,' Silcox said.

Mullenger refilled Thorne's cup and talked about the best way to proceed, if and when Thorne made the journey to Spain himself. He seemed confident that the man who used to be called Alan Langford would be known to Spanish-based SOCA operatives and local drug-enforcement officers. Thorne's job, working with them, would simply be to establish that the criminal in question was indeed Langford, and then to find something for which he could be arrested and brought back to the UK for trial.

'Piece of piss, then,' Thorne said.

'We'll hook you up with one of our agents in Malaga or Marbella,' Mullenger said. 'Probably easier for him to brief you when you get there.'

Thorne agreed, knowing that his contact might turn out to be a copper, a customs officer or even, God forbid, a taxman. In an attempt to create a British FBI, SOCA had been formed as an amal-gamation of the National Criminal Intelligence Service and the

National Crime Squad, but had also taken staff from HM Revenue and Customs and UK Immigration. Thorne knew that the agency had officers embedded within many police forces and that the arrangement was reciprocal. He also knew that their powers were wider-ranging than those of their counterparts; and that, unlike regular coppers such as himself, they were exempt from the Freedom of Information Act.

They didn't have to tell anybody anything.

'We've got some shit-hot agents over there,' Mullenger said. 'You'll be working with good people.'

Thorne smiled. To be fair, this *was* an agency, so those who worked for it were, strictly speaking, agents. But Thorne saw how much Mullenger relished saying the word; imagined that it made him feel like a proper G-Man. Thorne worked regularly with people who had the same affectations. One DS on a parallel team to his own had once visited Quantico and had somehow managed to acquire an official FBI lanyard from which he proudly suspended his Met Police swipe card and ID. On the lanyard it said: *Fidelity, Bravery and Integrity.*

It should simply have said: *Knob.*

'I don't want to spoil a beautiful friendship,' Thorne said. 'But what are the chances that this corruption you were talking about might involve some of these "shit-hot agents" of yours?'

Silcox and Mullenger looked at each other.

'I know,' Thorne said. 'You go that extra yard with the biscuits and then I go and bring the mood right down.' He smiled, but he was thinking about the speed with which the killings of Monahan and Cook had been sanctioned and executed; about an exchange of information. Those jungle drums. 'Only, if I was Langford, or somebody *like* Langford, they'd be the first people I'd be looking to sweeten, you know?'

Mullenger gathered together his photos and maps. 'It's a fair question.'

'Bad apples in every barrel,' his partner said.

'Absolutely. Who's to know?'

'You can drive yourself mad worrying about that stuff,' Silcox said. His voice was louder than it had been all afternoon. 'I should worry about things you can do something about, like how many pairs of shorts to pack.'

A few minutes later they walked him briskly back to the lift and said perfunctory goodbyes. There were handshakes, one firm and one less so; and, as the lift doors closed, Thorne took a final look at the pair of them.

It did not feel quite as childish as it had forty-five minutes before.

If it came to it, Thorne knew he could take Mullenger with one arm tied behind his back. But he was less sure about Silcox. The shorter, older man had the kind of eyes you worried about and would almost certainly fight dirty.

Outside, he switched on his phone and saw that there had been another text from Anna Carpenter: *we still need to talk about donna!*

He looked at his watch. It was hardly worth going back to the office now.

And Vauxhall was only two stops from Victoria.

TWENTY-FIVE

With more than half an hour until going-home time, Anna was delighted to answer the intercom to what sounded like a potential client. If Frank stuck to his usual routine and took the man across the road to discuss business over a drink, then there was every chance he would let Anna leave early. As it was, the man at the front door had no interest in waiting on the street and insisted on talking to Frank in the office, so somewhat disconsolately, Anna buzzed him up.

Having hurriedly cleared the worst of the clutter from his desk, Frank opened the door and showed his visitor to a chair. He immediately apologised for the mess, which he put down to working too hard on cases to have time for cleaning, and for Anna's bike, which was propped against a radiator.

The man seemed unconcerned and keen to get on with it.

Frank handed over a folder filled with laminated testimonials – many of which he had written himself – and told the man a little about the business as he flicked through it. Only then did he introduce Anna, as his associate. The man looked at Anna for the first time and nodded a hello.

Anna smiled and said, 'Nice to meet you.'

'I gather that you specialise in matrimonial work,' the man said, turning his attention back to Frank.

'It's one of several areas—'

'A friend of mine used you and said you were very good.'

'Oh . . . who was that?' Frank asked. 'It's always nice to hear about another satisfied customer.'

'I'd rather not say.'

'I understand,' Frank said. 'And you can be sure that discretion is very much part of the service we provide.'

'Honey traps, right?'

'Some people call it that,' Frank said. 'We prefer to think of it—'

'Yes or no?'

'Yes,' Frank said. 'Definitely.' He glanced across at Anna, who tried not to look too disgusted at the excitement in his face. The job he had mentioned to her on Friday had failed to materialise. Another in a long list of clients who had gone elsewhere after learning that other agencies provided a more efficient service. 'We can definitely do that.'

'As long as we're clear. So, how much does it cost?'

'It all depends on the circumstances and so on . . .' Frank was beginning to look a little flustered. 'But there's something I'm not clear about.'

The man looked at Frank, waited.

Frank cleared his throat. 'We're talking about your wife?'

'Girlfriend.'

'Fine, girlfriend. But that still leaves us with the same problem.'

'Which is?'

Frank tried to mask his discomfort with laughter, but it looked and sounded forced. 'Well, normally it's the *women* who come to agencies like ours, you see, wanting to make sure their husbands aren't playing away from home. We don't actually have any male operatives. I mean, there's *me*, obviously, but I don't really . . . I'm hardly likely to trap anybody, so . . .'

'It's not a problem,' the man said.

'I don't follow.'

209

The man nodded towards Anna. 'I presume it's your associate over there who normally does this kind of work.'

Frank told him it was, and that Anna's record in such matters was impeccable.

The man turned to look at Anna again, but she reddened and looked away. 'Well, we should be fine, then.' He raised an eyebrow at Frank. '*She*'s just my girlfriend's type.'

Frank's mouth fell open a little, and his cheeks flushed the same colour as one of the rosés he favoured. 'Right, got it. So . . . she . . .'

'Swings both ways,' the man said. 'Either that or I've turned her into a lesbian, I'm not quite sure. I was hoping you might help me find out.'

'Well, I won't lie to you, it's a new one on me, but I don't see any reason for us not to take it on.' He reached for a pen and paper to start taking down the necessary details, but the man stopped him.

'I'll need a word with her alone first,' he said. 'With . . . Anna, was it?'

'I'm not sure—'

'A few details are a bit . . . embarrassing, you know?'

'Right.'

'It would be easier if it was just the two of us.'

'It's fine, Frank,' Anna said. 'I'll take him across the road.'

The man thanked her and promised it would not take very long.

Frank was quickly on his feet, seemingly relieved to have an awkward conversation taken off his hands. He told the man that they could talk about costs, run through the different procedures for this kind of operation and so on later. There was no hurry, he said, though that did not stop him barking at Anna to get a move on as she paused at the door to dig around in her shoulder-bag for lip-salve.

The man looked daggers at Frank.

'Well, it's all chargeable time,' Frank said. 'No point in wasting your money, is there?'

Anna led F.A. Investigations' newest client down the stairs, not stopping to release the laughter she had been struggling to contain until they were safely out on the street with the door closed behind them.

'What the hell was *that*?'

'What?'

'You're off your head, you know that?'

'I suppose I *could* just have showed him my warrant card,' Thorne said. 'Told him I needed to talk to you.'

Anna laughed again. 'Frank's face . . .'

'But then he would've wanted to know what was going on at some point, and I'm guessing you've still not told him about the case.'

'What case?' Anna said, the laugh trailing away.

'Right. That's what we need to talk about.'

For ten seconds or more, she clearly found it hard to sound as angry as she felt, so she watched the traffic and let it build. 'I don't have a case any more, do I?'

'No.'

'Not since you told Donna to sack me.'

'Let's go and get a drink,' Thorne said.

They walked across the road and into Frank's favourite bar. Thorne bought a Diet Coke for himself and a glass of wine for Anna, and they chose a table by the window. It was still a little early for those wanting a quick one on the way home, or several slow ones after a hard day, so the place was relatively quiet. The muted, hesitant exchanges between the two people by the window did little to change anything.

'What am I supposed to tell Frank?' Anna asked. 'When I go back to the office without his new client.'

'Anything you like,' Thorne said.

'That's helpful.'

'Tell him I was just wasting your time. That I was some kind of freak or whatever.'

'*Control* freak.'

'Listen—'

She leaned towards him. 'Why the hell does everybody think they have the right to run my life?'

'I don't think that.'

'That I'm somehow incapable of deciding what's best for me.' Anna

211

was drinking quickly, half her large glass of red gone in two gulps. 'First it's my stupid bloody mother. Now it's you.'

'This isn't about what's best for *you*,' Thorne said. 'It's about what's best for my case. I've got a job to do and, to be honest, you're really not helping.'

She blinked slowly, took another drink.

'I'm sorry, but the fact is . . . you're a liability.' Guessing correctly that Anna would react badly if she thought she were being patronised, Thorne had decided on a harder approach, but he had not banked on seeing her face fall quite so far.

How bad it would make him feel.

'Oh, cheers,' she said.

'You said yourself, you're still learning the ropes.'

'And . . . ?'

'And part of that is knowing when to step back and admit that you're out of your depth.'

'What did you say to Donna?'

'I didn't say anything.'

'You're a bloody liar.' She emptied her glass and, without a word to Thorne, got up, walked to the bar and bought herself another. Thorne watched, beginning to wish that he had done this over the phone.

Anna started talking before she was back in her chair. 'Donna said that, because the police were now so heavily involved in trying to find her ex-husband, she didn't need my services any more, or some shit like that. But I knew damn well that you put her up to it.'

'I asked her to do me a favour.'

'Because I'm a "liability".'

'Because it's *dangerous* . . . Jesus!' Thorne took a breath and lowered his voice. 'You're not stupid, Anna. You know very well what we're dealing with.'

'I told you I wasn't scared after Monahan was killed.'

'Right, and I told you that you should be. And I told you to back off, because I knew that was never going to be the end of it.'

Anna grasped the implication straight away. 'Who else?'

Thorne told her about Howard Cook, taking care to mention the bloodstains on the road outside his house and the brain-matter found baked into the shattered windscreen of the burned-out car. He did his level best to describe how devastated the man's widow was.

'That's horrible,' Anna said, finally. 'But it doesn't really make any difference.'

'What?'

'This man you're after is only killing anyone who can hurt him, witnesses or whatever. He—'

'Don't try to make him sound *reasonable*.' Thorne's voice was quiet, but there was steel in it. 'He's *anything* but reasonable.'

'He's a businessman, right?'

'He has people killed, Anna.'

'But there's no reason why he would ever—'

'You can't presume to know what the likes of Alan Langford are willing to do,' Thorne said. 'Basic rule. You *never* presume.'

Anna laughed, but it was aggressive, like a slap. 'You presume all the bloody time!' She smacked down her glass, splashing wine across the tabletop. 'You presume that I'm scared and out of my depth and that I'll screw things up. You presume to take work away from me, then sit there like some . . . *authority*, when you're clearly as much of a fuck-up as anyone.' She stood up, shaking her head, then bent to dab at the spillage with a napkin while scrabbling for her bag and jacket with the other hand. 'And worst of all, *stupidest* of all, you presume that I like you enough to let you get away with it.'

Thorne watched her leave, pushing past a couple in the doorway, searching for a gap in the traffic then running across the road. Her hair was flying and her bag bounced against her hip as she went.

Unpleasant as it had been, Thorne presumed he'd done what he came for.

TWENTY-SIX

Louise's basement flat in Pimlico was very different from Thorne's place in Kentish Town. Bigger and more modern, with clean lines and furniture that looked and felt less lived-in than Thorne's ten-year-old Ikea collection. It was also considerably less tidy than Thorne's, a fact that surprised nobody more than Thorne himself. He had become rather more house-proud since Louise had started staying with him, but the same could not be said of her. Thorne could never equate the ruthlessly efficient Kidnap Unit DI with the woman who kept a large cupboard entirely stuffed with plastic bags and whose bathroom – though it smelled nicer than his – looked like an explosion in a cosmetics factory.

It seemed to Thorne that they always reacted differently to each other when they were staying in Pimlico, that the dynamic between them was subtly altered. He guessed that he was the same way when the situation was reversed, but recently Louise had seemed a lot more comfortable whenever they were staying at her place; more at home, in every sense.

Or maybe he had simply never noticed it before.

With both of them now so at ease in their own places, Thorne wondered if the idea of them getting somewhere together would – or *should* – ever be discussed again. They had talked about selling one flat and renting out the other, as Thorne still had money left from the sale of his father's house a couple of years before, then buying a place further north, in Hertfordshire maybe. But perhaps the moment for all that had gone.

Louise cooked pasta, added a tin of tuna and some black olives to a Sainsbury's arrabiata sauce, and they ate at the small table in the kitchen.

'I meant to say, Elvis was sick again this morning.'

'Shit,' Thorne said.

'You need to get her to the vet.'

'Did you leave her plenty of food?'

'A couple of bowls of the dry stuff,' Louise said. 'For tonight and tomorrow morning.'

'She's probably just picked up a bug or something.'

Thorne had inherited the cat from a murder victim many years before, a woman who had named the cat without realising she was a female. He had no real idea how old Elvis was, but she must have been pushing twelve or thirteen, and while she had never been a big cat, Thorne had noticed, picking her up a day or two before, that she was feeling skinnier than usual.

'If nothing kicks off at work, I'll try to take her in at the weekend,' he said.

They continued to eat. Louise told Thorne that she had put the rubbish out before she'd left his flat that morning and that he was almost out of milk. Thorne told Louise how good the meal was, and thought that this was what couples who had been together for a year or two talked about: bin collections and cat sick.

Tried to convince himself that it could be a whole lot worse.

When they had cleared away the plates, they took glasses of wine through to the living room. There was a Champions League match that Thorne fancied watching, but he said nothing as Louise exercised home advantage and put on a CD: some woman from the West

Country who thought she was Dusty Springfield. Thorne made himself comfortable on the sofa, but when Louise came across and sat facing him on the matching footstool it was clear that she wanted to talk about more than taking out the rubbish.

'Hypothetically,' she said, 'what would you think about me getting out of the Job?'

Thorne sat back and puffed out his cheeks. Said, 'Bloody hell.'

'I said "hypothetically".'

'Where's this come from?'

'I think we need to do something.'

'*We?*'

'Change something, I mean.'

'But you love the Job,' Thorne said. 'More than I do, anyway. You can probably make DCI this year.'

'I think maybe the Job had something to do with losing the baby.'

'You don't know that.'

'I'm damn sure it didn't *help*. Come on, you know how stressful it is . . .'

Thorne could hear something in her voice: anger, urgency. He just nodded and took a drink.

'And it's probably got something to do with the fact that it hasn't happened again.'

'Well, maybe if we actually had *sex* a bit more.'

'Right, if the sodding Job didn't wear us both out quite so much, and if our shifts didn't mean that we're like ships in the night most of the bloody time.'

There was not too much Thorne could argue with. He sat back. The West Country Dusty was getting worked up, bleating about her lover being drunk and faithless.

'It just seems a bit . . . radical,' Thorne said.

'We need to *do* something, Tom. If we want this to go anywhere—'

'*Go* anywhere?'

'Maybe we both need to get out of the Job.'

'*What?*'

216

They had talked about it once before, their fantasy future. But that had been when there was a baby on the way.

'Are you really going to sit there and tell me everything's fine?'

'You're the one with all the opinions.'

'That's part of the problem.'

'Everyone has ups and downs, whatever, but you're talking like everything's *fucked*.'

'I'm trying to be realistic.'

'You're being ridiculous,' Thorne said. 'And melodramatic.'

Louise shook her head and laughed, just once, exasperated. 'It's so typical.'

'What is?' Thorne had been careful to say whatever was necessary, in whatever way was necessary, to keep Louise from losing her temper. Now, he was in danger of losing his own.

She swallowed a mouthful of wine, still shaking her head. 'When it comes to work, you'll do whatever it takes to get the right result. You'll go the extra mile, take stupid risks. You'll *push* it. With other people, other people's lives and problems, you do what needs to be done without even thinking about it. But with your own life, *our* life, it's a different story.'

'This isn't fair, Lou . . .'

'With us, it's just about the path of least resistance, about doing as little as possible. It's like the Job's taken all the fight out of you or something, and when it comes to personal stuff, to *this*, you'd rather just bumble along and settle for a quiet life, no matter how bad it is.' She was sitting on the edge of the stool, her knees pressed against his shins. 'Well, I think you've got it arse about face. I reckon your priorities are wrong, and if you really give a toss about how things are going to work out between us, you need to think about what's more important. Decide what you want.' She emptied her glass, looked at him. 'Well?'

Thorne stared at the carpet, wanting more than anything at that moment to turn off the music. To pull out the wannabe Dusty's tedious CD and smash it against the wall.

217

The doorbell saved him the trouble.

Louise swore and stood up, walked across to the CD player and turned it off. 'If that's the stupid cow from upstairs, she can piss off. There's no way that was loud enough to disturb her.' She looked at Thorne as though she were waiting for him to go and answer the door.

'*I*'m not going,' he said. 'She's your bloody neighbour . . .'

He switched off the film and faded up the lights with the same remote. He always got a buzz out of that. When the home cinema had been installed, he'd made sure it came with all the bells and whistles, and it had been worth every penny. He had all the big dishes, so he could watch Premiership football whenever he wanted, the BBC news, all that. But mostly he just watched films. He had quite a library now: war movies, Westerns and a full set of Laurel and Hardy; a decent porn collection that he and Candela dug into every now and again.

Just to keep things interesting.

He'd had it built down in the basement, so it was also the coolest room in the place. Most nights, when he wasn't out somewhere or entertaining, he ended up here, with the sound turned up good and loud, stretched out in shorts and a T-shirt until his eyes began to close. He would usually call it a night then, but sometimes he would nod off and wake up sweating at three or four in the morning, with the screen still bright and the speakers hissing. For a moment or two, he might not remember where he was.

Which time, which country.

Then, once he'd sorted himself out, he would pad slowly back through the villa to the kitchen, pick up a bottle of water from the fridge and go to bed. Happy enough, all things considered, at the way things had turned out.

Until now . . .

It was hassle he simply did not need, not to mention a lot of money he could have done without spending. The precautions he'd taken to make sure the situation could not seriously hurt him had not come cheap. The people he was using had to be paid decent money, on top of what he'd been shelling out every year anyway, just to keep his sources sweet.

It wasn't all about the money, though. He'd *earned* the life he'd made for himself, and, bar a minor hiccup or two, until recently it had been relatively stress free. He wasn't getting any younger and he'd been counting on life staying the way it was until he went toes-up. Golf and boats and a spot of clubbing. Parties and shagging until he couldn't get it up any more and a bit of business every now and then, just for the mustard.

Who wouldn't want that? Do whatever it took to protect it?

He picked up the remote again, dimmed the lights and restarted the film.

But he couldn't get his mind off that copper. The one who looked like he might enjoy a bit of digging . . .

He looked at his watch. On the screen, Stan and Ollie lay asleep in bed, a feather floating back and forth between them as they snored in turn.

The UK was one hour behind. Things should start happening soon enough.

And with a bit of luck, that would be the end of it.

TWENTY-SEVEN

Thorne had heard the voices and was already on his feet when Louise walked back into the living room with Anna Carpenter. Louise was smiling and saying something about a drink, but as soon as she caught Thorne's eye she stared good and hard. Said, 'Visitor.'

'Right,' Thorne said.

'I'll put the kettle on.'

She walked towards the kitchen, her mouth set, the muscles working in her jaw. Thorne put a hand on her arm as she went past, hoped that her irritation was due to nothing more than having an important conversation interrupted.

'This is obviously not a great time to be dropping in,' Anna said, trying to smile. She stood in the middle of the room, shifting her weight from one foot to the other. She had not taken off her coat or put down her bag.

'How did you get this address?' Thorne took a step towards her.

'Look, I'm sorry—'

'And don't tell me it was your mate at the DVLA . . .'

'Your chief superintendent,' Anna said.

'*What?*'

'He gave me his number last week and told me to call if I needed anything, so—'

Thorne had already turned away and was moving towards the kitchen. He stuck his head around the door and told Louise not to bother with the coffee. When she opened her mouth to speak, he told her that he was sorry and that he would not be gone long. Then he lowered his voice and told her they could continue the conversation when he got back.

He walked back into the living room and grabbed his leather jacket from the arm of a chair.

Anna adjusted the strap of her shoulder-bag.

'Let's go for a walk,' he said.

Anna had to hurry a little to catch Thorne, then settled into step with him and did her best to keep up. 'Where are we going?'

Thorne was unable to answer as he did not have the slightest idea.

'OK, how about *why*?' She turned to look at him. 'I'm guessing you didn't want to shout at me in front of your girlfriend.'

Again, Thorne said nothing, unwilling to think about his reasons for wanting to get out of the flat – wanting to get Anna out of the flat – for too long.

'Sorry, I don't know her name,' Anna said.

'Tell me about Jesmond.'

As they walked, Anna told Thorne that his chief superintendent had called her the day after she had visited Thorne at Becke House. Jesmond had been extremely friendly, she said, and keen to let her know that he and his team would do whatever they could to assist her.

'I'll *bet* he was keen,' Thorne said.

Anna had been told she should not hesitate to contact him if there was any question she needed answering or anything he could do to help. She explained to Thorne that she had already been to his flat in Kentish Town earlier that night, and not knowing where else he might be, she had phoned Jesmond. He had called back a few minutes later and given her the address Thorne had signed out to for the evening. Anna said he'd been happy to help.

Thorne swore and upped his pace.

'I didn't know what else to do.'

'Why didn't you just call *me*?'

'I needed to talk to you in person,' she said. 'There's some things I need to say . . .'

Thorne looked at her properly for the first time since they had left the flat. He saw the colour in her cheeks as they passed beneath a street lamp and watched her hitch up the strap of her shoulder-bag to prevent it slipping. He slowed down a little.

She puffed out her cheeks and nodded, grateful.

'Go on then,' Thorne said.

She took a few seconds, shrugged, took a few more, then said, 'Just . . . sorry, really. I said a few things in the bar that were probably out of order. I mean, obviously I was fuming, but that's no excuse. That stuff about you being a fuck-up . . . I don't know what I'm talking about, so . . .'

Thorne stared ahead.

'And mostly you've been really great, which makes it even worse. You didn't have to take me along to see Monahan, or Donna, and I know I was a pain in the arse.' She waited. They were now little more than strolling. 'You can contradict me, you know.'

'I *can*, but I'm not going to.'

'Anyway . . . sorry for that. And . . .'

Thorne nodded. 'I said a few things I didn't necessarily mean as well, so . . .'

'It's OK, I know what you were trying to do,' she said.

'Good.'

'But that's the thing. Because what I'm most sorry about is that I'm not going to listen to you.'

Thorne stopped. '*What?*'

'I've thought about it and I've decided to see it through.' She saw that Thorne was desperate to speak, so answered the question she knew he was about to ask. 'Because I need to stick at this. If I just walk away whenever things get tough, it's like admitting I was stupid to all

222

those people who thought I was mad to get involved with this kind of thing in the first place. So, sorry, and thanks for being concerned, but I'm not quitting. I've already spoken to Donna.'

'Oh, for God's sake . . .' Thorne started walking again.

They passed the Chelsea College of Art and Design and then turned left towards the river. As they walked past buildings similar to Louise's, Thorne glanced down into the windows of the basement flats, caught glimpses of people eating or watching TV.

'I always do that too,' Anna said. 'There's always the possibility you might see someone naked.'

They crossed the road at Millbank and headed down into Riverside Walk Gardens. The light shining up on to the centrepiece sculpture spilled across the park's braided grass terraces and glinted off a row of metal benches just shy of the embankment wall. Thorne walked across to one, the slats still damp from a downpour an hour or so before. Anna handed him a wad of tissues. Thorne smiled and began wiping away the moisture.

'What?'

'I was just thinking about you in the park the other day,' Thorne said. 'Giving that bloke the tissues.'

They sat.

'I don't back away from a row.' Anna shrugged. 'Always been my problem.'

Thorne nodded, said, 'Alan Langford's not just some bloke letting his dog crap on a footpath.'

'I know that.'

A woman jogged past, red-faced and panting, an iPod strapped to her belt.

'Who's she kidding?' Anna asked.

'Jesmond's just trying to keep you sweet, by the way.' Thorne turned to look at her. 'You need to know that. He's shitting himself in case you decide to go to the papers, tell someone how we screwed up the original inquiry.'

'Why would I do that?'

223

'He tends not to let common sense get in his way. Same as someone else I can think of.'

'Am I going to get another lecture now?'

Thorne took a few seconds, let the flash of anger and impatience fade a little. 'Is this about proving something to your mother? This refusal to do the sensible thing.'

'No.' Anna looked away, watched the jogger run on the spot for a few seconds before turning and heading back the way she had come. 'Well, not *just* that.'

'You don't need to prove anything.'

'I know.'

'To yourself or your mother. Or me.'

'It's about feeling something. Making a difference or whatever. God, why do I always sound so wanky when I'm talking to you?'

'Look, I'm not going to tell you that you're wrong – or stupid – for wanting any of that. It's probably what I wanted, once upon a time.'

She looked at him. 'You told me you weren't . . . hardened. The other day, when—'

'I'm not,' Thorne said. 'Not that.'

Anna waited.

Thorne decided to try another tack. 'OK, forget how dangerous all this is. Forget that Langford has already had three people killed. *At least* three. Forget that he's clearly willing to do whatever it takes to hold on to the life he's carved out for himself. I've told you all that until I'm blue in the face and it's obviously not working.'

Anna smiled. 'Fine. I've forgotten it already.'

Thorne looked hard at her. Made sure she knew he was serious. 'Listen, whether you're trying to catch men who are cheating on their wives or trying to find Donna Langford's daughter, you're slopping around in other people's misery and you can't just wash it off. Do you understand?'

She nodded.

'When there's a murder, when there's someone out there I need to find, I *have* to switch off. I'm disgusted by it, by what's been done, but

I can't afford to have feelings towards whoever it is I'm trying to catch. I can't afford to hate the person I'm after. I mean, I don't love him either, but I have to at least try and understand him. So I can get him. Afterwards, it's different . . .' His voice had dropped and he could see Anna straining to hear above the wind blowing across the water. He cleared his throat. 'Afterwards, in the interview room, across the court-room or whatever, I'm . . . hateful.' He saw the confusion on Anna's face and shook his head. 'That's not the right word. I'm not sure if there *is* a word. I'm . . . full of hate . . .'

He wrapped his fingers tight around the edge of the bench, then moved them away when he felt the small clods of dried chewing gum underneath.

'There's a man called Adam Chambers. The case I was working on before.'

'I know,' Anna said. 'I read up on it.'

Thorne nodded. 'So. Just the thought of him out there, or Langford, or a dozen others who are walking around because they got lucky or someone screwed up. I imagine them sitting in the pub, watching TV like the people in those flats we passed, *sleeping*. I remember the things they did and I'm full of it. Full to the fucking brim with hate.' He conjured a half-smile, then an unconvincing laugh to go with it. 'And I hate it.'

They both stared ahead for half a minute, legs stretched out in front of them, hands pushed into jacket pockets. The temperature was dropping and there was more rain in the air.

'Look, I'm not saying I want to be your shadow or anything,' Anna said.

'That's a relief.'

She moved a little closer to him. 'Seriously, I'm not expecting an access-all-areas pass and a promise that I can be there when you make an arrest.'

'Good, because you wouldn't get it.'

'Just keep me informed, OK?'

Thorne turned to her. He could see that this was as big a concession as she was prepared to make.

'I'd rather hear what's going on from you than from Jesmond.'

'Fair enough,' Thorne said.

'I've got a feeling I wouldn't get the full story from your boss. He sounds a bit slimy.'

Thorne said, 'More than a bit,' and looked out at the river. In one way at least she showed remarkably good judgement. But he still felt uneasy about the situation.

Perhaps he was just unused to giving so much of himself away.

He stared at the shifting, black water, at the lights moving slowly in both directions under Vauxhall Bridge, and for the second time that day, he wondered if life would be easier aboard one of those boats. He could turn his face to the wind and empty his mind of all this. The notion was just as incongruous as it had been earlier, staring down from the briefing room at SOCA, not least because Thorne was anything but a natural when it came to the water. He had first learned that as an eight-year-old on a mackerel-fishing trip with his father, when he had thrown up ten minutes out of Brixham harbour. Since then, anything but a millpond would have his guts churning, make him crave solid earth beneath his feet. Yet he still loved the *idea* of boats, of drifting away on one, however disappointing the reality always proved to be.

Like so many other things in his life, it was a good idea on paper.

He let his head fall back, felt the first spatters of drizzle on his face, but it was not unpleasant.

'We should probably go,' Anna said.

'Right.'

'I should let you get back to . . . Sorry, I still don't know her name.'

Like so many other things . . .

'Louise,' Thorne said.

Walking back, they talked easily, taking their time as the streets narrowed and grew quieter. They argued about football when it emerged that Anna was a closet *Match of the Day* viewer. Like far too many Londoners, she was a Manchester United supporter, but Thorne tried not to take it too hard.

226

'Could be worse,' he told her. 'Could have been Chelsea.'

Their pace slowed even further when they reached Louise's road, walking back towards the flat at a fraction of the speed they had left it.

'Sorry for being such a nightmare,' she said.

'I'll get over it,' Thorne said.

Halfway along the street, a pizza-delivery scooter beetled past, its engine whining like a swarm of angry wasps.

'Bloody hairdryer on wheels.' Thorne spoke without thinking. It was something his father used to say.

Anna laughed. 'Pizza sounds good, though. My stomach thinks my throat's been cut.'

The rain was coming down far heavier now, and they were no more than half a minute from Louise's flat. Thorne thought about asking her inside and cooking her something. 'Do you want me to call you a cab?' he asked.

'It's fine. I can jump on the tube.'

Thorne watched the scooter reach the end of the road, turn around and start moving back the way it had come. He reached out instinctively towards Anna. 'You sure?' He kept one eye on the scooter. He had presumed that the driver could not find the right address, but there was no attempt to look for house numbers.

'Honestly, it's not a problem.'

Thorne felt a tingle build and spread at the nape of his neck. 'Let's get inside.'

The scooter slowed, wobbling a little as it edged towards the pavement; as Thorne moved his hand to the small of Anna's back and pushed.

'*What?*' she said.

The man on the scooter, his face obscured by a blacked-out visor, was now steering with one hand, and without needing to see what was in the hand that was hidden by the fuel tank, Thorne urged Anna forward. '*Move!*'

The rider raised the gun and Anna shouted, took hold of Thorne's arm and told him to watch out. Thorne half shoved, half dragged her the last few feet until they were level with the low railings that ran along the front of the building, Louise's door was still ten feet below them as the first shot was fired.

Just a pop, no louder than the scooter backfiring.

Anna said, 'Christ,' then spoke Thorne's name as the scooter accelerated, a few more seconds of wasp-whine, until it was all but level with them. There was no time to move those last few feet to where the steps wound down from the pavement and, in the end, Thorne could do nothing but push himself against her; pressing her back against the railings, feeling the tremble take hold in his arms and legs, and the rain running down his neck.

He heard his own name screamed again as he turned to see the gun come up a second time.

PART THREE

COAST OF LEAD

TWENTY-EIGHT

A few minutes before beginning its descent into Malaga, the plane hit a patch of clear-air turbulence and dropped suddenly. Thorne sat back hard and opened his eyes, aware from the look on the face of the woman next to him that his gasp had been audible. He felt embarrassed, knowing – because he'd read it somewhere – that such fraction-of-a-second drops were actually of no more than a few feet and were insignificant in the scheme of things.

He mouthed a 'sorry' and smiled at the woman. She nodded and went back to her magazine.

Thorne closed his eyes again and waited for it to get a little less bumpy. Although he knew well enough that the sick feeling, the wet and peppery knot in his stomach, had nothing to do with turbulence. He had not been asleep, but the images and snatches of remembered conversation might easily have been fragments of a nightmare.

Eight weeks since the shooting.

Before the man on the scooter could fire again, Thorne and Anna had gone crashing together over the metal railings and down hard on to the steps. He felt a searing pain in his shoulder, guessing as he struggled to move that his collarbone had gone and dimly aware of the engine noise, the high-pitched drone as the scooter accelerated away. Aware of Anna moaning beside him, the cold, wet step against his face, Louise opening the door and screaming when she saw the blood.

Eight weeks . . .

Two since the funeral.

Thorne had felt stared at; observed, at the very least. Inside the church, in the grounds outside, and most of all afterwards, at the Carpenters' house in Wimbledon. It was probably all in his head and certainly nobody had said anything. None of those with every right to do a damn sight more than stare at the copper who had spent two weeks with his arm in a sling while the girl beaming out at them from the order of service had bled to death in the back of an ambulance.

I don't back away from a row. Always been my problem.

One person who *did* stare was Frank Anderson, recognising Thorne as the man who had stood in his office with a cock-and-bull story about a skirt-chasing girlfriend. But even Anderson resisted the temptation to say anything, while Thorne, in turn, fought the urge to say a few of the things *he* had been bottling up. All the same, he imagined it, standing in the church and staring at the dandruff speckling Frank Anderson's collar. He imagined taking a handful of the man's hair, ramming his face down into the pew and demanding an explanation for the way he had treated Anna. For the things he had made her do.

Do you know how much she hated it, you spineless little twat? How it made her feel? Have you got the slightest idea?

Instead, Thorne stood and sang 'How Great Thou Art' and listened to a moving eulogy from an elder sister he had known nothing about. He spoke to her afterwards at the house, learned she was a successful lawyer. Thorne asked himself if, in taking the job she had hated at the bank, Anna had been trying to compete with her, or be different from her, every bit as much as she had been trying to please her mother. He silently rebuked himself. What right did he have to pass any sort of judgement, to jump to any conclusions about what had been going on in Anna's head?

232

Walking slowly out of the church, he had seen Donna up ahead of him. Outside, while people talked quietly and lit cigarettes, the two of them exchanged nods, but she seemed in a hurry to get away and Thorne was grateful to avoid the conversation. The clumsy dance around guilt and blame.

At the Carpenters' house, he downed a glass of beer and helped himself to another. After all, he was not there in any official capacity, so he could put away a drink or two. Surely he had every reason to put away more than a few and make an arse of himself.

It was a bright day, and out in the garden Thorne spoke to Anna's friends, Rob and Angie. They were sitting on a low wall, balancing plates of cold ham and salad on their laps.

'She mentioned both of you,' Thorne said. 'Said what a good laugh you always had.'

Rob nodded and pushed his coleslaw around.

'She mentioned you, too,' Angie said.

There was not too much more to say after that. Had someone older died, someone whose death had not been totally unexpected, one of them might have said, 'It was a nice service, wasn't it?' or told a funny story. But it was simply too hard for any of that, for the pleasant lies, and instead, they focused all their energy on keeping themselves together.

Thorne had watched the mother and father all day. The man's hand on the woman's arm almost every time Thorne caught sight of them: stepping out of the shiny Daimler; moving into the church; drifting between the groups of friends and relatives in their kitchen and sitting room, glassy-eyed, as though they could not quite believe they were able to put one foot in front of the other.

To stay upright and engaged. To speak without howling.

There had been a cursory greeting at the church, but back at the house, hovering between the buffet table and the sitting-room door, Thorne finally got a chance to speak to them properly. With Thorne in hospital, other officers had dealt with Robert and Sylvia Carpenter in the days following the shooting. So, although he felt sure they

233

knew exactly who he was, this was his first opportunity to introduce himself.

'You're the one who was there,' Sylvia said. 'The one who broke his collarbone.'

Thorne swallowed. Said that he was.

The one who failed to protect my daughter.

The one they were after.

The one who should be in that box.

'How is it now?' Sylvia asked. She reached a hand out towards him. 'They can be a pig to set. A cousin of mine had all sorts of trouble.'

Thorne stared. If she were intending to be snide or sarcastic, it was not there in her voice or her eyes. On the contrary, her face was set in an expression of almost manic concern.

'Clavicle.' She said the word slowly, emphasising each syllable. Her hand was still stretched out, the fingers fluttering a few inches from Thorne's chest. 'That's the proper name for it.'

'Sylvia . . .' Robert Carpenter gently laid a hand on his wife's arm. She turned her head slowly to look at him, then abruptly moved away, staring intently at the platters of cheese and cold meat as she walked the length of the buffet table.

The two men watched her go, then Robert Carpenter turned back to Thorne. He looked down at his shoes for a few seconds then raised his eyes. 'It's hit her very hard,' he said.

'Of course,' Thorne said.

'I mean, obviously, it's hit all of us.'

Thorne could say nothing, aware of the inadequacy of the platitudes he might have been expected to trot out. Indeed, *had* trotted out in countless similar situations. Looking at Anna's father then, it struck him that, in recent years, the influence of American TV shows had crept into the language of condolence every bit as much as it had been felt elsewhere.

I'm sorry for your loss.

That final word set Thorne's teeth on edge. Surely it implied the possibility that, some day, whoever had been lost might be found.

Keys were lost and mobile phones. Dogs and wallets and telephone numbers. Those wrenched from their families by violent death were *gone* – plain, simple and terrible, but they were anything but *lost*.

Thorne and the rest of those under Robert Carpenter's roof had gathered together to mourn Anna's absence.

'Did she tell you she was not her mother's favourite?' Robert asked suddenly.

'No,' Thorne said.

'She always thought that. The stupid thing is that she was.' He shook his head and lowered his voice still further. 'She really was . . .'

Thorne wondered what else Anna might have told him, given time.

'There's no news, I suppose?'

'I'm sorry?' Thorne said.

'Your colleagues have all been very good, keeping us informed and what have you. But I haven't heard anything for over a week, so . . .'

'We're doing everything we can.'

'Of course, I do understand that.'

Thorne had been at home for a fortnight following the shooting – compulsory leave in the wake of an incident involving a firearm, if not strictly merited by the severity of his injury. There would be counselling sessions too, a little further down the line, the thought of which filled Thorne with horror. Reminded him of a few other things that you could lose.

Your diary.

Your way, en route to the counsellor's office.

The will to live.

During those two weeks away from the office, Thorne had stayed in touch with the investigation: talking to Brigstocke, Holland and Kitson half a dozen times a day; phoning Gary Brand to see if any of his contacts had heard any whispers. Keeping on top of things. So, he was acutely aware of the lack of witnesses, the deafening silence in response to numerous appeals, the absence of any forensic evidence on the abandoned scooter. He was intimately acquainted with each brick wall and dead end in the search for the shooter.

'She told me about the case she was working on,' Robert said. 'This man everyone thought was dead.'

'Right.'

'She was excited about it. I told her how much I enjoyed seeing her like that.' He paused and the smile slid from his face. 'He did this, I suppose?'

Tried to kill you and killed my daughter instead.

Should have organised something a little more efficient than a gun fired at night from a moving scooter.

'We think so,' Thorne said. 'Or at least paid to have it done.'

Anna's father was studying his feet again, glancing up every few seconds towards others in the room. 'Well, I'd better . . .'

'Thank you,' Thorne said.

He was not sure what he was thanking the man for. For his hospitality? For not pushing him against the wall and screaming into his face with grief and fury?

For Anna?

Thorne spent another half an hour or so wandering between kitchen, sitting room and garden. He caught Rob and Angie looking at him and did his best to smile. He looked at the collection of family photographs on a dresser: Anna and her sister on holiday somewhere warm; the family at Anna's graduation; Anna and her mother, their postures and expressions almost identical. Reaching across the buffet table for more food he did not really want, he felt the ache in his collarbone. He felt it spread into his shoulder, and he felt again the weight of her as they lay together at the bottom of the stone steps.

Her breath bubbling and shallow against his chest and her blood leaking through his fingers.

He spoke to Robert Carpenter one more time that day, as goodbyes were being said at the front door. Anna's father was thanking people as they left, braced for the final litany of condolence, taking hands in his own. Thorne searched for the right words. He said he was glad he had come, mumbled something about how good the food had been, then found himself blurting out, 'She told me you liked bluegrass.'

236

Robert Carpenter smiled and nodded, then handed Thorne a hand-kerchief.

'The captain has turned on the seatbelt signs, so . . .'

Thorne stuffed his newspaper into the pocket and pressed his knees hard into the back of the seat in front to remind the selfish bastard in the row ahead of him to raise his seat into the upright position. The woman next to him said something, having clearly decided that with no more than a few minutes left before landing, it was safe enough to strike up a conversation.

'Sorry?'

'Holiday?'

'Not really,' Thorne said.

The woman nodded and said, 'Looks like you could do with one.'

Thorne closed his eyes again and did not open them until the plane's wheels screamed against the runway.

Standing at the luggage carousel, he felt the pulse in his collarbone again and pictured a bare-chested man raising up a beer glass. Smiling and squinting against the sun. Would that smile be summoned quite as easily now, Thorne wondered, after everything the man had done to keep his place in the sun?

Probably . . .

From the moment Thorne had returned to duty, he had badgered Brigstocke, had even gone cap in hand to Jesmond, begging for the go ahead to travel to Spain. Initially, there had been reluctance, with little more in the way of real evidence than there had been on the night Anna was killed. Three dead now. Four, including the unidentified body from ten years before. But still nothing to tie the man they all knew was responsible to any of the killings.

Eventually, Thorne had been given the nod; out of sympathy, as much as anything, he suspected. But it didn't matter. He would take whatever was on offer if it meant a chance to get up close and personal with Alan Langford. He would do whatever he could. He would find Langford and wait, rely on others back in London to furnish him with whatever was needed to bring the fucker back in chains.

'I hate to sound like the captain in *Starsky and Hutch*,' Brigstocke had said. 'But I can only give you a couple of weeks.'

Holland had driven Thorne to Luton Airport. 'We'll be busting a gut,' he had said. 'You know that.'

Pulling up outside the terminal, Thorne had said, 'Find out who was in that Jag, Dave. He's the key to all this.'

Thorne's suitcase came out early. He was happy to take it as a good omen.

He grabbed the case and wheeled it out quickly through the automatic doors, reached into his carry-on bag for sunglasses, and stepped into the late-April Spanish sunshine.

Full of hate.

TWENTY-NINE

Not so much 'shit-hot', Thorne decided, as 'lukewarm'.

Within a few minutes of meeting DI Peter – 'call me Pete' – Fraser, Thorne was convinced that the agent assigned by Silcox and Mullenger as his guide and liaison for the Spanish leg of the inquiry was probably not one of SOCA's finest.

'Welcome to the madhouse,' Fraser said as they walked towards the airport car park. He grinned and lowered his head, peered at Thorne over wraparound sunglasses. 'From what I've heard, you should slot in quite nicely.'

He was not much taller than Thorne, but looked a good deal fitter. His hair had the kind of blond streaks that Louise called 'bird-shit highlights', while the three-quarter-length shorts, beaded necklace and salmon-pink shirt made him look more like a small-time drug dealer than a big-time secret squirrel. Perhaps that was the idea, Thorne thought. He pictured his own, more conservative collection of shorts and polo shirts, bought a few days earlier with his warm-weather allowance of M&S vouchers. He guessed that anyone with an eye for such things would mark him out for what he was straight away.

He decided that he didn't much care.

'Good flight?' Fraser asked.

'It was easyJet,' Thorne said.

They sat in Fraser's Punto for a few minutes, waiting for the air conditioning to kick in before heading away. Listening to the agent's easy chatter, Thorne wondered if, first impressions aside, he should perhaps give the man the benefit of the doubt. Hadn't he taken an instant dislike to Andy Boyle? Hadn't he thought that Anna Carpenter was a pain in the neck when he had first been lumbered with her?

Perhaps Fraser would surprise him, too.

The SOCA man watched as Thorne held sticky palms towards the air vents. 'This is *chilly*, mate,' he said. 'You want to try being here in August. I promise you, you'd be sweating like a rapist.'

Perhaps not . . .

The road from the airport was clogged with traffic, squeezing between building works every quarter-mile or so that narrowed the lanes. The carriageways were separated by a seemingly endless line of palm trees and, for the first twenty minutes, snaking slowly through the built-up outskirts of Malaga, drab-looking apartment blocks and retail strips crowded in from both sides. Furniture stores, DIY warehouses and restaurants, with as many English signs as Spanish.

Fraser took a call and, in a London accent that was sounding increasingly affected, told whoever he was talking to that Thorne was in the car with him. He said his passenger was clearly feeling the heat and laughed at the response. He hummed his agreement to a few things and promised to call back later. After hanging up, he turned the radio on and found an English station; some Radio Essex reject proudly announcing a programme of back-to-back eighties classics.

Spandau Ballet gave way to Kajagoogoo.

'We should probably give you a day or two to get settled.'

'I don't need a day or two,' Thorne said.

Fraser shrugged. 'You might want to feel your way into things is all I'm saying. There's not much on today, anyway.'

'You got more stuff for me to read?'

'Oh yeah, we'll go through everything tonight over dinner. But you know, softly-softly-catchee-monkey, all that.'

'Way past that with Alan Langford,' Thorne said.

Fraser looked at him, placed a finger to his lips. '*If* he's who we think he is, you start saying that name too loudly and we might just as well be wearing pointed hats.'

Thorne nodded. As Brigstocke had guessed might be the case, SOCA suspected that Alan Langford was a man they had been observing for some time, and information about him had been faxed through piecemeal in the weeks since the shooting. Details of the new life Langford had made for himself in Spain. Some of his nice new friends and not so nice business associates.

His new name.

The traffic had eased and, despite the high-rise sprawl of Torremolinos in the distance, their clear view of the coast – arcing south-west towards Gibraltar – was spectacular. The sea was shining to the left of them, crashing against the beaches in waves far bigger than Thorne had expected.

'Nice, isn't it?' Fraser asked.

'*Looks* nice,' Thorne said.

Five minutes later, Fraser drifted across to the right-hand lane and Thorne clocked the sign for the turn-off.

Benalmádena.

'Where the photographs were taken,' Thorne said.

Fraser nodded, said, 'Seems as good a place as any for some lunch. You hungry?'

Thorne had found it easy to resist the lure of easyJet's in-flight catering service. But even if he had fancied something on the plane, he could not have justified using up a fortnight's expenses on one cup of coffee and a sandwich.

'Yeah, I could eat,' he said.

They found a small restaurant in a parade of shops and bars just across from the beach, where people were sharing tapas around large upturned barrels. Fraser told Thorne that he'd do the honours and, having put away one small beer and asked for another, ordered food for both of them in fluent Spanish. Thorne let him get on with it. He was happy enough, for the time being at least, to let the SOCA agent play his games, as well as a little relieved at having been spared giving a demonstration of his own ignorance.

Waiting for the food, Thorne watched an old man a few feet away pulling a large octopus from a vat of boiling water. He snipped off pieces with large scissors, laid them on a wooden plate alongside slices of waxy-looking potatoes and, after a liberal sprinkling of salt and paprika, drizzled the dish with olive oil.

Pulpo a feira.

The reason why the boat in the picture had been in Benalmádena. The one clue that had helped them find Alan Langford. *If* they had found him . . .

Thorne nodded towards the old man. 'Can we try some of that?'

'We've got plenty coming, trust me.' Fraser noticed Thorne watching him as he finished his second beer, said, 'It's not even a third of a pint.' He winked. 'It's all about fitting in, right? Looking the part.'

Thorne shrugged and went back to his sparkling water.

'Listen, don't think this isn't hard graft,' Fraser said. 'Trust me, mate, I'd rather be in Tottenham.'

'Right.'

'Straight up. It's mental here, I'm telling you.' He stabbed at the top of the barrel with a finger, counting off a predictable list of the criminal fraternities. 'We've got the Albanians, the Russians, the Irish, the Brits . . . and the locals aren't exactly Boy Scouts, either. Gun-running, vice like you wouldn't believe and multi-million-pound property scams in every resort you can name. The armed robbers could teach the lads back home a thing or two, and I don't need to tell you about the drugs.'

He didn't, but he proceeded to anyway. Thorne was given more or less the same lesson he'd received from Silcox and Mullenger, but he sat and listened politely. He'd already decided that 'innocent abroad' might be a useful persona to hide behind.

Fraser pointed out to sea. 'Ninety miles up the coast, Africa's so close you can almost swim across. They usually drown, so who cares, but we've caught a few with lifejackets stuffed full of all sorts.'

'Jesus.'

'I swear.'

Thorne could easily believe it. He knew the lengths people would go to for drug money, and he couldn't help wondering if some of those who risked their lives in such a way might be working for Alan Langford. He knew that those further down the chain recruited their mules and dealers from the streets of British cities: no-hopers in Nottingham or Sheffield peddling wraps of coke outside downmarket nightclubs who would jump at the chance of a free plane ticket and a few months in the sun. Who wouldn't think it strange to be asked if they were strong swimmers.

The food came and they both got stuck in. Thin and crispy shrimp tortillas and fiery Padrón peppers. Deep-fried anchovies and huge clams eaten straight from the shell with lemon and salt.

A hundred yards away, on a corner, Thorne could see the sign for a Burger King. He sucked down another clam and nodded across. 'Why the hell would anyone want to go there when you've got this?'

'To be honest, you can get a bit sick of the local stuff,' Fraser said. 'Sometimes you just want a decent bit of stodge.'

'Right, like a nice kebab back in Tottenham.'

Fraser took off his sunglasses and stared. He was clearly unsure if Thorne was taking the piss and, despite the smile that eventually appeared, Thorne could see that, whatever else Call-Me-Pete might be, he certainly wasn't soft. As soon as the shades went back on, Thorne looked away, and Fraser followed his eye-line to where two women were standing topless at the edge of the beach.

Fraser broke into a grin. 'OK, forget what I said about Tottenham . . .'

Once they had split the bill and Thorne had tucked the receipt for his half into his wallet, they walked slowly back towards the car. Having shown off his mastery of the language, Fraser was now keen to play the know-it-all tourist guide. He pointed out the town's four-teenth-century tower and the remains of its ancient sea fortifications. Thorne made a fine job of feigning interest, but he was far more inter-ested in the familiar line of hills running down to the coast that he recognised from the pictures sent to Donna Langford.

243

Fraser pointed to a bar called Hemingway's. 'You know, the writer? He loved all this Spanish stuff – seafood and bullfights and what have you. Ever seen a bullfight, Tom?'

Thorne said he hadn't.

'You should go to Ronda,' Fraser announced. 'Definitely.'

'What, in Wales?'

Again Fraser hesitated, uncertain whether Thorne was winding him up. 'It's an old town up in the hills. Everyone raves about it.'

'Not been yourself, then?'

'Not had time, mate, but it's supposed to be fabulous. Oldest bull-ring in Spain, something like that. Orson Welles was mad about the place, had his ashes scattered there, by all accounts. You know, the fat bloke who advertised sherry?'

'Yes, I know.'

'Seriously, you should go.'

'I'm not here to go sightseeing,' Thorne said.

Fraser nodded a 'whatever'. 'Look, it's like I was trying to say in the car, right? Nothing's going to happen very quickly. Never does here. All I'm saying is don't be surprised if you find yourself with a bit of time on your hands, OK?'

Thorne looked hard at him. 'I'm really hoping that doesn't happen.'

If Fraser got the message, he showed no sign of it. 'Anyway, you're waiting on stuff happening at home, right? Even if he is your man, you've got sod all on him until then, so . . . Where are you . . .?'

Thorne was already stepping off the pavement and walking back towards the beach.

Fraser went after him, pointing back towards the street where they'd left the Punto. 'We're up there, mate.'

'I want to find the place where the photos were taken.'

'What's the point of that?'

Thorne had no good answer, but he kept on walking. Behind him, he heard Fraser say, 'I'll wait in the car.'

After ten minutes, Thorne had walked the length of the beach without success. The line of hills stayed ahead of him, but it was impossible to pinpoint the location he was after. The place where Langford had posed for the photographs could have been any one of half a dozen beach bars and restaurants.

Thorne stopped and breathed in the sea, stared out across a small bay towards the hills. Although he had exiled himself through necessity rather than choice, it was not hard to see why Langford liked it here. It was clear in the shark-smile he had turned on for the camera, the glass raised in a toast to his new life.

Enjoy it while you can, Thorne thought.

Sweating, he walked back to the road and kicked the sand off his shoes against the kerb. He bought himself an ice-cream from a café near the place where they'd had lunch, then ambled back past the tower to the car park. Fraser was waiting with the engine running, drumming his hands impatiently on the wheel.

Thorne climbed in. 'Sorry for keeping you waiting, Peter.'

Fraser yanked the gearstick into reverse. 'Pete,' he said.

Kate was having lunch in town with a friend, and that suited Donna perfectly well. Things between them were a damn sight better than they had been for weeks, but they still kept out of each other's way as much as possible, eating separately more often than not and sometimes going for a day or two without speaking a word.

They hadn't touched one another in almost two months.

Donna drank tea in the kitchen, flicking through a magazine without taking in a word. She glanced towards the hall every few minutes. She turned on the radio, then switched it off a minute later, scared she might not hear the phone ringing.

Definitely better that Kate wasn't here, she decided. There would only be a row if she overheard, or disapproving looks at the very least.

Fine one *she* was to talk about secrets, mind you.

They were both silly, stubborn bitches, that was the problem. That, and the fact that one of the things they had both learned inside, learned *together*, was that you never gave an inch.

There was very little shouting any more, not since the big blow-up when Thorne had come marching in like God Almighty and dropped his bombshell. When it had all come out about Kate meeting up with Ellie after she'd left prison. For a day or two back then, Donna had really lost it, had been steaming with rage in a way she had not been for a good many years. Maybe not since Alan. But then she'd noticed the change in Kate and the anger towards her partner had slowly begun to cool. Donna had stopped feeling as though she could hurt her when she'd seen how *damaged* Kate had been.

Thorne had thrown Kate's past in her face like boiling water laced with sugar. A 'wet-up', they called it in prison, and it was designed to scar. He had made snide suggestions, *accusations*, and, since then, Kate had seemed wary and reserved. Donna had never seen that before. One of the things she had loved about Kate when they'd first met had been a fearlessness, a 'bring it on' attitude that was impossible to resist.

She missed that. She missed *her*. And she hoped the day would come when she felt able to tell her, and to forgive her for lying about Ellie. As it was, anger towards Kate had given way to the acid of resentment coupled with something close to pity.

The rage was still in there somewhere, though. A few days earlier in the supermarket, a woman had barged in front of Donna at the check-out as if she did not exist. The snotty cow had her daughter with her, eight or nine, and the little brat had looked up at Donna with the same tight-arsed expression as her mother. Then she had smiled, like she wanted to know what Donna was going to do about it.

That hadn't helped.

Donna had forced herself to look away, then breathed and breathed until she was sure she would not scream and smash the woman's perfectly made-up face down on to the conveyor belt.

Sometimes that inch had to be given, to save you from yourself.

She was thinking there was nothing she would not give to save Ellie, to get her girl back, when the phone rang. She put down her cup too fast, spilling tea across the work surface, then walked into the hall, praying it was the call she was expecting from Spain.

THIRTY

Fifteen minutes west of Benalmádena, Fraser turned off the main road and they began to drive up into the hills.

'We'll get you settled into your hotel,' Fraser said. 'Then we can meet up later and get the ball rolling.'

'Where am I staying?' Thorne asked.

'It's a nice place. They don't do food, so you'll need to find somewhere to have breakfast, but aside from that—'

'*Where?*'

'Mijas,' Fraser said. 'Mijas Pueblo, as opposed to Mijas Costa. It's a really gorgeous village. Proper old Spain, you know?'

'How far?'

'Fifteen minutes or so. It's a nice drive.'

'I thought I'd be in Malaga.'

Fraser glanced across.

'That's where you're based, right?'

'We decided you might prefer to be somewhere quieter. A bit less conspicuous . . .'

'Would have been nice to be consulted.'

'Look, it's no more than half an hour from anywhere we're interested in. Puerto Banus, Torremolinos, Malaga, at least two of the golf resorts our man's got his fingers in. Trust me, it's a good location, so don't start feeling left out or whatever.'

'Who said I was?'

'Anyway, you might prefer being somewhere that isn't wall-to-wall full English breakfasts and live Premiership football.'

'Nothing wrong with either of them,' Thorne said.

'You're Spurs, right?'

Thorne held Fraser's look for a second longer than he might otherwise have done, acknowledging that the agent had done his homework. Not long enough to let him feel like he'd scored any points, though.

'Who are you?'

'Man U, mate, who else?'

'You're a Londoner.'

Fraser nodded, as though that were perfectly acceptable. 'Still the team to beat,' he said.

Thorne blinked, remembered the rain coming down as he and Anna had walked back from the river. When she had revealed her affiliation and sung Wayne Rooney's praises, laughing as Thorne grew increasingly exasperated.

'You're just jealous because your lot never win anything.'

'At least the people who support "my lot" live in the city where they play.'

'Right. We are definitely going to the next Man United–Spurs game. A tenner says we stuff you.'

'Only another five minutes,' Fraser said.

The climb had not felt particularly steep, but looking to his right as they swept around a corner, Thorne could see the sea far below them. The landscape fell away gently towards it on either side, rocky and dotted with trees then getting greener, dip by dip, as it neared the coast. They passed several signs warning of bulls in the road and then finally Thorne saw a field of them. Eight or nine: big and black and looking well capable of breaking through the fence and taking on a Punto.

'So, whose ashes are scattered in Mijas, then?' Thorne asked.

'Come again?'

'The Milk Tray man? That bloke off the Mr Muscle adverts?'

'That's funny,' Fraser said. He laughed, but it sounded like something he'd learned.

In reply, Thorne's modest snort of laughter was genuine enough, as he imagined Fraser being casually tossed into the air by one of the bulls they had just driven past. The wraparound sunglasses stomped into the ground and the beads flying off his ponce's necklace.

Olé . . .

The main road was closed just before it entered Mijas, and a police officer on a motorbike waved them towards a diversion that ran downhill and around, into the newer part of town. Thorne asked what was going on and Fraser said that he had no idea. With all available parking space taken by a fleet of tourist coaches, they had little choice but to leave the car in a grim-looking multi-storey. Then Thorne followed Fraser back towards the cluster of white buildings high above them. He hauled his suitcase up a long, steep flight of steps and through a warren of cobbled streets until they finally emerged into the main square.

'Nice, right?' Fraser said.

Thorne just nodded, happy to stand and take the place in for a minute or two. He was sweating again and needed the time to catch his breath. A large, covered food market took up most of the square, and crowds were flocking up and down row after row of stalls selling fruit and vegetables, fish, dried meats and cheeses. A large and equally crowded bar ran down one side and those not shopping seemed content to stand around, talking and drinking. A few were dancing unselfconsciously to what sounded like live music, though Thorne could see no sign of the musicians.

'Market day,' Fraser said, as though Thorne needed an explanation. 'That's a bit of luck.'

Thorne looked at him.

'I don't know, you might want a bit of fruit for your room or something . . .'

Despite the number of coaches they had seen down by the car park, Thorne couldn't hear any language being spoken but Spanish. One or two people were pointing cameras, but they had not passed any tacky souvenir shops and the place felt nothing like a standard tourist trap. No football shirts were being worn either, so Thorne guessed there were not too many Brits around and regardless of what he'd said to Fraser on the way up, he was not unhappy about it.

The ones he was interested in had not come to Spain to buy castanets and get sunburned.

'We should get you sorted, mate.'

Though Thorne thought it had come a little late, he accepted Fraser's offer to take the suitcase and followed him, the wheels clattering across the cobbles as they walked through the crowds, around the square and up another short flight of steps at the far corner. Fifty yards or so on, after three or four tight turnings, Fraser stopped at a pair of dark wooden doors behind a trellis wound with ivy and bougainvillea. He pushed at the door and shook his head. Said, 'Don't worry.'

Thorne watched as Fraser pressed a button on the intercom then leaned down to begin a conversation in Spanish with the woman on the other end. Thorne heard his name mentioned several times.

When Fraser had finished, he looked up. 'Siesta time.' He winked. 'Spanish yoga. Don't worry, though.' There was a buzz from the intercom and Fraser pushed open the door.

Thorne followed him into a tiny and dimly lit reception area with the outline of a staircase beyond. The place was deserted and Thorne's voice echoed slightly when he spoke. 'Where are they?' he asked.

'Not the faintest idea, but it's fine. Here you go . . .'

An envelope with Thorne's name and a room number written across it lay waiting on the reception desk. Thorne shook it and felt a key rattle inside. He nodded and stepped towards the stairs. An automatic light came on.

'You should do what the locals do,' Fraser said. 'Try and get your head down for a couple of hours.'

'What are you going to do?'

'Oh, I need to get back to the office. Tell them I got you here in one piece.'

'Expecting snipers, were we?'

Fraser looked at his watch. 'Three hours. How's that?' Without waiting for Thorne to answer, he backed away to the front door and said, 'So, I'll pick you up at half seven.'

Thorne took a few steps up, then lowered his case and turned. 'What about the villains?' he asked. 'Do they bother with siesta time? When in Rome, all that?'

'Yeah, I should imagine,' Fraser said. 'But they probably sleep with one eye open . . .'

The room was on the third floor, with further lights coming on as Thorne climbed higher. It was fairly basic: two single beds pushed together, a small bathroom, a portable TV, metal shutters over full-length windows and a balcony not quite big enough to step on to. Thorne reckoned it was good enough, or at least was not in the right frame of mind to care.

He opened the shutters, then unpacked quickly and was surprised to find a mini-bar in the cupboard beneath the TV. With beer only three euros a pop, his mood improved a little. He opened a bottle and checked for new messages on his phone.

Nothing.

He set the handset's alarm for 6.15 p.m., then showered. It was the usual hotel dribble, but it was hot and it felt good to wash the dried sweat away. Afterwards, he wrapped a towel around his waist, turned up the air conditioning and lay down on the bed. He rolled on to his side and looked across at the grey net curtain moving gently back and forth at the window.

Next thing he knew, he was scrabbling across the bed to answer his phone.

'Hello? *Hello?*'

Thorne looked at the small screen, struggling to focus. It was not a call. It was six-fifteen and all he had done was switch off the alarm.

THIRTY-ONE

Twenty minutes later than promised, Fraser arrived to pick Thorne up with a plain-clothes Guardia Civil officer named Samarez in tow. The Spaniard mumbled a greeting, then hung back a little as they walked away from the hotel, his expression non-committal as Fraser explained that the two of them had been working together for the last few months. That Samarez was 'a top bloke' and 'a good copper' but most importantly 'a right laugh, once you get to know him'.

'Something to look forward to,' Thorne said.

Judging by his reaction, Samarez wasn't as good with languages as Fraser, just cocking his head a little when Thorne turned to look at him. He was taller than both Thorne and Fraser, with dark hair cut very short and a five o'clock shadow that suggested he probably needed to shave a couple of times a day. He did not look the sort who smiled a great deal, but perhaps that came from working with Fraser. Or perhaps, Thorne thought, he just had bad teeth.

'There's some business to go through later,' Fraser said. 'But a bit of bonding wouldn't hurt, would it?'

Thorne and Samarez shrugged in unison.

'I reckon a few beers is a good idea if we're going to be working together. Three fucking musketeers, yes?'

They found a restaurant in a small square a few minutes' walk from the market place. Thorne ordered for himself this time, or at least made his choice known, then sat back as Fraser did the talking. He wondered if the waiter found Fraser's expansive mateyness as irritating as he did, and if the SOCA man spoke Spanish with a mockney accent.

They were sitting close to a large pair of open doors, and Thorne was glad he had brought along a jacket. He pulled it on, looked around the dining room. 'Not very busy in here,' he said.

It was gone eight-fifteen and the place was almost empty. Aside from a man with a newspaper a few tables away and an elderly couple talking in hushed voices near the kitchen, they had the restaurant to themselves.

'The locals don't eat until much later,' Fraser said. 'Stupid, if you ask me. I mean, I know a lot of them had their heads down in the afternoon, but even so. Bad for the digestion, apart from anything else, not to mention putting the weight on.' He grinned and prodded at the small roll of fat falling across his belt. 'This is just a few too many San Miguels, mate, don't worry. Get that shifted easy enough.'

Over a few more beers they talked, or at least Fraser did, about Job background and families. About the ups and downs of working away from home. For much of the time, Fraser spoke to Samarez in Spanish and Samarez nodded as he listened, his eyes on Thorne until he leaned in towards Fraser to say something himself.

Still no sign of the man's teeth.

Thorne was hungry as well as keen to crack on towards the business that needed to be done, so when his meal came he got stuck in quickly. *Huevos estrellados con morcilla, chorizo y patatas.* Thorne had recognised two out of the four ingredients, and the English translation on the menu had told him the rest.

'All traditional Spanish ingredients,' Samarez said. 'But it's basically the big English breakfast you all seem so fond of.'

Thorne looked up and stopped chewing for a few seconds. Until that moment he had presumed that Samarez spoke next to no English. He smiled, trying to mask his surprise, and swallowed. He said something about how they must have known he was coming, but now he found himself wondering what Fraser and Samarez had been talking about earlier.

'Is it good?'

Thorne said that it was.

'Christ on a bike,' Fraser said. 'How many Spaniards go to London and order paella?'

'*I* do,' Samarez said. 'No offence, but it's sometimes difficult to find anything very good over there.'

Despite the language thing, which was almost certainly nothing more sinister than a gentle wind-up, Thorne was starting to warm to his Guardia Civil colleague. There was a dryness he liked. It might have been wishful thinking, but Thorne also suspected that Samarez thought Fraser was as much of an idiot as he did.

They all moved their chairs a little closer to the table when the coffees arrived. Lowered their voices. Samarez produced a large envelope from his briefcase and, once there was room, laid out a series of photographs for Thorne.

An Alan Langford gallery.

'So, it seems we are all interested in a man called David Mackenzie.' Samarez pointed to a couple of the pictures. 'Though we now understand he used to be called Alan Langford.'

Thorne stared at the dozen or so shots: Langford/Mackenzie walking along a street with another man; smoking outside a restaurant; talking on the phone behind the wheel of a silver Range Rover. Most looked as though they had been taken with a long lens, some even from the air, above the grounds of a luxurious villa. Clearly, the operation in Spain ran to helicopter surveillance.

'It's a nice place.' Samarez pointed at a photograph of Langford by his swimming pool. He lay on a sunlounger, two fingers raised lazily towards the photographer high above him. 'Up in the hills above Puerto Banus. One day I hope to see the inside.'

Fraser laughed. 'We've not had an invitation as yet.'

'You know how it works down here?' Samarez asked Thorne.

Thorne did not need another version of the Costa del Crime primer he had been given twice already. He nodded and said, 'I can guess what he's up to.'

'There's not much Mr Mackenzie *isn't* involved in,' Samarez said. 'Over the years, he's done very well for himself. He's made a lot of influential friends, and if he's made any enemies, they don't appear to have been around for very long.'

Thorne raised an eyebrow, but Samarez shook his head.

'We can prove nothing,' he said. 'We've had him under surveillance on and off for the last few years. We've been monitoring his mobile-phone calls, but it is clear he knows we're on to him, so he does all his business on a secure line that we have no access to.'

'He's bound to slip up some time,' Thorne said.

Samarez took a slurp of coffee and leaned further forward, towards Thorne. 'He is a cut above most of those in the same business, you understand?' A smile suddenly appeared, but it was cold, wolfish. 'This is a man who is *seriously* careful.'

Something else Thorne did not need telling.

'Bastard hasn't put a foot wrong,' Fraser said, 'and he *never* puts himself on the line. Always the silent partner, whatever the deal. Drugs, half a dozen clubs and restaurants between Marbella and Malaga, and he's got his paws into several of the big golf resorts and the gated communities, some of which are still being built.'

'It's all very mysterious.' Samarez widened his eyes sarcastically. 'I don't know how he does it, but the building firms that get these contracts are never the most attractive bidders.'

'Maybe he's just lucky,' Thorne said, equally facetious.

Samarez shook his head. 'This is the one thing Mackenzie is definitely not, because he does not believe in luck. He does not commit himself until he's weighed everything up very carefully. It does not matter what kind of profit he stands to make, if it's a high-risk enterprise, he simply will not get involved.'

Fraser nodded. 'I know for a fact that he's said "no" to bankrolling a couple of the armed-robbery firms over here because he knows they're not careful enough. He thinks a long way ahead, does Mr Mackenzie. Plays the long game, because he's seen plenty go down over the years that have taken the easy money and paid for it.' He waved over a waitress, asked for more coffee, then waited until the girl had left. 'Look, he definitely knows how to put the squeeze on if he has to, and there's obviously a good few people afraid of him, but the bottom line is, in terms of anything we can actually prove, he's clean as a whistle.'

'This is your problem, Mr Thorne,' Samarez said.

'One of them.'

'Yes, of course. You need evidence that Mackenzie and Langford are one and the same man.'

'Can't be too hard, can it?'

Samarez gathered up the photographs and produced a second batch from his case. Four or five different women, some alone and others with Langford outside clubs or cosying up by the pool. 'He has a number of women he sees, but there is one semi-regular girlfriend.' He pointed to a photograph of a tall blonde woman in a red bikini. 'She is the one I think we can make use of for your purposes.'

Thorne pulled a series of three photos across the table and stared down at them. Langford in a car with a different girl; young, dark-haired. The same girl getting out. Langford's hand in the small of the girl's back, guiding her towards the front door of the villa.

'Tasty,' Fraser said.

'This is his daughter,' Thorne said. 'This is Ellie.'

Fraser shrugged, evidently not thinking it made any difference to his assessment.

Samarez nodded. 'The mother hired a private detective to find her, yes? Miss . . . Carpenter?'

'Anna,' Thorne said. He looked up, saw a small nod of understanding from Samarez, of sympathy. The Spaniard had clearly been comprehensively briefed.

Fraser continued to stare at the photographs with more than professional interest, until Samarez cleared them away. Then he called for the bill. 'We going on somewhere else, then?'

'Early start tomorrow,' Samarez said.

'Tom?'

Thorne shook his head without bothering to look up. He was thinking about the call he would be making to Donna first thing the next morning. Had things turned out differently, he would have been happy to let Anna make it. But, despite the twist in his gut caused by thinking about that, he was looking forward to giving Donna the news and confirming her suspicions that Ellie had been taken by Langford. The prospect of trying to answer her first question was not quite so pleasant, though.

What would he say when she asked, as she surely would, what he was planning to do about it?

'Looks like I'll be drinking on my own, then,' Fraser said.

Thorne guessed that he was used to it.

Back at the hotel, Thorne called Louise. She sounded as though she had just woken up. Thorne looked at his watch, saw that it was not yet 10.15, 9.15 in the UK, but he said sorry anyway, that he hadn't realised it was so late.

'It's OK, I was waiting for you to call.'

'What's up?'

'I had to take Elvis to the vet.'

'What's the matter with her?'

'I don't know, but it's not good. She wouldn't even get up when I came in and she'd been horribly sick again. There was blood round her mouth as well, so . . .'

'Shit.'

'I've left her in overnight, but the vet didn't look very hopeful.' After a few moments' silence, she said, 'Are you still there?'

'I'm sorry that you've been lumbered with this.'

'It's fine. How was your day?'

'You know. Long. Flying anywhere's a pain in the arse.'

'I'll leave you to it, then,' she said. 'Those roaming charges are such a rip-off anyway.'

They both knew that calls home were not covered by Met expenses, so it was a useful get-out when neither had a great deal to say. Thorne said he would phone the following day to find out how the cat was doing. Louise told him she'd sort things out, one way or another, and said goodnight.

Thorne lay on the bed and searched for something to watch on TV, but the only thing in English was a BBC World financial report. Then he found a channel showing hardcore pornography, the screen divided into four quarters featuring a variety of clips to suit every taste. There was a quick-fire voiceover and a number for anyone who wanted to hire one of the movies, though try as he might, Thorne could not figure out why anyone would *need* to pay anything.

He was too tired to take even the most perfunctory advantage of the free entertainment. But once the lights were off, he still found it a lot harder to sleep than he had just a few hours before.

THIRTY-TWO

For almost forty years, since its lavish opening, the well connected, the super rich and the showbiz elite had flocked to the marina complex at Puerto Banus. These days, the surrounding streets were more likely to be filled with pissed-up stags and hens than movie stars, and the hookers outnumbered the millionaires . . . just. But the marina itself remained as astounding a display of conspicuous wealth as Thorne had ever seen.

Upwards of five hundred yachts were moored. Line after line of dazzling white Sunseekers, many with smaller boats attached or a brace of jet-skis, and a few the size of small cruise-ships, complete with helipads, gymnasiums and swimming pools.

'How the other half lives,' Fraser said.

'*Half?*'

They walked the length of the marina and back. Fraser pointed out the yacht belonging to the King of Saudi Arabia. Said, 'Bit over the top, though.'

Thorne wondered what might constitute *way* over the top. A diamond-encrusted toilet-roll holder? Panda-skin cushions?

The cars parked alongside were as high end as the shops that lined the surrounding streets. Though there seemed to be nowhere anyone could buy anything as basic as boating supplies, there was no shortage of designer outlets from where shoppers in need could pick up those essential four-figure handbags, five-figure stereo systems and sunglasses that cost more than Thorne's monthly mortgage repayment.

The villas and apartments available in SuperSmart Homes reflected the lifestyles of those who would not need to bother with mortgages. Those who could probably pay with cash and would certainly appreciate being shown round a property by someone as beautifully refurbished and well-appointed as Candela Bernal.

'I don't actually care if a woman's had her tits done,' Fraser said. 'Doesn't bother me.'

'Thanks for sharing,' Thorne said.

Sitting in a car across from the estate agent's where she was based, they were now waiting for Langford's girlfriend to arrive for work. Fraser held up the picture of a bikini-clad Candela Bernal he had been examining. 'I mean, people go on about plastic surgery, but it's no different from wearing glasses when you think about it.'

Thorne thought about it.

'I don't understand.' Samarez leaned forward from the back seat. 'Are you saying that if a woman has her breasts enlarged, it will improve her eyesight?'

'No, don't be daft, I'm. . .' Fraser caught the look on Thorne's face and realised that Samarez was mocking him. 'Oh, piss off.'

'You're going to *need* glasses if you're not careful.' Thorne snatched the picture and turned to continue looking across the street. SuperSmart Homes sat between Tod's and Versace. The window was filled with ads for the kind of place David Mackenzie lived in, that in another life he had lived in when he was still Alan Langford.

That he once shared with the woman who had tried to have him killed.

Thorne thought about his early morning call to Donna Langford. He had told her that he had seen Ellie, or at least pictures of her and that, as far as anyone could tell, she was fine. The news had not elicited quite the reaction Thorne had been expecting. The relief was there somewhere, but surprisingly muted, and the barrage of questions, of *demands*, had not been forthcoming.

'She's fine, Donna,' Thorne had said again.

Nothing for a few seconds. Then, 'No thanks to the likes of you . . .'

'Well, I've not got a problem with plastic surgery,' Fraser said. 'That's all. I mean I *desperately* need a penis reduction, but if something needs doing, you—'

'There she is,' Thorne said.

'Half-past ten,' Fraser said, looking at his watch. 'Nice work if you can get it.'

They watched as Candela Bernal stepped out of a white, soft-top Mini and stood on the pavement, pulling her long blonde hair back into a ponytail. She was somewhere in her early twenties and, for a moment or two, Thorne felt a tug of sympathy for her. For the life she had fallen into. For the trouble he knew was coming her way.

Samarez had explained earlier that morning how they were planning to use David Mackenzie's girlfriend to establish his real identity. How her bad habits had given them what he hoped would be sufficient leverage to ensure her cooperation. 'I'm sure we can persuade her,' he had said.

'She's going to be very scared.'

Samarez agreed, but assured Thorne that she had plenty to lose either way. 'We have made the arrangements for tomorrow,' he had said.

Now she was talking to a woman outside Tod's. Her smile reminded Thorne of someone else's, and he remembered why he was there.

His sympathy quickly evaporated.

Her conversation finished, Candela walked to SuperSmart Homes' door. A banner was hanging in the window beneath the agency's sign: *Paraiso de los sentidos*.

Paradise for the senses.

'Bloody hell, you're not kidding,' Fraser said. 'No wonder Langford's smiling in most of those pictures.'

Samarez nodded, unable to argue.

261

'One more reason to hate the fucker.'

Thorne said nothing, simply watched as the girl disappeared inside.

He had plenty of reasons already.

'No pressure, Dave.'

Langford looked up and smiled at the man who would be about ninety quid poorer any moment. 'Wanker.'

You think *this* is pressure?

He sniffed and bent over his ball again. He had three putts to win the match on the sixteenth.

He needed only two.

'Played, mate . . .'

Langford shook his friend's hand and gratefully pocketed the hundred-euro note. He would get a decent bottle of something with it later at the club. Do some sniffing around while he was there.

Get some feedback.

The big step he had needed to take a couple of months earlier – *needed* rather than *wanted* – had gone seriously pear-shaped, and now the trouble had come a little closer to home. Now, it was all but knocking on his bloody door. Not that it would get that far, obviously, but to nip it in the bud, to regain some control over the situation, it would help at least to get the measure of the man who was making such a nuisance of himself.

A man who seemed to enjoy chasing lost causes and now had a very good reason to be taking things personally.

'Staying for a quick one?'

His friend – a fat builder who was less adept at cutting corners on the golf course than he was where it really counted – hoisted his clubs on to the back of his buggy and climbed aboard.

Langford climbed on to his. 'Can't do it,' he said. 'Got a lunch meeting.'

They began to drive back towards the clubhouse.

He had been monitoring developments back in the UK via the usual channels, so had known Thorne was coming for a week or so.

Having another crack at him so soon after botching the last one was not a viable option, so he had been unable to do anything to stop him. Taking out a copper was not something anybody but an idiot did without a very good reason, and certainly not once the copper in question knew he was a target. It was not something you did *at all*, not unless you wanted it raining shit for the foreseeable future, so Langford had done some hard thinking before giving the nod. Prior to Thorne, he'd done it only once before, when it was the best option available to him. But for a businessman who was as careful and as far-sighted as he prided himself on being, it was the last of all last resorts.

Now, thanks to some useless twat who couldn't shoot straight, he would have to think again. Reassess the situation; reorganise. Above all, he would need to stay calm.

'That hundred euros,' the fat builder said. 'Double or quits. First one back to the clubhouse.'

'Well, we already know you're not Tiger Woods,' Langford said. 'But now you think you're Lewis fucking Hamilton.'

'Up to you, mate.'

Langford put his foot down.

They watched the estate agent's for a little over an hour before Candela Bernal re-emerged. Fraser started the car, ready to follow, but instead of heading for her Mini, the girl turned towards them, then walked all the way to the far end of the marina, across the road and on to the beach.

'All right for some,' Fraser said. 'A cup of coffee, an hour gossiping with the other girls, then a quick dip before lunch.' All three climbed out of the Punto. 'I think I'm in the wrong job.'

Thorne glanced at Samarez and told Fraser he couldn't disagree.

As Samarez was due to be involved in the following day's business with Thorne, he drove his own car back to Malaga to ensure that everything was being set up properly. Thorne and Fraser followed Candela to the beach and took up a position in a bar thirty feet or so from the water's edge. Fraser ordered a bottle of water. 'Don't want any more of your dirty looks,' he said.

It had been overcast first thing, but the cloud had quickly burned away and now Thorne was sweating again. Fraser was wearing a different combination of shorts and loud shirt while Thorne – even though he'd left his jacket in the car – still felt overdressed in a polo top and chinos. As he'd been packing, Louise had told him that he would probably need no more than a single pair of long trousers, but he had not listened.

Whenever he imagined himself standing in front of Alan Langford, he wasn't wearing shorts.

'So, you didn't give much away last night,' Fraser said. 'About your set-up back at home.'

Call-Me-Pete, on the other hand, had babbled all the way through dinner about his wife and three kids; about the place they might buy in Estepona one day if she didn't piss it all away in TK Maxx before they got the chance. 'Maybe this Spanish piece we're going to watch tomorrow could give me a few property tips,' he had said.

Samarez had smiled and said, 'I think you will need to do a little more overtime.'

The arrangements on the beach were as high end as everything else in Puerto Banus, and after slipping off her thin dress and sandals, Candela settled down on a thickly cushioned, rattan sunlounger. She removed the bikini top and lay down on her front with a magazine. It made Thorne feel sleepy just watching her.

He closed his eyes for a few seconds, enjoying the sensation of the sun on his skin, the rumble and shush of the water. He remembered what the woman on the plane had said about him needing a holiday and thought she was probably right. His last time abroad had been when he and Louise had gone to Greece the year before. When the baby she went on to miscarry eight weeks into a pregnancy had been conceived.

They had not discussed holidays since.

'I meant what I said about the fake tits.' Fraser wiped the lenses of his sunglasses, replaced them, then continued staring appreciatively at Candela. 'They really don't bother me.'

'I'm sure she'll be very pleased,' Thorne said, not bothering to open his eyes.

Fraser looked across at him. 'Come on, you can't be *that* disinterested. I don't see a wedding ring, so I'm guessing you've been spared that particular nightmare.'

'You should be a detective.'

'Girlfriend? *Boy*friend?'

'One of those,' Thorne said.

After fifteen minutes or so, a waiter walked down to the sunbed with a glass of wine and some kind of salad. Candela sat up, covering her breasts with one arm as he laid the tray down on a low table. She reached into her bag for some cash and he nodded, smiling, clearly grateful at being told to keep the change.

'You've obviously got a bit of a hard-on for our friend David Mackenzie,' Fraser said.

Thorne looked at him.

'I'm not surprised, mate.'

'No?'

'If somebody took a pot-shot at me I'd not be best pleased either.'

'A *pot-shot*?'

'I'm just saying . . .'

'A girl died,' Thorne said.

'Yeah.' Fraser nodded and left what he obviously thought was a suitable pause. 'You knew her a bit, then?'

Thorne pictured the flush in Sylvia Carpenter's face as she talked about his damaged shoulder and the tremble in her hand as she reached out towards his chest.

'Yeah, I knew her.'

Thorne turned away and watched Candela as she picked at her food, placing what was left back on the tray when she'd finished and waving to the waiter, who quickly came across with a second glass of wine. After another ten minutes of sun, she stood up and tied her bikini top back on, then walked gingerly across the hot sand and into the sea until it was up to her waist. She stood facing the beach, staring almost directly at Thorne and spreading her arms out wide. She gave a little jump and a yelp of excitement each time one of the big waves broke across her back.

She looked as though she did not have a care in the world.

Thorne thought: She soon will have.

THIRTY-THREE

The roads into Mijas Pueblo were still blocked, so Fraser dropped Thorne off by the car park just after five-thirty. His own place, like those of most of the SOCA agents, was in an apartment block in Malaga, though he told Thorne that if things went the way he was planning, he'd end up getting somewhere far better.

'If I can swing a permanent job over here, then the wife and kids can come out for good. You get a nice house, private education for the kids, top-notch health insurance, the lot. Knocks the Met into a cocked hat, I'm telling you.'

He told Thorne he would pick him up at nine the following morning.

'I want to hire a car,' Thorne said.

'There's no need, mate. I'm perfectly happy to run you around.'

'I'd be happier looking after myself.'

Fraser seemed uncomfortable.

'What's the problem?'

'Well, really, I'm supposed to . . .'

'Keep an eye on me?'

'It's a joint operation, that's all. I mean, when you get down to it, the Met doesn't actually have any jurisdiction here.'

'What about all this free time I'm going to have? If I'm going to visit these fantastic places you keep telling me about, I can't keep expecting you to chauffeur me about.'

'OK, let me see what I can organise.'

'I can sort it out myself, Peter,' Thorne said. 'I'm a big boy.'

Fraser unconsciously felt for the phone he kept clipped to his belt. Before he drove away, he told Thorne it would be a good idea to wear something smart the following day. To look like he had a few quid.

Thorne walked up towards the newer part of town and saw immediately why the traffic had been diverted. A carnival was in full swing, with stalls running the length of the main street and an enormous carousel in the park. At first, it looked like the kind of funfair Thorne was used to back at home. The same tawdry gathering of old rides and dodgy stalls he went to as a kid in Finsbury Park; where he would drink cheap cider with his mates and fail to meet girls. Then he saw that, as well as the candy-floss and the toffee-apples, the stall-holders were selling spooky-looking Mexican wrestling masks and small guitars, and that people seemed to be *enjoying* themselves. Crucially – despite the fact that every shop he passed seemed to be selling a bewildering array of knives – there did not appear to be a better than average chance of someone getting stabbed.

He watched as three different marching bands in handsomely decorated uniforms gathered around the edge of the park. Dozens of men, women and children were arranging themselves into lines, the sun bouncing off the rims of the drums and the highly polished brass. Thorne bought a bottle of water and sat down for a while. Then, when the music struck up and the bands began to move, he fell in step and followed the first one as it wound its way towards the market place.

The Plaza de la Constitución was even busier than it had been the previous day. Hundreds of people were dancing in the shadow of the huge awning across the market and the bar was four or five people deep. The group on stage stopped as the procession snaked into the square, their up-tempo sing-along replaced by the drums and blaring brass of the marching bands, whose arrival was greeted with tumultuous applause.

Thorne queued for a beer, then found a seat outside one of the bars a dozen steps up from the square. He shouted above the noise to ask a man at the next table what was going on.

The man struggled to hear, then to understand. '*Feria*,' he said, eventually. He pointed to a poster in the bar's window and Thorne went to take a look.

Feria Virgen de la Peña.

He guessed that '*feria*'was 'fair' or 'festival'. Did '*peña*' mean 'pain'?

There was an effigy of the Virgin, and some details of the ongoing festivities that Thorne could not understand. The dates were clear enough, though. Thorne had arrived in Mijas during its biggest festival of the year. Four days of it.

He took another beer back to his table. Walking across the bar, he noticed a man reading a Spanish newspaper; the same man he had seen the night before in the restaurant when he had been discussing the case with Samarez and Fraser. Mijas was not the biggest place in the world, but Thorne still doubted that it was a coincidence. When the man glanced across at him, Thorne raised his glass.

Give my best to Alan . . .

Five minutes later, when he turned to look again, the man had gone.

Thorne watched and listened and let an hour drift by. The bands primarily played traditional Spanish tunes, although, for reasons Thorne could not fathom, one broke briefly into the theme from *The Flintstones*, and the biggest cheer of all was reserved for a stirring rendition of 'Y Viva España'. Presumably ignorant of the song's crass English lyrics, the crowd joined in noisily with the hook and men hugged unashamedly each time the chorus rolled around. Women moved among the crowd in flamenco-style polka-dot dresses, bright purples and pinks to coordinate with the flowers in their hair. They wore high stilettos in matching colours and Thorne was amazed at how easily they moved across the large cobbles, handing out carnations from baskets that bounced against their hips.

'Sir, you want to eat something?'

Thorne looked up at the waiter, wondering if it was really *that* obvious he was English. He supposed it was, and decided that an early dinner, followed by an early night, was probably no bad idea.

Donna was in the kitchen when she heard the key in the front door. She ran into the hallway, began speaking before Kate had even unbuttoned her coat.

'Ellie's in Spain,' she said. 'Alan's got her.'

'You sure?'

Donna nodded, smiling stupidly. 'She's OK.'

Kate said, 'Thank God,' and moved to take Donna in her arms. 'It's what we always thought, right?'

Donna squeezed, then stepped away. The smile was still there, but it wavered a little. 'It's what *I* thought, but for a while I wasn't sure what was going on inside *your* head.'

'I never thought she was dead,' Kate said. 'I promise you.'

Donna took Kate's coat from her and hung it up carefully. 'I wasn't sure if I believed you.' She picked a few stray hairs from the sleeves. 'You can hardly blame me for that.'

'No.'

A few seconds later, when Kate raised her eyes again, Donna had already turned away and was walking back to the kitchen. Kate followed her and sat down. Donna flicked on the kettle.

'So, what are you going to do?'

'What do you mean?' Donna snapped.

'Nothing . . . Christ, Don.'

'What *can* I do?'

Kate shrugged. 'Just have to wait for more news, I suppose.'

'I suppose.'

When the tea was ready, Donna carried the mugs to the table and sat down. The smile had returned, her good mood peaking again, while Kate's wariness cranked up a notch or two in response.

'When Ellie comes back, it's really going to be all right, you know.'

270

Donna was nodding through the steam from her tea. 'The three of us can live together and it'll be great, I know it will. Here or somewhere else, whatever. Is that OK with you?'

'Whatever you want.'

'I want to know I can count on you for this,' Donna said. 'I want to trust you again. Because—'

'We should go out,' Kate said, suddenly enthusiastic. Desperate. 'We should go somewhere and celebrate.'

'I'm tired.'

'Just a quick drink, then. Come *on* . . .'

'What did you say to Ellie?'

Kate let out a long breath. 'Please, let's not start that again. Not now.'

'That day in the café.' Donna sat very still, blew on her tea. 'Just tell me.'

'I said nothing bad, OK?' Kate leaned forward and reached across the table, but Donna's hands stayed wrapped around her mug. 'On my life, Don. On *Ellie*'s life . . .'

There had been no shortage of things to look at, but still it had felt a little odd to be eating alone and Thorne had wished he had something to read. Anything to make him look a little less . . . sad. Before flying out, he had gone back to the sex-shop where he had met Dennis Bethell and picked up one of the thrillers he had been looking at. He had not so much as opened it yet, but had decided against walking back to the hotel to pick it up.

He had felt a little less awkward by the time he had finished.

After dinner, he moved to sit halfway down the steps with what was left of his beer. He had not previously noticed the arrangements of multi-coloured lights that now glittered above every street, strung between balconies where families gathered to watch the crowds below.

With a crash of cymbals, one of the bands launched into 'La Bamba'.

The waiter had brought olives before his meal arrived, and Thorne

271

had remembered Anna devouring a plateful at that bar in Victoria. She would have loved it here, he thought now. Stupidly excited at the idea of the two of them working the case together. She would have gibbered non-stop on the plane and joked about separate rooms.

She would have danced and looked a damn sight less English than he did.

She would have thought Call-Me-Pete was a tit.

He felt, rather than heard, his phone ring and when he saw the screen he caught his breath. He had forgotten to call Louise.

'God, I'm really sorry, Lou. It's been non-stop.'

'It's fine,' she said.

Thorne said nothing, wondering why people said 'fine' when things were anything but. Why he and Louise said it quite so much these days.

'It sounds noisy there.'

'Some kind of festival going on,' he said.

'Elvis had a tumour in her stomach.'

'Oh shit. What did the vet say?'

Louise said something, but Thorne was struggling to hear. He put a hand over his free ear and repeated the question.

'The vet put her to sleep this afternoon.' Raising her voice, she suddenly sounded angry as well as upset. 'He said it was the best thing to do.'

Thorne took a deep breath. A few feet from him a girl began squealing with delight as a man lifted her off her feet and swung her around.

'What was that?'

'Sorry, there are people everywhere, it's—'

'This is pointless,' Louise said. 'Can you call me back from somewhere quieter?'

Once he'd hung up, Thorne sat where he was for a while. He was cold suddenly and, as the minutes passed, a wash of loneliness settled over him that no page-turner, no amount of company, could relieve. He raised his glass then quickly dropped his hand as he felt a sob rise up fast into his throat and break. Then another. He lowered his head and let them come, the sound barely audible, even to him, above the drums and blaring trumpets.

'You OK?'

He looked up to see a large woman in a red polka-dot dress standing above him. She smiled and asked again.

He nodded.

The woman reached out and handed Thorne a carnation. Then she leaned down to kiss him on the cheek.

He woke just after 2 a.m. to what sounded like a war outside.

The explosions rattled the glass in the window frames, and for a few seconds Thorne was genuinely alarmed, until he saw the flashes of red and green through a gap in the shutters and heard the mournful whistles as the fireworks began falling to earth. Between each *crack* and *whoosh* he could hear the trumpets somewhere nearby, but now the cheerful music of earlier had been replaced by something far slower and altogether more ominous. A tumbling, minor cadence that rose from the street and prickled against his skin.

It sounded like misery.

Thorne closed his eyes and lay there, shaken and sweating, the sheets pasted to his chest and each explosion sudden and terrible, like a fresh blow to his heart.

Just a pop, no louder than the scooter backfiring.

THIRTY-FOUR

Candela had shown more than enough people like this around properties to know that being overly inquisitive was not a good idea. Many of her clients described themselves as 'businessmen', and if that's what the Englishman chose to call himself, she was far too smart to ask any other questions.

Far smarter than most people took her for.

He looked rather more thuggish than his friend, she thought. The type who would not think twice about screwing someone in any way possible to get what he wanted. Probably had a vicious temper on him, too. She wondered if the tall Spaniard was his minder. He didn't smile or say a great deal, but she knew that sort were rarely employed for their personality or intelligence.

Not that she was under any illusions herself. She knew exactly why David kept *her* around.

In truth, Candela didn't care too much what either of them did. Any of them. Commission was commission, and although she was well taken care of, she enjoyed making her own money. This one would keep her in D&G for a long time.

'Here is the master bedroom suite,' she said. She waited for the two

274

men to follow her through the door. 'Very nice, as you can see. The view is very beautiful, like in the other rooms.' She smiled and corrected herself. '*From* the other rooms.'

The Spaniard nodded.

'Lovely,' the Englishman said.

The block was a new build, and the penthouse apartment was the most spectacular and expensive property of the lot. Three beds, three baths and a huge living space, with private security and use of the gymnasium and pool complex.

'The whole place is lovely.'

Candela smiled, pleased with the way things seemed to be going. 'If you wish, you can keep the furniture that is already here, but of course that will cost a little extra.'

'Of course.'

'Or you can take it empty and choose things for yourself. Perhaps your wife might prefer to do that . . .'

'I'll ask her.'

'Women like to choose their own things.' She fingered a button on her ivory blouse. 'I know that *I* would prefer it.'

The Englishman flicked once more through the brochure she had given him, then walked across to the huge window. 'We'll need to talk about the price, though.'

'We can talk,' Candela said, laughing. 'But not too much. There is a waiting list already and offers have been turned down three times.' She walked across to join him and stood close. 'You can almost see Africa if the day is nice and this does not come cheaply. This block is ideal for getting anywhere on the coast, too, near to the motorway and the airport. What is it you say in England? The location, the location, the location?'

'Something like that.'

'There is a TV show also, yes? I saw it when I came to London.'

'You've been to London?'

'Of course. I went last year with a boyfriend.'

'This would be Dave Mackenzie, would it?'

Candela felt the colour leave her face and stepped quickly away from the window. 'No.' She shook her head. 'Not . . . Why are you asking me about this?'

'I thought we were friends,' the Englishman said.

The Spaniard stepped towards her then, reaching into his pocket, and she felt the flutter of panic expand and take hold. She had heard several horror stories during the two years she had been doing the job. Most of the agencies employed a few girls like her; girls who could show off a property well enough and give just a hint of something extra at the same time . . . as long as an offer was made quickly. It made them valued employees, but also easy targets for the odd lunatic.

She tried to control herself, managed to smile. Then began to panic even more when she saw what the Spaniard had been reaching for.

Russell Brigstocke stuck his head around the door of the small office that Holland and Kitson were sharing while Thorne was away.

'He called again,' Brigstocke said. 'First thing this morning.'

Holland looked over at Kitson and raised his hands in despair. 'Jesus, it's not like we're sitting on our backsides.'

'I know that.'

'We're doing everything we can,' Kitson said.

Holland sighed. 'We've *done* everything we can.'

'Just letting you know,' Brigstocke said, before he left.

The two of them had been working flat out since Thorne had left, checking and rechecking the same missing persons reports from ten years earlier that they had examined back in February. They had worked long hours, poring over the mispers files, cross-referencing them with the PM report on the body in the Jag; eliminating many but following up any that looked even remotely likely, including some that had been discounted during the previous search.

The day before there had been a result of sorts, though not one that would interest Thorne.

They had not been looking for bodies, of course, but the discovery of a simple clerical error had given them all they needed to match a missing junkie – reported as such one week after the Epping Forest Barbecue – with a previously unidentified corpse that had been found in a park in Kingston. The 'Celtic ring' listed under the body's personal effects had actually been a tattoo, described in the Distinguishing Marks section of the original mispers report. So they had been able to give the Kingston corpse a name, and were now in a position to inform the next of kin, but Holland had not yet called the dead man's mother.

'Come on, Dave, it's not like she doesn't already know he's dead,' Kitson had said.

'Right, but it's not like there's a grave she can visit, is it?' Thus far, despite several reports to the appropriate mortuary and coroner's office, Holland had been unable to establish what had happened to the body. 'It's not exactly good news.'

'It's closure.'

'Is it hell.'

That said, Holland was starting to believe that the dead junkie's mother would end up with a damn sight more 'closure' than Robert and Sylvia Carpenter. That Thorne would be coming back from Spain with nothing more than a bottle or two from Duty Free.

A few minutes after Brigstocke had left, Kitson said, 'It's not like you've let him down.'

Holland looked up.

'Thorne.'

'I wasn't thinking I had.'

Holland had spoken more sharply than he had meant to, but Kitson did not seem offended. 'Yes, you were . . .'

Holland could see there was no point in denying it any further. Kitson knew him well enough. He had worked plenty of cases where no amount of solid police work could produce the result that everyone wanted. It was part of the Job and the frustration was necessarily fleeting. When it was one of *Thorne's*, though, there was always more pressure. And when things did not go the way they should, Holland invariably felt like a schoolboy who had missed a last-minute penalty in a vital football match.

277

'Don't worry, he does it to everyone some time or other,' Kitson said.

'That's something, I suppose.'

'Harder for you, though.'

'Why?'

She smiled. 'Well, you've clearly got a father-figure thing going on.'

'That's rubbish,' Holland said, turning back to his computer screen.

Stepping up again. Getting ready to balloon the ball over the cross-bar . . .

They were *all* vital to Thorne, of course, and everyone understood how much the Adam Chambers verdict had hurt him. Perhaps that was why this case had become so important to him. But, whatever the reason, Holland knew how much Thorne needed something solid to pin on Alan Langford. How little anything else had come to matter.

Since Anna Carpenter's death, it had become personal.

'You really need to make that call, Dave.'

Holland looked up to see Kitson waving the report on the junkie who was no longer missing. He nodded, well aware that he had put it off too long already. Perhaps she's right, he thought. After all, having a loved one go missing, not knowing whether to hope or mourn, was probably as bad as it could get. The truth had to be some kind of good news.

Holland picked up the phone.

He only wished he had some to give Thorne.

THIRTY-FIVE

Candela Bernal spent nearly a minute examining the identification cards produced by Thorne and Samarez. Taking just long enough, Thorne thought, to gather her thoughts and compose herself.

She sat down in a chocolate-leather Barcelona chair. 'So stupid of me,' she said. 'I should have known who you were, because cops and criminals are very much alike.'

Thorne sat down opposite her. 'You think?'

'We want to talk about David Mackenzie,' Samarez said.

It seemed to Thorne, in the few seconds the girl took to say anything, as though she were deciding whether there was any point in claiming no knowledge at all of that name. The look on *his* face clearly made it an easy decision for her. Told her that she would simply be wasting time if she started lying.

'OK, we can talk, but I don't know anything, so . . .'

'You don't know *anything*?' Samarez said. He nodded slowly and walked around the back of her chair. Sat down on the edge of a side table, so that Candela was between himself and Thorne. 'You don't know, for example, that David Mackenzie is not this man's real name?'

She shook her head. 'I don't understand.'

'You don't know where all this money he spends on you comes from?'

This time, the shake of the head was more dramatic but far less convincing.

'It doesn't matter,' Thorne said. 'I don't really care if you're lying or not, because we don't need you to tell us anything.'

There was relief on Candela's face, then alarm. 'So, *what*, then?'

What they would be asking of her was straightforward enough, but there would certainly be some risks. And the fact that she and Langford always got together at his place rather than hers was an added complication. It might have been about caution or control, or perhaps Langford simply preferred a big bedroom when he was on the job. But in the eight months he had been seeing Candela, he had not so much as set foot in her apartment, despite paying the rent on it.

'We would like you to get something for us,' Samarez said. 'And don't worry, we do not mean secret files or anything like that. You will not have to break into Mr Mackenzie's safe.' He smiled, leaned towards her. 'Just a . . . cup, maybe?' He shrugged, as though it were nothing. 'Something like that; nothing too difficult for you. A glass or a spoon, something you have seen him touch.'

'Something with a fingerprint,' Thorne said.

'These days we can get fingerprints off human skin,' Samarez said. 'But we do not want to put you to that much trouble.'

Candela spat a word at him in Spanish. Seeing Samarez suck in a fast breath, mock-wounded, Thorne did not need a dictionary to know that she had called him something very unpleasant.

'Can you do it?' Thorne asked.

She turned to him, pushed her hair back from her shoulders. '*Why* should I do this?'

'Because we've asked you nicely?'

She stood up and told Thorne that he was not funny, that she was going to leave and that they could not stop her. But she was watching as Samarez produced a sheaf of photographs from his briefcase. He laid them out on the coffee table and she slowly sat down again.

'These were taken three nights ago in the Shades nightclub in Puerto Banus.' Samarez pointed at a picture of Candela talking to a man on the edge of the dance floor. 'That is a very nice dress, Miss Bernal.'

Candela stared at the floor.

'Did you have a good evening?' He waited, but got no response. 'Well, it is certainly one you will remember, because later you handed this man two hundred euros in exchange for two grams of cocaine. I know all this because this man is an undercover police officer.'

She muttered more words in Spanish.

'We have more photographs as well as a voice recording of the transaction.'

'Lucky for us that cops and criminals are so alike,' Thorne said.

When Candela finally raised her head she tried to smile, but the panic was clear enough around her mouth and in the eyes that darted between Thorne and Samarez. Finally, she nodded slowly.

Samarez did the same. 'That's very good.'

'You will need to protect me.'

'Yes, of course,' Samarez said.

He and Thorne were happy enough to offer at least a degree of the protection they had known Candela would demand. It had come as no surprise that she was afraid of Langford. And they were pleased to see no sign of loyalty to the man she was being asked to betray.

Earlier, Thorne had glanced at Samarez when the girl had talked about her trip to London. Samarez had given a small shake of the head. The Guardia Civil would have known if Langford had travelled to the UK. More significantly, Candela had said '*a* boyfriend'. It was apparent that Langford was not the only one with several partners on the go, that she took what she needed from their relationship just as much as he did.

If she had been in love with him, they might have had more of a problem.

'When are you seeing David Mackenzie next?' Samarez asked.

She leaned towards him and spoke low in Spanish. Samarez shook his head, having previously agreed with Thorne that all conversations

281

must be in English, but Candela ignored him, talking fast and sounding increasingly desperate until he waved at her to shut up.

'In English,' he said, firmly. 'Now, when are you seeing him next?'

She reached down to her bag and took out a pack of cigarettes. Smoking in an agency property was probably against the rules, but Thorne knew that holding on to her job was now the least of Candela Bernal's worries.

'Tonight,' she said.

On the way down in the lift, Thorne asked Samarez what the girl had said to him.

'She offered me money,' Samarez said.

'After that,' Thorne said. 'She said something else after you shook your head.'

'She offered me all sorts of things . . .'

By mid-afternoon Thorne was back in Mijas, where the streets were just as busy, though thankfully a little less noisy than they had been the previous evening. There were still many people in outlandish outfits, some wearing elaborate masks or dressed as giants with papier-mâché heads and oversized boots. In the main square, some kind of competition was in progress. An enthusiastic and vocal crowd had gathered in front of a stage to choose between half a dozen different couples in traditional costume.

Thorne found himself standing next to a middle-aged man with a Liverpool accent. '*Mr and Mrs* kind of thing, is it?' he said.

The man laughed and began to describe the crowning of the *feria*'s King and Queen in such detail that, within a few minutes, Thorne was wishing he had not bothered to ask. The man, who turned out to be not only a resident of the village but one who prided himself on his extensive local knowledge, went on to deliver a potted history of the *feria* itself: the original sighting of the Virgin by two shepherd boys and the carving of her shrine into the rocks above the village by monks in 1548.

'That's where the name comes from,' he said. '"Virgin of the Rock". It's quite funny, as it goes, because a lot of people get it wrong. They think "*peña*" means "pain", but it's actually "rock". Or "cliff", if you want to be strictly accurate, like.'

'Might as well get these things right,' Thorne said.

The man pointed Thorne towards the site of the shrine, and Thorne seized his chance to escape, following a group of Japanese tourists up a gentle, winding slope until he reached the cave. It was predictably small and crowded. The entrance was blocked by those taking pictures, but Thorne could just see the candles throwing shadows on to the rock walls and across the statue of the Virgin, which would – so Thorne had been reliably informed by his know-it-all Scouse tour guide – be paraded through the village the following evening.

Thorne had no desire to go inside, so he walked across to a small wooden balustrade from which a few people were pointing video cameras. He squeezed in next to a young couple with two noisy kids and looked down into the valley.

'Stop that, Luke!'

'Don't climb on there, Hannah, that's really old . . .'

He thought about the past, both recent and long distant; what you honoured and what you tried to put behind you. He wondered if Alan Langford thought about his past quite as much as he did about his future. Thorne knew how carefully Langford planned his moves, how he always tried to anticipate what might lie ahead. But once those things had happened, once they had become part of his history, did they stay with him as much as they would with those whose lives he had ruined in the process?

At the side of him, the mother yanked one of her children down from the first rail of the balustrade, then swiped at the back of his leg.

How carefully Langford planned his moves . . .

What had Donna and Fraser said to him?

Alan never did anything by halves. He planned things out, thought them through . . .

He thinks a long way ahead, does Mr Mackenzie. Plays the long game . . .

Thorne moved away from the couple and their kids, took out his phone and called Holland. 'Have a look through the original case notes and find out when Donna first met up with Monahan.'

'What?'

'The date,' Thorne said.

Holland needed only half a minute. 'In court, she said she couldn't remember the exact date, but it was the last week of June.'

'Right, and they killed whoever was in that Jag at the end of November.'

'OK . . .'

'Five months later.'

'I'm not with you,' Holland said. 'We know that.'

'What if Langford found out early on what Donna was up to? We don't know when he got the tip-off, but if it was right after that meeting, he might have snatched whoever ended up in that car straight away. Someone he wanted to get rid of. I mean, he didn't know Donna was going to keep losing her nerve and putting it off, did he?'

'I suppose not.'

'If Langford knew all along who was going to take his place in that car, he might have been holding on to the poor bastard for months, waiting for Donna to give the go-ahead, keeping him holed up somewhere.' The more Thorne thought it through and talked it out, the more it made sense. The more it seemed screamingly bloody obvious. 'We've only been looking for people who were reported missing a couple of weeks either side of the killing,' he said. 'We've not been looking back far enough.'

He told Holland to get the mispers reports dating all the way back to early June ten years before. To start working through them with Kitson straight away.

'Before you go,' Holland said, 'the DCI wants a quick word.'

As soon as Brigstocke came on the line, Thorne told him what he had just been discussing with Holland. Told him that the time frame

284

made sense; that Langford was smart enough and *cold* enough. Brigstocke sounded pleased, but Thorne heard something in his voice, an enthusiasm that sounded forced.

'What did you want, Russell?'

'Adam Chambers,' Brigstocke said.

Thorne tensed and began to walk back down the hill. 'I hope you're going to tell me he's been hit by a bus.'

'There's some stupid campaign been started up to clear his name.'

'*What?*'

'The press have got hold of it and now some twat of an MP has jumped on board. It's all over the news.'

Holland and Kitson spent the rest of the day making all the necessary calls and computer searches, gathering together the relevant mispers files so as to begin the process of elimination all over again. They worked well into the evening, poring over report after report, watching as one shift was replaced by another and eating pizza ordered by phone and delivered to the gate.

Thorne called twice, and was told twice by Yvonne Kitson that he wasn't helping.

The search parameters remained broadly the same. They were looking for missing Caucasian males of approximately six feet in height. The age of the victim was somewhat trickier. At the time of the post-mortem, there had been no reason to suspect that the body in the car was anyone other than the man identified by Donna Langford as her husband, and therefore no reason to examine bone fragments and tissue samples for an accurate assessment of the victim's age. So, Phil Hendricks had re-examined the samples he'd taken during the PM ten years earlier. He established conclusively that the victim had not been drugged, but the damage caused by the fire meant determining a precise age was impossible.

'Between twenty and fifty years old,' Hendricks had told Holland. 'But even that's just a guess, and make sure you-know-who *knows* that.'

★

285

Thorne had to sit through twenty minutes of Far East business reports on BBC World before the main news bulletin came on.

It was the second item.

Thorne was shocked to see that the MP Brigstocke had mentioned was a woman – young and earnest in a nicely cut business suit. She was standing outside Scotland Yard, the iconic sign revolving slowly behind her as she outlined the aims of the campaign.

'Yes, Adam Chambers is innocent in the eyes of the law,' she said. 'But that is not enough. He has been traumatised by the experience of being falsely accused of such a terrible crime and is finding it desperately hard to rebuild his life. Mr Chambers is as much a victim as anybody. In fact, as far as anyone has been able to prove, he is the *only* victim in this entire shambolic investigation.'

Thorne was sitting on the edge of the bed, no more than a couple of feet from the small screen. 'Bollocks,' he said.

'What do you want to see happen now?' the interviewer asked.

The woman half turned towards the building behind her, skilfully alternating her tone between concern and outrage. 'At the very least, Adam Chambers is owed an official apology, but I will be lobbying hard to see an independent inquiry launched.'

'Do you have a message for the parents of Andrea Keane?'

Now the concern was even clearer in the studied nod and the lowering of the voice. 'I have nothing but sympathy for the unfortunate parents of the missing girl. And I can assure you that Adam Chambers feels exactly the same way. But . . . on his behalf, on behalf of anyone who truly believes in justice, I'm demanding that those who sanctioned such a ridiculous and expensive prosecution be called to account.'

'Can you tell us how Mr Chambers is coping?'

In the background, Thorne could see one of the Scotland Yard security officers watching, a machine-gun slung against his hip. He leaned forward to grab a beer from the mini-bar, slammed the door shut and heard the remaining bottles tumbling inside.

Imagined the officer taking aim and delivering a message of his own.

THIRTY-SIX

Thorne woke with an idea.

He called Yvonne Kitson and asked her to dig out Langford's file; to look through the list of his blood relatives and get dates of birth and phone numbers for any who were still alive. When Kitson called back fifteen minutes later, he scribbled down the information on a scrap of hotel notepaper.

'Sorry about this Chambers thing,' Kitson said. 'It must feel like a kick in the teeth.'

'It'll blow over,' Thorne said.

Then he called Samarez.

He gave the Guardia Civil officer the significant dates and numbers and explained what he was looking for. Samarez said he would check the phone records and get back to him later in the day.

'I don't need telling that Mackenzie is Langford,' Thorne said, 'and I know this probably won't stand up in court. But until we've got the print evidence, it'll have to do.'

Samarez told him that they would not have too long to wait for the fingerprint match. 'Candela met up with Mackenzie in a nightclub last night. She told him she had a headache and left early with Mackenzie's champagne glass in her handbag. So, with luck . . .'

'I hope she was careful.'

'She is not stupid.'

'Neither is Langford,' Thorne said.

They talked for a few minutes about how the inquiry might best be taken forward, both skirting around the fact that until there was some new information, either in Spain or from the UK, it was likely to go precisely nowhere. Samarez said that he was busy on other cases for the rest of the day, and that Fraser had called in sick. He asked Thorne what he was planning to do and Thorne said he had no idea.

'You should get up to Ronda,' Samarez said. 'It's really very nice.'

'So I hear.'

'It might do you good to relax for a few hours.'

Coming from Samarez, the suggestion seemed less like an attempt to get Thorne out of the way than it had done from Fraser. Thorne wondered if Samarez might be right. There was nothing else that could usefully be done while they were waiting for Forensics to lift a print off the glass Candela Bernal had provided. To scan the results and send them through to London for comparison. A trip would certainly kill some time and might help take his mind off Langford for a while.

Off Anna Carpenter and Andrea Keane.

'I'll see how I feel,' he said.

He left the hotel and found a café. He drank two cups of milky coffee and made short work of scrambled eggs, fried potatoes and chorizo. Then he walked down towards the commercial area of the village to collect his hire car.

The enthusiasm in Thorne's voice had been clear enough when he had called the previous afternoon. His voice always rose a little higher when he was fired up and he talked faster. Everything he had suggested made sense, and Holland and Kitson had gone about their task with all the dedication they could muster. But Holland could not help but feel that increased hope would only lead, in the end, to increased disappointment.

That penalty kick he was destined to fluff had just become even more important.

Going back as far as Thorne had requested had eventually yielded another eight candidates. Having made certain that each one was still missing, Holland and Kitson had arrived at work that morning to begin the laborious process of contacting the next of kin, making appointments, and arranging wherever possible for DNA samples to be collected. As with the list they had worked through in February, most of the stories were simple yet terrible. The reasons why these individuals might have vanished without a trace, for the holes left in other people's lives.

Drugs. Abuse. Mental illness.

Or nothing at all.

A case that fell firmly into the last category caught Holland's eye halfway through the morning. Just for a moment or two, it made him feel as though he might have his penalty-taking boots on after all. Having talked to Brigstocke, he and Kitson decided they would not tell Thorne until they were sure there was really something to get excited about. But everyone agreed that it looked promising; that they should focus all their attention on this case.

Find out who was in that Jag, Dave. He's the key to all this.

It seemed to Holland as if it had risen up from the stack of files like a card from one of Brigstocke's magic decks.

The car was stifling and smelled plasticky when Thorne picked it up, but once the air con had been running for ten minutes, the drive up into the hills was pleasant enough, although the concentration it demanded left little time to take in the scenery. It was a far steeper climb than the one up to Mijas, with alarming drops on his left-hand side and more than a few hairy corners. Thorne was amazed to see signs warning of snow on the road, which were not only incongruous, considering the hot weather, but made him wonder how in hell any driver managed the climb – and worse yet, the descent – in freezing conditions. Chuck in the risk of rock falls and the occasional wandering goat, he thought, and it would be astonishing if anyone made it up or down in one piece.

It took him the best part of an hour to reach Ronda, and within a few minutes of parking the car and starting to walk towards the centre of the 'white town', he was out of breath. He stopped and looked down from one of the bridges into the canyon on which the town was perched, carved out by the river which now divided it in two. He took a minute. The view was undeniably spectacular, and he was content to put the breathlessness down to the fact that he was several thousand feet above sea-level, rather than blaming the several pounds he could do with dropping.

The big breakfast might have been a mistake, he thought.

He picked up a map from a tourist information office and followed it past rows of small shops and quirky museums to the historic bullring that Fraser had mentioned. There were far fewer visitors around than there had been in Mijas, but Thorne put that down to the *feria*. This town had a different atmosphere, too, something almost reverential, and it was certainly quieter.

He paid his four euros and walked through a turnstile into the empty bullring. The sandy floor sloped very gradually up towards the centre and was harder than he had expected. A couple was taking photos on the far side, and more people were moving in the stands, but despite their presence, and the late morning sun overhead, the place felt strangely cold and spooky. Resonant of a past that made Thorne uncomfortable. He found himself wondering how many animals had died there . . . and how many men. How much blood had soaked into the floor beneath his feet over two hundred and fifty years.

Standing in the centre of the ring, looking towards a pair of scarred, white, wooden gates, it was easy to imagine the heat and the roar of a frenzied crowd. Thorne could almost taste the adrenalin, coppery in the mouths of those waiting to face the bulls. He tried to gauge the distance between the centre and the edge, asked himself if he would make it, should he ever find himself running from a charging bull. He still fancied himself as reasonably quick if he needed to be, in short bursts at any rate.

He decided he would not even get halfway.

He spent a few minutes walking around the bullring's museum, taking no more than a passing interest in the old photographs and mounted bulls' heads. He looked briefly at the antique suits of lights displayed behind glass and wondered why vintage clothes always seemed so small, before walking across to a bar on the edge of the main square.

He waved to attract a waiter's attention and was ignored.

On the table, he laid out a handful of leaflets for some of the town's other attractions. There was certainly no shortage of museums, but each exhibition seemed more gruesome, more bloodthirsty, than the last.

A history of hunting.

Torture during the Spanish Inquisition.

Five hundred years of capital punishment.

Looking at pictures of some of the exhibits, Thorne was not sure that Ronda was quite as 'nice' as everyone kept telling him.

It was hotter now, and Thorne turned again to look for the waiter. The bar was busy and he cast an eye across the customers, half expecting to see the man with the newspaper he had spotted twice already. But when he heard a chair being scraped back, he spun around to see an even more familiar figure.

Thorne could only watch as Alan Langford dropped casually into the seat opposite.

THIRTY-SEVEN

'You mind?' Langford raised a hand, and within a few seconds a waiter was at the table. Langford looked at Thorne. 'What do you want?'

Thorne said nothing.

I want to drive a glass so far into your face that it won't matter what you call yourself, because nobody will ever recognise you again. I want to twist and push and feel the flesh shredding and I want to hear you scream. I want you to say my name, same as she did . . .

'I fancy a beer,' Langford said. 'Not one of those poxy little ones, either.' He ordered two beers in Spanish, then sat back to look at Thorne, shaking his head and smiling, as though they were two old friends who had fallen out over something so trivial that neither of them could even remember it properly.

I want your blood to wash away hers.

When the beers arrived, Langford put away half of his in one gulp, then sat back again and began methodically peeling the label from the bottle. 'There's nothing for you here,' he said. 'You need to know that.'

Thorne reached for his own bottle. He had no desire to drink with this man, but suddenly his mouth was dry and his tongue felt sticky.

He hoped the beer might steady the tremble in his legs and help him fight the urge to do exactly what he had just imagined doing.

'*You're* here,' he said.

'Right. I'm here minding my own business.'

'And we all know what that is.'

'Listen, I don't know what you *think* you know, but the only thing you're getting in Spain is sunburn. So all I'm saying is, why don't you just toddle off home and save us all a lot of trouble?'

Langford's hair was greyer than it had looked in the photographs, and too much sun had left his face lined and leathery. Despite the bravado, Thorne could also see that he was anything but relaxed. The smile showed only teeth that were too big for his mouth, and too white.

'For someone who's minding his own business, you seem awfully worried,' Thorne said.

'I'm *irritated.*'

'Well, I must be doing something right.'

The teeth flashed again. 'It's a lot of trouble to go to, though, don't you think? To come all the way out here, costing the taxpayer God knows how much, to check up on a retired businessman.'

'You're not exactly retired, though, are you? And I'm doing more than checking up.'

Langford puffed out his cheeks, then exhaled slowly. 'A man finds out his wife is planning to have him killed, so he thinks it might be a good idea to start again somewhere else. End of story. I can't see the Crown Prosecution Service getting very excited about that a decade down the line, can you?'

'They're pretty keen on people who leave bodies behind.'

'Well, course they are, but I wouldn't know anything about that.'

'You don't know how a man came to be burned to a crisp in your car?'

'I thought you'd caught the man who did that,' Langford said. 'Isn't he in prison?'

'He *was,*' Thorne said. 'Until he got carved up in his cell a few months ago.'

293

'Dangerous places, prisons.'

'Then the prison officer who colluded in his murder got hit by a car.'

'Nasty.'

'Very. But you wouldn't know anything about that either, right?'

'I'm a bit out of touch over here,' Langford said. 'Unless it's in the sports pages . . .'

His hand dropped to his waist, reaching idly beneath the white linen shirt to scratch. Thorne caught a glimpse of the scar Donna had mentioned, pale against the brown belly.

'Retirement must get a bit boring, though, surely?' Thorne said. 'How much golf can you play, how many laps of your pool can you do?'

'You sound jealous, mate.'

'It's perfectly understandable, that's all I'm saying. Wanting to keep your hand in, I mean.'

'I just want a nice, quiet life.'

'Course you do, but sometimes things need doing to *keep* it nice and quiet.'

Langford was still picking at the label from his beer bottle, rolling the pieces into balls between his fingers and dropping them into the ashtray. He shook his head and his eyes drifted away, as though he had momentarily lost the thread of the conversation.

Four or five skinny, feral cats were sniffing around near the tables, yowling for food then fighting over any scraps thrown their way. Langford held out a hand towards one, made kissing noises in an effort to draw it towards him, then gave up. He turned back to Thorne, said, 'Little buggers are more suspicious than you are.' Then, 'What were we talking about?'

'Howard Cook and Paul Monahan.'

Another shake of the head.

'Names not ringing a bell, Alan?'

'David.'

'Well?'

'Sorry,' Langford said. 'Are they footballers?' He leaned back and finished his beer, snapped his fingers as if he'd just remembered exactly what they were discussing. 'Hang on, what about that body in the car you were talking about?' Keeping his eyes on Thorne, he held up the empty bottle to let the waiter know he wanted another beer. 'I'm guessing you still don't have a name for that one.'

'We're working on it.'

'Best of British.'

'Thanks.'

'I mean it.'

'You'll be the first to know how we get on, don't worry.'

A couple at the next table got up to leave and Langford leaned across to grab one of their plates. He picked up the pieces of fat and gristle that had been left and tossed them one by one towards the cats. They immediately began rushing for every morsel, hissing at one another whenever they managed to grab a piece.

'What about Anna Carpenter?' Thorne asked.

'What about her?'

'You know *her* name, then?'

Langford narrowed his eyes, as though the name were familiar but would not quite come to him. As though he had almost placed the woman, then lost her. Finally, he shook his head again, defeated. 'No idea,' he said. 'She's not that tennis player, is she?'

I could end this now, Thorne thought. End all of this and go home. I could reach across the table and use that dirty knife.

End it.

This fucking stupid game.

My fucking stupid career.

'You know, I keep hearing from everyone how good you are at planning things out,' Thorne said. 'Weighing up the risks. Donna told me—'

'You don't want to believe anything that stupid bitch tells you.'

'Well, that's just it, because I think she's wrong. I think they're all giving you way too much credit, because you make plenty of mistakes. You certainly made one when you took Ellie.'

295

'You really don't know what you're talking about, do you?'

'I've seen photos of her.'

'Have you?'

'And you made a *big* mistake with the girl. With Anna Carpenter.'

If Thorne's words – the way he said them – had any effect, it was well hidden. Langford did not so much as blink. Thorne slowly let his fists unclench beneath the table, but he could not bear to let Langford walk away from this thinking that he had won.

That he had scored any points at all.

'Oh, and you're not really on the ball when it comes to hiring staff, either,' Thorne said.

Langford sniffed. 'Really?'

'Really,' Thorne said. 'Whoever you had watching me made a shit job of not being spotted.'

'Well, thanks for the advice, but at the risk of repeating myself, you don't know what you're talking about.'

'Right.'

'Seriously.' Langford shook his head. 'I don't need to watch you.'

Thorne tried not to look shocked, because, for the first time since Langford had sat down, Thorne believed he was telling the truth. He stood up quickly and stepped away from the table. He watched the cats scatter, then turned back to Langford. 'You were wrong, by the way,' he said. 'I'm more than suspicious. I know *exactly* how dangerous you are.'

Langford looked at him for a while. He smiled and raised his hands in mock-surrender, then waved one of them dismissively. 'Listen, don't worry about the bill, I'll sort it out.'

Thorne moved quickly back to the table. He gathered up the tourist leaflets and tossed them into Langford's lap. 'Try a couple of these exhibitions if you've got some free time,' he said. 'Though I'm guessing they might be a little tame for you.'

Before Thorne was halfway back to the car, Samarez called. 'I've got the information you wanted,' he said.

'Right.' For a few seconds, Thorne had trouble recalling what he'd asked Samarez to do.

'I checked Langford's phone records, and there is a match for one of those dates and names you gave me.' He told Thorne which one. 'Same day every year for the last few years. Very clever of you, Tom.'

Thorne mumbled a 'thanks' for the information and the compliment, although he was still finding it hard to think straight, still reeling from the conversation with Langford.

Then, as if to show how clever *he* was, Samarez said, 'So, did the two of you have a pleasant chat?'

'*What?*'

Samarez laughed. 'He is still under surveillance, so obviously he was seen talking to you.'

It made sense, though if the Guardia Civil had been aware that Langford was in Ronda, or on his way there, Thorne wondered why Samarez had not seen fit to warn him. 'OK . . .'

'So much for your relaxing day off.'

'I guess your men are better at keeping themselves out of the way than his are,' Thorne said. But even as he spoke, he was thinking about Langford's reaction to the suggestion that he was having Thorne followed.

If Langford hadn't hired the man with the newspaper, who had?

'So, what did you talk about?'

'His retirement,' Thorne said. 'The people he's had killed, that kind of thing. It was all very friendly.'

'No nice, easy confession, then?'

'Most of it seems to have slipped his mind.'

'Of course.'

'At least he's not denying who he is, so we're halfway there.'

'You knew that anyway,' Samarez said.

Knowing was not proof, though, and an unverifiable conversation would not count for a great deal either. But the fingerprint evidence, if and when it came through, would do the job, and until then they had the phone records. The calls to the key number on a crucial date. There was something on paper.

'This trick with the dates and the phone numbers is something I need to remember,' Samarez said. 'You have tried it before?'

'No, but I'll certainly try it again.'

Thorne was grateful that in an uncertain and mostly unfair world, there were some things you could rely on. Politicians lied, British trains broke down and Germany won penalty shoot-outs.

And an old-fashioned London villain would always call his mother on her birthday.

He had little choice but to take the drive down slowly. Negotiating the sharp corners and perilous drops that were now only a few feet away on his near-side, his mind was not where it needed to be. His knuckles whitened on the wheel during some of the steeper sections as he fought to concentrate, to forget Langford's mock-innocent smirk when Thorne had mentioned Anna's name.

Some idiot in a Mercedes was on his bumper for a mile or two. Thorne feathered the brake at every opportunity, ignored each blast on the horn and gave the driver a good, hard stare when the Merc finally took the chance to overtake.

She's not that tennis player, is she?

He was still several miles up from the coast when his mobile rang on the seat next to him. On any other road, at any other time, he would not have thought twice about taking the call. Now he let it ring, listened to the alert as a message came through and waited five minutes until he had the chance to pull over.

He saw that the call was from Dave Holland and called him straight back without bothering to listen to the message. Glancing down into the valley as he waited for the call to connect, Thorne could see the lush fairways of a golf course highlighted against the surrounding browns and greys; splashes of green in an otherwise arid landscape.

Kitson answered Holland's phone. 'Dave's just nipped out, Tom.'

'I hope this is good news, Yvonne. It's not been a great day so far.'

'Dipped below seventy degrees, has it?'

'Put it this way, I'm about ready to twat the next poor sod who so much as looks at me funny.'

'You should do it, if it makes you feel better.'

'So, what's happening?'

'Chris Talbot,' Kitson said. 'Thirty-five years old, reported missing about four months before the body was found in Epping Forest. Right height, give or take the same build. His wife – ex-wife, whatever – lives up in Nottingham, so Dave and I are driving up there first thing in the morning. It looks good, Tom.'

From where Thorne was standing, it looked better than good. 'Can't you get up there tonight?'

'We tried, but she's not around until tomorrow.'

'Well, call me as soon as you've seen her.'

'Listen, I haven't got to the best bit yet. You know we talked about the victim being someone Langford wanted out of the way. The whole two-birds-with-one-stone thing?'

'I'm listening . . .'

'Chris Talbot was a copper,' Kitson said. 'Serious and Organised.'

THIRTY-EIGHT

By the time it had begun to get dark, the rush of optimism that Thorne had felt after speaking to Kitson had faded. Sitting in his hotel room, with the now familiar sound of trumpets and applause drifting up from the town square, he felt restless and oddly disconnected. He couldn't decide whether he needed reassurance or company.

He flicked through the TV channels, but it was too early for the easy distraction of porn. He picked up the thriller from his bedside table, read the first few pages then put it down again.

The fictional detective was *way* too bloody miserable.

He called Samarez and asked him if he wanted to have dinner. Samarez lived a good hour away on the far side of Malaga and said that it would be difficult for him to get there. He said that his wife was cooking and Thorne told him that sounded like a far more attractive proposition.

He called Phil Hendricks.

'Have you bought my sombrero yet?' Hendricks asked. 'I want a great big, fuck-off one, OK? I also want one of those bullfighting posters with my name on it.'

'No problem at all. It's not like I'm busy or anything.'

'Just put "*El Magnifico*".'

'I was thinking "*El Poofo*",' Thorne said.

'Yeah, that'll work.'

The conversation cheered Thorne up, but only slightly. 'I'm out of my bloody depth here, Phil.'

'They're only Spaniards, for God's sake.'

'I don't mean *Spain*, you tosser. The case. Langford . . .'

Thorne told him about the meeting in Ronda. He was used to villains fronting it out. Sometimes it was the only option they had left. But Langford had seemed genuinely confident and relaxed, even when Thorne had made his feelings about Anna Carpenter's murder abundantly clear.

Thorne was the one who had walked away shaken.

'Cocky's good,' Hendricks said. 'It's the cocky ones that fuck up.'

'As long as I don't fuck up first.'

'There's nothing wrong with being a bit . . . jumpy, all right?'

'Even if this missing copper *does* turn out to be our mystery body, I'm not sure where that leaves us.'

'Don't worry, it'll pan out, mate.'

'I hope so.'

'I reckon you're owed one anyway.'

'After Adam Chambers, you mean?'

'Listen, Tom. Langford's the one who's out of his depth, because he doesn't *know* you. If he did, there's no way he'd think he could wind you up and walk away.'

Thorne just grunted, non-committal. Praying his friend was right.

'You listening?'

'Yeah . . .'

'It's not just the case, is it?'

The music was getting louder, and there was a bell ringing, sombre and sudden, every few minutes.

'It's ridiculous,' Thorne said. 'I'm three hours from home, but it feels like the other side of the world. Like I'm thousands of miles away.'

'It must be heartbreaking, being away from me,' Hendricks said. 'I understand that.'

'Yeah, I don't know how I'm getting through the day.'

'I was sorry to hear about Elvis, by the way.'

'You spoke to Lou . . . ?'

'Not that the furry little bastard ever wanted much to do with me.'

Thorne swallowed hard, smiled at the memory of the cat assiduously avoiding Hendricks at every opportunity. 'She was a good judge of character.'

'Lou was upset, so I went round.'

'Thanks, Phil.'

'Not a problem.'

'Was she OK?'

'I don't think it was just about the cat. You know?'

Thorne grunted again and this time Hendricks didn't press it. 'How did Spurs get on last night?'

'Lost two–one at home to Villa,' Hendricks said, gleefully. 'Now *they* really are out of their depth.' There was a blare of trumpets as if to acknowledge the joke that Thorne had just ignored. 'What's that racket?'

Thorne told him about the *feria*, the celebrations on the village's big night.

'So, why the hell are you sitting there and moaning at me?'

When he and Hendricks had finished, Thorne tried to call Louise. There was no reply from either Kentish Town or Pimlico and her mobile went straight to voicemail. Thorne left a brief message, told Louise that he missed her.

Then he grabbed his jacket, left the hotel and walked towards the noise.

THIRTY-NINE

It did not take her long to pack.

Candela Bernal felt a little depressed that she had so little to take, so few possessions she could not leave behind, but she knew she needed to move fast and that this was not the time for sentiment. She took clothes mostly – shoved roughly into a pair of Louis Vuitton suitcases – some silly knick-knacks she had kept since childhood and half a dozen family photographs. She would also take the jewellery David had given her, of course. She was many things, but she was not stupid. She had earned it, after all. Besides, she knew that the time might come when she would need to sell some of it. Bracelets and fancy wristwatches were only *things* at the end of the day, to be admired rather than cared about. Staying safe was far more important; safe and well, assuming she could finally kick the cocaine habit.

Another thing David had given her. Another good reason to get as far away as possible.

They had talked about protecting her – that animal Samarez and the English cop – but Candela knew that it was *just* talk. They said she would be looked after in return for her cooperation, but she could see very well what they thought of her, that they had more important things to worry about than some mobster's girlfriend. Some druggie slut. They were like most of the men she had known, David Mackenzie included. Happy to promise you anything, to tell you whatever you needed to hear until they had got what they wanted.

When she had finished packing, she stood waiting at the window with a cigarette and her third glass of wine. She blew smoke against the glass and stared through it at the lights of the marina far below. She would not miss much about the place, certainly not the richer-than-you-are bullshit, but she would be sorry not to see the ocean every day, and the girls in the office. She had told them that she would need to skip the usual drink after work today. She had given each one an extra-long hug when she had left, and told them hay fever was making her eyes water.

She looked at her watch: the taxi was a few minutes late.

She had worked out the schedule to allow for traffic, leaving at least fifteen minutes to catch the train from Malaga to Córdoba, where she would be spending the night with an old school friend she had called the night before. Just *one* night, to be safe, then north from there – to Toledo or Madrid. She would decide later, once she was on her way, although perhaps somewhere smaller would be a better idea. In the cities, where David Mackenzie did so much business, where there were so many people keen to get into his good books, someone always knew someone.

And she knew he would be looking.

When the bell went, Candela turned from the window and walked to the intercom. She spoke briefly to the taxi driver, then buzzed him up to collect the cases. She took a last look around the apartment. Thought that, once she felt a little less terrified, it might even be fun to start again.

She had been pretending to be someone she was not for far too long anyway.

It took Thorne fifteen minutes to squeeze around the edge of the square until he found a space on some steps leading up to a bar. But he still had trouble seeing much, and had never been particularly happy crammed up against other people. He put his hands in his pockets, wary of thieves.

The crowd had left a corridor that was just wide enough for each of the marching bands to pass through. They came, with no more than a minute or two between them, the music of each fading into the next as the bands moved on to another part of the village. The uniforms were even more spectacular than the ones Thorne had seen before, but tonight the music was far less celebratory. The drummers beat out a rhythm that was almost funereal, and Thorne began to feel more than a little out of place. As if he were trespassing. Though every face he could see was open and happy, with the onlookers straining to get their first glimpse of the Virgin, Thorne started to find the whole thing positively *spooky*. He felt the same way about almost every religious ceremony, the tribute paid to anything that was outside simple human experience. He had once been unnerved watching a small group of Morris men in a Cotswold village. Their dancing had seemed aggressive, frenzied; the leader black-faced and sweating, glaring at the spectators, his hat shaped like a slab of rotting cheese.

When the crowd suddenly began applauding, Thorne looked to his left and saw the effigy swing into view and start its slow journey down the hill towards the square. This was way beyond clattering sticks and waving hankies.

Thorne had not got a good look at the statue up at the cave, but from where he was standing now, it seemed as though the entire shrine had been removed. The scale was breathtaking – twenty feet by ten, at a conservative estimate – and the weight evidenced by the fifty or so men needed to bear it upon their shoulders.

Thorne caught sight of a hand waving just a few feet away and watched as the Liverpudlian he had met the previous afternoon pushed his way towards him. The man seemed pleased to see Thorne and began raving about how lucky they were to be there.

'Has to be seen to be believed . . . Once in a lifetime . . . Real privilege.' All that.

Keen as ever to pass on information, he told Thorne that the men carrying the effigy – each dressed in immaculate white trousers and shirt – were all local police officers. He carried on talking while Thorne watched the enormous display moving down the hill and imagined every crime in the village over the next few days being investigated by distinctly lop-sided coppers.

'Do you fancy a pint?' The Scouser was now pressed up against Thorne, shouting in his ear. Then, as though his invitation were not clear enough, he made the universally understood drinking gesture.

Thorne fancied a pint very much, but he was less keen on having his ear talked off, or spat in, any more. He said, 'No, but thanks,' and edged his way through the crowd until he was at the corner of the square, at the bottom of the hill.

After twenty minutes, when the effigy and the hundred or so villagers who were following it had passed him, Thorne stepped into the street and joined the back of the procession.

Candela stubbed out her cigarette and finished her wine. She carried her luggage to the door and opened it.

'Just two bags,' she said.

Then she looked up and stepped back fast, tripping over one of the cases as she moved away from the door.

'Going somewhere, love?'

Directly behind the platform on which the effigy was mounted, a group of middle-aged men were carrying staffs topped with elaborate crosses. They were followed by the penitents, some barefoot or blindfolded, with candles stuffed into makeshift, tin-foil holders to prevent the hot wax falling on to their hands. Thorne moved along slowly with everyone else, the sense that he was intruding heightened when he was nudged gently but firmly to one side by someone clearly more deserving of a place ahead of him in the procession. Yet he felt compelled to follow, if only to see what would happen next.

He still felt uncomfortable, but the spectacle was hypnotic, the devotion oddly moving. The Scouser nodded to him from the steps of the bar and Thorne nodded back.

The huge platform swayed from side to side as it was carried, the bearers moving in a choreographed rocking motion that Thorne presumed made their progress easier. Every few minutes a man would turn to ring a bell on the front of the platform and it would be set down. It was not clear if this was part of the ritual or simply a way of giving those carrying it a break, but it gave Thorne the chance to move through the crowd and get close to the effigy itself.

He took out his phone and tried to get into a good position to take a few pictures. He thought Louise might like to see them.

The platform was thick with flowers: garlands of pink roses arranged around the ornate silver candelabra which twisted up towards the statue. The effigy stood beneath a silver canopy, with more flowers twisting around the struts and arranged on the top.

The Virgin was smiling.

She was five feet or so tall and had a doll's face. Her lips were bright red, as though freshly painted, but the pale flesh of her cheek was peeling a little in places and there were cracks on the hands that gripped a sceptre and cradled an even more doll-like infant. Her long, brown hair seemed too modern, though, falling in curls across her shoulders and Thorne thought the wig looked a little out of place beneath the sunburst of a huge golden crown.

But her expression was simple enough, and dazzling.

Thorne put his phone away and stared as the bell was rung again and the platform was hoisted back on to the police officers' shoulders.

A young girl's face, trusting and content. But with eyes cast down in understanding, or perhaps in expectation of the suffering that was so many people's lot in life, and the cruelty that seemed so much a part of others'.

As the platform moved, swaying its way out of the square on its journey around the village, the statue began to wobble, but Thorne kept his eyes on the face.

Andrea Keane's face and Anna Carpenter's.

A live band started to play, although Thorne could not see them, and those who had not already begun to move away sang along. Thorne felt cold suddenly. It was not a slow song, but the voices sounded sorrowful, as though the Virgin's expectations had been fulfilled.

For those few, terrible seconds before he reached her and clamped his hands around her neck, Candela understood what was happening. She knew how stupid she had been to give the police what they had asked for. How naïve she had been to think that she could run.

His face showed nothing. He did not speak as he pushed her back hard against the window. He calmly moved one hand from her throat to reach for the handle on the sliding door, and she knew that there was little point in struggling.

But instinct made her fight anyway.

She kicked at his legs and ripped her nails across his arms. She desperately tried to move her head so that she could bite him, but then she heard the hiss of the door gliding open behind her and felt the wind move into the room.

Her bladder went at the same time as she staggered back, on to the balcony.

A jumble of thoughts and pictures in those last few moments. It was cold and she was only twenty-two and there was blood in her mouth where she had bitten through her tongue. She thought about her mother and said, '*Perdóname, Mama,*' in her head, or perhaps it was out loud when she felt the metal rail pressing hard into the small of her back.

She was over then – tumbling and gone. Those lights in the marina rushing up at her and the wind like icy water.

She screamed all the way down.

FORTY

'We're gonna chase these fellas clear down to Texas . . .'

It was late and Langford was in his cinema room, sprawled out in one of the leather recliners, the volume almost as high as it would go. He'd installed top-of-the-range speakers and he liked it good and loud, liked to feel each punch and gunshot go through him. He reckoned *Unforgiven* was the last great Western ever made. He had lost count of how many times he'd watched it and now it was just getting to the big shoot-out at the end which was hands down his favourite part. Where it's pissing with rain and Clint walks into the bar to sort everyone out for killing Morgan Freeman.

He reached down to the cool-box and took out a bottle of Mahou. He was still sweating, still rushing from what had been an eventful day.

He'd had a couple more beers up in Ronda after his chat with Thorne, had enjoyed the afternoon and driven home a little pissed. It wasn't something he worried about a great deal. He'd been stopped twice in the past and both times the mention of a high-ranking local cop had seen him waved on his way.

A nice quiet life, that was what he'd said to Thorne, and Thorne had been right when he'd come back at him. Sometimes you had to do whatever was necessary to keep it that way.

Some things went beyond business, hurt you in all sorts of places.

In the bar, Clint cocks the rifle and everybody turns to look at him. He tells them he's there to kill Little Bill, that he's killed just about everything that walks or crawls at one time or another. That gets their attention all right.

What had Thorne expected him to say when he'd reeled off those names? Monahan, the bent screw and the girl Thorne obviously had a thing for. 'Fair enough, mate, we'll finish our drinks and then you can pop me on a plane back home to face the music'?

Probably just looking for a reaction, for a weak spot or whatever.

Well, he'd be looking a bloody long time, same as everyone else.

Clint shoots the owner of the place, but Gene Hackman knows he's only got one round left, so he isn't that worried. Then the classic misfire and all hell breaks loose and after he's shot Gene, Clint just gets himself a drink, cool as fuck. Says he's always been lucky when it comes to killing folks. And Clint hadn't even wanted to get involved, that was the thing. He had his own nice, quiet life, didn't he?

He hadn't started it . . .

Those fucking photos, it all came down to them, and whichever spineless ponce had stuck them in the post.

He was only reacting to the situation he'd been put in, after all. He hadn't asked for any of it, done anything to warrant all the aggravation. But now the shit was flying at him from every direction and all sorts of people had to be sorted out.

Only Gene Hackman isn't really sorted out, not yet. Says he doesn't deserve to die. Clint tells him that 'deserves' has got nothing to do with it before he finishes him off, up nice and close. He walks slowly into the rain then, past his mate's body, and one by one all the hookers come out too, the whores like Candela who started it all. They all stand there and watch him ride away, even the one with the messed-up face.

310

Fucking priceless.

Langford waited and let the credits run, because he believed it was rude not to. Then he reached for another beer and pointed the remote so he could watch the scene one more time.

FORTY-ONE

Alison Hobbs, who used to be Alison Talbot, had remarried three years earlier. Six months after her first husband Chris had finally been declared legally dead. When she answered the door, there was a toddler peering from behind her legs, and her new husband was waiting for them when Holland and Kitson were shown into the living room.

Stuart Hobbs had a firm handshake and gave a suitably solemn nod.

Alison went to make tea, leaving Holland and Kitson to fill an awkward few minutes with small talk while her husband wrestled his small son on his lap. The drive up from London had been pretty good, despite the average speed checks on the M1. The toddler's name was Gabriel, and the 'terrible twos' were kicking in. They were waiting on a quote to have the kitchen extended.

Everyone looked happy when the tea arrived.

'It'll be a relief, actually,' Stuart Hobbs said, 'if you *have* found Chris. It's not been particularly easy for either of us.'

Holland said he could understand that. 'Like I said on the phone, though, we can't make a positive identification at the moment. That's why we're hoping you can answer a couple of questions that might help.'

Alison sat down next to her husband. He took her hand. 'Fire away,' she said.

'Did you know much about what Chris was working on?' Kitson asked.

She shook her head. 'He didn't really talk about it and I didn't really want to know. Not once he'd moved into plain clothes, anyway. I knew there was a good deal of secret stuff, some seriously nasty people they were after, but he didn't bring it home with him, if you know what I mean.'

'Sensible,' Kitson said.

Hobbs shifted his son gently to one side and leaned forward. 'I thought this was just about . . . identification.'

'It is,' Holland said. He had already put a call in to Chris Talbot's former DCI at Serious and Organised, but was still waiting to hear back. So far, Alison had certainly said nothing to suggest that the work her former husband was doing would *not* have brought him into contact with Alan Langford ten years before.

'You think the fact that Chris was a copper is important?' Alison asked.

'Yes, it might be.'

'Might have had something to do with what happened, you mean?'

'Well, as I said before—'

The door to the living room opened suddenly and a boy walked in – twelve or thirteen, with shoulder-length hair and a My Chemical Romance sweatshirt. He stopped as soon as he saw that there were visitors, shifted awkwardly from one trainer to the other. 'My *World of Warcraft* account needs topping up,' he said, looking at the carpet.

'I'll sort it out later,' Hobbs said.

The boy mumbled a 'thanks' and left quickly.

'That was Jack,' Alison said.

Holland and Kitson nodded; the maths was easy enough. Chris Talbot's son.

'Stupid bloody computer game,' Hobbs said.

There was a slightly uncomfortable silence until Alison got up, saying 'oh' as though she had remembered something and going to fetch a cardboard box that Holland had seen at the bottom of the stairs on their way in.

'I got this down from the loft,' she said. 'It's a few of Chris's things. I thought they might be useful.' She laid it on the carpet in front of Holland and he leaned down to look at it. 'There's a few photos and some other bits and pieces. Not much, really. Considering.'

'That's great,' Kitson said. 'Thank you.'

Holland lifted the flaps of the box, tried to make his question as casual as possible. 'I don't suppose you'd know if Chris had his appendix out,' he said.

Alison looked taken aback, then nodded slowly. 'I think so. I mean, there was a scar, but you should probably check with Chris's mum. I can put you in touch with her, but we don't really talk much these days.' She shrugged, summoned a thin smile. 'She wasn't exactly thrilled when Stuart and I got married.'

Kitson said, 'It's difficult.'

Alison squeezed her husband's hand.

'Did he ever have an operation to put pins into his leg?' Holland asked.

'Yeah, Chris smashed his leg up playing rugby, the silly sod,' Alison broke into a smile. 'He was pretty good, actually. Played for the Met's first fifteen a couple of times.'

Holland nodded, impressed. He reached down and began rummaging in the box, but could not resist a glance across at Stuart Hobbs.

'I play football,' Hobbs said.

Holland looked up at Alison and he could see then that she knew they had found Chris Talbot's body. He had no idea what she still felt for the man to whom she had been married and whom she now knew to be dead, but the swell of sympathy he felt was not just because of her loss. He could see that the woman simply did not know how she was supposed to react. Sitting there as wife and widow, ten years on, with her new husband and his firm handshake.

314

Alison laughed softly, remembering. 'He used to have all sorts of problems with airport X-ray machines . . .'

'Be even worse these days,' Hobbs said.

Holland pulled a framed photograph of a rugby team from the box. He looked for Chris Talbot's name at the bottom and found him halfway along the second row. His arms were folded high on his chest and his ears stuck out. Holland could not detect much of a resemblance to the boy he had seen a few minutes earlier.

Kitson started to say something about Jack and DNA, but Holland was no longer paying attention.

He was staring at the photograph.

Two along from where Chris Talbot was standing was a face Holland recognised.

Ten minutes later, he and Kitson were walking back towards the car.

'We have to tell Thorne,' Kitson said.

Holland held up a hand. He already had his phone out and was listening to a message. 'Sonia Murray,' he said. 'Asking me to call her back urgently.' He shook his head, unable to place the name.

'I've seen her name somewhere,' Kitson said.

Then Holland remembered an attractive black woman, the barrage of abuse as she walked along the landing.

Sonia Murray was the police liaison officer at Wakefield Prison.

FORTY-TWO

Thorne's mood had been bad enough already when he'd got the call from Fraser . . .

He had managed to find a copy of the previous day's *Daily Mail* and having bitten back the bile – he had only been looking for a report on the Spurs–Villa game anyway – had taken it to the café to read over breakfast. The match report had been brief and uninformative, probably because there was no scope to make any comment on illegal immigrants or dole scroungers, but flicking through the paper he had come across a double-page article written by Adam Chambers' girlfriend.

Natalie Bennett had been charged with attempting to pervert the course of justice. Although there was little doubt she had lied, the charges had been dropped following her boyfriend's acquittal. In the article, beneath a caption that read 'Picking up the Pieces', she movingly described her efforts to rebuild her life after the trauma she and Adam had endured. There was a photo of her smiling bravely.

If Thorne had been served his breakfast by then, he would have heaved it up across the table.

Even more disturbingly, Bennett mentioned that she and Chambers were currently working on a book that would 'lift the lid' on the abysmal failings of the police investigation and in which the full extent of their suffering would be revealed. Thorne read on, thinking things could not get any worse, until he spotted that the book was being co-written by a hack journalist and true-crime writer called Nick Maier. Thorne had had dealings with Maier in the past, and the thought of him profiting in any way from what had happened to Andrea Keane turned his stomach still further.

By the time he had thrown the paper away, his appetite had all but gone and the call from Fraser killed it altogether.

Now, he was stepping gingerly through a crime scene, in the apartment from which Candela Bernal had fallen to her death the night before.

'You seen many jumpers?' Fraser asked.

'She didn't jump, *Peter.*'

'Just saying. They take their glasses off, did you know that? I saw it in an old episode of *Inspector Morse.*'

'She didn't wear glasses,' Thorne said, 'and she didn't fucking *jump.*'

'I know, OK? Just making conversation, Christ . . .'

The sliding door that led to the balcony was open and there were more officers working outside. A blue tarpaulin that had been secured to the railings snapped and fluttered in the wind.

'Why was nobody watching this place?' Thorne asked. 'We told her there would be protection.'

Fraser raised his hands. 'Nothing to do with me, mate.'

'Well, *somebody* screwed up,' Thorne said. He considered everything Silcox and Mullenger had told him back in London. 'Or looked the other way.'

'Come on, we couldn't have guessed it would be so quick.'

'*Couldn't* we?' Thorne was as angry with himself as he was with Fraser or any of his colleagues. 'Langford probably sussed it when she told him she had to go home early. He might even have seen her put the champagne glass in her bag.'

'Look, none of this was my idea, all right?'

Thorne moved away, but Fraser followed, a pace or two behind, his hands stuffed sulkily into the pockets of his plastic bodysuit. Thorne stepped across a local scene of crime officer who was on his hands and knees, scraping at the carpet. The officer muttered something in Spanish that was almost certainly not 'Good morning and how are you?' as Thorne walked over to where the two suitcases lay near the door.

'She was trying to leave,' Thorne said.

'Looks that way.' Fraser moved alongside him, nodded at the door. 'No sign of forced entry, so maybe she knew him.'

'You should check with all the local taxi companies.'

'Wouldn't she just have taken her own car?'

'Too easy to trace,' Thorne said. 'She'd have known Langford has friends in high places. Including police officers.'

'I don't know what you're trying to suggest, mate,' Fraser said.

'I'm not *suggesting* anything.'

'One or two of the local boys might be a bit dodgy, fair enough, but . . .'

Thorne had already stopped listening to him. He was staring at a small, glass-topped side table next to the sofa. There was an empty wine glass and a beer bottle minus a label. In the ashtray, dark gobbets of rolled-up paper lay scattered among the lipstick-stained cigarette butts.

'Langford did this himself,' Thorne said.

'Come again?'

'He killed her.'

'No way,' Fraser said. 'You've said it yourself, he doesn't get involved in the messy stuff.'

'Messy' was the only way to describe the scene on the street seventeen floors below. By the time Thorne had got there, the area had been sealed off and hidden from the public, but there was still a good deal of cleaning up to be done. They would be lucky if there was enough of Candela Bernal left for a post-mortem.

'He's rattled,' Thorne said. 'His girlfriend does the dirty on him and he takes it personally. He's already had the job on me go wrong and he's fired up enough to do this one himself.'

'I can't see it.'

Thorne pulled Fraser across to the small table and pointed. 'He had a drink with her, OK? Or sat down and helped himself to one after he'd killed her.'

'Jesus . . .'

Thorne remembered the terror on the girl's face when they confronted her, and what she had said about cops and villains. The difficulty in telling one from the other. She had not been given much of a choice in the end, but she had still picked the wrong side. 'Make sure you get prints off that bottle,' he said. 'Match them with the ones from the glass Candela brought in.'

'Doesn't matter if his prints are all over the place,' Fraser said. 'This is his girlfriend's flat.'

'But he'd never been here, remember?'

'Yeah, but the only person who can corroborate that is the girl and she's pavement pizza, so what's the point?'

There was a sudden burst of laughter from the balcony.

'The Spanish are even more hard-arsed about this stuff than we are,' Fraser said. 'Some of the *jokes*.'

'Just get the prints.' Thorne turned and began unzipping his body-suit as he walked quickly towards the door.

'Where are you off to?' Fraser asked, two steps behind him again.

'A bit more sightseeing,' Thorne said.

The villa was at the edge of one of the countless golf resorts that had been developed beneath the Sierra Blanca, and it was more exclusive than most. At the highest point of a winding road, Thorne could not see any neighbouring properties, and though he had not followed the perimeter fence for any distance, he guessed that there was a fair amount of land attached to it. Plenty for a man to stroll around and feel good about himself.

However hard that might otherwise be.

319

There were solid metal gates at the end of the driveway, and from what Thorne could remember from the helicopter pictures he had been shown, it was about a quarter of a mile from them to the house itself. Thorne could not see any security cameras, but he did not much care if he was seen anyway.

He rang the bell and waited. Rang again, then stepped back and walked a few yards along the perimeter fence. Densely cultivated firs obscured the view, so he moved back to the gates, pushing the sweat out of his eyes with the heels of his hands. He pressed the bell one more time, then leaned down to the speaker that was built into a concrete post. He had no idea if anyone was listening.

'You made another mistake, Alan,' he said. He could hear nothing but the low buzz of power lines overhead and the humming of cicadas. 'Your last one . . .'

He turned at the sound of a vehicle approaching and watched a white VW Golf coming around the steep bend that led to the villa. The car slowed when the driver saw him, then stopped altogether. Thorne took a few casual steps and recognised the man he had seen watching him on his first two nights in Mijas. The man who may or may not be working for Alan Langford.

Thorne and the driver looked at each other for ten seconds before Thorne began walking quickly towards the car. The gravel spat as the driver immediately threw the Golf into a three-point turn. Thorne started to run, but there was never any chance of him catching it. He made a mental note of the number plate and was repeating it to himself as the Golf disappeared around the corner and his phone rang.

It was Holland.

'How did it go in Nottingham, Dave?'

'Chris Talbot is definitely our man,' Holland said. '*Was* our man, whatever. But listen, there's a photo you need to see.' He told Thorne about the rugby picture, about the man whose face he had recognised.

Thorne felt what might have been a bead of sweat, or an insect crawling across the nape of his neck. He had already forgotten the

VW's number plate. 'It's not *that* strange, is it? Considering the team.' He began walking back towards his car.

'Not if it was just that, but Sonia Murray called from Wakefield. They did a random search of Jeremy Grover's cell last week and found a mobile phone.'

'Last *week*? So why are we only hearing about this now?'

Holland explained standard HMP protocol in such circumstances, as it had been explained to him by Murray. The phone had immediately been sent to the prison's security department in case it contained pictures of officers or keys, and from there to an outside technical support unit. The techies had extracted data from the SIM card, including the numbers of all incoming and outgoing calls, and had then passed the information on to Murray.

'If she hadn't been on the ball, we might never have heard about it,' Holland said. 'But she thought we might be interested in the calls made and received in the few days before Monahan was killed. And *on* the day . . .'

'You've checked them out?'

'One number came up repeatedly.'

'Whose?'

Holland told him. The same man he had seen in the photograph at Alison Hobbs' house. A mobile registered in his wife's name.

'Grover sent a text the day he killed Monahan,' Holland said. 'And he was called back a few hours later. The same thing happened the day after Cook was killed.'

Thorne reached the car and leaned against it for a few seconds.

'There's your jungle drums,' Holland said.

Thorne opened the door and climbed in, turned on the ignition and waited for the cold air. He ran through conversations from two months before. Let the pieces fall into place.

'Sir? Tom . . . ?'

'We use him to get Langford,' Thorne said. He was thinking aloud, but he knew it was the best chance they had. The only chance. 'We can use him, but we need to get him *here*, all right?'

321

'How do we do that?'

'Piece of piss,' Thorne said.

Suddenly he knew exactly what needed to be done. And he knew just the man to do it.

FORTY-THREE

'For Christ's sake, drink your beer,' Langford said. 'And relax, will you?'

A clink of glasses, or bottles maybe, and the sound of something ticking fast in the background.

'I don't know how you can be so calm. We're in trouble here.'

'I don't agree.'

'How can you—?'

'Getting worked up doesn't do anybody any good.'

'They're really turning the screws on Grover.'

'Everything can be sorted. As long as you've been careful.'

'Course I have.'

'So, no problem then.'

'Thorne's not going to give this one up, I'm telling you.'

'He'll have to, eventually. Chasing lost causes always pisses the brass off in the end. Well, *you* know that.'

'You should never have done the girl.'

Just that ticking for ten seconds or more then the scrape of a chair against the tiles.

'You're sweating like a pig, mate,' Langford said, laughing. 'Take your shirt off, have a dip in the pool.'

'I'm fine.'

A throat cleared loudly . . .

'If he takes his shirt off, we're in big trouble,' Samarez said.

Thorne shrugged. 'Not as much trouble as *he'll* be in.'

They were sitting in the back of a van with blacked-out windows and the name of a plumbing company on the side. It was parked in a small turning a hundred yards or so from the gates, but with a clear view of them. The conversation at the villa was coming through loud and clear, with the voice of the man wearing the wire only a little more distinct than Langford's. He'd been told to get as close as he could.

'It's a decent enough microphone, though,' Thorne had told him as the wire was being fitted. 'So, no need to sit on his lap . . .'

Now, up at the villa, Langford was telling his visitor how warm the pool was. 'Like a bath,' he said.

The other man said he wasn't much for swimming.

'We have not discussed what we should do if this does not . . . work out,' Samarez said.

'Damn, I knew we'd forgotten something,' Thorne said. He pretended to think about it for a few seconds, to *give* a toss. 'I suggest we just sit here and listen to him getting battered.'

'Well, for a while, perhaps.' Samarez was wearing the headphones, while Thorne was sitting close to a small speaker on the table next to the receiving equipment.

Next to him, Andy Boyle shifted his folding chair nearer to the speaker. 'He's pushing it too hard, if you ask me.'

'Maybe,' Thorne said.

They listened for another minute.

'How do we know the tosser's not writing notes?' Boyle asked. '"Say nothing" or whatever.'

Thorne shook his head. 'He's deep in the shit and this is his only chance of keeping his head above it.'

'Hope you're right,' Boyle said.

★

Thorne had met the Yorkshireman at the airport two days before. Boyle had shaken his hand, said it was a damn sight warmer than Wakefield.

'Thanks for doing this, Andy,' Thorne had said.

Boyle had glanced at the man he had brought with him. 'An absolute fucking *pleasure*, mate.' Still holding on to Thorne's hand, Boyle had leaned in close to Thorne and said, 'Really sorry about the lass.'

'I know . . .'

Then, as if embarrassed to show too much of a soft side without so much as a single drink inside him, Boyle had stepped away and pointed an accusing finger. 'Oh, and you never sent my pants back by the way . . .'

Thorne had not spoken to Boyle's fellow passenger – the one in plastic cuffs – until a couple of hours later when Thorne had felt good and ready. Only once he, Boyle and Samarez had had a chance to put their heads together and Gary Brand had been given an hour or so to stew in a Guardia Civil safe house.

'Not quite as clever as your boss, then,' Thorne had said. 'Very careless all this phone business, but I'm guessing you were stitched up by somebody else.'

Brand was sweating in a grey suit. They had deliberately not given him the opportunity to change out of it. They wanted him hot and bothered. He said nothing for a few seconds, then sat back and folded his arms. 'Cook was a twat,' he said. 'A *greedy* twat. Like he wasn't getting paid well enough anyway.'

'He took the phone in.'

Brand nodded. 'He was supposed to give Grover a clean handset every week and get rid of the old one, but he thought he'd make a few extra quid by selling them to other prisoners. So . . .'

'Can't get the staff,' Thorne said.

He had put it all together over the week or so it had taken to arrange for Brand's transfer to Spain. The nuts and bolts of Brand's deception. The extent of his own stupidity.

'Mind you, Langford's probably not the easiest employer to work for, right?'

'He was not my *employer*,' Brand said.

Thorne smiled, sour. 'Well, not in the sense of holiday pay and a P45, maybe, but in all the ways that mattered, he *owned* you.'

It was now clear that Brand had been in Langford's pocket throughout the original investigation and probably for a good while before, that once the new inquiry had begun, he had cleverly wormed his way back into Thorne's confidence. Brand had turned up in the Oak the night of the Chambers verdict and 'bumped into' Thorne, maintaining his trust from that point on through a series of conversations – many instigated by Thorne himself – and by feeding Thorne useless names to check out. He had convincingly portrayed an officer – a *friend* – with as much interest in putting Alan Langford away as Thorne, while he was busy making the arrangements for Monahan and Cook to be killed.

And Anna Carpenter.

'Let's talk about Detective Constable Chris Talbot, shall we?'

'This isn't a formal interview.'

'Just a chat.'

'So, nothing is admissible in court.'

'Plenty of time for that,' Thorne said. 'So, was it your idea to use Talbot?' He watched Brand thinking.

Brand already knew that he could not escape serious corruption charges, but he was treading carefully, reluctant to say anything that might lead to him also being charged as an accessory to murder.

'We know you knew him.'

'So, I knew him. And . . . ?'

'And I'm guessing that he was getting too close to your pal Alan. Or maybe he found out that *you* were.'

'I played rugby with a lot of people, all right?'

'Either way, he was the perfect choice to take Langford's place. You needed a body *and* you needed Talbot out of the way. You might even have been there when he was put in that car and burned alive.'

'That's bollocks.'

'You might just as well have been.'

'I wasn't . . .'

'Same as you might just as well have stuck that shiv into Monahan or fired the shot that killed Anna Carpenter.'

Brand visibly tensed at the mention of Anna's name, as though well aware that they were stepping into extremely dangerous territory. 'I knew nothing about that.'

'Really?'

'I swear—'

'You're a lying cunt.' Thorne leaned forward fast. 'Now, give me the name of the shooter and I *might* not come across this table and rip your head off.'

Brand held Thorne's stare, but not for long. 'We need to talk about how this deal is going to work,' he said.

'You're going to prison,' Thorne said. '*That's* how it's going to work. Even if you get Alan Langford marching out of that villa with his hands in the air confessing to half a dozen murders and begging us to nick him, you're going to prison. But it's all about *which* prison. You do this the right way, and you might not end up sharing a wing with some of the people you've put away. Men with a few grudges and plenty of time to get a toothbrush nice and sharp.'

'How long?'

'Not my decision, mate, but if you end up in the wrong place, that won't really matter, will it?' Thorne sat back again, giving Brand a few moments to take it in. 'You should consider yourself very lucky that there's *anything* you can do to make your life a bit easier, and you can be sure that's only because I want Langford even more than I want you.'

'Don't expect me to be grateful.'

'What you should be is careful,' Thorne said. 'Because if you don't do this right, I'll happily throw you to the fucking wolves.' There was a gratifying flash of panic for the first time in Brand's eyes. 'Nothing to worry about, Gary. Like you said, this isn't a formal interview.'

Just a chat . . .

★

Langford was now telling Brand about some of the development projects he was involved with and Brand was saying very little. Thorne imagined him sitting there nodding, trying to look relaxed, wondering how he could get Langford to admit anything, waiting for an opening. Brand had been instructed that he should not force the issue under any circumstances, as much to avoid the suggestion of entrapment further down the line as anything else, but he was clearly running out of ideas.

'So, what about Grover, then?' Brand asked.

In the van, Thorne, Boyle and Samarez looked at one another.

'What about him?'

'You want me to organise anything?'

'I'm going to organise a couple more beers . . .'

Samarez grunted in frustration while Thorne kicked out at the side of the van.

'Langford's cagey as fuck,' Boyle said. 'You think he might be on to it?'

Thorne knew that it was possible. Brand had never been to visit Langford in Spain before, so his 'insistence' on making this trip could easily have given Langford serious misgivings. They had briefed Brand as thoroughly as possible in the time available. He had been instructed to talk about Candela Bernal and to reveal that evidence was mounting against Grover, who was finally starting to crack under pressure from Andy Boyle, but even that might not be enough to draw Langford out. Thorne recalled the man who had joined him at the bar in Ronda. He was certainly confident, and Thorne wondered if that was bred not just of the power he possessed, but of a faith in his own ability to sniff out danger.

'Yeah, he might be,' Thorne said.

The evidence Brand had already provided was sufficient to get Langford arrested and extradited for trial in the UK, but without an admission on tape, Thorne could not bank on a conviction. He knew better than anyone that even the most solid of cases could fall apart, that any half-decent brief might persuade a jury that Brand was no more than a bent copper trying to save his own skin. There was every chance that Langford would be back in Spain before his tan had begun to fade.

There was no way Thorne could let that happen. He owed it to himself and to too many others.

'Here you go, mate,' Langford said. 'A nice cold one.'

'Cheers.'

'You sure you don't fancy a swim?'

Gary Brand was the only shot Thorne had.

FORTY-FOUR

Langford sipped his beer and wondered what Brand's game was. He'd always been able to sniff out anything iffy, had prided himself on the fact, and though he couldn't be sure exactly what was happening, something was definitely starting to stink.

All the same, he had to tread carefully.

'What happened to that girl you were seeing?' Brand asked.

'I see a lot of girls.'

'Yeah, but one was a bit special, wasn't she?'

'I chucked her,' Langford said.

Worst possible scenario, the arsehole had grassed him up to save himself and was wearing a microphone. All that shit about not being much for swimming. But dealing with it would be tricky to say the least. There were consequences to be considered whichever way it went, and until then he just needed to watch his temper, to keep his wits about him. There was not a great deal he could do for the time being, other than mind his Ps and Qs and let things play out.

What else could he do? Rip the sneaky little fucker's shirt off then and there?

If he was wrong, he'd risk losing someone who had been a valuable source of information for over ten years. Brand was very useful, no question about it, and Langford didn't particularly want to piss him off by coming on like some paranoid nutcase. If he was right, though, things might get even more complicated. He'd been kidding himself, thinking he could play this whole thing like Clint Eastwood or whatever and stay calm. He should have seen that back when he was slapping that silly fucker in the club who'd used his real name. He was still capable of losing his rag, same as anyone else . . . same as he'd done the last time he'd seen Candela . . . and if he *did* find out that Brand was having him over, he could easily end up having to push a bottle into the mongrel's face or seeing how long he could stay underwater.

It would feel good, course it would. It would feel *merited*. But if the conversation *was* being monitored, if his new friend from Ronda was listening in, it might not turn out to be the smartest thing he'd ever done.

He needed to keep on his toes, simple as that.

He'd always loved that line from *The Godfather*, the one about keeping your friends close and your enemies closer. Something the Pacino character had been taught by his old man. Loads of good stuff in that movie of course, but that bit was right on the money.

If Brand was no longer a friend, Langford needed to keep him as close as possible.

'How long you planning on staying, Gary?'

'I'll go back tomorrow,' Brand said. 'In and out.'

'That's good. Presumably you can't just waltz off to Spain without your bosses getting suspicious, can you?'

'I had some holiday owing, so . . .'

'That's a bit of luck.'

Brand took a long swig of beer. Then another to empty the bottle.

'Got yourself a decent hotel?'

Brand swallowed fast. 'A place in Malaga. In the old town.'

'What's it called?'

'The hotel?'

'Yeah, I've stayed in quite a few places down there, might be able to recommend a couple of decent restaurants.'

'It's one of those boutique-type places,' Brand said. 'There's a chain of them, I think. Room Mate? Something like that, anyway. Nice enough.'

No real hesitation. Well briefed or on the level, it was hard to tell the difference . . .

A young girl stepped on to the deck from inside the house. She wore a thin, pale blue sarong over a white bikini and a sullen expression. Brand turned to look at her.

'You remember Ellie?' Langford asked.

'Course I do.'

'Last time you saw her she'd have been what, seven or eight?'

Brand said hello. The girl mumbled it back at him.

'Go and get us another couple of beers,' Langford said. 'There's a good girl. Actually, make it four, will you? I reckon we're on for a heavy session here.' He pointed at Brand. 'You hungry, mate? We could rustle up a sandwich or something . . .'

'I ate on the plane,' Brand said.

The girl turned and went back into the house without another word. Langford watched her go, then grinned at Brand.

'She's grown up,' Brand said.

'She looks so much like her mother did at that age it's not true.'

Brand nodded. Langford finished his beer. They both looked out across the swimming pool for a minute or more.

'Listen . . . we really need to talk about what we're going to do,' Brand said. 'That police liaison officer – Murray . . . she's been getting far too cosy with Andy Boyle and it's starting to look like they've got some serious ammunition to use on Grover, you know? Organising something at Wakefield is obviously going to be trickier now that Howard Cook's gone, but—'

Langford cut him off. 'Of course, I would have been happy to put you up here, but I don't think that's a clever idea.'

Brand took a few seconds, and Langford saw frustration on his face that was every bit as obvious as the sweat patches under his arms. He had few doubts now about what was happening; fewer still that disposing of Brand would be even easier than getting rid of Candela had been.

Another one he would happily handle himself.

'The hotel's fine, honestly.'

Laughing, Langford nodded towards the house. 'Some of the locals are already wondering what I'm doing shacked up with a girl who's young enough to be my daughter. Last thing I need is them thinking I'm on the bloody turn!' He laughed again, louder. 'So, we probably shouldn't spend too much time together.'

'No.'

'Especially now that we've got the Met's finest running around the place.'

FORTY-FIVE

Especially now that we've got the Met's finest running around the place.

In the van, Thorne bristled slightly. For a second or two, he thought Langford had worked it all out and was cheerfully taking the piss. Thought the last remark had been meant specifically for him. He glanced at Samarez and Boyle, and could see that they were thinking much the same thing.

'So, what do you want to do?' Thorne asked.

'Not much we *can* do,' Samarez said.

'We sit it out, then.'

'Right.' Boyle lifted the bottom of his T-shirt and flapped it, revealing a generous roll of pallid beer-gut in his efforts to cool down. 'Let's see if Langford gives us what we want before we roast to death.'

Brand had arrived at the villa in a taxi driven by a Guardia Civil officer, but Thorne and the others had been in position well in advance of that. By now, they had been there almost two hours, and the inside of the van was baking and airless. As an observer, Boyle had seen no reason to wear anything even remotely formal, but Thorne had felt unable to dress quite so casually for this sort of operation. He was sweating in khakis and a short-sleeved shirt, sucking in warm air that tasted of sweat, while Samarez, who was wearing a similar outfit, did not look a great deal happier.

'Perhaps we could just arrest him,' Samarez suggested. 'Confront him with what Brand has told us.'

'Arrest him for what?'

'We can come up with something.'

'He knows that Brand isn't a reliable witness,' Thorne said. 'And anyway, whatever Brand might say, he knows we've got nothing concrete to tie him into any of the big stuff.'

They listened for another few minutes. Again Brand said how worried he was about what was happening back at home, that he needed Langford to tell him what to do. Langford ignored him, refusing to bite and began talking about some film he'd seen. Told Brand he *had* to get the DVD out when he got home.

'I think we're stuffed,' Boyle said. 'He hasn't even admitted knowing who Grover *is* and we haven't got him within a million miles of the Anna Carpenter killing.'

'All we need is one slip,' Samarez said.

Thorne drank deeply from a bottle of water that was already warm. His shirt was pasted to his back and he was starting to catch the smell of his own sweat.

One slip . . .

You're not much of a detective, are you?

The first words Anna ever said to him.

A radio squawked and Samarez reached for the handset next to the speaker. He talked in Spanish for a few seconds, then told the others, 'There's a car coming.'

They waited, watching the gates, knowing that any vehicle passing the Guardia Civil car positioned down the hill could only be on its way to the Langford villa. After a minute or so, a white VW Golf pulled up outside the gates.

'I know that car,' Thorne said.

He recognised the driver, too, but could not get a clear view of the woman sitting next to him. Then the passenger door opened. The woman got out and walked up to the gates.

'Donna . . .'

Samarez looked confused. 'The *wife?*'

'What's she doing here?' Boyle asked.

They heard a faint buzzing through the speaker: the microphone picking up the noise of Donna ringing the bell. Langford said, 'Won't be a minute,' then there was nothing but Brand's breathing.

Thorne realised now that the man watching him had been working for Donna. She had clearly hired herself another detective. He had probably been watching Samarez and Fraser, too. Then, as soon as he had found Langford's villa, he had fed the information back to his client.

'Oh, Jesus,' Thorne said. 'She's here for her daughter.'

There was a minute of muffled conversation, then silence until Langford returned to the pool and Donna climbed back into the car.

'It's my ex-wife,' Langford told Brand. 'Why am I so popular all of a sudden?'

'*What?*'

Thorne watched as the gates begin to swing slowly open.

'You'd best make yourself scarce, Gary,' Langford said. 'She might recognise you. You wouldn't want that, right?'

'What the hell does she want?'

'Well, I don't think she's popped by for tea and biscuits, do you?'

In the van, they could hear the rasp of Brand's breathing and the sharp scrape of his chair against the tiles. As he walked away from the pool and moved inside the house, Brand whispered into the microphone, 'This is all going tits up.'

'You're telling me,' Boyle said.

The Golf was disappearing from view, heading up the driveway, when Langford shouted Ellie's name somewhere in the house. Thorne moved quickly towards the rear of the van.

'Where are you going?' Samarez asked.

Thorne was already opening the doors. 'This could all get very nasty very quickly,' he said.

'What about Brand?'

'I don't care.' Thorne jumped down on to the path, talking fast. 'Langford's not exactly predictable right now, and if Donna's come for Ellie, I can't see him just handing her over, can you?'

'We do not have enough,' Samarez said.

Boyle shook his head. 'We don't have *anything*.'

'Keep listening,' Thorne said, slamming one of the doors. 'He might get careless now that he's got something else to worry about.'

He slammed the other door before Boyle or Samarez could argue and sprinted towards the gates. He stopped momentarily when he reached them, to check that the Golf was out of sight, then slipped through just before they closed with a clang.

He waited for ten seconds, fifteen, his hands on his knees, panting. His mouth was dry and the spit he sucked up tasted coppery.

Like he was waiting to face a bull.

Then, still breathless, Thorne began jogging uphill towards the house.

FORTY-SIX

It took Thorne three or four minutes to reach the house, but it felt like a lot longer. The Golf was parked outside, and though Thorne would have loved to tell the man in the driver's seat precisely what he thought of him, there wasn't time. He settled for a hard stare and the satisfying look of panic on the private detective's face as he walked past the car.

The door to the villa was open and Thorne could hear shouting from inside. He stepped into a large, vaulted lobby. There were acres of white marble, potted palms whose leaves almost brushed the glass roof and a staircase that swept up and around to his right. He walked beneath it, his breathing and heart-rate finally beginning to slow a little, and followed a tiled corridor towards the far side of the villa, towards the screams of rage and frustration that echoed off the tastefully decorated walls.

'Well, you've wasted your fucking time . . .'

'Christ, what's he done?'

'What's *he* done?'

'Please . . .'

'You really are a stupid bitch, aren't you?'

Just before the corridor ended, Thorne passed a room whose door was slightly ajar. He pushed it open and saw Gary Brand, sitting and flicking through a newspaper as though it were a doctor's waiting room. Brand looked up, alarmed, and opened his mouth to say something.

Thorne put a finger to his lips as a glass shattered somewhere near by.

'You've lost it, love.'

'Just tell her to go . . .'

Brand tried to stand up, but Thorne pushed him back into his seat. Told him quietly but firmly to shut his mouth and stay where he was. Then he stepped back into the corridor, took another few paces and peered around the corner.

'You heard what she said.'

'I'm not going anywhere.'

'Maybe I should call the police . . .'

Thorne was now at the entrance to a large, open-plan seating area. There was a pool table and a white piano beyond the L-shaped sofa. On the far side was what looked like a well-stocked bar, with rows of bottles in gleaming optics and vintage movie posters framed on the wall above.

The Dirty Dozen. Where Eagles Dare. The Italian Job.

The room led directly out, through an open pair of sliding doors, to the pool, and from where he was standing, Thorne had a clear view of the action.

Langford was sitting on the edge of a sunlounger, with Ellie standing behind him. A few feet away, on the other side of a glass-topped table, Donna stood, her fists clenched at her side and her eyes fixed on her daughter's right hand, which was resting on Langford's shoulder.

'I was struggling not to laugh out loud,' Langford said, 'when that copper accused me of "taking" her.' He glanced up at Ellie. 'She couldn't wait to get over here, could you, love?'

'I *dreamed* about it.' Ellie squeezed her father's shoulder, but spat the words across at her mother. 'Just had to wait until I was eighteen, so nobody would bother looking too hard.'

'For ten years, you were all I thought about,' Donna said.

'Oh, I thought about you, too. Only not quite in the same way.'

'That last day I saw you, before the trial, you cried and cried and begged them not to take me away.' Donna's voice was weak and cracked. 'You wouldn't let go of my arm.'

'I was a kid,' Ellie said. 'I was stupid.'

'No . . .'

'I didn't know what you'd done. What you'd tried to do. I didn't know what a vicious cow you were, did I?'

'But I did it for *you*.'

'You tried to kill my *father*!'

'For *us*.'

'You didn't think about *me*, how I would feel.'

'That was *all* I thought about, I swear. All those years . . .'

'Funny,' Langford said. 'I thought you were too busy becoming a rug-muncher to give a shit.'

Even from his vantage point twenty feet away, Thorne could see the hatred etched into Donna's face.

'When did you contact her?' she asked.

Langford thought about it. 'About eighteen months after I got here, once I was settled. I got word to her, had a few friends keep an eye out, passed on some money whenever she needed it. We started making plans for you to come out here fairly early on, didn't we, love?'

Ellie nodded.

Donna was shaking her head as though trying to make sense of what she was hearing. 'I don't understand,' she said. When she looked across at Ellie, it was as if Donna herself had become the child. 'I don't understand . . .'

Thorne had seen and heard enough. He stepped into the open and watched as Langford spotted the movement, focused on him . . . then smiled.

'I thought you must be knocking about somewhere,' Langford said.

Donna and Ellie both stared at Thorne – the daughter looking straight through him, the mother ashen.

Langford held out his arms. 'Come and join our happy family reunion.'

Thorne walked on to the pool deck and across to Donna.

'Careful of the broken glass,' Langford said. He nodded towards the green shards at the edge of the pool, the remains of a beer bottle. 'My ex has been playing up.'

'I don't understand,' Donna said again. 'What about the photos? Somebody sent me those photographs . . .'

'You're even more stupid than I thought,' Ellie snapped.

Thorne had already worked it out, but it took Donna a few seconds. 'You?'

Langford looked up at his daughter. '*What?*'

'I was going to explain—'

'*You* sent the pictures?'

Ellie nodded, opened her mouth again to speak.

'Have you *any* idea what you've done?' He pushed her hand away from his shoulder. 'How much fucking trouble you've caused. How much you've *cost* me?'

'What trouble might that be, Alan?' Thorne asked.

Langford turned slowly and glared at him. He said nothing, but the blood that had rushed to his face was clear enough, even through the tan.

Donna was still looking at her daughter. 'Why?'

Ellie sniffed, spoke as though she were telling someone the time. 'Because I wanted you to know that you'd been sitting in prison for killing someone who wasn't dead. I wanted you to see what a great life he was living while yours had turned to shit. I wanted you to *suffer.*'

It was clear that Ellie Langford had got her wish. Donna took a faltering step forward but then had to lean down and hold on to the table to keep from falling.

Thorne moved forward and laid a hand on her arm. Said, 'I think it's time to go.'

'Yeah, look after yourself, Mum,' Ellie said.

Thorne stared at her, saw the sarcastic sneer replaced by the same

341

sullen pout he had seen in the photographs of Ellie as a young teenager.

She cocked her head. 'What?' A challenge.

Donna gently removed Thorne's hand from her arm. She still seemed bewildered, disoriented. 'But the photos were posted in London.'

'Jesus, I've still got *friends* in London.' Ellie nodded dismissively at Thorne. 'I would have thought PC Plod could have worked that one out.'

'But it was like you'd been . . . *taken*. You just vanished.'

'Nice clean start,' Langford said. He was trying to sound calm, but was obviously still shaken by Ellie's admission. 'Best way. Same thing I did.'

'Plus, *he* didn't want anyone sniffing around over here,' Thorne said. 'That's why her passport was left behind, why he got her out of the country on the quiet.'

Langford smirked. 'What? Are you going to do me for people smuggling?'

'If I have to.'

'Bring it on,' Langford said, aggressive suddenly. 'Sounds like fun.'

'Why didn't you at least tell your foster parents you were all right?' Thorne asked.

The girl seemed more concerned with a few stray hairs that had been loosened by the breeze than with the devastation she was casually wreaking.

Thorne tried to keep the disgust from his voice, not wanting to give her the satisfaction. 'Have you any idea what they've been going through?'

Ellie shrugged. 'Not that it's any of your business, but I would have told Maggie and Julian eventually.' She spoke their names mockingly, like a bad comedian taking the piss. 'They'll survive, don't worry. They've got their precious Sam, anyway. I was always going to be second best once he came along.'

Now Thorne could see the extent to which this pretty, dark-haired teenager was dead inside. Cold and hard as stone. Sending the pictures had been only part of it. Not letting the Munros know she was alive and well had all been in the cause of torturing her mother, and she had been happy for Donna to believe that she was dead. Thorne watched her tuck her hair behind her ears and realised that, although Ellie Langford had inherited her mother's looks, all the things that defined her had come from her father.

Donna was staring at the floor, muttering.

'You'll have to speak up, love,' Langford said.

'You've no idea,' Donna said. She raised her head and looked at her daughter. Pleading. 'What it was like with *him*. The things he did, the things he made *me* do, the way he made me feel. What was I supposed to do?'

'God, here we go,' Langford said.

Donna lurched towards Ellie, and for a second panic replaced boredom on the girl's face. 'He did *this*,' Donna screamed. She reached out to show the flash of pink, puckered skin across the back of her hand. 'Look at what he did to me . . .'

Ellie had already recovered herself. She shrugged. 'That routine didn't work in court, so don't try it on me, OK?'

Donna let her arm drop and turned her head to stare across the pool. She looked hollowed out and hopeless.

Thorne took a step towards her. 'Come on now, Donna.'

She didn't move.

'Christ, she won't take a hint, will she?' The girl's voice was raised suddenly, shrill and contemptuous. 'It's not like I didn't make it clear enough when I spoke to her "girlfriend".' The distaste was obvious. 'I told her I never wanted to see the bitch again, that I'd happily let her die in prison. I told her I didn't even *have* a mother.'

There were a few seconds of silence then, save for the sound of the pool cleaner sucking its way across the bottom of the pool, ticking and slurping at the end of its long hose. Donna finally turned away from her daughter and began to walk slowly towards the sliding doors, listing slightly as though she were a little drunk.

'I need a drink,' she said. 'Some water . . .'

Thorne watched her disappear inside, sympathy fighting for space with guilt now that he finally understood what Kate had kept from her . . . and why. It had been a small lie – a simple and tender not-telling – to protect the thing that Donna cherished more than anything else.

He knew better than most that love could cause as much damage and death as hate ever did.

'So, what do we do now?' Langford asked. 'You fancy a dip, Mr Thorne?'

Thorne said nothing. He would not rise to Langford's bait, and besides, he was too busy wondering if the people-smuggling charge might provide some sort of starting point. If there was anything he could feasibly nick the daughter for.

'I wonder where your mate Gary's got to,' Langford said. 'Still skulking around inside somewhere in case Donna sees him, I suppose. Not that it really matters much any more.' He watched Ellie as she calmly lay down on an adjacent sunbed, then pointed to his ears. 'Hear anything interesting, by the way?'

'Just bullshit and bravado,' Thorne said. 'The sound of someone running out of time.'

Langford lay back on his sunbed. 'Yeah, the pressure's terrible.' He reached for a paperback on a small table, then, almost as if he'd forgotten that Thorne was there at all, said, 'You can let yourself out.'

Thorne watched, feeling the hate bubble up and the blood beating in his veins. Then he saw Langford glance towards the doors and sit up suddenly. He heard Ellie say, 'Dad . . . ?'

Donna walked calmly on to the deck, pointing a gun. Her eyes were wide and unblinking, and when she spoke her voice was flat and low, almost robotic. 'Old habits, eh, Alan? Always slept with one of these near the bed. Always thinking ahead.'

Langford climbed cautiously off the lounger and backed away, his arms held out towards her. Ellie stood up too and edged towards her father. Thorne stayed where he was.

'This is stupid, Donna,' he said. 'Give the gun to me.'

He could not be sure if she heard him, if whatever voice was guiding her was simply too loud. She held the gun out further, two hands trembling around the butt as she continued to point it at Langford.

'He's right, it's stupid,' Langford said. He stepped towards Ellie and, for a second, Thorne thought he was going to use his daughter as a shield. He could not help but wonder, as time seemed to stand still, which of them would be the greater loss to the gene pool. 'What's the point of this, Donna?'

'I'm giving Ellie what she wanted,' Donna said. 'She wanted me to spend the rest of my life in prison and this seems as good a way as any. The best way, as a matter of fact.'

'I didn't mean it,' Ellie shouted.

'She didn't mean *any* of it.' Langford took a tentative step towards his ex-wife. 'The photos were just a bit of fun, that's all, love. Just a joke, for Pete's sake.'

Donna nodded slowly, said, 'Not funny,' then shot Langford in the chest.

Time had caught up with itself and then sped ahead long before the ringing in Thorne's ears had died down. Ellie screamed and kept screaming as Donna lowered the gun. Langford took two paces back and dropped, first to one knee, then on to his back at the side of the pool. Thorne heard Samarez shouting, 'Armed police!' and 'Drop the gun!' and watched Donna do as she was told, her face as calm as the water in the pool while the weapon slipped from her hand and clattered on to the deck.

Just a pop . . .

Samarez, Boyle and Thorne all ran to Donna, while Ellie rushed towards Langford and dropped to her knees beside his head. He was still moving, rocking up on to his side before collapsing back again. As soon as Donna had been restrained, Samarez walked back into the living area and took out his phone.

'Is someone going to *do* something?' Ellie shouted.

Thorne could hear Samarez talking fast, calling an ambulance or doing something far more important, such as letting his wife know that he'd be late for dinner. Gary Brand was standing near the piano, saying, 'What the hell happened?' as Boyle started to lead Donna inside. She mumbled a thank-you and there was the suggestion of a smile as she passed Thorne, although she never looked up at him.

Ellie Langford lifted her father's head off the ground and on to her lap. She removed a sliver of green glass from his neck and pressed her fingers to the wound as blood began to bubble and pulse. Not as much as was pouring from his chest, though, already dark and shiny against the cream tiles and spreading towards the edge of the pool.

Thorne walked slowly across and while the girl screamed abuse at him and reached up to pull at his shirt, he leaned forward to watch the first drops of Alan Langford's blood slide over the edge, plop quietly into the water and start to sink.

Each one breaking up just a little as it went down.

And between the sobs and the groans and the shouting from somewhere inside, the sound of the pool cleaner, still ticking and slurping as it went about its business.

PART FOUR

ALL RIGHT
TO TELL

FORTY-SEVEN

The swings were every bit as rusty and the goalposts still had no nets, but the small park in Seven Sisters now felt a little more like a place where someone might actually want to stroll or to sit for a while. The weather helped, of course. A spot of sunshine and a few clumps of daffodils always made things *look* better, no matter how much pain people were in.

'I'll wait for her, you know,' Kate said.

She and Thorne were on the same bench that he, Donna and Anna had chosen almost three months earlier. The day Anna had confronted the man with the dog. Thorne couldn't even hazard a guess as to when Donna might have the chance to sit there again. She was on remand in Holloway Prison, awaiting trial for the manslaughter of Alan Langford.

'You might be waiting a while,' he said.

'It's fine,' Kate said. 'Least I can do.'

'You shouldn't feel guilty.'

'Shouldn't I?'

'None of it was your fault.'

'If I'd told her, things would never have gone as far as they did.' She leaned back. The tattoo was partially visible above the collar of her black T-shirt, the first few letters of Donna's name. 'If I'd told her what a bitch her daughter was.'

'She would've been devastated,' Thorne said. 'And she would've hated you for it.'

'If I'm honest, that's what I was really afraid of. I keep telling myself that I kept my mouth shut to protect her, but really I was trying to protect the both of us.'

'Nothing wrong with that,' Thorne said.

Three boys ran on to the grass from the other side of the park. One of them kicked a ball high into the air, and there was a good deal of swearing as they argued about who would be going in goal.

'Your friend might still be alive as well,' Kate said.

Thorne said nothing. He was not interested in blaming anyone but himself. Anna was *his* scab to pick at.

'Donna was really upset about that. She really liked her.'

'There was a lot to like.'

Kate looked at him. 'You two were close, yeah?'

'She was a friend, that's all.'

'And that was all you wanted, was it?'

'Yeah, I think so. I don't know.' Thorne watched the kids playing football, two Arsenal shirts and one bare-chested. 'I didn't know her long enough for it to be anything, really. It was all just . . . silly.'

'You should have said something.'

Thorne shook his head.

'Best to be honest, trust me.'

'Maybe,' Thorne said. Whatever his feelings for Anna had been – and beyond a few moments of sheer fantasy, they had never been overtly sexual – they had been a symptom of something else. It was time to be honest with *himself* . . . and Louise. 'So, what are you going to do?' he asked. 'While you're waiting.'

Kate shrugged, smiled. She looked much older than the last time Thorne had seen her, and she would be a damn sight older still before she and Donna could be together again. 'Go to see her. Make sure she knows I'm not going anywhere, you know?'

'She knows,' Thorne said. He believed it, but he also believed that prison was exactly where Donna wanted to be right now. It was the only place where she felt she truly belonged.

'Fancy a drink?'

'When?'

'Now? The pub, or I've got a bottle indoors.'

Thorne glanced at his watch and said that he needed to be getting back. Kate told him that was fine, that she had things to do herself. It was clear that she knew exactly where he was going. The case against Donna was still being prepared, with statements being taken from all those present at the killing and Thorne himself as the main prosecution witness.

He would not lie about the shooting, of course, but nor would he hold back when describing the extent of the provocation Donna Langford received from her ex-husband and daughter; the mental torment that drove her to pull the trigger.

Best to be honest . . .

'What about tonight?' Kate asked.

'Sorry, I can't,' Thorne said. Andy Boyle was down from Wakefield and Thorne had promised to take him for a drink. It was likely to be a heavy session. 'I'll call you and we can fix up a night next week, maybe.'

'It's fine,' Kate said. 'I know you're busy.'

They sat for a few more minutes, then stood up and shook hands.

'I meant to say sorry,' Thorne said. 'That day when I was going on about what you did twenty years ago.'

Kate nodded, uncomfortable.

'You said I was out of order and you were right.'

'Just doing your job.'

'I shouldn't have dragged all that up.'

'It's not like I'd *forgotten* it,' Kate said. 'First thing I think of when I open my eyes in the morning.' She took a step away, then stopped. 'Maybe the second thing, now . . .'

Thorne was halfway back to Colindale when his mobile rang. Brigstocke told him he was in Jesmond's office and suggested, if

Thorne were not hands-free, that he might want to think about pulling over. Thorne laughed and said it sounded serious. Then Jesmond cut in. His voice was tinny on the speaker-phone, but the severity of his tone came through loud and clear as he calmly told Thorne that Andrea Keane had walked into a Brighton police station at ten-thirty the night before.

FORTY-EIGHT

'Where have you been, Andrea? I mean . . . the best part of a *year*.'

They were sitting in one of the briefing rooms at Becke House. It was not a formal interview, although Jesmond was seriously looking into bringing a charge of wasting police time against her.

'It might make us look a little less like bloody idiots,' he had said.

The Chief Superintendent had said a number of things since Andrea Keane's reappearance that Thorne would remember for a while. His favourite was: 'Well, the good news is she's alive. Hip-hip-hoo-bloody-ray. The bad news is we're fucked. All of us, but especially *you* . . .'

'Andrea . . . ?'

She was sitting across the table from Thorne, holding hands with her father. She looked very different from the girl in the pictures that had been so widely distributed after she had gone missing ten months before. She was at least a stone lighter and her hair had been cut short and dyed black.

She looked terrified.

'Have you any idea how much effort went into looking for you?' Thorne asked. 'Never mind the cost . . .'

'I'm sorry.' She looked at her father. He squeezed her hand. 'I don't know what else to say.'

'Just tell us the truth.'

Jesmond cleared his throat. He was sitting next to Thorne, though not quite close enough to hold hands. 'Take your time, Miss Keane. I know this must be difficult.'

Thorne could not resist a sideways glance. He felt like leaning across the table and letting Andrea and her father know what the caring–sharing chief superintendent really thought. Perhaps he could pass on a few of his senior officer's more sensitive pronouncements:

'OK, we lost the case, but with her alive we've lost the moral high ground as well.'

'What's going on around here? Why the hell can't the dead stay dead?'

But Thorne said nothing, largely because, deep down, he shared many of Jesmond's frustrations. He was not sorry that Andrea was still alive, never that: the look on Stephen Keane's face was enough to cheer anyone with an ounce of humanity. Even so, Thorne was sickened by the thought of the field day Adam Chambers and his high-powered friends would be enjoying right now. The self-righteous bilge that the newspapers would print over the days to follow. The shocking final chapter in Nick Maier's nauseating exposé.

'I was in Brighton for a while,' Andrea said. 'At Sarah's. Then I moved around a bit after that.'

'You were staying with Sarah Jackson?'

Andrea nodded.

Thorne sighed and looked at Jesmond. 'We interviewed her. *Twice.*'

'She's my mate, so she lied.'

'She deserves an Oscar, the performance she gave.'

'Is she going to get in trouble?'

'Maybe,' Thorne said. He watched Andrea nod slowly and try to blink back the tears that were brimming. 'What have you been doing? How did you live?'

'I just stayed at Sarah's flat for the first few months, until things had died down. Then she helped me get a cleaning job, cash in hand, so I was able to give her something for putting me up. Hiding me, like.'

'You've no idea,' Stephen Keane said.

'No, I haven't.'

'What she went through.'

Thorne nodded, said, 'You are going to have to tell us *why*, Andrea.'

'Yeah, I know.' Her voice was suddenly very small. A child's.

'It's all right, baby.' Stephen Keane leaned across to whisper and squeezed his daughter's hand again. 'It's all right to tell.'

She started talking fast, as though it were the only way she would be able to get it out, her eyes fixed on the edge of the desk and the hand that was not clasped inside her father's wrapped tight around the arm of her plastic chair. 'That night, I went back to his place . . . to Adam's place, after the lesson had finished. We had a couple of drinks, talked about other people in the class, just chatting, you know?' She took a deep breath, then ploughed on. 'I fancied him, if I'm honest. He was fit and he seemed dead nice. I knew he had a girlfriend, but he said things weren't so great between them, so I didn't feel too bad about it . . . Like I said, we had a few drinks, listened to some music. He was pretending he knew a lot about wine, sniffing the cork when it came out of the bottle and stuff, and I knew he was full of shit but I didn't really care. He put his arm round me and I let him. I *wanted* him to.'

She glanced up at Thorne, then turned to look at her father. He smiled and nodded. Said, 'It's OK.'

'We were kissing or whatever for a few minutes and then suddenly his hands were all over the place.' Her own hand moved from the arm of the chair as she spoke, passed lightly across her chest and down to her lap. 'They were everywhere, you know . . . his fingers. I told him I had to get home because I had an early start, but really I was starting to feel like it was a big mistake, like I'd really messed up, even though he was whispering and telling me how great it was going to be. How long he could . . . keep going. I told him to stop.' She looked up again and suddenly there was strength in her voice. 'I *told* him to stop and I *wasn't* drunk. It was just a couple of glasses and I was . . . *not* drunk.

355

'But he was really strong, you know? He used to show off during the lessons, bench-pressing and all that, using a few of the girls like they were weights, so when he started to get rough there was nothing I could do. He kept talking to me . . . while he was doing it, saying he knew how much I wanted it, that his girlfriend used to pretend that she didn't like it rough, but he knew *she* was a lying bitch as well. I just closed my eyes until it was over, tried not to make any noise, but . . . he hurt me.

'He hurt me . . .

'Then I got dressed and he was watching me, saying there was no point telling anybody, because I'd wanted to go back to his flat and I'd been drinking and nobody would believe that I hadn't been begging him for it.'

She paused and Jesmond began to say something about how sensitively offences of this nature were now handled. But Thorne was not really listening and neither was Andrea Keane.

'When I left,' she said, looking at Thorne, 'he just sat there, sniffing his fingers, same as he'd done with the cork. *Appreciating* it. Like I was just some . . . bottle he'd opened.'

Her father moaned next to her.

'I couldn't go home, I couldn't bear facing anyone for a while, so I called Sarah and she drove up to collect me. I didn't mean to stay away for so long. I mean, it wasn't like I had a plan or anything, but when I knew everyone was looking for me it just got harder and harder to come back. Then I saw that he'd been arrested, so . . .'

She looked up and it was clear that she'd finished. Now her father's face was streaked with tears. Jesmond reached into his pocket for a handkerchief, but it was ignored.

'So, why now?' Thorne asked. 'Why did you come back now?'

'Because he got off. Because he walked out of that courtroom like butter wouldn't melt and I watched him on the TV and saw him in the papers and it felt like he was doing it to me all over again. Like he was doing it to *everyone*.'

'What if he hadn't got off? Would you have done nothing and let him go down for murder?'

356

'Like a shot,' she said. 'Even if it meant staying away for good. Knowing he'd been punished for *something* would have made that worth it.'

'What about your parents? How could you not have told them you were OK?' Thorne blinked as he remembered asking Ellie Langford almost exactly the same question a few weeks before.

'I would have let them know,' Andrea said. 'And they would have understood.' She looked at her father. 'They'd have kept the secret.'

Stephen Keane nodded, sat back and wiped his face. 'So . . . that's it.'

'Right,' Jesmond said. 'Thanks . . .'

As the chief superintendent started to talk about taking statements, sympathy and determination seemed to be etched in equal measure across his puffy features. But Thorne knew how skilled the man was at showing people what they needed or wanted to see. In reality, Jesmond was feeling nothing but pure and simple relief.

Thorne felt something a whole lot darker.

FORTY-NINE

Thorne and Kitson were sitting in an unmarked car outside a house in Cricklewood. The street was quiet, lined with flowering oaks. Adam Chambers had moved in only a few weeks before, and Thorne wondered how much assorted publishers and tabloid editors were contributing to the mortgage.

'What are you waiting for?' Kitson asked. She did not receive an answer. 'Come on, we know he's in there.'

'There's no rush.'

'Really? You must have averaged sixty miles an hour all the way here . . .'

Thorne stared at the house. He tried to sort things out in his mind, to compartmentalise, but it was impossible. A few months earlier, Andrea Keane had become Ellie Langford, then Candela Bernal, and now, however much he tried to be professional and pretend otherwise, all of the victims were blurring into one. A young woman who had not been cut out to work in a bank. Who talked too much and told stupid jokes, and who had been absolutely right when she'd called him a fuck-up.

There was no point kidding himself.

This was for Anna every bit as much as it was for Andrea.

He got out of the car and slammed the door. A few seconds later, Kitson did the same, and the sun bled butter through a gash in the clouds as they began walking towards Adam Chambers' front door.

'He'll wish he'd killed her,' Thorne said.

Acknowledgements

I am hugely grateful to the many people who have helped make this book so much better than it would otherwise have been . . .

The input and support from everyone at Little, Brown has been invaluable as always, most notably of course from the peerless David Shelley, while the 'furniture' that my agent Sarah Lutyens continues to supply just gets lovelier with each book.

There is at least one bookshop in which I will always be stocked!

Thanks probably come a poor second to lavish gifts or cold hard cash, but they are due nonetheless to Wendy Lee, Peter Cocks and Victoria Jones. And to the two people whose names I did not discover: the dodgy-looking man who wanted to buy my hat in a bar in Mijas and could easily have been Alan Langford, and the girl on the beach in Puerto Banus, who became Candela Bernal.

And to Claire, of course. It goes without saying.

While all those mentioned above have contributed enormously to *From the Dead*, the mistakes remain entirely my own work. On that subject, I would like to point out that I am well aware that the *feria Virgen de la Peña* takes place every year in Mijas Pueblo in September and not in April. Having experienced the festival myself in all its hypnotic and spooky splendour, it was not something I could deny Tom Thorne. So I hope that those who are – even now – reaching for their green pens to write me angry letters will forgive me taking liberties with the calendar in the interests of the story.